Clichéd Love

A Satirical Romance

Also by Lynn Galli

Virginia Clan

Forevermore

Finally

Blessed Twice

Imagining Reality

Wasted Heart

Aspen Friends

Life Rewired

Something So Grand

Mending Defects

Other Romances

One-Off

Full Court Pressure

Uncommon Emotions

Clichéd Love

A Satirical Romance

By Lynn Galli

Penikila Press

CLICHÉD LOVE: A SATIRICAL ROMANCE. Copyright © 2016 by Lynn Galli. All rights reserved.

This is a work of fiction. Names, characters, events, and incidents are a product of the author's imagination or are used fictitiously. Any resemblance to actual events, locations, or persons, living or dead, is coincidental. The opinions expressed in this manuscript are solely the opinions of the author and do not represent the opinions of the publisher.

Cover photo © 2016 Masson/Shutterstock.com. All rights reserved. Used with permission.

No part of this book may be reproduced, scanned, or distributed in any printed or electronic form without the publisher's permission. For information address: Penikila Press, LLC at admin@penikilapress.com. Criminal copyright infringement, including infringement without monetary gain, is punishable by law. Please purchase only authorized electronic or print editions and do not participate in or encourage electronic piracy. Your support of the author's rights is appreciated.

ISBN: 978-1-935611-13-4

Printed in the United States of America.

Synopsis

Vega, a journalist by trade and a cynic for life, came up with a brilliant pitch for a series of articles. Recount the tales of lesbian and gay couples to assure the heterosexual population that the institution of marriage isn't at risk now that gay marriage is legal. Her editor loved the idea. Vega loved the notion of a long-term assignment that paid regularly. What she didn't realize until too late was that she'd have to sit through every one of these often banal, regularly nauseating love stories without wanting to hurl herself off the nearest cliff. So much for her brilliant idea.

By the time she arrives in Seattle, she's already had enough of interviewing couples, but she's determined to see it through. After all, if the readers of a national newspaper can recognize a love story as a love story, regardless of sexuality, she might change a few minds out there. Helping to temper the discontent is new friend Iris, who seems to know everyone's story and, more importantly, shares Vega's take on them. As the interviews continue and her friendship with Iris grows, Vega wonders if her lifelong cynical attitude toward love might be softening a bit.

1

Entering the bar, I wondered again if this was the most ill-advised pitch I'd come up with in my career. Sure, it was a job. A good paying one. One that would no doubt be interesting and, done well, important. Yet in only my fourth city, I was already mostly tired of these interviews. I hadn't thought through the whole thing when I'd pitched this assignment. How often these women would say the exact same thing over and over. How much I'd feel like those characters on *Airplane* while listening to Striker's long-ass, boring story.

A nice looking brunette wearing what seemed to be the ubiquitous lesbian bartender uniform of tight tank and hip hugging jeans was using both hands to make four drinks behind the bar. My head shook, rejecting her as the owner of this establishment. She was too young and pert to be the raspy-voiced owner. Not barely-legal young as is often required for bartenders in an establishment like this. Late thirties, possibly older, petite height and slim with nicely shaped shoulders and arms. She was the only one working on this slow Thursday night. Dead Thursday night, more like. All of seven patrons were scattered around the tables, on bar stools, and at the pool tables in the back. Perhaps I'd chosen the wrong place to use as my home base.

The bartender caught my eye and smiled like any good food service rep who mostly depended on tips to live. Adjusting the strap on my messenger bag, I headed over.

"What can I get you, babe?"

Babe? In San Francisco the women in the bars had used more sexually charged endearments. I'd been downgraded. "Is Charlie in tonight?"

"She's in the back. She expecting you?" Brown eyes swept over me, slowly inching back up to meet mine. In a matter of seconds, she'd sized me up and probably knew more about me in that time than all of my college roommates combined. At my nod, she asked, "What's your name?"

"Vega." I placed a twenty on the counter and pointed to the tap for a local draft. She poured the beer for me and smiled extra bright when I waved off the change. It was a write off, and I'd be using one of their tables often over the next few weeks. Plus, she had to leave her post to track down Charlie for me.

My eyes roamed over the interior. A few more people had entered and were settling at a table. Another couple came up to the bar and gave me a glance, then another. Seattle was a nice sized city, but a new face in a gay bar, no matter the population, always garnered a second glance. I just hoped the offbeat reputation of the city applied to the people who lived here. I was counting on it for my assignment.

"Vega?" The gruff voice startled me from my evaluation.

I turned and shook hands with the owner. She was in her fifties, possibly sixties, with skin that wore the marks of someone who didn't understand the damage sunshine can inflict. I wouldn't be surprised to find out she and I were both forty-six, but I looked like an embryo compared to her. Excessive exposure to the sun aged many a beauty before her time.

"What do you think of my place?" Charlie asked.

"Very nice. I appreciate you letting me set up shop here." My eyes slid back to an empty table near the center of the bar. Anyone interested would take notice if I camped out there.

"I'm counting on it bringing in some new faces." Her dark eyes, possibly blue but really not distinctive other than dark, skated out over the small crowd. A frown appeared as if she hadn't known how dead it was out here.

"I'll do what I can," I assured her, having posted this trip to Seattle on my social media accounts and received a few enthusiastic responses already.

"Any place you want to get comfy is fine. Lane is here for whatever you need."

My eyes flicked to the skilled bartender. Lane. Nice, fitting. She cut her boss a glance. It didn't take a mind reader to spot the annoyance at having her unspecified services offered, but Charlie remained clueless.

"Thanks. I'll try not to bother you with drink orders when you're slammed." I spoke directly to Lane instead of about her. I needed her on my side. One bad word from her might influence potential interview subjects.

The left side of her mouth quirked up. A practiced move she must've perfected before she tried it out on the lesbian population. It oozed sex appeal while ramping up her attractiveness, and she knew it. Probably filled her tip jar every night.

"I know a perfect couple for your article," Charlie made another unsolicited offer.

I felt my head nod to save my mouth from having to decline. Her couple could go either way. If they didn't make the article, she might be upset. "I'll just take a look around and get settled in for tonight. Thanks again for letting me become a barfly at your place. I really appreciate it."

Beer in hand, I wandered over to watch as one woman attempted to make pool appear interesting for the three who couldn't play. One television screen showed the Storm game and the other showed the Sounders game. Both teams were losing, one pretty badly, but the one fan in the foursome only cared if the "smoking hot guard" was on the court at the moment. Her date didn't seem to mind the open lust this woman was showing.

All four were in cargo shorts, two in tank tops and the other two in novelty t-shirts. Tank Tops both had short hair, one brown, the other almost black. Their companions had longer hair in blond and medium brown. Despite the cargo shorts, the women in the novelty tees were both quite feminine with dangly earrings, highly styled hair, and made up faces.

I began to rethink my appearance. Perhaps dressing down was the way to go. My slacks fit my slender, five-seven frame nicely. Under a lavender top, I wore a white camisole that showed off my prominent clavicle bones and a hint of cleavage. Tonight I wore a trace of makeup to even out my T-zone and eyeliner to highlight my olive green eyes. Golden blond hair hung to my shoulder blades in one straight length. No curls, no waves, it was one of the things I didn't like about my appearance growing up. Thankfully, puberty added the kind of volume that women paid hairdressers to dry with a roll brush. I might have wanted curls growing up, but I was okay with the blanket of straight locks now. I'd cut it short once, but with my oval face, narrow nose a touch too long, and high forehead, it looked better long. In the stifling Chicago heat of the past two summers, I'd kept it perpetually off my neck in a ponytail or bun. If today was any indication, I wouldn't need to employ the bun once during this Seattle summer. Overall, I was going for professional without looking too dressy.

"You want in?" the best player asked me.

"You're new," the blond one who thought the guard was smoking hot said. "First time?"

First time in a gay bar or first time in town or first time getting hit on by a woman who should be paying more attention to the woman who brought her here?

"Baby," the low voice of her companion spoke volumes with the one word. Guess she had cared that her flirty girlfriend noticed anyone with a pulse.

"Just being friendly, sweetie," the woman pouted, pushed out bottom lip and all.

"She is that." The butch girlfriend relented at the fake pout. Her brown eyes flicked to mine expectantly, thinking I'd melt at her girlfriend's obvious antics.

I was getting too cynical for my job. For life, really. I saw right through this couple. Butch partner let femme partner wind her around her finger and thought femme would never look elsewhere because butch was a goddess in bed. All the while, femme was keeping her options open in case butch lost her job or stopped succumbing to her whims.

"In town for a month or two. Thought I'd check out the local flavor."

Butch partner nodded approvingly. Femme partner gave me a second swipe of her eyes.

"You got a name?" Butch Two asked after taking an abysmal shot.

"I don't. What's your preference?" I realized I was jerking her around. The day had been trying so far. My two-hour flight this morning had been delayed three hours. The hotel didn't have my room ready when I finally arrived, and the property agent couldn't see me at the later hour to search for a short-term rental. It probably wasn't the best night to start this assignment here.

But the foursome thought my snide comment funny and chuckled in various volume levels and laugh types. Once again, I'd been saved by the good nature of lesbians in a gay bar. It was why I thought this article might fly. The sisterhood seemed happy to let me invade their privacy. Happy to have their stories published for the whole world to see. I'd always differed from my peer groups on many things. On this matter, I was in a completely different universe.

"She looks like that hottie from *Alias*," the first femme told her butch.

"You're getting your actresses mixed up again."

"No, I'm not."

Yes, she was. I didn't look like the hottie from *Alias*, unless she meant the hottie that came in during the last season because the original hottie was pregnant. Even then, I didn't look like that hottie, who went on to some science fiction show and wasn't as hot as the original.

"You're thinking of another show that guy did," the other butch offered when it looked like first femme would get snippy at her girlfriend.

"What guy?"

"That guy who does all those shows, only he doesn't really do them. He works the first couple of seasons and then abandons them to direct some sci-fi movie. Anyway, he had another show with another law enforcement hottie. That's who she looks like." Butch Two's convoluted explanation didn't immediately register with her friends, but I was pretty sure I knew which hottie she was talking about. While it was flattering to be compared to her, no possible way. She was the definition of hottie.

"I'm Vega," I said to stop the comparisons to various kickass chicks on cancelled TV shows. People weren't comfortable unless they placed everyone in boxes.

"I'm Riley." First butch stuck out her hand. "What brings you to town?"

"A little work," I answered with a handshake and turned to meet her girlfriend, Adrian, and their friends, Devon and Sawyer.

"What kind of work?" Second femme spoke up for the first time.

"Have you all lived here long?" I deflected, not ready to get specific. If I could learn more about couples before I let on to my purpose here, I could save myself a lot of grief or boredom in listening to stories that would never fit in my article.

They responded with various numbers, none of which equated to their whole lives. They all worked together and have been couples for a while. By a while, I meant the first butch got the number of years wrong, which incited the pouty girlfriend into a tirade about how she clearly didn't care enough to remember how long they'd been together. Second butch gave me a look of exasperation, but her hesitation at answering the question told me she'd barely escaped the same fate with her girlfriend. So far nothing about them was individual enough to make my article, but I'd keep them on the back burner in the event of a slow night.

"I've enjoyed the company." I escaped before first femme started with the crocodile tears.

Lane's eyes tracked me back to the bar. Her beautiful mouth held that sexy lopsided smile as if she knew exactly what I'd just witnessed even way over here out of earshot. "Another?" Her glance shifted to my half empty beer.

"A different one, please." My hand indicated another tap. The one I'd chosen had been too bitter. I set the glass on the counter and placed another bill beside it.

"Are they going to be your first?" Lane's head tipped in the direction of the foursome. My eyes went back to see first femme being comforted by the beefy arms of first butch.

"Don't." A woman spoke up from my left. "I don't know what you're talking about and it's none of my business, but they are not to be the 'first' of anything unless you're looking for a fantastic demonstration of drama."

A laugh slipped out as I swiveled to take in the voice's owner. Tall and lean, the woman wore nicely fitted dark jeans, not too tight or stark, not worn and frayed, not dress up, jeans that she stepped into many times for a night out. Her top was a short sleeve button-down in checks of green, not plaid or western style, unfussy checks. It too fit nicely, no cleavage, partly because her bust was fairly flat, but also because she left only one button open. She had a tan that took me all summer of controlled sun exposure to obtain. If she was close to my age, I'd guess this was her natural skin tone as opposed to time in the sun. It wasn't just that her skin didn't have the same telltale signs that Charlie's bore. It was more that I hadn't seen the sunshine yet today. In late May, when it was sunny in every other city in America.

Blue eyes peered at me from beneath sandy brown eyebrows. Her short, layered hair stopped just below mid-neck in a wash-and-go style with wisps pasted into chaotic order. The cut followed the frame of her heart shaped face. Like Lane, she had an interesting mouth that was precisely symmetrical to her teardrop nose and understated cheekbones. If she had a practiced smile as well, she might never spend a night alone.

Force of habit had me trying to pin down her type. Apparently I wasn't comfortable unless I had a box for everyone, too. She had a similar athletic build to mine. Amazing posture, no slumping at all. Not femme. Nothing about her said femme, but she wasn't anything like the butches I just met. They'd been solid, short haircuts, baggie clothes, and probably hadn't even walked down a makeup aisle before. This woman exuded authority without aggression and zero masculinity.

Lane smacked her arm and tsked at her comment. The epitome of a good bartender. No bad words would be spoken about her paying clients, but the affectionate grin she flashed said they were friends. Possibly more. "Don't listen to her." Lane waved her off. "You need all sorts, and you'll get all sorts in here."

I reached for the new beer she'd set down, taking a sip. My eyes shifted from Lane back to the other woman. We all fit the not femme but not butch category. Androgynous didn't really apply either. Our features were too distinctly feminine. My hair was longer than both of theirs, and I was often mistaken for femme until someone spent time with me. Sporty could fit, although Lane might just look this way at work for the tips it could generate.

A finger tapped my shoulder, and I turned to find the couple I'd set up to interview tonight. In each new city, I started out by interviewing friends. When locals saw another couple spilling their story to me, they were less hesitant to share their own. The shorter of the two hugged me while her partner shook my hand. I gestured to the table I'd scoped out and reached for my beer.

My eyes shifted back to the witty woman. I considered her remark and felt my lips curl up. "Thanks for the tip."

She tilted her drink and let her smile pull widely. I liked that she wasn't shy with her smile. She wasn't playing coy or keeping things close to the vest. She spoke up when she wanted and smiled when she pleased.

As I followed the couple over to the table, first femme from the pool tables sidled up to me. She'd apparently gotten over her pouting fest and had something to say. "Stay away from her if you don't want your heart broken, sweetie."

My brow furrowed. "Who?" And which one was she? Adrian or Sawyer?

Her finger pointed surreptitiously over her shoulder at the woman with the sharp wit. "She beds anyone that moves."

Okay. For her to warn me like this meant she'd been one of the woman's love 'em and leave 'em victims. For her to warn me like this meant she was still bitter about it and not over her. Perhaps that's why the alleged lothario warned me about her drama prone ways.

I didn't need to worry. Despite the wit and slamming body, the sporty andro wasn't my preferred type. Not that I'd been looking for a relationship or a roll in the sheets in a while. I looked down at pouty femme and repeated what I'd said to witty woman, "Thanks for the tip."

As she drifted back to her girlfriend, I couldn't help but check over my shoulder again. Wit caught my glance and smiled. She didn't seem at all concerned that Pouty had been whispering in my ear. If what Pouty said was true, she should be worried about the burning in her ears. Instead, she gave me an unaffected smile that didn't tip her thoughts. There was no agenda in that smile, and I liked that quite a lot.

2

Fran & Yvette

No sooner had we sat, then my old college friend, Fran, started gabbing. "I can't believe you're finally visiting. You look younger every time I see you. How's that possible? Did you make a deal with the devil?"

"Explains her success," Yvette, the usually silent, disinterested one, commented.

"Oh, you." Fran knocked her on the shoulder. She pursed her lipstick lined lips, trying to suppress a smile at her partner's joke. "Tell us what you've been doing."

"Same as always," I replied vaguely. People our age didn't usually get my lifestyle. At forty-six, I didn't own a house or furniture, didn't have a girlfriend or partner, didn't have any pets, and wasn't looking for any of those things. My life as a journalist had always been about chasing stories and the experiences that come with that. It afforded me many more life experiences than most people, but because I wasn't settled and didn't have a home, I wasn't relatable.

"You're not dating anyone?" She asked what she thought was the most important thing someone can ask another after not seeing her for two years.

"I'm not." My hands reached into my messenger bag and pulled out a recorder, pen, and notepad. I took my time arranging them on the table. It was as much for show to draw attention from potential interviewees as a stall tactic to get off the subject of me.

"You're not printing our story, are you?" Yvette's eyes tracked every one of my movements.

Interesting. I wouldn't have guessed she'd react as I would to having part of my life put in print. She'd never warranted much thought because, as partners went, she was a bit blah. Fran had personality, a little grating at times, but Yvette just followed along except in the areas she needed to lead: driving, home repair, finances, and the bedroom. Everywhere else, she let Fran do whatever she wanted. And all the talking.

"I won't unless you want me to," I assured her. "I appreciate you playing the shills tonight. This always helps to draw interest. People should be stopping by all night if they follow the same patterns I saw in St. Louis, Phoenix, and San Francisco."

Yvette nodded, but Fran frowned at her. "You don't want our story public?"

Oh, brother. Spare me the pouty fit right now. "I'd want to keep mine private, too. Just between me and the love of my life." I crossed my fingers and hoped the B.S. would work.

Fran pondered that, then gave Yvette the benefit of my words. "Well, she knows our story anyway."

Only I didn't because I hadn't paid attention to the dull, drawn-out saga Fran had told me over the phone when she'd met Yvette. It was kind of a habit with me, which was why I was so shocked that the idea for this article had even occurred to me. Listening to how people got together and stayed together was as uninteresting to me as someone's coming out story. Those were nearly impossible to avoid. Maybe I didn't have friends with interesting coming out stories. They were all the same: crushing on a girl in high school, or kissing a girl in college, or being fixated on the tough, but hot female police detective on her favorite show, and how it all felt so much more intense than it did with boys. Since there was never a doubt in my mind that I liked women, I didn't have one. Even if I did, I wouldn't feel the need to share it any more than I wanted to hear others. Landing me back again in wonderment over how I'd ever come up with this idea and thought to pitch it to a national paper as a freelance series.

Flipping to a blank page in my notebook, I jotted their names, the location, and the date at the top of the page. I reached for the recorder and turned it on before tossing out the first of my set interview questions. "Tell me how you met."

Fran spoke up, shocking absolutely no one at the table, and proceeded to tell me about how they'd met—at work—how Fran thought Yvette was handsome—an exaggeration in my opinion—how Yvette found excuses to come by her cubicle until she finally suggested they get lunch together—big spender—how Fran had jumped her on the walk back—big surprise for the sex-crazed Fran—and finally, how they both called in sick and spent the rest of the day in bed and never slept alone again. I vaguely remembered the part about leaving work early to boink like bunnies, and of course, the decision to move in together immediately. That was the part I reacted to when she'd called to share her news. Not verbally, I'd simply held the phone away from my ear and silently screamed what I wanted to scream at her. I honestly thought the U-Haul joke was a massive exaggeration. Every other lesbian I knew waited at least a month before they officially moved in together. These two had fallen into bed and become roommates on the same day. If it weren't for Yvette's go-along attitude, I doubt they'd still be together.

Throughout the telling of the story, we had to break for various curiosity seekers. The shills were working. After tonight, it shouldn't be hard to get people interested in being interviewed.

"Is Lane throwing shit again?" Riley, from the pool foursome, interrupted Fran's narration of when they'd first declared their love for each other—after their second round of sex before dinner that first night. Nothing like waiting for the perfect moment.

While I'm certain Lane would love to throw things at some of her customers, I doubted she'd resort to tossing feces. My questioning glance made Riley rephrase. "You're a reporter?"

"I'm a writer," I corrected because the other word often had a bad connotation. Plus, reporters went after news stories. This article series would be in the personal interest section.

"About lezzie stories?"

Lezzie. Charming. "It's centered on lesbian and gay subjects, yes."

"How we all got together?"

"About relationships in the community."

"Were you interviewing us back there?" Her hand waved toward the pool tables.

"I was not."

An affronted face now. She was everything I thought she could be if I interviewed her. "Why not?"

"I enjoy chatting with people as much as the next person, but you'd know if I was working." Dazzling smile to show I meant no offense at not interviewing her when I had the chance.

"Lane didn't know if you were looking for others?" She couldn't hide her curiosity.

The warning from the witty woman crossed my mind. "I have several lined up already, but thanks for your interest."

Her eyes lingered on me, stumped for a moment. "Let us know if you need others."

"Will do, thanks." It was entirely possible that I would interview her to fill out a night, but I didn't want her asking every night I was here.

It happened again when I went up to place a dinner order for our table. A short, skinny number approached and stopped me before I got to the bar. "Heard you were collecting coming out stories for a book or something?"

The Telephone Game was in full effect tonight. I was fairly certain Lane hadn't said anything more than I was a writer in town for a story. The rest was generated by people lurking within earshot of our table.

"Close."

She beamed. "I've got a great story to tell."

"I'm interviewing couples actually."

"No problem, I'll bring my cuddle-boo."

Cuddle-boo? Mental eye roll. "I'm Vega." I held out my hand.

She shook it without aggression. That I could work with. "Blake. Should I tell her we're on?"

I had to start somewhere. "Can you make it tomorrow at six?"

"Better make it six-thirty. The 520 is a nightmare to cross after work."

I acted like I knew what she was talking about. "See you tomorrow, Blake."

"How's it going?" Lane shifted over from another customer.

"Yeah," I responded without answering her question. It was still rumbling around in my head at the moment. The shills were working, but I wasn't sure there'd be the same number of usable interviews here as there'd been at the bar on Polk Street in San Francisco.

A muted golf clap sounded from my left. Witty woman was delicately slapping her palms together and repeating, "Good answer. Good answer."

I laughed again. Obscure reference to a game show from the seventies that was, like all of television these days, resurrected when it shouldn't have been. My eyes strolled over her again. I might have guessed wrong on her age. She didn't look to be in her mid-forties, but then again, neither did I. "Wasn't much of one, was it?"

"Let me guess. 'It's going all right.' That about what you would have said?"

My lips pulled inward. She had me pegged after exchanging only a few words. "Predictably, it was."

"You lose points on innovation, but even with the East German judge, you'll get a 5.6 overall."

East German? Now, I really looked her over. She had to be close to my age, otherwise she would have said German. What I hadn't noticed before, cowboy boots, not the fancy kind, broken in cowboy boots, finished out her look. Cowboy boots on a woman who lived in a West Coast city was a noteworthy choice.

"Generous, thanks. I'll perfect my dismount before trying again."

A grin flared on her face, making her impossibly more attractive. "You do that."

An inebriated patron brushed up against her, trying to get Lane's attention. The woman shifted to help with her balance and suggested coffee instead. She was smooth, not aggressive or bossy, and within seconds had the woman changing her martini order to a coffee.

I tipped my chin in parting and headed back to the table. Fran and Yvette were having a heated discussion regarding how much to reveal about their first hookup. Worse than pouty was the sexual overshare. I waited for them to settle their decision before I discouraged them from telling me the details. As I waited, I watched witty woman escort boozy woman out the door.

Perhaps Adrian/Sawyer had been right. Not that I'd judge. Nothing wrong with a little no strings fun. It was certainly better than spending the evening listening to the details of my friends' sex life.

3

BLAKE & KERRY

The property agent pulled her minivan to the curb in front of another high-rise condo not too far from last night's bar. On our third showing of the morning, I was eager to find something before the official start of my interviews with Blake and her cuddle-boo tonight.

"This is Capitol Hill." The agent waved a bejeweled hand toward the windshield. Two same-sex couples strolled by hand-in-hand, a dude clinging to an eighties' Mohawk walked toward us, and four adult skateboarders attempted elaborate tricks nearby.

"Interesting," I commented as we exited the kiddie shuttle.

She launched into another lengthy discussion about her two talented toddlers as we headed up to the unit. I'd already heard plenty about her "amazing" family, which sounded pretty ordinary to me. This was my curse. People shared things with me, often without prompting. The curse that I'd turned into a career.

Upstairs, I breathed a sigh of relief. We'd found the place. The furniture was clean and comfortable, and the view of downtown Seattle and Elliot Bay closed the deal. "This is good," I said after a quick check of the bedroom and bathroom.

"Don't you want to see the amenities?" The agent didn't hide her surprise at my swift decision.

"I'll check out the gym while you get the contract ready."

At ten-thirty on a weekday morning, only one woman in basketball shorts and a clingy t-shirt was working out. She kept a brisk pace on the treadmill, barely any perspiration showing on her tan skin. Her thighs were muscular and gorgeous. Her arms equally so. She turned at the sound of the door opening, and that smile that I'd liked from last night at the bar flared again.

"You live here?" We both asked at the same time.

She shrugged her shoulders while still maintaining her jogging pace. "I just use the gym."

Uh-oh, what kind of building security allowed someone off the street to use the gym?

She must have seen the concerned look I was trying to hide because she offered, "I worked for the building's owner. This is my payment."

Gym privileges in lieu of money? My reporter instincts kicked in, overwhelming me with questions I wanted to ask. But she didn't deserve an interrogation. "Did you get the better deal on that one?"

She tipped her head in acknowledgement of my tease. The strands of her hair curved upward as much as the three-inch lengths would allow, giving the style more body. With no product this morning, they were free to flounce and settle with each of her steps on the treadmill. Last night they'd been sectioned into chaotically styled chunks with a few swipes of her hands. She didn't bother with meticulous pampering to make it look just so. This morning, the bouncy wisps looked just as good. As did the rest of her.

Her mouth opened to respond to my tease, but the agent called me over to sign the lease. When I looked back, she was watching me leave. It was possible she was watching my ass leave, but I couldn't be sure. Even without being my type, an attractive lesbian checking out my ass made my day.

That gratified feeling stayed with me through getting settled into the new place and on my return to the bar. I looked for her as soon as I stepped inside, but the dense crowd was making it difficult to spot anyone. At least Lane had company behind the bar. A cute guy with shaved hair on one side and multiple earrings stood beside Charlie, and two servers were working the tables.

Lane greeted me with a raised glass. I indicated a tap and nodded at Charlie when she came over. After a brief handshake and announcement to the people around us as to why I was there, Charlie moved on to the next patron as if she were a local celebrity everyone was dying to meet. Witty woman was nowhere to be found, much to my disappointment. Neither was Blake. Lane set the drink in front of me and pointed to an empty table she'd reserved for me. While setting up, I got a few curious stares and one loud Riley smacking my back in greeting.

Blake came through the door holding the hand of an Asian woman in tight jeans and an even tighter top. Blake wore an outfit that I swear I saw draping a mannequin in the Eddie Bauer store I'd passed on my walk through downtown today. Not just the pants or top, the entire ensemble including belt, socks, shoes, leather wristband, and small tote.

"Meet my cuddle-boo, Kerry," Blake said as she approached.

I stood to shake hands with the raven-haired beauty and offered them seats. "I'm happy you could make it."

"I couldn't believe it when Blakie told me what we were doing tonight. Are we really going to be part of a book?" Kerry asked, her dark brown eyes sparkling. They were just one of the remarkable features on her face.

"Right now it's a series of articles." Articles that I and my sponsoring paper hoped would assuage the rampant fear about marauding bands of gays and lesbians kicking down the doors of traditional marriage now that the Court had handed down its decision. A series of articles depicting the way a sampling of homosexual couples got together and stayed together should prove that marriage was marriage regardless of sexual orientation.

"Not a book?" Kerry's face fell, which did nothing to ramp down her attractiveness.

"It could become a book, but right now, it's a series of articles for a national newspaper." If I could stand rewriting these stories in book format with an overriding theme, I'd give it a go. Staying in one location for a while without having to work at a news desk for a paper had a lot of appeal. Slightly more appeal than having to rehash these stories, so the book was still an option.

"Which one?"

I named the nationally recognized paper that was often slid under hotel room doors every morning and received raised eyebrows from both women. That should put an end to any disappointment.

My eyes caught sight of the witty woman making her way up to the bar. It was a little crazy that seeing a woman I wasn't sexually attracted to and had only met twice would lighten my mood. In my lifetime, I'd made one instant connection: my current editor. Over the years of our friendship, she'd been responsible for some of the best assignments in my career and was the obvious choice for this freelance series. The way I'd been reacting to this woman, I wondered if I'd found another.

"Where should we start?" Kerry brought my attention back.

"Anywhere you like." It was just as interesting to hear where people decided was the beginning of their story.

"Camping!" They both declared with big smiles.

I listened to the start of their nine-year love story discovered in the wilderness under the stars or something like that. I refrained from rolling my eyes in some places, especially with the Truth or Dare game played around the campfire by their group of friends. I almost guessed how they'd end up together, but I waited for them to tell me.

"It rained one night, and Blakie's tent had a tear in it. She woke up soaking wet and screeching—"

"I was not—"

Kerry grinned as she corrected herself, "Bravely griping about getting wet as if it were melting her—"

"I was soaked!"

"So I invited her to share my tent." Kerry's eyebrows fluttered suggestively.

"And her sleeping bag," Blake added with her own eyebrow flutter. "Mine was soaked, remember?"

"Fortuitous," I commented, but meant fortunate for her.

"We were so loud we woke up the rest of the group." Kerry's hands came up to cover her face. "We'll never live that down."

"And we've been happily ever after since." Blake wound her arm around Kerry and pulled her in.

I jotted down answers to a few follow-up questions. It was one of a few other camping stories I'd heard, but the first one with rain causing them to sleep together. The others were about forgetting a tent or an extra two people showed up so they had to double up, but not the rain soaked tent. That alone might help push it to the top of my available camping stories.

They barely glanced at the release allowing me to publish their story. Two quick signatures on the forms, and I stood to prompt the end of the interview. Blake took the hint first and shook my hand. Kerry insisted on the handshake that turned into a hug as if we were longtime friends. As they left the table, my eyes immediately went back to the bar. I was starving and hadn't had time to order food.

Lane glided over as soon as I stepped up with my repacked bag. She looked like she could use a break, but the crowd had doubled in size. She took my order, and I grabbed one of two remaining open stools. Someone brushed against me as she took the one next to me.

"Did you get the rain soaked story?"

My lips pursed, trying to hold in the smile as I turned to the witty woman. Her short hair was styled again. I couldn't decide if I liked the natural wisps or the pasted wisps better. I had the urge to touch both and test the springiness of those waves. That would be a step too far, even if I felt like we had an instant connection.

"What rain soaked story?" I played stupid to see which way she'd go with this.

She let out an amused breath. "They tell it to everyone."

"Known them long?" I'd met three couples here, and she knew them all.

"A while." She turned to face me fully. "What they didn't tell you was that Blake cut a hole in her tent and let the rain soak her to get Kerry to issue an invitation."

My eyes widened. Now that would shoot the story to the top of my list for all stories, not just the camping ones. Manipulative, but ingenious without being skeevy. "Did they tell you?"

"Blake did. She gets braggy when she drinks too much."

"Good to know." I'd have to confirm this version with Blake to see if she'd be willing to let me print it. If she really did get braggy, Kerry probably already knew about the manipulation.

"What made you choose Seattle?" she asked, and I really liked that she didn't ask me to confirm what I did or if what she'd heard about the writing was true.

"I've been through a few times. Always liked it."

"Did you end up signing the lease?" Her smile flared at my nod. "You'll like it."

My eyes skated over her casually clad body. Only her well-defined arms showed tonight. Her pants hid those enviable thighs. I'd bet a year's salary that her abs could be counted from twenty feet away. "Will I find you there some days?"

"That's the real reason you'll like it."

If she hadn't delivered that perfectly, it would have sounded seriously arrogant. Instead, I laughed. "Is that so?"

Her shoulders lifted briefly. "You'll like me as a friend."

"Will I?" It was too amusing not to prod her further.

"Ask Lane." Her hand gestured to Lane.

"Ask me what?" Lane joined the conversation, placing my burger in front of me. In another tank top and jeans ensemble tonight, she took the sexy bartender thing to another dimension.

"I make a great friend." Blue eyes tinted violet more than ocean sparkled at her friend while we waited for what we both thought would be an instant response.

A long silence stretched out. Lane's cinnamon brown eyes blinked slowly, plump lips puckered in thought. Neither woman broke until customers started clamoring for Lane's attention. She shot us the cool lip twitch and admitted, "She does." Then she was off to make more drinks.

"Testimonial evidence right there." Wit leaned in, and I caught a whiff of lemongrass. "I am also the keeper of the real stories."

"Like the Blake-made hole in her tent?"

"Exactly like that."

"We'll see about that."

She grinned but stopped when someone bumped into her. She recognized the pretty redhead pushing her way up to the bar and helped to steady her. Again, she worked her boozy whispering and got the woman to skip ordering another drink. Her eyes sought mine in apology as she stood to help the woman outside to a ride. When she didn't return, disappointment hit me again. She was attractive enough to have major game, but she didn't strike me as the kind who took multiple women home every week or took advantage of tipsy women.

"Know what you're getting into with that one, Vega," Blake said as she pushed in beside me to order a round of drinks. "I feel like we're friends, so I should warn you. She's only interested in one night. It'll be a good night, but only one. For a woman who's collecting love stories, you're probably not into the casual thing."

If there was one button someone could push to make me instantly annoyed, it was when she thought she knew me after one meeting in which she'd talked most of the time. After subjecting myself to often nauseating love stories all day, a one-night stand might be the best medicine. Blake didn't know anything.

I found myself mystified by my defensiveness of a woman I didn't consider dating material. Based on the "friend" comment, Wit wasn't into my type either. Both of the women she'd left with were pretty with more makeup, perfume, and spiky heels than most of the city's female population. I didn't own spiky heels or perfume, and my makeup wasn't meant to be noticeable. What confounded me was that these strangers felt the need to warn everyone off her. Or warn me off her. They hadn't done anything to stop the two tipsy women from leaving with her.

Curiosity definitely piqued.

4

Jay & Dakota | Montana & Mac

Wind whipped at my face as I walked past the Seattle Central campus on my way back to the bar Sunday night. What possessed me to think I should walk to the bar tonight when the temperature had dropped ten degrees since this afternoon, I'll never know. People on the street wore t-shirts and shorts. Only a few were more covered like me with cotton pants, long sleeved shirt, and lightweight jacket. I'd been in town four days already and no sign of the infamous endless rain yet. Cold and overcast, sure, but not even a sprinkle.

Riley was getting out of her truck as I passed the bar's parking lot. She beamed at me and stepped down from the biggest truck I'd seen in the city thus far. There weren't a lot of full-sized pickups in this part of the city. My feet dragged as I tilted back to check. Yep, she'd taken up part of another compact parking space in the lot. That explained why there weren't that many pickups around.

"Yo," she exclaimed and slapped me on the back again. "Back for another?"

"For a while, yep." I was hoping to cut off the question before she decided to ask it every time she saw me.

"Got people lined up tonight?" Sincerity darkened her light brown eyes. None of the bravado she'd shown in front of her friends stood between us tonight. It made her more likeable.

"In about an hour."

"Oh, good, then you've got time for my friends. I told them about you."

Sigh. Then again, the more stories I collected, the sooner I could move on to the next city. Not that I had much choice, since

Riley used her vice grip hand to clamp onto my arm and drag me inside. I would have protested if the heat hadn't soothed me once the door closed behind us.

"There they are." Her finger pointed to a table of six women, all different shapes and sizes, but very much like Riley and her girlfriend, Pouty, or whatever her name was. One butch, one femme to a couple.

"I'll meet you over there. Can I get you something?"

Her eyes widened. Perhaps no one had ever bought her a drink before. She was probably used to paying for Pouty and any of Pouty's friends. "A Bud Light. Thanks."

Lane appeared as if she'd sensed me from the other end of the bar. She raised an offering glass.

I indicated the soda nozzle and Riley's beer tap. "Do you ever get a night off?"

"Tomorrow," Lane of few words said.

"You're closed tomorrow."

"My night off." She didn't elaborate on whether she got her only night off when the bar was closed or the bar closed because she needed a night off. Seeing as the boss put in a minimal amount of effort even when they were slammed on Friday night, I'd guess it was more the latter.

Placing my order, my eyes automatically searched for Wit. She hadn't shown at the condo gym yet either. I'd been looking forward to that promised good friendship but hadn't had the opportunity to learn anything more about her. Adrian/Sawyer waved at me from one of the pool tables. I couldn't remember if she was the pool shark or Riley, and I couldn't remember if she was Adrian or Sawyer.

I walked Riley's beer and my soda over to the table. Riley sprang up from her seat and introduced me around. There were two state names, a few nicknames, and one Geo. Not Georgie, or Gigi, Geo. For a woman. And she said it wasn't short for anything. If it wouldn't make me a jerk, I'd ask to see her birth certificate.

As I was prepping my workspace, the door opened and Wit strolled through. Two steps in, her eyes found mine and crinkled. My stomach warmed, knowing she'd searched me out. I'd get the chance to see if she proved right about the friendship thing. Although with three couples to listen to, I hoped she'd stick around long enough.

One of the state names one started out. Dakota and her sweetie, Jay, met in high school, secretly crushed on each other but didn't do anything about it. Not until the ten year reunion when they finally confessed their secret crushes and did the deed in the principal's office while the rest of their class was boogying to some Justin Timberlake tune.

My eyes rounded a few times while listening to their story. Not that there was anything original about the secret crushes and nervous eagerness at the reunion, but the getting down and dirty on the high school premises during the reunion upped the ante a bit. Perhaps everyone did this at a reunion. I wouldn't know, having never even been back to my home town of Frederick, Maryland, let alone return for a high school reunion. My parents did me a great favor when they relocated to Arizona the year after I graduated high school.

The other state was up next. Montana let her spouse, Mac, do most of the talking. College sweethearts, really by default, since they'd been assigned the same dorm room and, over time, realized that their feelings for each other were more than just good friends. Or more likely, being horny college kids, figured out how much easier it was to have sex with the roommate instead of trying to find an interested woman every week.

I took a break after their story and made my way up to the bar. Neither of the stories was original enough to make the article and confirmed my theory that most romance stories were pretty uninspired. I'd been treated to a few gems, all of which would end up in the series, but they were hard to find.

"Can you even imagine being with someone from high school?" Wit asked from right beside me after I'd placed the table's drink order.

"What makes you think I'm not?" I faced her, wondering where she'd gone to high school. My eyes dipped down to her legs, a different pair of jeans tonight, but the same cowboy boots. Completely stereotyping, I didn't think cowboy boots belonged to a woman who'd grown up in Seattle. They looked damn good on her, but if the stereotype held, she'd be from somewhere else.

Her eyes slit with amusement. "You're not." She didn't bother to drop them to my left hand to check for a ring. She must have done that already. Which reminded me. Nope, no ring on her finger either.

Normally such a certain statement would grate on my nerves. Arrogance was probably my least favorite quality in a person. She, however, pulled off the borderline arrogance laced with unpretentious humor and turned it into a completely new personality type. One I rather liked. "I'm not."

"You didn't do your roommate in college either." Her eyes focused on Montana before returning to mine.

Now it was getting a little scary how well she could read me. "How do you know?"

"I just do."

And she did. Most likely because she knew if you screwed your roommate and it didn't work out or it was lousy, you'd have to continue living with that person for the rest of the semester.

"Maybe I should just interview you since you know everyone's story."

She shrugged. "Wouldn't be right."

Very true. "Or printable without a firsthand description."

"You both good?" Lane asked as she came back our way. Her eyes lingered on Wit for a long moment before the nodding reply was enough for her to get back to her other customers. My head tilted. No. They didn't act as if they were together. Perhaps something had happened earlier in the day and she was just checking on Wit.

"What's your name?" I should probably know it if we were going to be friends. My fingers crossed in the hopes of hearing a good one. A stupid habit, but as a writer, names carried significant weight.

An eyebrow spiked. "Four meetings and you're just now asking? You're a true original. I'm liking that."

Best compliment ever. I'd been called weird mostly, a little off occasionally, but a true original never. She waited for me to say something, but I was still feeling giddy from the compliment. Her eyes sparkled when she realized she'd said something I really liked. My hand gestured for her to respond.

"Iris."

Breath pushed out in relief. "Oh good. You've got a woman's name."

She laughed and looked at the table again, then over to the foursome at one of the pool tables. "This from the woman with the rare first name."

My eyes rounded. So, she'd found out my name. Although the way some of these women talked about each other, it was probably hard not to hear about the writer with the oddball name that only belonged to fictional characters. Female fictional characters, at least. "Granted I've only met a dozen women here, but they've all got unisex or men's names. Is that a West Coast thing?"

A know-it-all sparkle livened her eyes. I'd let slip I wasn't from the West Coast. Not only that, since I'd used West Coast instead of Seattle, she must realize I was from the East Coast. As someone used to knowing a lot more about the people I speak with than they know about me, this was a little disconcerting.

"I think it's a generational thing. Although some of those women go by middle names because they don't like their feminine first names."

"Geo?" My gaze shot to the stocky woman with her arm around the voluptuous brunette at the table.

"Georgianna, but don't tell her I told you that. She'll key my car."

I felt like giggling, and I never felt like giggling. Sporty types didn't giggle, but this woman was funny and likeable. And comfortable because of that instant connection thing. We'd make very good friends. "I'll make sure."

"You working out tomorrow morning?"

A smile touched my lips. "Plan to."

"Maybe I'll see you there."

"You can tell me then how you got gym privileges."

"That won't make your article."

"I should hope not, Iris." I tipped my chin at her and headed back to hear Geo, of the Georgianna car-keying fame, and her partner's story.

Everyone reached for their drink when I set them on the table. Dakota leaned close to me. "She's a player, just so you know."

I squinted at her as I took a swig of my soda. "Who?"

"Tall, dark, and handsome over there." Her chin jutted over to the bar.

My eyes went back to Iris. She was above average in height, but not basketball tall. Her barely brown hair and lightly tanned skin tone couldn't be described as dark. Handsome didn't fit either. Attractive, alluring, hot, but handsome belonged to someone with more chiseled features, more coiffed hair, more masculine everything. Iris wasn't masculine. She wasn't feminine either, but handsome didn't work for her. Neither did pretty or conventionally beautiful. Good-looking and charismatic, both old-fashioned descriptors, but they fit this one.

"What kind of player?" I didn't plan to take her word for it, but she was intent on warning me like Adrian/Sawyer and Blake before her.

"The kind that just needs to look at a woman and her skirt drops."

Iris must have some real game if she's got three women telling me about her conquests. What I couldn't figure out was why they all felt they needed to warn me. I don't come across as delicate or innocent, by any means. They must feel they've made a connection with me after revealing so much of themselves and needed to play the protective friend.

My eyes flicked back to the bar, but Iris was gone. A quick glance around and I caught her leaving with yet another beauty. Three nights at the bar and three different women taken home. She really must have game.

5

Mornings at the condo gym were pretty quiet. Flexible hours let me dodge most of the gym hounds in this building. Waiting until mid-morning assured no one else came by.

The door opened behind me, causing my lips to twitch. Almost no one.

"Iris," I greeted without turning around.

Her footsteps halted. Several seconds passed before her eyes found mine in the reflective surface of the machine to my left. "Vega."

She set her towel and water bottle in the holder of the treadmill beside the elliptical I was on. Finally standing rather than sitting next to her, I could size up her height at an inch taller than my five-seven. Wearing another pair of basketball shorts and an exercise shirt that clung to her fit torso, she looked like she could haul a grown man in a firefighter's carry. Her arms had muscle definition, more so than mine. Mine were toned, defined even, but hers showed muscles even when not active. Not overdone weightlifter muscles, more like professional tennis player definition. Her thighs were the same. Exercise was important to her, while exercise allowed me to eat what I wanted.

"You've been busy," I commented on not seeing her in the gym until today.

"I had some work."

I waited to see if she'd say anything else. She didn't, so I told her, "Now you pretty much have to tell me what kind of work."

"Do I?" She grinned that grin that would be cocky on someone else, but self-assured on her.

"Seems right after mentioning the work and all."

"Private investigator."

My laugh surprised us both, a sharp, almost bark. "And I'm a reluctant but brilliant surgeon, who's secretly seeking my stern father's approval because he's an even more brilliant surgeon on the board of my hospital."

She blinked a few times before her lips turned up in amusement. "What?"

"I thought we were trading typical lesbian romance themes." I gave her my own amused smile. "Or maybe I'm a workaholic CEO, who has more money than whole continents, but I can somehow find time to woo a financially strapped, gorgeous lesbian, who is the guardian of her dead sister's toddler, giving me that instant family I've secretly craved."

She was laughing now. "Read a lot of lesbian romances, do you?"

"I read a lot of everything." Goes with the whole writer thing. Nerd thing, too, but she didn't have to know that about me right now.

"I imagine you do."

"So, what do you really do?"

"Private investigator."

"Good one." I appreciated that she was trying to make light when I felt like smacking her at her inability to collapse under the pace she was maintaining. I thought I'd been putting in a good workout until she came along. I waited for her to break, give up on the joke. She didn't, so I called her on it. "You expect me to believe that?"

"I do."

My chuckle turned into a cough because unlike the android next to me, I couldn't catch my breath. Fingers touched buttons to lower the resistance and slow the pace for a conversation. "Have you ever, in your entire life, met an actual private investigator? Just by happenstance. Not someone saying she's a private investigator to get chicks."

"I have and not to get chicks."

"At the weekly meetings of your association, PIs R Us?"

The tease brought out a grin. "In my former work."

I gauged her expression. She wasn't kidding, but that had to be one of the rarest occupations out there. Despite what a lot of mystery novels portray, private investigators spend the majority of their time taking photos of cheating spouses. She didn't seem the type to hang out in seedy motel parking lots, hoping to catch a cheating spouse.

What had she said? Her former work. Oh. "How long were you on the force?"

Blue eyes widened, and those lips quirked up again. "What makes you ask?"

"I know very little about the PI biz, but I do know you can't get a license without many, many hours of investigative work. It's almost impossible to get them outside a police department. Same with the military and the flight hours needed to become a commercial pilot."

"Research?" she guessed, looking even more impressed.

"I do a lot when I'm not reading a lot."

"You're right. It's easiest to get your license after being a police detective."

A million questions came to mind, but I wasn't interviewing her. I was getting to know her, so I started with the most obvious. "Why did you leave the force?"

"I put in my twenty-five for the full pension, and it was time."

"What division?"

Her head tilted, and she gave me a long look. A police detective look, meant to get me to open up without her having to talk, to bend to her will, to slip up and confess. I didn't do any of those things. I just waited until she had to answer or tell me to go to hell.

"A few. I was a rover at first, so I had a taste of everything."

A rover by choice or more probably because twenty years ago when she first became a detective she might have been the only female detective in her division. No one would have wanted her permanently on their squad. I could ask, but that would be better saved for when we were the friends she promised we could be. "And your favorite?"

Her eyes flared momentarily. She was pleased by my question. I wanted to know why, but I could wait on that as well. "Fraud."

My mind sifted through all the other possible departments. Any detective who worked homicide would have named that. Robbery had to be a close second, but she liked fraud. Fascinating.

"You're surprised."

My eyes widened. No one could read me that quickly. As journalists we're paid to be neutral. Blank expressions were our default setting. "You said you roved, so I'm assuming you've worked the more..."

"Prestigious?"

"Yes, and you chose fraud. It's interesting."

"Not really." Perspiration beads finally began to dot her forehead and neck, dispelling the earlier android theory. "Homicide is horrible, robbery can be shocking, narcotics is unsympathetic, missing persons is usually hopeless, and sexual assault is...unspeakable."

I swallowed and turned the elliptical off, walking through the cool down with no resistance. She'd worked them all, and she had an opinion about them all. I'd probably pick fraud over those, too.

"Everyone else asks me about homicide or sex crimes. They like gruesome from afar."

"But I didn't," I finished for her, which was why she'd been surprised earlier.

"No."

"Another thing you like?"

Her eyes drifted over me. "Yes."

"Good."

"Good?"

"Sure. You said you'd make a good friend. If you like some things about me, maybe I'll get to find out."

She nodded, delight evident in her expression. "Great friend," I said. "And you will get to find out."

* * *

Her smile engaged. It was the only way to describe it. When people saw it, they didn't just see it. They noticed it. They took it in and let it ignite them. It was probably one of the reasons so many women followed her home from the bar.

"What?" Iris asked from across the net, halting her service motion.

My eyes flicked back over to the women who finally shut the fence gate after taking their damn sweet time leaving the court next to us. They'd practically tripped over themselves as soon as Iris politely smiled at them on their way past our court.

"Potent," I commented.

"My serve? Hell, yeah. Without it, you'd be kicking my ass."

That was true. She wasn't as fast or accurate with ball placement, but her serve and powerful forehand were keeping her in this game. It wasn't what I'd been talking about, though. She had potent charm. It would explain her success at the bar. Out here on one of the twelve public courts with women in cutesy tennis dresses wearing enough makeup to be televised, Iris and I looked out of place in our standard gym attire. These other women were pretty, damn pretty. If I had to guess, all were straight, all probably bored housewives, which was how they had time to be out here mid-morning on a weekday. I doubted any of them were writers or PIs with flexible schedules, but I probably shouldn't put them on an episode of *Desperate Housewives* just because they looked like they could have been cast on that show.

Comparatively, Iris didn't hold up in looks. In fact, she looked rather plain when put in this backdrop. Stick her in a lesbian bar, though, and her looks, demeanor, and figure were striking. I didn't compare to those women either, but my long blond ponytail gave me a girl-next-door look. With her short hair and muscular arms, Iris really didn't fit. And yet, she was still attractive compared to these Stepford wives batting around tennis balls next to us.

Comparatively? No, it couldn't be that easy, could it? But it really could. And this was why I loved my job. I'd been thinking about this article for months now. Doing research and conducting interviews even before I left my staff position in Chicago. Then just like that, I had a better angle. An angle that the paper would flip over. That readers could interact with.

"Now what are you smiling about?" Iris paused again after having won the last point while my thoughts were elsewhere.

"Just found the angle for my articles."

She looked as thrilled as I felt. "Can you tell me?"

"A competition." It was that easy.

"People love competitions."

"That's what I was thinking."

"Does it mean more work for you?"

I swallowed as reality hit. Yeah, it would be more work. But worth it. I hoped I could endure listening to straight people talk about how they got together. It probably wouldn't be much worse than all the clichés I'd been sitting through thus far. For comparative purposes, it would be necessary. I'd write two stories per article and let readers vote in an online poll on which couple they thought was gay or straight. Generalize pronouns, take advantage of all these unisex names, and hopefully prove that all this fear over gay marriage ruining the institution was unfounded because people couldn't tell the difference between homosexual and heterosexual love stories. My editor would love it. I hoped the paper would as well.

"You can handle it," Iris encouraged. "Look at all this free time you have right now." She waved her tennis racket around to indicate our current leisure time.

"You're right." I didn't need to tell her about the two hours spent writing this morning. I preferred to ease people into knowing about my nerdish tendencies.

"You'll find I usually am."

Had it been accompanied by a smug smile, I probably would have served a tennis ball right at her face. Yet, she maintained a perfect balance between arrogance, sincerity, and humor. For the first time in years, I knew it would be hard to walk away from this daily friendship when I left town.

6

ALEX & ALEX

The couple sitting across from me could have been twins. Same short hairstyle, same minimal makeup, same popped collars on their polo shirts, same cargo shorts, same fanny packs, and same black socks with Birkenstock sandals. They even had the same name, and when they got married, one took the other's last name. So now there were two of them in this world.

They'd been talking so long I couldn't discern their voices anymore. Together sixteen years, the longest of my couples so far, they talked in fits and spurts, taking up where the other left off as easily as if this were scripted. My head shook after almost everything they said. I had limited personal experience with long-term relationships. One lasted three years, but that was only because I was away on assignments most of the time. Had we been in the same town for the duration, I wouldn't have lasted a year with her. It made envisioning sixteen with the same person a little difficult. I do know that I never, and I can't stress how much I mean never, want to be in a relationship where the person cuts me off to fill in the rest of my story.

"So, there we were on the courthouse steps—"

"City Hall steps—"

"Yeah, that's what I meant—"

"With thousands of other gay and lesbian couples—"

"Waiting to celebrate history."

"Get legally married," Alex One or Alex Two corrected the other. I'd long since forgotten which one I'd labeled as Alex the First. Oh, and another thing, if I'm getting hitched to someone for the rest of my life, I'm making sure that she has a different name.

Think about it for a sec. Do you really want to call out your own name during sex?

"Yeah, that's what I meant," the other Alex said.

"Thousands of other couples?" I kept my voice even, not wanting to tip that I knew the number was closer to three hundred. Nor did I let on to my horror at the idea of standing in line with dozens of others to go through what most would consider a sacred event.

"Thousands," One repeated.

"Maybe hundreds," Two allowed.

"This was what you'd always wanted for your ideal ceremony?" I was getting pretty good at keeping my tone judgment-free. My thoughts were a different matter.

"Hell yeah," One agreed.

"Well, a big wedding would have been nice," Two allowed, her eyes downcast.

"You wanted a wedding?" I latched onto Alex the Second. I'd already heard a version of the courthouse steps story in San Francisco. I needed something a little different.

"Well, sure. I'd always dreamed of a big wedding." She shrugged.

My eyes flicked to Alex One. Nothing in her expression told me she caught on to her wife's wistful tone. I barely knew Alex Two, yet I was certain she was the type to want a wedding. They'd been together twelve years by the time they were able to legally marry in this state. She'd had twelve years to plan the perfect wedding. Eloping would not have been part of that plan. It worked for a lot of people, especially in this circumstance where couples wanted to one day tell their kids they got married on the first day it was legal. If I were the wedding type, I'd consider a City Hall ceremony as well. It was as good as any other place. But for a partner who wanted an elaborate wedding, maybe eloping wasn't the best way to get married.

"I'd wear a beautiful white gown, and Alex would be in a tux with the whole morning coat and top hat and everything."

Ugh. Something about a woman in a tux. Not that I'd be the one in the dress, but I definitely wouldn't wear a tux. Suits made me look like I was playing dress up in my brother's clothes. Luckily, I had the kind of job where I didn't have to shove myself into jackets that did nothing for me.

"But we made history, baby," Alex One said.

"No you didn't," I muttered and realized too late that it was loud enough to be heard.

"Yes, we did." She flashed challenging eyes at me.

Which was why I didn't back down when a gracious person would have. "Washington wasn't the first state to legalize gay marriage."

"So?"

"So, you didn't make history." Blank stares came at me from across the table. "Do Vermont and Massachusetts ring a bell?"

"Well..." Alex Two looked at her spouse. "But..." Now her expression was one of dejection.

"We made history, baby." One's arm came around her wife's shoulders.

"State history with a thousand others across the state," I muttered at a much lower volume, which they both chose to ignore. It probably wasn't a good idea to point out that Alex Two had been cheated out of her dream wedding by Alex One's idea of self-importance.

"And we're living happily ever after."

As clones in some socks and sandals cult, but whatever. At least their shirt colors were different.

"You sure are," I agreed because I'd already insulted them without thinking and would insult them further by not adding them to my article. The midnight City Hall marriage license grab and group elopement with several other couples would make it too clear that they were the lesbian couple in the story. If I worked hard I might be able to piece together enough of a story without mentioning the details of the elopement to include them. I should give that a try because their clonelike appearance was starting to appeal. It would be so much easier to have my partner's outfit for the day dictate what I'd be wearing.

"There now, gumdrop, she's listened to hundreds of couples and agrees that we're living something amazing," Alex the First told her.

Dozens, but exaggeration was Alex One's superpower. I clicked off my recorder and shut the cover of my notebook. "Thanks for your time and sharing your story with me, Alex." I shook One's hand and turned to Two. "Alex." She felt a hug was necessary.

They went up to the bar after more pats on my arm and back as they were leaving. I needed a drink but didn't want to follow for fear that Alex Two would launch into another "cute" story about her wife. A wife who had completely ignored her wishes for a big wedding and dragged her down to a government building to stand in line in the cold, dark, and probably wet night until after midnight when they could be shuttled through, one couple after another, and given an impersonal "ceremony" just to make "history."

My head gave a full shake this time. I needed to end these snide thoughts. It wasn't fair to my subjects. They didn't know how ordinary and sometimes boring their stories sounded. They thought they were living something original. And of course, they were, since no two stories were identical, but damn, some of them were very similar.

A hand landed on my back. Not the sharp slap that Riley usually gave. Not the soft caresses that Adrian/Sawyer sometimes gave. Not Lane's quick tap whenever she delivered a drink. This was a gentle hand placement meant to both alert me to her presence and a greeting.

"Tough one?" Iris sat next to me and took her hand back.

"I was kind of an ass, actually."

She tipped her chair into a balance on its back legs, amusement livening her face. "Because you don't think waiting in line for hours outside with a group of people only to get married at the same time as four other couples is the most romantic idea for a wedding?"

I let out a relieved laugh. I might have been an asshole, but at least someone else shared my critical stance. "It wouldn't be my choice, no, but I do understand how it would work for those people who waited years to be legally married and didn't want to wait anymore. As long as eloping is fine for both partners, have at it. It was heartening to read about all those couples who married the first day they could in this state. They have a story to be proud of for the rest of their lives. My main hang up with those two was that one partner wanted a real wedding and her spouse-to-be seemed more interested in making a statement than marrying the love of her life."

Iris contemplated that with a nod. "You know the worst part? There's a three-day mandatory waiting period after obtaining your marriage license in this state. They had time to plan for something more intimate with their friends and family. It might not have been everything Alex wanted, but it wouldn't have been any less important than going down to City Hall."

The waiting period was news to me. Made me feel worse for Alex Two, also known as Alex Who Didn't Get Her Wedding. My gaze traveled over Iris. "You really do know everyone's story, don't you?"

"Only the best ones." She looked me over. "Missed you in here last night. Took a night off?"

"Nope, doing the other side of the competition."

Her mouth drew into a thin line of concentration. "I could make you tell me, you know."

"You could just detect it, private eye lady."

That got a laugh. "Still don't believe me?"

I shrugged to give her a hard time.

"Come out with me tomorrow."

I started forward in my seat. "What?"

"I'm doing surveillance work tomorrow. Come out with me."

"Like a stakeout?"

She laughed at the excited look on my face. "Exactly like that."

"Really?" I had work to do, but suddenly I didn't care. I'd never been on a stakeout before. As a journalist, I'd done a lot of research and been in some tight situations, but I hadn't done a stakeout before.

"It'll be fun."

My eyes narrowed. I'd seen enough cop shows to know that couldn't be true.

Her hand waved off my skepticism. "Maybe not fun, but fun to have you around."

"Yeah, okay." I tried to tone down my excitement, but she saw right through it.

"I'll swing by your building at ten tomorrow morning." She patted my back and headed over to chat with Lane. I stopped watching as soon as another tipsy patron caught her eye and she worked her magic again.

"She's not the marrying kind," Alex Two spoke from a foot away.

I wanted to groan out loud, but since I'd already been rude to her before, I turned with a polite smile. "What makes you say that?"

"She's never once had a long-term relationship."

Neither had I really. Did that make me the "not marrying kind" also? "You know her that well, do you?"

"Well, no, but she's in here every night and has been for years."

Which proved absolutely nothing. "Is it possible that she doesn't cook or that her best friend is the bartender?"

She contemplated that but brushed it off almost as quickly. "Just a warning, babe."

Not her babe, and she didn't have the right to warn me. "Don't need it, thanks."

"She's taken an interest in you," she persisted, her hand coming down to grip my shoulder for emphasis. "When she sets her sights, she doesn't relent."

"We're friends." Clearly these women didn't know Iris well enough to know when she was being friendly and when she was on the hunt.

"That's what I said about Alex when I met her, and look where we ended up?"

On the steps of City Hall, settling for a ceremony among a hundred and fifty other couples when she wanted a real wedding. I barely managed to keep from asking, "Did you wear socks and sandals at your wedding too?" Instead, I smiled and nodded like she made any sense.

7

Hazel eyes stared up at me from the photo I'd checked a hundred times already. I tried to memorize the sweep of his dark hair, the stoop of his shoulders, and the set of his jaw, so if he did show up on the street we were watching, I could spot him. If ever in this lifetime he showed up. Stakeouts were boring. If not for Iris, I'd have willfully returned to listening to Alex and Alex's entire life story.

"Believe me yet?" Iris offered the last of the grapes she'd thoughtfully packed.

As with our other outings, we'd had no trouble coming up with topics of conversation to fill the hours sitting in the car. She also understood the intent of every comment I made. Never once did I fret about offending her with whatever snarky thing I said. Now, she was asking if I believed she was a PI again, somehow reading my mind.

"This would be a pretty elaborate set up if we weren't really here to watch this guy. Why are we doing this, by the way?"

"Three hours in, and you're just now asking?" She gave an amused shake of her head. "I like the way your mind works, lady."

My eyes caught on four people leaving the apartment building we'd been watching. All men, all tall enough, one with dark hair and a little stooped. Possibly our target. I'd brushed up on my cop show lingo last night in preparation.

Iris sat up straighter and grabbed for her camera, using the telephoto lens to zoom in. "Not him." She set the camera back on the console between us.

"He's wanted for staying indoors too long?" I guessed.

She laughed. "Insurance fraud. I get calls from a few adjusters I know when they have suspicions but not a big enough settlement to justify assigning their in-house investigator."

"What's his fraud?"

"Slip and fall. He's racking up chiropractor bills to make him appear more injured than he is." She methodically closed the empty grapes bag and placed it into the small cooler she had in her backseat. Her car's interior was spotless, probably because she spent years at a time in the car, surveilling people who NEVER CAME OUTSIDE.

"How do you know he's not?" My reporter's habit of playing devil's advocate often helped me get all sides of a story.

"That's why we're here." She didn't feel the need to get defensive, which propelled her upward a few rungs on the ladder of admiration. "The insurance adjuster had a feeling after talking to the guy. He asked me to look into it."

"I thought most PIs spent their time trying to catch cheating spouses."

She cut a glance at me. "Most do, but I don't take those kinds of cases."

"Must be nice." What I wouldn't give to be able to pick and choose my assignments. Of course, that's why I'd pitched this freelance series. It could pave the way for more work of my choosing rather than scrambling to find another paper to staff.

"I make enough with these claimant and employee fraud cases to cover my expenses. I don't need to work sixteen-hour days to close active investigations anymore. Once my pension kicks in at fifty-five, I can cut back even more if I want."

Having worked plenty of sixteen-hour days, researching, interviewing, investigating, and writing, I always appreciated when I could take a break from that and live on savings or write unessential pieces that didn't take the same amount of effort. "Does your ass ever fall asleep?"

Her eyes dropped down to my ass, or my hip because I was sitting on my ass. "It's a learned skill," she said in a steady voice, looking away to hide the fact that I'd caught her trying to check out my ass. "Need another break?"

"I'm good for now. I'll walk to that sandwich shop over there and get us some lunch in a little bit."

"May not have to." Iris grabbed her camera again and checked the guy walking out of the apartment complex's door. "That's him." She snapped several photos of a guy who walked with ease down the street. He didn't look injured, but that wasn't always evident.

"What did he injure?"

"Back, neck, hip, and shoulder according to the insurance adjuster. He showed up for his interview in a neck brace and shoulder sling and needed to sit with a pillow at his back."

I made a disbelieving sound. He definitely didn't look that injured now. Before I could ask what she had planned, she adjusted a tiny video camera suctioned to her dash, handed me the digital camera, and reached for her door latch. "What?"

"Just keep taking photos." She dropped out of the driver's seat of her SUV and went around to the back hatch. With a soft grunt she hauled a cumbersome looking box from the cargo area and onto the ground a few steps away. "Don't let him see you."

It took a few seconds before her words dawned on me. "Oh, come on. You're not going to *Silence of the Lambs* him, are you?"

"Don't make me laugh, or I'll blow it."

"I'll move over there."

She followed the direction of my finger point to the alcove of another apartment complex. "Careful shutting the door. I don't want him to look over and see you."

I slipped out of the car. Adrenaline surged, which was ridiculous since I'd been on dangerous assignments before. All I was doing here was positioning myself for a good shot if she managed to get this guy to fall for her creep-with-a-heavy-object-that-needed-to-get-into-her-creepy-van bit. My hands trembled as I brought the camera up to my eye. One at a time, I shook them out to steady them.

As predicted, the guy noticed the cute woman bent at the waist—or noticed her ass sticking up—trying to struggle the large parcel into the back of her car. My breath held as several emotions flickered across the guy's face. He liked the ass, liked her whole body, but was it worth the hassle of helping her? When she stood up, wiped her brow, and let out an exaggerated groan, he decided that he'd probably never get a better chance to be a hero to some attractive woman. So, that was why she'd worn makeup today. At most I'd seen her in eyeliner, but she was wearing that, shadow, some base, and colored lip gloss today. The scoop neck tight shirt showed a good amount of skin, and the slacks molded to her ass. This guy didn't stand a chance of resisting.

"Hey there, need some help?" He offered, jogging over to her.

My finger pressed down on the shutter release as Iris played her part perfectly. If I didn't know she wasn't planning to push him into the back of her SUV and throw him down a well where she'd force him to put lotion on himself, I'd be a little frightened at how easily she could take this guy right off the street.

Not only did she convince him to solely lift the awkward and heavy package up and into the cargo area, but she had him jump up there to tie it down, bending this way and that with absolutely no grimaces of pain or stiffness showing. This dude was such a faker I wouldn't be surprised if he lied about his name, too.

After getting what I assumed was a bogus phone number for Iris, he gave a deep bow when she applauded him, and sauntered off, not one limp or back seize in his step. All the while, I'd been taking snap after snap of his show of strength and flexibility. And fraud.

"Get in, we're following," Iris said from the now open driver's side window.

I rushed forward as if avoiding a sniper. I had no idea why I was crouched and darting. It must be the adrenaline making me do weird things, including jumping into the passenger seat as if the car was in motion. At least the window wasn't open, or I might have tried getting in *Dukes of Hazzard* style.

I faced her as she cranked the ignition. "I can't believe you almost made him put the lotion in the basket."

She laughed loudly and flipped a U-ie, heading to the intersection where the guy had turned the corner. We crept along because he was on foot, but found it wasn't necessary when he ducked into the second building on the block.

"His gym," Iris said when she pulled into a parking spot across from the wide expanse of windows that allowed us an unobstructed view inside the gym. "Jeez, this guy is an idiot."

"Do most people do this? So blatantly?" I handed her the camera.

Her eyes flicked to me before looking through the viewfinder. Our guy was starting into a run on a treadmill that faced the street. Big surprise he'd chosen a machine that allowed him to be noticed by everyone walking by. She started taking photos, sparingly unlike me, and set the camera in her lap. She clicked through some of the photos I'd taken. "Did you lift your finger at all?"

Heat touched my cheeks. "I didn't want to miss anything."

"You did well, thanks. And to answer your question, yeah, when they think they've gotten away with it, they're blatant as hell. One interview, fill out a few forms, they think they're in the clear."

"So his doctor is in on it?" I felt my mouth pinch in distaste.

"Chiropractor. That's the key." She caught my look of distaste and nodded approvingly. "A doctor takes x-rays or MRIs, makes note of the patient's pain, but once the scans come back clear, a doctor won't keep writing prescriptions. Chiropractors depend on repeat business. Chronic pain that can't be explained. They aren't prescribing medication. They're giving temporarily relief to chronic pain. It's an ambulance chaser's dream."

That made sense and wasn't as sinister as when I'd thought it might be a medical conspiracy. "I see. Get adjustments three times a week, rack up the medical bills to make the injury legit? Let me guess, he's not able to work either?"

"Exactly. You could run the fraud division now."

I sat up straighter. Damn right, I could run the fraud division. I had a stakeout under my belt and could stealth with the best of them. Then again, maybe not. "I could never entice someone into the back of my creepy van."

Her eyes drifted over me as she laughed again. "You'd need a van first."

"This was fun."

"It was. I appreciate the help."

"Glad to." Genuinely. I hoped to do it again.

"I'll buy you a beer tonight if you're going to the bar?"

"Tomorrow night." I was already feeling the disappointment of not being able to collect on that beer tonight. "I'm stuck interviewing at another place tonight."

She cut a sly look at me before raising the camera to snap a few final photos of Captain Uninjured America across the street. "You'll tell me about the angle soon. I can feel it."

I could, too. She was becoming a good enough friend to drop my guard around her.

8

GAYLE & PAUL

Their story began with him falling out of an elevator on top of her. Oh, the romance of it all. I shiver to think something that blissful might happen to me one day.

"And then I go, 'Yo, babe, you make a good pillow.' She totally fell for me." The balance-challenged guy, Paul, came across as a typical jock. Or former jock, I should say, since his protruding belly indicated he no longer played sports. Or he was pregnant.

My eyes shifted to take in Gayle. She didn't look as enamored by the "meet cute" story he was spinning as she must have been when they'd first gotten together. "He really fell out of the elevator right on top of you?"

Paul didn't let her answer. "I was sloshed. Just came back from this killer party at the frat I was rushing and could hardly stay upright."

If he'd been a woman, he probably wouldn't have made it out of the house without being repeatedly molested. Instead, being a guy, he was able to leave the party unharmed and somehow find a woman to fall on top of.

"I was waiting to get on the elevator. He fell out as soon as the doors opened," Gayle clarified.

"On top of you?"

"Toward me. I tried to break his fall, but we both ended up on the ground."

Ah. The real story. Not on top of her, but onto the ground while reaching for anything to break his fall and blindly lucked into a woman half his size. Charming.

"You've been together ever since?"

"We dated on and off for a few years, but yeah," Paul agreed.

On and off? No doubt code for: I slept around but she better not have, or we wouldn't be together now. My eyes flicked to Gayle again. Hers wouldn't meet mine. This was likely her permanent expression whenever she took her husband out in public and let him talk.

"Did you live together first?"

"Hell yeah," Paul said. "I wasn't marrying someone who can't handle how I am around the house."

Translation: I lounge in front of a television in my boxers every weekend and eat whatever she fixes for me and fart whenever I feel like it with no regard for my girlfriend in the room. Yeah, I knew guys like this. I even knew a woman like this. She'd added a tank top to her boxer clad body, but all the rest—doing whatever she wanted and farting freely because she didn't want any falseness between us—yep. One afternoon of that, and I decided I was completely fine with "falseness" if it meant I didn't have to listen to or smell gassy emissions from the woman I was seeing. Call me uptight, but I didn't see anything wrong with keeping up a polite veneer, at least until we were hopelessly in love. Even then, really, but that was my own preference. There was even a study that showed how much more likely those kinds of habits caused couples to break up. Nothing like stats to back up my uptightness.

"For eight years," Gayle relayed the length of time living together. Resignation still dripped from her voice. She probably thought he'd never propose.

"Married for six years," I said after checking my notes. Neither of them looked ecstatic with the arrangement anymore. Inertia and laziness probably kept them together more than love these days. "What was your wedding like?"

"Oh, here we go. Strap in; she'll never shut up about it." Paul sighed and stopped a passing waiter, not ours, to place another drink order.

Gayle donned a dreamy look. Uh-oh, Paul might be right about this. I glanced over at the bar and sighed to myself because my friends weren't here. This was a touristy chain restaurant downtown. I'd much rather be listening to Riley and Adrian's story with the chance to chat to Iris or Lane before the night ended. If my editor hadn't blown out my eardrums with her screams of excitement over the competition angle to the story, I would have abandoned the premise. Instead, I'd signed up for double the amount of happily-ever-after stories.

To hasten our exit, I went up to pay the bill at the hostess stand. Lingering to avoid meeting up with Gayle and Paul at the elevators, my eyes wandered the mall outside the chain restaurant. They snagged on Iris as she walked past the theater across the way. I blinked and gave a head wobble. It had to be wishful thinking screwing with my vision. Just the same, I darted out front to make sure.

It was Iris. She was on her way to the down escalator of this multi-level upscale mall. What was Iris doing at Pacific Place? She didn't like shopping, and her clothes lent themselves to department store over some of the designer shops in this place.

Downstairs, she stepped into one of the stores. A second later, her face appeared in the window front. Ah, so she wasn't here to shop. She was following someone and doing a good job of it. In attire set to blend with the other women here, she looked good lightly made up, hair wisps styled purposefully, shirt and trousers that both differentiated her look yet conformed to the trends in the mall. No cowboy boots tonight, which made sense. Black lace up flats that, if I had to guess, had rubber nonslip pads attached to help dampen any noise they made. The perfect getup to stay inconspicuous in a crowd of female shoppers at a high-end mall.

I took the escalator down, caught between wanting to watch this play out and knowing I could blow her unassuming manner. With that as a possible outcome, I decided to continue on my way to the exit. Then her eyes landed on me in one of her sweeps of the area. She quirked her lips and tipped her head back once. I took that to mean that I should head over to say hello.

She reached out and pulled me to her as soon as I entered the store. "Hey."

"Hi," I matched her low tone. "Who's your mark tonight?"

Her eyes widened. "Should have known you'd see it."

I puffed up a smidge at her compliment. "Another insurance fraud guy?"

"No, this one's a cold case. I worked it seven years ago but couldn't get the evidence I needed."

My eyebrows rose. "What do you think he did?"

"Killed his ex-wife."

Breath pushed out audibly. This was a far cry from slip and fall fraud. Before I could say anything, her hand clasped mine and pulled me out into the mall. I didn't have enough time to document the pleasant feel of her smooth hand before my attention focused on the guy starting toward the down escalator again. We followed, letting several people get on in front of us and moving onto the same step.

She leaned closer and spoke. "His alibi was his new wife. It's the only thing that kept us from getting an arrest. Everything else pointed to him. No more child support, no more shared custody, no more threats for full custody. He'd beaten her to within an inch of her life when they were married, but she never pressed charges. It was heartbreaking."

We got off at the next level and followed him around the escalator bank to the next set that took us down to the street level. A rather inconvenient layout for surveillance, but it forced people past more shops on their way down each flight.

A hand squeeze stopped us when he window-shopped the Cartier store on the first floor. She maneuvered me against the railing that overlooked the ground floor, her back to him with me peeking over her shoulder. She placed a hand on the railing beside me and moved close. She smelled of lemongrass again. Something else, too, not quite powdery but something in that family. The fragrance was faint, not strong enough for a perfume or even a lotion. Scented soap, probably. After the long day and even longer story, I hoped I still smelled as pleasant as she did.

"What else?" I figured if he did glance our way it would look less conspicuous if we kept talking. My heartbeat sped up again.

This was even more interesting than taking photos of an insurance faker who was too stupid to know he was being set up.

"The thing about murderers is that their stories usually hold up as long as they can tell it the way they want." She fished out her phone and turned on the video camera, angling it to watch him behind her. "The minute you show up for more questions, all of a sudden it's, 'I told you everything the last time. I can't help anymore. I think I should get a lawyer if you want to talk again.' It's almost always the suspect that trips himself up." She paused when he moved to the next window, eyeing the display of engagement rings. "When you've got three good suspects, and two of them have no problem answering your questions, but the third gives a statement, then asks for an attorney, he's almost always the guilty one."

My eyes shot to him again. "That's this guy?"

"To a T. What he doesn't know is that his now second ex-wife no longer feels the need to protect him with the false alibi she came up with while they were married."

"How do you know?"

She glanced over her shoulder. In the next moment, her hand was back in mine, tugging us into motion as he walked toward the exit. "Don't judge me on this, but once a month I check the divorce records for the names of the suspects in all my unsolved cases."

"All right," I said because I couldn't think of what else to say. That was brilliant and tedious and obsessive and brilliant again.

"Break a woman's heart, and she's no longer so protective of you." She fluttered her eyebrows at me, making me wonder if she had plenty of experience with that. Judging from the comments some of the bar patrons made, she must have broken a few hearts in her lifetime. "We closed a few cases that way while I was still on the force. I left a handful of unsolveds when I retired. If you know anything about a detective, we can't let those unsolved cases go."

"How many have you closed since you left?" This was giving me an idea for another article. Retired detectives who worked on unsolved cases after leaving the force. Might bring some notoriety to their quest to find the perpetrators.

"Two so far. This would be my third."

My feet stopped moving. She'd only been retired for a year, and her PI duties were a full-time gig. "That's incredible."

Her chin dipped at the compliment. "Not really. We aren't given much time to follow leads to their conclusions on active cases. If nothing gets resolved in a few weeks, you have to start concentrating on another case. There's never any overtime money to surveille the suspect unless you've got a tip that something is going to happen. When you retire, you finally have the time to follow anyone and everything for as long as you want. Sometimes you get lucky."

Up ahead, the guy raised his hand in a wave. Iris guided us across the street in between the standstill traffic, so we could watch this play out. He came up on a pretty, way too young for him, woman and leaned down to kiss her hello.

"Not ex number two?" I guessed as we watched them clasp hands and enter the restaurant in front of them.

"That's what I was afraid of."

"What?" I took in her worried expression.

"New girlfriend. It wasn't long after he'd started an affair and gotten divorced to marry his second wife that his first wife ends up murdered."

My eyes flicked back to the restaurant. Could the guy really be that stupid? He got away with the first murder, but if another ex-wife turns up murdered, he had to know he'd be the only suspect.

"I'll walk you back."

I was jerked out of my thoughts. "You don't need to see what happens?"

"I just wanted to confirm what his second ex-wife suspected. With that gander at the Cartier shop window, he's possibly looking at another proposal."

Her meaning dawned on me. "Which would move up the timeframe on anything else he might be planning?"

"You could have been a detective." She winked and placed a hand on my back to turn us around.

My shoulders lifted and dropped. "Don't like guns." Even if I went for extensive training, I wouldn't be comfortable carrying one.

She smiled in understanding. "That would be a problem."

"Not in the UK."

Now she was laughing. "Yes, okay. You could be a detective constable for the Met. No guns necessary."

"Or I could just write about people who use guns."

"Much better idea." She squeezed her arm around my shoulders. "Keeps you here, anyway."

I warmed at her tone. It felt good to hear she wanted me to stick around as much as I was starting to feel like sticking around for a while.

9

Shawn & Wesley | Drew & Finn

My eyes blinked and kept blinking as the story these women were telling me continued on. All four at once. My preference would have been two at a time, but they were all best friends and wouldn't think of talking to me without the others. Not that I anticipated the story they were going to tell.

"You all came out here together from Iowa?" All of them, together, like a migration pattern of lesbian, tattooed, pierced geese.

"Shawn was the one who got offered the job first. We were together then, so I quit my job and came with her," the one who wasn't with Shawn anymore said.

"Yeah, and I applied as soon as Shawn was offered a job because we worked at the same place back in Des Moines. Figured they'd probably want me, too," Cocky, confident, zero humility told me.

"And did they?" I had to ask.

"Um, well, not there, but I did get a job with their competitor," she said with the exact same confidence as if she'd turned down the unoffered job.

"And I came out here with my partner," the last one who wasn't Shawn spoke up.

I was having a hard time following who was the first and with whom. "You two were together back in Iowa?" I clarified, pointing to the two with opposing arm tattoos.

"And we were together back then," the other two with lip piercings said.

Two couples in Iowa moved out to Seattle together. Maybe not so odd, except for the twist that only seems to happen in lesbian circles.

"And now we're together," Lefty Tattoo said, gripping Stud Lip Piercing.

"And we're together," Righty Tattoo said, matching the possessive pose with Hoop Lip Piercing.

Yeah, they traveled almost two thousand miles to dump their partners for their best friends. All of them. Not just one of the couples breaking up because one of the partners had a thing for her best friend who was with their other best friend. No, they swapped partners. And one of them was pregnant at the time.

"Okay." I couldn't think of anything else to say whenever I heard about women dating everyone in their group of friends because they somehow must feel there weren't any other lesbians out there to date. One of my heterosexual friends once went after the ex-girlfriend of another friend of ours. Those guys still aren't speaking to each other even after the one guy broke up with the ex-girlfriend. The dating carousal just didn't happen as often in heterosexual circles.

"So now we're all one big happy family," Hoop Piercing Wesley declared.

Who have all seen each other naked and spent years in committed relationships that didn't stay committed through a venue change. Yeah, happy family.

"And you have the baby?"

"She's twenty-eight months now, but yes," Left Tattoo Finn said. "Of course, Shawn is still her other mommy. She's got three mommies and a stepmom."

"Wow." What else could be said about someone who leaves a pregnant woman to get together with her best friend whose partner decides that she really always wanted the pregnant woman so it all worked out? Even with the baby, who was supposed to be brought up by pregnant mommy and her partner only now she's got pregnant mommy and her new partner but still the old partner? I was confusing myself.

"Do you think we'll make your article?" Shawn, the quiet right tattoo, said.

It was hard to say. As much as I would want everyone to read about their partner swap and baby raising quartet, it would be difficult to separate out these couples into two articles with two other heterosexual couples. "It's up to my editor." I happily passed on their impending disappointment to someone else.

"How will we know?" Drew, the cocky stud piercing, asked.

"You'll have to read the paper or subscribe online." Might as well get a few more customers for the paper out of this.

They took turns shaking my hand and trying to needle me about being in the article but finally vacated. I was packing up when Iris took the seat next to me. I hadn't seen her come in, which was surprising since I was facing the entrance.

"Here's what I'm thinking," she began and tipped her chair back, a sly grin on her face. "We should move to Nebraska or someplace like that, find out we're miserable together but too afraid to be alone, so we'll take our best friends with us and couple up with them instead. Sound good?"

I snorted and she laughed, pointing out that I snorted. "Judgey."

"Oh, please, you were wearing a flowy black robe and holding a gavel right with me."

I checked over both shoulders, spotting the foursome moving over to the pool tables with Riley and her crew. All were currently making more racket than the rest of the bar combined. "How do you know?"

"Almost everyone in here thinks the same thing."

"How'd you get all this info?" I'd been meaning to ask her this for days now. A lot of people chatted with her in the bar, but it wasn't long enough to get their entire stories. Certainly not as long as I'd been sitting with these couples to hear them.

"Despite what you see in here, the Seattle lesbian community isn't really that small."

I'd never thought it was, but the same faces were in here night after night.

"With this as your base, you're missing out on thousands of others." She leaned close and spoke in a low voice. "Charlie's rubbed some people the wrong way, and others just aren't into the bar scene anymore."

Unlike her, who seemed to be into the bar scene every night. Or every night that I was here, at least. Even back when I was into the bar scene, I stayed home four nights a week. Then again, I didn't have as much game as she did. Didn't want to have as much game as she had.

"Check out Green Lake on a Sunday afternoon," she advised. "There's an entire league of women playing softball. Almost all are lesbians. Or head to a Mariners game and find the section that hosts a revolving group of lesbian season ticket holders. Same with the women's roller derby and soccer matches. Most of those women don't come in here. If they hit a gay bar, it's the trendier one a few blocks over. See what I'm saying?"

"Yes, you're saying that you stalk these women so you know their stories."

She snorted this time. "It's like you're a comedian."

"Without the obligatory vest, though, right?"

"Right. You haven't worn a vest once yet. Guess you're not funny enough to become a comedian."

I leaned back, enjoying our banter. Several pairs of eyes flicked our way before glancing off again. Since I'd completed an interview already, I should be spared requests to take down any other stories tonight. These glances weren't checking if I wanted another interview. They showed hesitation at joining me with Iris there. It bothered me that I hadn't pinned down the dynamic in here yet. Iris had left the bar with someone more often than not, but she never talked about leaving with that person. So if she didn't brag about her conquests, why were so many people ready to warn me about her? I couldn't believe she'd slept with everyone who warned me off her or even all the women I'd seen her go home with.

I glanced at her and caught a curious stare. If she could read my mind, I'd blush, so I asked, "You following someone again tomorrow?"

"You want me to follow you?" She held out her hand and ticked off each finger. "Gym, library, coffeehouse, library again, and back here to the bar."

A flush heated my cheeks. She'd been joking, but she had part of my days mapped out. "Just wanted to know if you'd had a break in your case."

"Listen to you, all mystery novel dialogue and all." Her hand shoved against my shoulder.

"I've been boning up."

"Very good." Her face grew serious. "Possible break. Enough to pass on to my former protégé. She'll follow-up, and fingers crossed, have an arrest soon."

"That's great. Really, Iris, good work. You must feel proud."

Her face turned away, embarrassed by my compliment. "Like a weight has been lifted." She looked back at me. "Want to celebrate by letting me kick your ass on a tennis court tomorrow again."

"Again? I seem to remember beating you last time."

"I let you win." Her nose wrinkled. "It's my hustle."

I laughed. "It's not a hustle if you tell me about it."

"Oh," she looked self-conscious for a second before cracking up. "Tennis. Prepare to be spanked." She rose from the table and headed to the bar.

Ten seconds after she left, Hoop Pierced Lip slipped into the seat Iris just vacated. "Don't go kinky with her, Vega. She won't let you go back to regular, if you know what I mean."

I didn't, and how the hell would she know? She'd been with Stud Pierced Lip, then went to Right Tattooed Arm the next night. Unless she cheated on one of them with Iris, she shouldn't know anything about how kinky Iris may or may not be.

Iris, kinky? Hmm, kinda fun to think about, but none of my business. Of course, it might be an entertaining topic to go over the next time we were on a stakeout together.

10

Bailey & Dusty

My mind was already several steps ahead of the couple sitting with me. They were telling a version of my least favorite get together story. The business trip, two colleagues who weren't supposed to get together, but circumstances and loneliness pushed them together. They thought they were clever because of the tiny little hiccup that wasn't so tiny and happened way too often.

"We get to the hotel," Bailey, the busty femme of the twosome, started the predictable part of the story.

And they only had one room available, I thought to myself.

"I made the reservations myself," Dusty, the lanky butch of the twosome, interrupted. She'd probably interjected that little tidbit every time this story came up.

Of course you did, I snarked inside my head.

"And instead of the two rooms that Duster booked, there was only one."

How amazing that could happen at a hotel where you didn't double check the reservations that your colleague made on your behalf. My snark was turning to snide.

"Couldn't believe it," Dusty-Duster was shaking her head as if she hadn't been the puppet master behind that little hiccup.

"And get this," Bailey leaned her bust—herself—forward and gripped my arm.

"There weren't any other rooms available in the whole town," I finished for her.

She jerked back, disappointment painting her face. Crap, I should have said that one to myself as well.

"No, there weren't," she agreed, a little deflated now. "There were four other conventions in town."

"Happens sometimes." I tried to soften my earlier guess.

"We didn't know what to do." She flung up her hands to prove she hadn't known what to do.

"Oh, I let that desk clerk have a piece of my mind," Dusty spoke up, her hand rubbing a circular pattern on her wife's back hard enough to tunnel through.

It didn't matter that I felt awful for taking the wind out of Bailey's story. I still wanted to let my snark free as I imagined how Dusty berated the front desk clerk all for show when she'd been the one to cause the problem.

"She was trying to preserve my honor. I almost fell in love with her right there in that hotel lobby." Bailey's breasts pushed up against Dusty as they swiped their noses against each other.

I swallowed the gag I felt rise and looked away. Lane was slammed again tonight as the only bartender. My plan halfway through this story was to wrap it up quickly and get something to eat. By the look of the crowd in here, I'd have to go someplace else. I was getting sick of the only thing the cook made well, anyway.

My lips curled up when I saw Iris pulling beers for some of the patrons. The bar's owner couldn't be bothered to help, so Lane's best friend pitched in. From the wrong side of the bar, which was fun to watch.

"Almost?" I encouraged Bailey to continue or I'd never be done with this interview. Never. I'd age in place at this very table.

"Maybe a little." She winked at Dusty. "But not only did they not have other rooms." She leaned forward again to grip my arm.

The room only had one bed, I guessed silently.

"We got up to our room, and there was only one bed."

Gasp!

"It was the last room they had, us getting in late and all." Dusty had the grace to look sheepish. She must have known I guessed that she was to blame for the room mishap.

"And I'm sure the chivalrous Dusty slept on the floor?" I couldn't help baiting.

"Oh, gosh no." Bailey's bust heaved at the scandalous suggestion. "I couldn't make her do that. We had a big presentation the next day, and she has a bad back."

A bad back? Now that was a new angle. I'd heard many excuses before for needing to share the only bed in a hotel room, but a bad back was a new one.

My eyes drifted away to avoid rolling rudely. They landed on Iris leaning over the bar top to fill four beer mugs for Riley. Another woman stood close, talking to Iris's back. Riley kept twisting away to hide her laughter at the woman's attempt to get Iris's attention. Dressed in a smart suit tailored to fit her lithe frame, the mystery woman was attractive enough to get anyone's attention. Yet, Iris wasn't biting. I so wanted to be over there, getting that story instead of listening to this one.

At least I could look forward to another tennis game tomorrow. It was becoming a regular once a week thing for us, sometimes more often. While Bailey droned on about Dusty's need for a comfy bed, I reflected on how these past few weeks had been easy and fun. I hadn't made the kind of friendships I'd made here in years. I'd planned to stay one more week, but with Portland a three-hour drive away and Spokane not much farther, I could use Seattle as a base for another month. Cultivate my tennis game and enjoy more time with these new friends. Good stuff all around.

"...in her arms," Bailey was saying as my attention came back. "I snuggled up against her sometime in the night. I'm a snuggler, don't ya know."

"I can't resist a good snuggle," Dusty admitted, fondness for her spouse evident on her face. She might have manipulated how they got together, but she was still dedicated to her after several years together.

"One thing led to another." Bailey turned to Dusty, gave her another nose snuggle, then kissed her—with lots and lots of tongue. My eyes didn't stop the roll this time.

I slammed the cover of my notebook closed and shot out of my seat. No need to prolong the impromptu voyeurism. "Thanks so much. I've got what I need. Nice to meet you." I fled before they started humping each other right there on the table.

"Beer?" Iris asked, starting her lean toward the unmanned taps as Lane was busy filling eight orders at once.

The attention seeking woman sighed loudly at the interruption. She pulled out a business card from her expensive purse and slid it onto the bar top in front of Iris. "Call me, Iris. We don't have to be exclusive." She slipped off the barstool, tipped her head at me, and headed for the exit.

They didn't have to be exclusive? Wow. So many questions marched across my mind. I wanted to laugh. As passes went, that one was definitely original. My eyes came back to look at Iris. She didn't look embarrassed to have deflected a pass in front of me. She looked perturbed.

"Not your type?" I watched as the woman hailed a cab out front.

"She's a lawyer."

I swung back around at the angry tone. "Don't like lawyers?"

"Not that one. I've come up against her in court a few times. She's damn good. Made me doubt myself on the stand." Distaste pinched her expression. "Now she thinks I'll forget that just because she's throwing money at me?"

Wait, money? She propositioned Iris? A former police detective? Something was off here. "Why is she throwing money at you?"

Iris focused on me. "For a job. Like I'd even consider working for a defense attorney to help clear the kind of clients I used to arrest."

Lane wandered by, glanced at Iris, and halted. "You okay?"

"Yeah, just Sharkie again."

She gave us the one-sided quirk of her lips. "Still stalking you?"

"This time, she said I didn't have to work for her firm exclusively."

Ah. Got it. Not a pass at all. "You could always take on a case, screw it up royally, thus making sure the client gets jailed, and the lawyer leaves you alone," I joked.

Lane snickered and sauntered away. Iris let a grin slip and gestured to the tap again. "Beer?"

"No, thanks. I'm going to grab some food somewhere and head home."

Her eyes flicked to the front windows of the bar before coming back to mine. "You're not walking, are you?"

The sudden change in her expression from amusement to worry forced me back a step. It was a pleasant night out, warmer than some of the others. Full dark, but a perfect night for a walk. Only she didn't think so. "I have a rental, but I thought I'd walk to that Thai place a block over. Have you been?"

Her eyes widened just a touch. "I have. Skip it. Try the place on Broadway around the corner from your apartment. Great curry and they spice it as much or as little as you like."

That sounded more like a warning against the place down the street than a recommendation for the place near my apartment. If I weren't so hungry, I would have made her tell me what had her so worried. As it was, I'd put in on the list of things to talk to her about while slamming tennis balls around. It was growing bigger and bigger for every outing.

11

My phone rang as I rounded the corner onto Iris's block. If I hadn't been expecting a call back, I would've let it go to voicemail. Checking the display, I took the call as I stepped onto the brick pathway up to the smallest house on the block. It only took thirty seconds to make me regret that decision.

"Bad news?" Iris called from the tiny stoop of her equally tiny house. Well, tiny might be exaggerating, but small for the neighborhood. On each side of her were mammoth boxes of homes, easily five thousand square feet and zero character. Not original to the neighborhood, either. Hers had probably been here since the early 1900s.

"Just got confirmation that one of my couples was lying."

She frowned as she waved me inside. "You're following up on their stories or someone volunteered that a couple was lying?"

My stride halted just inside the door. Iris bumped into me as I tilted back to check out the exterior again and then back inside. It looked much larger inside than out. On a swivel, my head took in every crevice. Sparsely furnished with the right sized pieces, it didn't feel cluttered or overburdened.

"I can't tell if you like it." She brushed past me and into the kitchen, ten steps away, to offer me one of the beers she'd set on the counter before coming to meet me at the front door.

"Nine hundred square feet?" I looked up at the low clearance loft space above the kitchen and down the hall just past the kitchen.

"Almost. There's a bedroom, bathroom, and laundry room back this way. I put in a deck out back, which is where I live in the summer."

"It's," I paused not quite sure what words to use. In the thirties and forties, every house on the block would have been this size. My condo in Chicago was much larger and yet, this didn't feel cramped at all.

Her eyes scrutinized mine, waiting for my review. For the first time, I spotted a touch of insecurity in her expression. She cared what I thought of her home. Not just because she took pride in it and would be insulted by anyone who didn't like it. She cared what I, her new friend, thought of the choice she'd made for a home.

"Perfect," I finished, my head nodding on its own. "The living room is just the right size, and the kitchen's big enough for two people. I don't know about climbing up and down those ship ladder stairs if that's where you're sleeping when you're eighty, but other than that, it's the perfect size and layout. An excellent use of space."

She smiled widely and my heart stuttered for making her that happy and erasing her earlier insecurity. "Thanks. I love it. Most of my friends thought I was crazy when I bought it. They were all getting brand new condos up here or in Belltown, all easily twice the size of this. Some paid three times as much. My cop's salary wouldn't stretch that far. I saw this place, small as it was, and something about it just grabbed me."

Something about it grabbed me, too. I could easily see settling into something this size when I found my next port of stay for more than a few months. "How long have you lived here?"

"Fifteen years. Had to replace almost everything over the years, new roof, new appliances, new paint, new floors, typical homeowner stuff. When most of those friends were ready to start families, they had to sell their shiny condos to get little more than the down payment for their mini-mansions in the suburbs. They'll be paying off their mortgages until they die."

"And you?" It was none of my business, but curiosity goes with the whole reporter thing.

"I burned those papers three months ago."

"Jeez, that's amazing, Iris. Forty-eight and no mortgage? Amazing."

"Thanks. It's why I knew I could retire from the force when I did."

Now the nonchalance about retiring early and only taking the PI jobs she wanted made sense. Admirable. Wish I'd bought something fifteen years ago. I could be in the same position. Instead, I was still a temporary migrant, flitting from story to story, city to city, and writing off my living expenses. It was a nice perk, but seeing this cute place with Iris settled into a second career and a ton of freedom, I was a little envious.

She led me outside to her back deck. We sat in two Adirondack chairs and took in the cottage style backyard. No lawn to mow, it was mostly low maintenance plants, trees, and rock gardens, but with plenty of space to allow for the same expansions her neighbors made to their homes. I could see why she spent so much of her time out here when the weather cooperated. I hoped to join her for many more nights like this. It felt that comfortable, both the spot and the company.

"Did you rent in Chicago, too? No permanent home?"

A breath pushed out as I thought about how to reply since most people didn't get my nomadic lifestyle. I was starting to admit that I didn't much get it anymore, either. "Don't have one. Chicago was okay, except for the brutal winters. When I stopped working for the *Trib*, I was ready for a change." Which accounted for the article series and the planned multi-city visit that was currently being delayed because I liked Seattle enough to stay another month.

"Thinking about something long-term, or do you have more of these assignments that will take you all over?"

The mindreading thing of hers didn't bother me as much this time. "Before I started this story, I would have taken the multiple assignments approach. Now that this series can be turned into a book, I could see myself stopping somewhere for a while. Maybe a long while."

"What about Seattle? Cold winters, cold springs, mostly cool summers, and pleasant falls, what more could you ask for?" She flashed a cheeky grin.

I shivered as a perfectly timed breeze whipped past us. "The weather is hard to resist. Will it ever become summer here?" More than halfway into June, the heat still hadn't been turned up yet.

"Just wait for the two weeks of the year when it edges up into the nineties. You'll be praying for this barely seventies weather again. Most homes don't have A/C. Try sleeping when you can't cool your house down."

After the grueling humidity and heat in Chicago last summer, this was very pleasant. So what if I needed to grab a coat before I went out to the bar at night. As long as my clothes weren't completely soaked in sweat before mid-morning, it was a sacrifice I was willing to make.

"We've got a little time before we need to leave for the baseball game." She was going to introduce me to a few of the lesbians with the group season tickets she'd mentioned the other night. "Tell me about the lying couple."

My mind snapped back to the phone call I'd received, and my good mood faltered. "They met using a dating site. Nothing like the great story they told me for the article."

"What was their story?" Original to a fault. Everyone else would have asked how I found out or why they lied. Iris wanted the story from the beginning.

"Halloween, five years ago. They were meeting blind dates."

"Do not say a costume party." Her hand reached to grip my arm.

I laughed. "Should I go British on your ass and call it a fancy dress party?"

She joined my laughter. "A costume party? Really?"

"Yep. They knew each other's names and what they'd be dressed as. Of course, others were dressed in similar costumes and had the same names. You can guess the rest."

She nearly spit out a mouthful of beer. "They didn't bother to check that the other vampire or whatever was their intended blind date?" Then she laughed even harder. "What am I saying? Of course, they didn't; it's a made-up story."

"Exactly, but I was right there with you, asking the same questions." It was too fun not to have asked. A blind date was tough enough. Add in costumes, and things go haywire quickly. "They claimed to be so enchanted with each other they didn't think that some other vampire and zombie might be the blind dates they were supposed to be meeting instead." They had been near the top of my favorites list, having met by chance when they'd been primed to meet other people.

"Where did it fall apart?"

"I ask every couple for numbers to talk to friends or families for some background info or objective observations. It's really so I can verify the stories."

"Interesting." She blinked a few times to process that. "So one of their friends gave them up?"

"Yep. Said they met using a dating site. Then I called four others. Two gave me their Halloween story; the other two confirmed the dating site."

"You believe the dating site version?" She shifted her chair to face mine and leaned forward in interest. I could feel her detective instincts kicking in.

"If one friend told me about the dating site, it might mean there's some petty jealousy there." That's what I'd hoped until getting that last phone call. "Two or more? I have to assume the dating site story is true, and the two who confirmed the costume story either don't know the truth or were told to lie to me to confirm their story."

"That sucks." She let out a sigh as if she were as frustrated by this as I was. "How much time did you waste on that?"

"Over an hour listening to it. Another five or six typing up a draft from the notes and calling around for confirmation." Just so I could now delete that particular article submission. Damn my anal-retentive, ethically based need for verification.

"You do that with every story?"

I shot her a sly grin. "You've been my verification on every story I've heard at the bar. Even if they exaggerate a bit."

"Like Blake and the tent?"

"Exactly, but if you'd told me they actually met bumping into each other at the bar, I couldn't publish that story."

She examined me, clearly curious. "Are you making other calls?"

"I did on the first few, but since we've become friends, I take your word for it. Two confirms is enough when you're involved."

"I'm honored." She clinked her bottle against mine. "Which dating site?" She almost choked on the last swallow when I told her the site's name. "You're interviewing straight people?"

My eyes widened. I hadn't told her that yet. "How did you know?"

"That site doesn't match gay couples."

I shoved at her shoulder. "You don't need to use dating sites. How would you know?"

She turned wide eyes on me and waited for me to say something else. Maybe explain my comment about not needing a dating site. But why would that need explaining? She didn't have any trouble getting dates. "I got familiar with all of them when I was in the fraud division. You wouldn't believe the fraud that goes on with some of the people on those sites."

"I didn't bother to look at the particular site, but you're right. They're a straight couple."

"You're getting stories from...ah, the competition." Her expression opened up as she nodded. "You're, what? Pitting straight against gay stories to see which readers like best?"

I liked her thought process. It might turn into that, but it wasn't my intent. "Even better, I hope. I'm using the whole unisex name thing to my advantage. One gay and one straight story, all names changed to unisex, no pronouns, and the readers vote on which they think is which."

"Damn." She sat back. "That's ingenious. Especially now with all these straight assholes thinking the world will end by the legalization of gay marriage. Wait till they can't tell the difference between the two stories."

"Exactly what I was thinking." Amazingly, again.

"Is there a prize in this competition?"

"A lavish wedding." I'd made the suggestion of a prize to my editor. She came up with the wedding idea and got the paper to go for it.

"Lavish?"

"Six figures." Or so the expense would be if the paper wasn't planning to send their own photographer, event planner, and caterer to save on those expenses.

She coughed, putting down her beer for good. "That would be one hell of a wedding. What if they're already married?"

"A nice trip somewhere." That had been my first suggestion. I didn't think the paper would go for anything more than that. "It won't be as much as the wedding, but it'll be a good deal more than what most people pay for a vacation."

"Nice job coming up with that angle. I can't wait to read them." She whistled her appreciation. "And the book you mentioned?"

I shrugged, still undecided. The biggest draw was being able to stay in one place for a while to finish and publicize it. "All the articles I submit have a limit on word count. With a book, I'd be able to use everything I've gathered, add readers' reactions, report on how the competition progresses, and tell the story of the winners. Should make for an entertaining book. Provided people take to the articles like I hope they will."

"I'm happy for you, Vega." She reached out to give my arm a squeeze.

Not just a polite response to someone's good news. She really was happy for me. Up until this point, those words from other friends hadn't meant much. Sitting with her in this gorgeous backyard, about to head to a baseball game where she'd introduce me to more people that will help my career, those words meant a great deal.

12

Max & Carter

On the bleachers at Green Lake, I watched the end of a softball game on a field to the left. My next couple was currently smooching through the chain-link fence of the dugout on the field in front of me. All throughout the last inning, Carter had been yammering in my ear about her sugar-pie and how talented she was. What I'd seen was a pretty average shortstop, who needed to be moved to second base because she was losing mobility with her age and added weight. Now that the game was over, Carter had fluttered down the bleachers and was showering her with praise and kisses like she was a superstar for the Mariners.

This was the second Sunday I'd spent watching the games. One of the couples I'd interviewed at the bar had introduced me to almost everyone in the stands. Iris had been right. Hardly any crossover among this lesbian set with the regulars at Lane's bar.

Yesterday, I'd been invited to a donut shop in Belltown where a group of gay men met every Saturday to play board games. I'd gotten two stories out of the couples there. Passable stories, different from what I'd heard in the past, but one might be too obvious that it described a gay couple. After the mess with the dating site, I was trying to pick my couples more carefully so as not to waste time. Next week, I had day trips planned up to Bellingham and down to Olympia. The week after, I would stay a couple of days in Portland. My plan originally was to move on to Denver next week, but with the new angle to the story and how much I liked it here, I didn't need many excuses to stick around.

"Let's make this quick. We have celebratory beers to down," Sugar-pie, also known as Max, grumbled as she lumbered up the bleachers to where I sat, notebook in hand.

"If you'd rather not be interviewed, I have other couples lined up. No big deal." I didn't bother to hide the smirk on my face. Carter desperately wanted in this article, and Max's ego needed it, too. She wouldn't pass this up.

"Sugar-pie!" Carter whined, complete with pout. She was a tall, lithe thing, but her careful clamber down the bleachers told me she didn't have one athletic bone in her body.

"Fine, fine. Ask your questions." Max pulled her baseball cap down low to indicate how put out she was to be missing the kegger with her teammates.

I started the interview the same way as every other. "Tell me how you met."

Over the next hour, they threw everything but the usual interview at me. It sounded like a badly written erotica novel, complete with every lurid detail imaginable. I kept looking around to see if I were in a high school locker room with the descriptive prose that came from Max's mouth.

"I swear, man, I was so hard the first time I saw Carter naked I nearly popped off when I rubbed against my jeans. Like a teenage boy on his first date, you know what I'm saying?"

No, actually I didn't. Why was it that some butch women insisted on describing their sex organs and sex acts as if they were men? And since she'd been a teenage girl on a first date at some point in her life and probably felt the same way as a teenage boy would have, she could have just said, "Like I was on my first date." I added this line to a dozen other doozies she'd spewed out over the hour. Perhaps she didn't understand that love stories were different from sex stories.

"I'm sure she doesn't need to hear that, sugar-pie," Carter crooned, gripping Max's bicep but shooting curious glances at me. She was trying to figure out if I wanted to hear this. I tried never to direct where stories went, but I had to steer it off the sex track.

"How long before you moved in together?"

"The next weekend." Carter smiled brightly, her teeth whiter than a lab rat. Veneers? That or she spent a lot of time having her teeth blitzed at the dentist's office every year.

"I couldn't get off work any sooner, and she had a lot of stuff to move, you know what I'm saying?"

I felt like responding, "I do know what you're saying, otherwise I would have asked you to explain." It might drive home how annoying her pet phrase was. If she'd mix it up with other pet phrases, it wouldn't be so annoying. On top of everything else she was so freely sharing, it grated my nerves more than usual.

"We've been so happy together ever since," Carter announced, planting a loud smacking kiss on her sugar-pie's face.

"How long?"

"Seven years now," Max said as if programmed to respond to this question. Seeing as how some of the other girlfriends at the bar missed the anniversaries and had gotten the silent treatment for it, I couldn't blame her.

"Nice." I added a period to my note as loudly as I could and slapped my notepad closed. This had gone on long enough. They'd met right here at the softball fields. While I didn't have a player-fan story yet, I wasn't sure I could wade through all the sexually explicit words to piece together enough PG-rated language to publish their story.

"Oh, is that it? You don't want to hear about our wedding night?" Max looked at me in surprise.

I really didn't. She'd already incorrectly identified the placement of both the hymen and the G-spot in her story so far. I didn't need to know if she got any other female anatomy parts incorrect. I could see how some less adventurous women might not have explored their bodies enough to find where their G-spot is, especially since so many romance novels made it seem like it was a mythical spot that sporadically appears only when she's excited enough. But to misidentify the placement of the hymen or even think that it was wholly intact by the time Carter reached twenty-three when they'd first had sex was pretty inexcusable.

Run a fricking Google search, Lady Who Loves To Brag About Sex Acts. Learn about your damn body so you don't sound like an inexperienced teenager the next time you overshare.

"Thanks, but I think I've got enough."

"Will we make the paper?" Carter asked, pushing a shock of black hair behind her ear.

"You'll have to subscribe to see. Remember, I'll be changing your names to keep the stories anonymous."

"Ooh, that'll be fun to try to pick out, won't it, sugar-pie?"

Another hat wiggle put it exactly where it had been before she adjusted it for the tenth time in the last hour. "Sure will, pookie-butt."

Pookie-butt? For serious? Gathering my bag, I kept the cackle buried deep inside me. I needed a drink after that story, and I knew just the place.

Iris was talking to Lane when I arrived. Several people waved at me as I made my way over to them. Focused on getting a dose of reality, I barely paused to acknowledge them before I dropped onto the barstool next to Iris.

"You look like someone took a swing at you," Iris commented and gestured to Lane, who pulled the tap of my favorite beer and slid the full mug to me.

"Someone just made me listen to an even more poorly written version of *50 Shades*."

Lane snorted as Iris grinned. "Even more poorly?"

"The original was complete trash, which makes any copy even worse." I was judgmental about books, too. Still stumped me how something like that became the omnipresent companion to practically every straight woman in this country for months after it was published. I could have recommended several better written D/s stories to fill out their fantasy lives. They would have learned a lot more and enjoyed the read.

"One of your couples was into bondage?" Iris faced me fully.

"They were into telling me every detail of their sex lives."

"Not joking?" Lane plopped her forearms onto the bar top in front of me. It was one of the first times I'd seen her stop working.

"Not."

Her brown eyes showed a mix of confusion and interest. "That's not part of your usual interview questions, is it?"

"It's not. This woman just volunteered. I get the impression she talks this way all the time. When she heard about my article, she must have assumed that's what I was asking about."

"Really detailed?" Interest overtook any confusion now.

"Excruciatingly."

She shared a look with Iris before turning to me and arching an eyebrow. "How detailed?"

I thought for a moment, then asked, "Okay, personal question that you absolutely do not have to answer."

Lane stood upright and stepped back. Her head swiveled, checking for any customers who might need a drink or food. Something. Anything. Since it was a slow night, she couldn't give in to whatever had made her react to my question that way by disappearing. I glanced at Iris, who'd watched the peculiar reaction and responded by placing her hand flat on the bar top. A gesture I didn't understand, but Lane's eyes went to her hand and stayed. As did she. With a quick check of her hair's messy bun, Lane expelled a breath and settled back at the tip of our conversation triangle. I was dying to question what just happened, but I'd let it sit. Lane was skittish about something personal. I wouldn't ask about it while we were at her work.

"Go ahead," Iris encouraged, her eyes moving between mine and Lane's. Her hand still rested on the counter, acting as a focal point for Lane's nerves.

I'd almost forgotten what I'd said, too engaged in figuring out what just happened. Riffling back a few seconds, I picked up where I'd left off. "When you think of, or if you're like this chick, describe your private parts, do you ever use words that would apply only to male genitalia?"

Iris did a spit take. Literally. A sip of beer sprayed out in a fine mist as she burst into laughter. Lane snickered, all nervousness vanishing. She reached for a towel and started wiping up the beer spray as a full laugh slipped out.

"No, seriously. Maybe I'm in the minority on this because it's certainly in enough lesbian romances. I've just never heard a woman actually use that language outside of a book until today."

Iris's hand gripped my forearm as she regained her composure. "What, like her clit is a mini," she paused and looked over her shoulder before continuing in a lower voice, "dick?"

"That very description, yes. Used that word and the other one. For her own body part. Not a toy, part of her own flesh."

"Oh, wow," Lane breathed out, completely back to normal. "Quite an afternoon, eh?"

I nodded, still reeling from how very descriptive and open Max and Carter had been. "So, it's not a Seattle butch lesbian thing, then?"

"What's not a Seattle butch lesbian thing?" Riley asked as she pushed in between Iris and me to order beers for her pool playing group.

"Vega was asking if everyone owned a Seahawks jersey," Iris lied, shooting a cautious glance at Lane before smiling at me. Something major was again unspoken in that glance. I didn't think it had to do with not mentioning sex in polite conversation. She didn't want the topic brought up with Riley, and she was overly concerned about Lane. I wanted to find out why, but with Riley here, it wasn't the right time.

"Oh, that's not just butches, babe. That's everyone." Riley slapped my back as she usually did whenever she got within reach of me. "Wait till the season starts. It becomes the standard outfit at work for casual Fridays in town."

"Has it always been like that?" I played along with the change in topic.

Lane snorted while Riley enthusiastically bobbed her head. Iris spoke the truth. "Only diehard fans even knew we had a team when they played in the Kingdome."

"She's exaggerating." Riley bumped my shoulder. "Give me a hand delivering the beers. There's someone I want you to meet."

Exhausted from the day in the sunshine and the oddly draining interview, I really wanted to stay put right where I was.

Then I noticed the five beers she had to carry, and my manners propelled me into motion.

"You're still talking to her, at least. I guess she didn't treat you badly when she kicked you out the door the next morning, huh?" Riley asked when we were out of earshot.

I stopped and sloshed some beer onto my hands, turning to face her. "What?"

"Iris. Remember, I tried to warn you about her. She's a one-night stand kinda gal. A total player. Hope you're not trying to win her back."

"We're just friends. There's nothing going on between us."

She gave me a disbelieving look, then shrugged. "Then you're open to meeting my friend. We weren't sure what your type was, but Greer is hot enough for you not to care."

Only my deep-rooted courtesy kept me from dumping the beer on her. First, she insults my friend, makes assumptions about me, then tries to set me up? What gave her the impression I was open to that? I hadn't minded the occasional chats we'd had in the bar, but this was overreaching on her part.

"Greer, meet Vega, the one I've been telling you about," Riley said from ten feet away.

The entire group turned to appraise me. A day in the sunshine had made me hot and sticky. I knew I looked a sight. It shouldn't matter, but for some reason, it did.

"The reporter, yes?" a short brunette asked from beside Riley's buddy Devon. She was attractive enough, but I so wasn't in the mood. Not only had it been a long and weird day, but I couldn't stand being set up.

"Writer," I corrected, handing the beers I was holding to Devon and Greer. "Nice to meet you." Then I turned and started walking back to where I'd been.

"Wait!" Riley said. "Don't you want to stay a while? Play a game?"

"Don't have time. I really just stopped in for a quick beer and to say hello to my friends." I pointed at Iris and Lane, realizing that I probably sounded rude since I hadn't counted her among my friends. "Have a good evening."

When I retook my seat, Iris nudged my shoulder. "Not to your taste?" Her eyes cast over the group and lingered on Greer.

"Wasn't my objective for the night."

Her gaze came back and ran over me, efficient and appraising. "Focused, secure, I get it and like it."

"Aren't you the same way?" My curiosity got the better of me. She didn't appear to discriminate in the women she took home from the bar, but I knew I wasn't seeing everything.

Those eyes studied mine for a long time. "We do have that in common."

I felt my lips twitch into the start of a smile. Wouldn't be examining why that response made me feel so good anytime soon. I'd just enjoy the shared moment.

13

LEE & EMERSON

Halftime at Key Arena generated a carousel of lesbians. That might be a slight exaggeration, but pretty much everywhere we looked women were holding hands. They were mixed among families, fathers with daughters in basketball jerseys, kids with painted faces, and basketball fans in every variety, but the carousel of women who loved other women was impressive. I didn't remember this phenomenon at my first WNBA experience in Chicago.

When the couple of the night suggested we do the interview at the game, I was hesitant. Halftime wasn't that long, but they assured me they'd stay if needed. Iris volunteered to go with me to the game, so even if the interview tanked, we'd have a good time. She was currently chatting with some women she knew in the makeshift club area outside of Section 110 after she'd secured one of the few tables for me. It had taken a dose of her customary charm to get the couple she knew to give up a table for my interview, but it was worth it.

Lee was a pretty pixie type. Her spouse, Emerson, was a long-limbed androgynous beauty. They were suburban soccer moms now, but they'd been circus performers when they met. Honest to goodness, circus performers. My mind had gone to lion tamers or elephant riders, but theirs had been the human circus variety, twirling on hanging drapes and lines, swinging, lifting, and stretching into unnatural positions. An aerial ballet. They'd lost some of their muscle tone, but both still looked like they could grab anything that dangled and get right back into their routine.

They spilled their story in ten minutes, concise and lovely. One of the few couples that had taken their time to fall in love. So far, the majority of my stories were about falling into bed, then mistaking those feelings for love. This one was nicely paced and set in the backdrop of traveling, performing, and high drama among their circus mates.

Surprisingly the story had been free of clichés, which I was learning to appreciate more and more as I talked to every couple. Other than moving to the suburbs, having two point five kids, and buying Subarus, they had an imaginative story.

"For me it was love at first swing," Lee admitted and a cute blush took over her cheeks. Together over ten years, and she still blushed when she talked about her partner.

Emerson laughed and snaked an arm around Lee's shoulders. This was their date night, and I was grateful they'd chosen to spend part of it with me. "I was the lunkhead. Took me a little longer to figure out she was the one."

"She wasn't convinced unconditional love could exist for her," Lee told me.

The smile I'd been flashing throughout their story faded as Lee dropped the first cliché of the night. Unconditional love doesn't exist except from pets and maybe some mothers who can be blind to the actions of their children. But from a partner, no. Every partner's love has conditions, whether she wants to admit it or not. *Don't change into a person I no longer even like ten years from now. Don't cheat on me. Don't disrespect me. Don't harm me or the people I love. Don't commit treason and force me to choose between backing you or giving you up to remain free to raise our children. Don't drink the last of the milk and put the empty carton back in the fridge.* Those are all conditions. Sure, some partners will overlook one or two of those conditions, but at some point, they will have had enough. I was fairly certain if Emerson flipped out and killed one of their kids, Lee's love wouldn't be so unconditional anymore.

My head tipped back, trying to eject my critical thoughts. It probably explained why none of my relationships had ever worked out. I'd actually laughed in the face of a girlfriend who once said, "I like you just as you are." Despite her actions to the contrary in our relationship—hinting that I should wear more makeup, secretly ruining some of my favorite clothes so she could pick ones she preferred, asking me to keep opinions on certain subjects to myself around her friends—the quote alone made me snicker. It drove me crazy when people quoted from movies, trying to be sincere but not realizing that they'd just quoted a movie instead of coming up with something on their own. Paraphrase, at the very least. Laughing at the girlfriend's Mark Darcy impression hadn't gone over too well. She dropped me soon after that conversation. Apparently she didn't like my cynical side just as it was.

"...in front of the whole crowd," Lee was saying.

My mind snapped out of the haze of cynicism to refocus. Something happened in front of a crowd that I hadn't heard and probably should. "Excuse me?"

"We were performers." Emerson shrugged as if that explained what I'd zoned out on.

"Could you repeat that?" I asked Lee, waving a hand at the end-of-halftime migration of fans going back to their seats.

"I said that she asked me to marry her as we were taking our bows after a performance in front of the whole crowd. Got down on her knee and everything."

"Wow." My eyes widened. So not how I'd want to be asked to get married, but I wasn't a big public displayer of affection. A public declaration of love/marriage wouldn't work for me. Not only that, the person was obligated to agree to the proposal to keep from looking like a jerk in front of a crowd.

"I knew she'd love it, and I just couldn't wait anymore. You know how that feels?" Emerson wasn't really asking. She just assumed I did. What person our age wouldn't?

But I didn't, and for the first time, I was a little sad about that. That was really why I was single. I'd never had that can't-wait-anymore feeling with anyone. "Thank you so much for the story. It's a keeper for sure."

Lee's eyes brightened, and she went in for a smooch from Emerson. "We'll make the article?"

"You will," I confirmed because they were two circus performers in love. Need I say more?

"This was fun." Emerson stood from the table. "We'd better get back to our seats before our friends think we decided to skip out early."

"The team *is* losing and telling our story has made me feel a little romantic." Lee's eyebrows wriggled at her wife.

I laughed and left them to decide if they'd go watch the rest of the game or sneak home to get it on while the kids were over at their parents' house.

"Good story?" Iris came over and handed me one of the sodas she'd bought for us.

I took a sip as we waited out the milling crowd, in no hurry to return to our seats. My eyes landed back on Iris. Casual tonight, she had on faded jeans and a t-shirt from a used sports equipment store in San Antonio where she'd worked in high school. The first time she wore it prompted all sorts of questions about her home town and why she'd moved here. She deflected most, as any good detective would, but I got enough to make me feel like we were on equal ground with what we knew about each other. My reporting skills had been failing me up to that point when it came to learning about her.

I looked away from her threadbare t-shirt and watched Emerson and Lee duck through one of the section tunnels. "It was, actually. They seem sweet."

"I used to see a lot of them when they lived up near me. Now they're in Maple Valley. I haven't seen them in more than a year." She pushed a hand through her hair. In the month I'd known her, sun exposure lightened it a full shade. The color could barely be qualified as light brown now. Not quite as blond as mine, but with more sunshine, the blond highlights could overtake the brown completely.

"I take it that's far away?" I asked, not having studied the area before deciding that Seattle would be a good stop on this interview tour.

She rolled her eyes at me. "I'm buying you a map. It's a suburb southeast of the city. When I was on the force, I didn't think anything of driving all over the region in a day. Now, I can't be bothered to drive ten miles to get together with people."

I often felt that way. "Age, huh?"

"Experience," Iris commented.

"Laziness," I added.

"Not worth it," Iris agreed.

As we started back toward the seats, I admitted, "Some people are."

Because I was pretty sure if I lived here permanently and Iris moved out to the suburbs, I'd make the effort to keep our weekly tennis date and hang out with her whenever I could.

14

Hunter & River

Halfway through tonight's story, I evaluated, yet again, the purpose of moving forward with this article series. Some of the stories were enjoyable, and I certainly appreciated meeting all these people and how generously they shared a part of their lives. I didn't, however, enjoy discovering how judgmental I'd become in my old age. At twenty-two, I couldn't have been this cynical. At thirty-four, I surely wouldn't have rolled my eyes upon hearing yet another trite tale. At forty-six, I hear how a woman roughly my age seduced a direct subordinate, who was twenty-five years younger, and I want to shake her silly. The age difference was forgivable, not something I'd go for, but forgivable. Some people were old souls and didn't fit with other people in their twenties. The direct subordinate thing, though, that needed to be stopped. Not only did it open the company up to lawsuits, but it was entirely unfair to the subordinate and her coworkers during and after the affair ended.

"She directly reported to you at work?" I asked Hunter, trying not to show my disdain for that action.

"She was my secretary," Hunter proclaimed proudly. "I know, I know, the boss has an affair with her secretary, right?"

Not really, but sort of right.

"And you were married at the time?" I clarified.

"Not legally." She managed to look both bothered and relieved about that.

Of course not legally, because we all knew when the state we lived in passed the gay marriage law or was swept up by the Court's decision. She'd been with her former partner well before Washington legalized gay marriage, but I never believed that legality had anything to do with marriage. If people were living together, sharing finances, sharing experiences, planning for the future as a couple, they're married. A legal contract shouldn't make them any more committed.

"You don't mind me writing about how you got together?" I wasn't sure she understood when she agreed to this interview what might be included.

"We have a great love story," River said dreamily, still in the I-can't-believe-I-bagged-my-boss stage of their relationship.

One that included adultery and violation of most corporate HR policies. Yeah, a love story for the ages.

I looked at Hunter. "You were married when you hired River, developed a romance with her while still married, and offloaded some of her responsibilities onto her coworkers so she could accompany you on business trips. Then when HR found out about your relationship, you had River's career path altered so you could continue to be together. Is that accurate?" I felt like I needed to confirm their story. They might feel blindsided otherwise.

"I wasn't *married*," Hunter enunciated like I was a moron.

"You were in a committed relationship with someone other than River, yes?"

Her eyes swept away from me. She shrugged. "I fell in love, what can I say?"

That you're a cheater, but whatever. "I'm saying that I'll be including those details in this story if you consent to continue."

Her eyes widened as she finally understood why I was being so particular. "Oh."

"But, baby, we didn't do anything wrong. Sheila's not mad or anything." River patted Hunter's bicep.

Bet she was at the time. Never met a woman yet who's okay with being cheated on.

"Our story needs to be shared," River whined.

"You're right, lambkin," Hunter told her. "We fell in love. No one can blame us."

You, you mean. No one can blame you, I wanted to say. River probably hadn't set out to make her boss break up with her partner. She just wanted a job, which she no longer had. She's probably the secretary to some other middle-aged asshole who thinks about leaving his wife for someone twenty-five years younger.

"Okay, then, thanks for sharing."

"When can we read it?" River asked, eyes glittering. She could practically taste the fame. I wouldn't be spoiling her fame-seeking motives by letting her know that her name wouldn't be published until after the series ended.

"The articles are starting up in about a month," I reported, not committing one way or the other. Likely, it would be included, if I could manage not to be too horribly Judgey Judgerson when I wrote it up.

Slipping my notebook and recorder into my bag, I escaped to the bar. Lane was mixing seven drinks at once, and Iris was in the process of standing from a barstool as I sat.

"Hey," I greeted both.

"The secretary affair? Don't you have a million of those stories already?" Iris asked, perching back on the stool to delay her exit.

"You could have warned me before I sat with them. And no, they're only my second, but the first with the added adultery angle."

"Why would they want that advertised?" Lane asked as she shook some elaborate cocktail up by her ear. "Hunter's been trying to convince people that she was already broken up with Sheila before she started with River. When that didn't work, she said that Sheila left her first."

My eyes shot to Iris, shocked that Lane had spoken an entire paragraph, and shocked again that she'd shared anything about her patrons. She was normally pretty tightlipped.

"Sheila's a friend," Lane explained when she caught my astonishment.

Ah, that explained it. "I let them know that I'll be writing about the whole story, not just the lovey-dovey part."

"Good," Lane said and went to deliver the cocktails.

"Where are you off to?" I turned back to Iris. She'd been about to leave when I first sat down. Wearing light grey pants, a blue cap sleeve shirt, those shoes from the other evening, and a hint of eyeliner, she looked ready to blend in again.

"New hire background checks."

My face scrunched up. "Exciting."

"Easy work and pays the bills," she said with an unbothered shrug.

"Do you use one of those identity services?" Too much was on those sites. What wasn't could be found on the applicant's social media pages because they often didn't realize they should take down anything questionable before applying for a job.

"For the initial assessment, yeah. This is the surveillance part of it."

Aversion to the perceived evening of boredom dropped from my expression. Now it was all interest. I'd been right about her outfit. She stood out in this bar, but on the street, she'd look like any woman in business casual attire. "You're following someone for a standard background check?"

"It's not standard. This firm likes to be certain about their new hires because they usually stick around until retirement."

"Smart, but expensive." Really expensive if they're employing a PI to surveil their applicants.

"Software company. They can afford it, and the applicants sign off on background checks."

"Nice." And it was. This was far better than following a suspected murderer. I knew she was good at her job, but being on her own to follow a guy who'd already killed one woman twisted my internal organs into a knot. "I'll walk you out."

"You drove, right?"

"What's this obsession with driving?" I teased.

She looked away, the tease not landing as I'd intended. "It's just not the safest area to walk."

"Oh," I sat back, strangely affected by her concern. I hadn't known it wasn't safe. Compared to some areas I'd walked in Chicago at night, this part of Capitol Hill didn't rate on the danger scale. "I walked."

Her eyes glanced to the front window. It was dusk, still light enough to make it home before full dark. "I'll drop you home."

"That's okay. I'll be extra aware."

"I'm glad, but I'll be driving right past your building. Let me drop you."

She wasn't relenting or explaining this sudden concern. "Okay. Thanks." We had a car ride for me to extract the story behind the concern. After all, I was a master interviewer. Then again, she was a master interrogator, so I might find myself on the stumped end of the conversation once again.

15

Eduardo & Norris

Dude ranches that catered to singles. Did such things exist? According to the two guys slurping the most complicated cups of coffee across from me, they did. Meeting at a dude ranch was different enough, but a dude ranch catering to singles? Gay singles?

"It was a gay singles vacation?" I clarified because if they just happened to be two single gay guys at a singles dude ranch, that would be pretty incredible.

"Oh, yeah. Twelve hot guys roping horses and sweaty, sexy ab flexing." Eduardo winked a dark eye and looped an arm around his partner. The partner didn't look like he'd kept up his sexy abs, if he'd ever had them, but he was cute enough with a full head of thick brown hair. Eduardo's black hair was thinning in a few places, but his sharp nose and sexy mouth took the focus away from his vanishing hairline.

"There was plenty of the sexy ab flexing," Norris confirmed, not bothered that his husband was beginning to drool at the memory.

"Had you been on a working ranch before?"

"Nope. Two of my friends were going and dragged me along." Norris came across as extremely easygoing. "I figured I could pet some horses and let them get their cowboy on, but it was pretty fun. You ever been?"

"Can't say that I have." A cousin of mine owned a working ranch in Maryland. I'd had enough ranch work in my lifetime. I didn't need to pay someone for a vacation version of visiting my cousin.

"We were both drooling over the same guy. A hired model, probably."

"We have no proof of that, babe." Eduardo probably had to insert this every time they told their story.

"Looked like a hired model. He was a ranch hand, totally unavailable, there to torment our single, desperate eyes." Norris heaved a heavy sigh.

I laughed at the dramatics. "But you found each other?"

"We bonded over our pathetic sexy abs crush," Eduardo confirmed. Wiry thin, he might never have had sexy abs either.

"Sweet," I commented because it rather was. And amusing. "No sexy abs crushes for each other?"

"Oh, please, I haven't seen an ab on my cubicle-dwelling stomach in, like, ever," Norris joked.

I laughed again. Eduardo didn't seem to mind missing out on sexy abs in real life. They were one of my favorite couples so far. Get rid of the crush on the same guy, and no one would guess them to be the gay couple in the article that week.

On my way back to my apartment, I passed Lane's bar. Eduardo and Norris had me in a great mood, and I wanted to share it with my friends. It felt especially nice without the added pressure of needing to get an interview while I was there.

Lane's customary twitch of the lips was much shorter than usual tonight. Not many people were around, Iris included. It could be the reason for Lane's unconventional greeting, but I didn't think so.

"Everything okay?" I asked her after pointing to the soda nozzle.

She shrugged and poured my favorite for me. Her eyes scanned the interior as if trying to drum up more business. When her glance shot to the back office three times on her sweep, I guessed whatever was bothering her had to do with Charlie. Lane wasn't easy to get to know. She'd joined us for lunch a couple of times, a movie once, and to a Mariner's game, but otherwise, our interactions were confined to this bar. She did deadpan better than anyone, and I liked her a lot. I'd also like to get to know her better, but she was a slow roaster. That suited me fine. I didn't mind waiting for something really good.

"What can I do to help?" I tried a different angle.

A frustrated breath left her mouth as she shook her head. The unruly knot of sable hair that formed her usual style looked more ruffled today. As if she'd adjusted it one too many times. Her brown eyes were pleading with me to drop it as much as they were asking me to continue pushing.

"Hey, Vega," Charlie's gruff voice interrupted us as she walked briskly from the back office. "How's the article going?" She was walking quickly toward the exit, not caring about my response. In the next second, she was outside, presumably leaving for the night.

"Does she ever work a full night?" I asked, then clamped a hand to my mouth. That wasn't a kind observation and certainly unprofessional in front of her employee.

Lane gave another frustrated breath and shake of her head. Instead of the usual open stance she took behind the bar, her shoulders were rounded, and she kept herself at an angle as if to deflect any attention. She was constantly in motion, prepping lemon slices, cleaning surfaces, taking and making drink orders. Tonight, she was also guarded.

"Something's wrong; I can tell." I focused on the swiping actions she kept making with the towel.

"It can wait till Iris gets here," she finally admitted.

My lips curled up. Just as I'd hoped. Iris would be coming in tonight. Pulling out my phone, I sent her a short text to tell her I was at the bar. A phone chime sounded from the entrance as Lane and I both looked up to catch Iris on her way inside. Her eyes crinkled when she saw us, not bothering to check the message on her phone.

"Hey there," she greeted and dropped onto the stool next to me. Her smile was bright at first, then it petered out when she faced Lane. "What's wrong?" On a swivel, her head took in the entire bar. She was looking for someone in particular. My posture stiffened. That sense that something was going on that only they knew about came over me again.

"No," Lane said, and Iris's posture relaxed. The one word didn't explain anything to me, but to Iris, it spoke volumes. "It's Charlie."

"What's she done now?" Iris groaned, clearly not surprised that Lane was upset by something Charlie had done.

Lane's eyes went instantly shiny. The brown shimmered in the low lighting of the bar. A lump formed in my throat at the unexpected emotional display. Iris's hand shot across the bar and grasped hers. It calmed her enough to explain. "She's selling the bar."

My mouth nudged open. Not that Lane couldn't get another job bartending someplace else, but this place was this place because of Lane. She pretty much lived here and took care of everything. Almost to the point of co-dependence. If she weren't so together otherwise, I'd be a little worried about her.

"Now? Dammit," Iris swore. "Did you tell her?"

"What's the point?" Lane replied.

"What's happening here?" I tried to get a handle on this conversation.

Iris looked at Lane for permission before speaking. "Lane's been saving up to buy this place from Charlie when she retires. It's supposed to be six more years. Charlie's been counting it down. Why the sudden change, did she say?"

"She had a doctor's appointment today." Lane stopped the busy wipe down of the back bar, not needing that extra level of comfort to talk to her best friend. "Likely he told her that her smoking and drinking was aging her too fast, and she's decided to reduce her stress to zero."

"What stress?" I scoffed and got a chuckle from Iris. "Seriously, Lane does all the work around here. She runs this place. Charlie's never around. How much stress could she possibly have?"

Lane's eyes shimmered again, but at least she appeared amused. "She didn't say anything, but she's been talking about how her doctor's been nagging her for years."

"Did she mention a price?" Iris asked.

Lane brushed the back of her hand against her cheek, stopping a tear before it fell. "She thinks she'll get three-fifty for it."

Three hundred and fifty thousand? For this place? My eyes scanned the bar for the millionth time. It had an identity problem, part cocktail lounge, part sports bar, part restaurant bar. Desperately in need of an update, it was still better than a couple of the others I'd checked out since arriving.

"She's out of her mind," I said, and they both stared at me in surprise. "Unless she owns the building?"

"She doesn't. Even at a realistic price, I'm out of the running now. I need more time, lots more." Lane's shoulders hunched. She must have had her heart set on buying this bar.

"I've got some savings, but not enough to cover what she's asking." Iris's perfect posture failed her. I popped upright, surprised by the offer. It was one thing to offer a friend money to help cover expenses if she's hit hard times. It was quite another to offer to help buy her a bar. "Sorry, Lane. This sucks." She reached across the bar top to squeeze her hand again.

"Yep," Lane managed but swallowed roughly.

"Close up," Iris encouraged, false levity in her voice. "Hardly anyone's here. Charlie's gone for the night. Send a text that you're sick and closing."

Seconds passed as her eyes stayed on Iris. Decided, she reached for her phone and typed in a message. Then she went into the back to tell the cook they were closing.

I looked to Iris for an explanation of Lane's intense melancholy. Her eyes flicked to the kitchen, and she shrugged. She wouldn't tell me more about Lane's upset without Lane there. I liked that about her as much as it frustrated me. Lane seemed far more upset than someone just losing a business opportunity. Surely there were other bars she could buy when she'd saved up enough money. Some in better condition than this one, which needed more than just a little lipstick added.

When Lane came back from the kitchen, Iris went over to a back cabinet to extract a stack of towels. She tossed them into the bar sink and reached for a disinfectant cleaner. I reached across the bar top and waited for Iris to hand over a cleaning towel. They both stared at me, Iris with a proud look and Lane with enough surprise to bring back that ghost of a smile. I could help her wipe down some tables. She needed a break. I didn't need to know her whole story to know she needed to get out of this bar as soon as possible tonight.

16

Dale & Kennedy

News had already spread among the bar's usual patrons. The mood somber as I sat through another interview. The regulars were worried, rightly so, that a change in ownership would mean no more catering to the lesbian and gay crowd. Finding another gay owner to take over the space was a bleak prospect.

My eyes caught on Iris, then flicked to Lane. She'd missed a day of work, shocking everyone. Iris had been absent, too. I'd stopped in to see how Lane was coping with the news a day later and couldn't believe neither of them was there. I liked the bar, but they were the draw for me in this place.

"I don't know what we'll do if it closes," Kennedy said with a sigh. She'd been doing this often throughout the interview tonight. "We love this place, and now it's going to close?"

"You don't know that, sweetie," Dale assured her with a pat to her wide back.

"I was so excited to tell Vega our story in our favorite place, and we find out it could be gone in a couple months." Kennedy sighed again and rested her blond head in her palm.

"Sweetie," Dale soothed again, the hand now rubbing circles on Kennedy's back. "Let me get you another glass of chardonnay. Vega, anything?"

"I'm good, thanks." I looked down at my notes to see where Kennedy had gone off topic. She'd been telling me about some competition they both entered that helped prompt their declarations of love to each other. Badminton? Hot dog eating? What had it been?

Another breathy sigh sounded from across the table. Kennedy was staring after Dale. "Doesn't she look exactly like

Xena? It's how I first noticed her. A living breathing Xena in a bowling alley in my neighborhood. I just had to meet her."

My teeth bit into my upper lip. Ah, yes, a bowling competition. And no, Dale didn't look anything like Xena. Not that I was a Xena fan, but I knew what the character looked like. Dale was five-five at most, had mousy brown hair, hazel eyes, and a conical shape to her body. She didn't look like anyone on that show as far as I remembered. Of course, to Kennedy, coming in at an inch under five feet, someone five-five would be pretty damn tall. If Dale wore blue, her eyes might look more blue than greenish hazel. Her light brown hair, though, was shaggy short, not at all long and black. Based on the conversation we'd been having, she hadn't ever been much for exercise. Yet, people found similarities wherever they wanted. Who was I to fault someone for thinking her sweetie was the embodiment of the ubiquitous lesbian fantasy woman?

"Which is your favorite episode?" she asked, her eyes still lingering on Dale up at the bar.

"Hmm?" I asked, scratching a random note on the page. It might have said: *Dale, in no way looks like Xena, but her delusional partner believes she does.* But my handwriting was a little hard to read. I could decipher it later. "Oh, uh, the one with, uh, what's her name, Gabrielle, yeah, and Xena around a fire pit."

"Which one? The," and she continued to summarize every episode where there was fire and the two main characters. I had no idea which one I'd been thinking of—the one and only episode I'd seen—but figured it would fill time until Dale got back, and we could conclude this interview.

A slender blond woman was shaking hands with Lane when I glanced over again. In the next instant she was following her into the kitchen. Iris was talking to a striking black woman with tight curls that spiraled out from her head in a fluffy crown. Beside her stood two blondes who kept changing their shade of blond every time they came into the bar, a butch who showed up with more piercings every night, a gorgeous Asian woman who often flitted from one group to the next, and another dark-haired butch who stepped right out of the fifties with rolled cuffs on her jeans and t-shirt.

"Ever written any fanfic?" Dale asked, making me realize that she'd retaken her seat. Probably a while ago, since she'd picked up on Kennedy's Xena-obsessed thread.

"No." I tried not to let anything shade my tone. One false note here might push Kennedy the wrong way. If Xena weren't a fictional character and could be stalked, Kennedy would be the lead trainer of that stalking class.

"That's how Kennedy and I first got to talking. I was an avid reader." Dale took a sip of her drink. "I can send you links to a few good sites, if you want."

"I've seen many of them." I haven't read more than one or two stories on the sites, but I've seen them. Years ago, I did a lot of research and wrote a story on fanfic authors, back when people wouldn't leave Mulder and Scully alone until they finally got together. Which, of course, ruined the show. Ha! Listen to me, sounding almost like Kennedy with her stalkee, Xena.

After a few more questions, I had enough to complete their story for my article. I'd leave out the delusional Xena lookalike comment so as not to tip off my readers, but otherwise, it was a nice romance. From the grand spectacle that was a neighborhood bowling alley.

"Hey, Vega," Iris greeted and gestured to the more condensed group of women she was chatting with. "Meet Cyrah, Ruth, and Cheryl." She pointed first to the striking black woman with the tight curls, then to the James Dean wannabe with short dark hair and almost translucent white skin, and finally to the gorgeous Asian woman who'd halted her duck-out when I approached.

"Nice to meet you." I shook their hands as Ruth's eyes wandered freely over me. The other two might have been doing the same, but Ruth's intensity brought my guard up. She opened her mouth, and Iris knocked the back of her hand against her chest, stopping whatever she was going to say. Ruth held up her hands in surrender and backed away, but not before her eyes ran up and down me again.

Iris turned to face me when they left to join their other friends. "Ruth would hit on a tree. Thought I'd save you the embarrassment." My eyes flicked over to Ruth again, happy not to have to fend her off, but Iris's worried tone brought me back. "Unless you go for that type? Did I just block you?"

A grin tugged at my lips until I realized that she wasn't joking. "You're worried?"

"What kind of friend would I be if I stepped on your toes when you could get your freak on?"

I laughed hard at that. "My freak on? Is that a thing here?"

"If you don't know, I'm not going to be the one to tell you about it. Call your mom and ask for 'the talk.' Or go hang out with some high school girls where you'll probably learn more than you want to know."

I laughed again as my eyes spotted Lane and the blond woman making their way from the kitchen over to the pool table area. Both came in around five-four, had the same slender shape to their bodies, and they looked good together. My eyes dipped down to check out the woman's calves under the long shorts she was wearing. They were more toned than mine, possibly even Iris's. I wanted those calves, not enough to work specifically on those muscle groups, but it didn't stop me from wanting the same tone. "Who's the fit blonde?"

"Is she your type?" Iris's eyebrows fluttered in jest.

"You going to block me again?"

"Afraid I am." A smile flared. "She's married, straight married, and happily."

"Ah." I wiggled my fingers for more information.

"You know the employer I run those background checks for?"

"The paid stalking you do? Sure, I remember," I kidded.

She smacked my chest this time. "That's her sister, Helen. She's a chef."

My brow furrowed, not following what a software employer and a chef sister had to do with walking around a bar. "Are you monitoring her? The software sister wants to make sure her chef sister is actually her sister?"

"There's that comedian thing again," Iris scoffed. "I'll get you a vest if you want to go out on tour."

"It's almost like you're clever." I flicked my hand toward Lane and the chef sister for the rest of the explanation.

"The software exec also does some venture investing. Lane was so crushed about the premature sale, I called and asked if she'd ever consider investing in a bar."

My heart sped up, happy to hear that Lane might get her wish. I searched the bar for the software sister but didn't see anyone paying the duo much attention. "Where's the investor?"

"She lives in Virginia, but her sister lives here and has food industry experience. She'll trust her judgment. If Helen likes the bar, she might go for it."

That easy? I hoped Lane wouldn't get ripped off in this deal. "What does a software exec know about the bar business?" Not that I knew much more, but I was feeling protective of Lane.

"She knows business. She'll look at the financials to see if it's profitable and wait on her sister's opinion of Lane and the operations around here. If both look all right, I think Lane might have herself a bar."

"Lane must be ecstatic." Provided the deal offered was a good one.

Tenderness showed on her face. Over the weeks, I'd moved from thinking they'd been together at one time to knowing with certainty that they'd only ever been friends. Very good, close friends. I envied that kind of friendship. As close as Iris and I were getting, they still had something very special. "She's trying not to get her hopes up. She's like that, but this would be the best thing to happen to her all year." She pushed out a hopeful breath. "She really needs it."

"I'll keep my fingers crossed."

"Thanks. I'll let her know you're pulling for her." Iris's tender smile shifted to me, and I felt as if she'd just swept me into their special friendship club.

17

After more than an hour of panicked searching of the apartment for my wallet, I finally got into my car and cautiously drove through the neighborhood's back streets, retracing the stops I'd made during the day. I hadn't noticed it was missing until after midnight when I was packing my messenger bag for tomorrow's interview. I checked all the usual places in the apartment before tearing it apart. I'd never lost my wallet, never left it behind. Never.

First stop was the QFC on Broadway. I'd used it to buy the week's groceries, but the store manager couldn't find a wallet in the lost and found. It still could have walked off with someone, but on to the next location.

The coffeehouse was still open. I dashed inside to look over the area where I'd conducted my first of two interviews this morning. I hadn't planned on conducting two today, but the straight couple needed to change their scheduled date. After hearing their story, I was glad I sat through two today. They'd spent time on opposing professional bicycle racing teams and somehow fell in love, despite their main riders absolutely hating each other to the point of minor sabotage efforts. They decided to ditch the competitive teams when one of those incidents produced serious road rash on a team rider. Retiring to a simpler life, they ran a small bicycle shop nearby.

After no luck at Tully's, I drove past the fast casual restaurant where I'd grabbed dinner. Closed. I'd have to check tomorrow if it wasn't at Lane's bar. I wanted to curse myself for the habit of paying with the business credit card and putting it in my pocket rather than into my wallet after every purchase. If not for that, I could be certain the wallet was at Lane's because I'd used the credit card there. Since it was still in my pocket, I was stuck checking all the spots from earlier today.

My eyes caught on the dash clock readout. At this hour, the bar would be closed, but my hands kept steering toward it. All the storefronts on the street were dark. Great. I'd have to wait until tomorrow to see if I'd left the wallet there. At least I still had two options to check tomorrow before I went through the hassle of cancelling my personal credit cards and applying for a replacement driver's license.

I was about to turn onto 12th to shoot down to Madison, when I spotted two women walking away from me. The streetlights were just bright enough for me to recognize Iris's stride. Pulling up next to them, I rolled the window down. "Hey, you two."

Lane whirled toward the street, face pale and tight. Iris must have been aware of my car creeping up on them based on her calm reaction. She gave a casual wave. "What are you doing trolling the streets at this hour?"

"I'll consider you my personal heroes if you'll let me back into the bar for a second. Please, pretty, please?"

Lane smiled, a full genuine smile that also seemed relieved. Not being a former police officer, she'd reacted as most people would when someone yells at her in the dark of night. "In desperate need of a pint?"

If only. "I think I might have left my wallet earlier."

She pointed toward the bar's parking lot. I reversed course and pulled in as they caught up to me and let me into the bar.

"Thanks so much. I'm sorry to hold you up, but I panicked when I didn't see it in my bag." I headed straight for the table I'd been sitting at. My hands searched the vacant chairs. I dipped down to look under the tabletop, like somehow it would be glued to the bottom of the table when it wasn't on the floor. I traced a path up to the bar, my eyes tracking every inch of the floor.

"I hate when I can't find mine," Lane admitted and went behind the bar. She ducked into the office and surfaced with a basket. In the next second her hand came up, grasping something small and brown and leathery with a zipper on top.

"Oh, thank you, thank you. You're definitely my hero." I reached for my wallet.

She whipped it back out of reach with a huge grin. "I don't know, Iris. What do you think? Should we look inside just to verify? The servers tend to chuck things into the office for someone else to deal with them."

"Verification would only be right," Iris double-teamed me.

"Funny." I made another swipe at the wallet. If not for the bar top between us, I would have been able to outreach her shorter stature.

"Anyone who leaves such a precious thing behind, we should really make sure it's yours. What if it's someone else's?"

Their teasing barely registered as the adrenaline from possibly losing my wallet started to drain. Irritation took its place at not being called when one of the servers found the wallet. They all knew I was Lane's friend. Tell her and let her call me. How hard was that? A simple peek inside and word to Lane wouldn't have been a lot of effort. "I swear I didn't leave it behind. I don't know how it got out of my bag. I've never lost a wallet before."

Iris smirked again. "Didn't I see Greer stop by your table after you finished interviewing your couple of the night?"

My eyes shifted between the two friends. "Yeah, what's that got to do with it?" She wasn't still pushing the "type" thing again, was she?

"Still fending off her efforts?" Lane took up the questioning. She'd never mentioned noticing how Greer always made a point of greeting me whenever we were in the bar together.

"I'm not fending off—what are you two up to?" My finger waved between them.

"If she doesn't get anywhere with you in person, she sometimes employs other methods," Lane said with a twitch of her lips.

"Is your phone password protected?" Iris asked. At my nod, she said, "Then your wallet might have some old school photos she'd like to see. Check to make sure you're really available since you aren't falling at her feet when she bats her eyes at you."

My head snapped back, eyes blinking in a daze. "She lifted my wallet to look at photos?"

"That and any other info that might be in there. In case of emergency contact, how many credit cards you have, cash you carry. It says a lot about a person." Iris tossed out these points as if we weren't talking about someone who committed a crime for absolutely no feasible reason.

Lane handed over the wallet, and I combed through it. Nothing looked different, except the current school picture I kept of my nephew was peeking out of its slot. All the cash was there. No, they had to be teasing.

"You're kidding, right?" They had to be because no one would be that stupid. Greer and I didn't even know each other. Stealing my wallet wouldn't do anything but tick me off. She had to know that.

"It's not the first time a wallet or phone has ended up in the lost and found after she's been in the bar." Lane flicked a questioning gaze at Iris when she noticed my bewilderment.

"Who turned it in?"

"One of her friends, as usual."

"That can't be right." I glanced at the former cop to see how she was reacting. Since nothing was stolen, it wasn't that big a deal. Disturbing, but not that big of a deal.

"Not to throw a wrench into your possible plans with her, but she gets a little clingy," Iris said.

"Stalker potential," Lane confirmed.

"Wasn't planning anything with her, and now, most definitely not." I waved the wallet at Lane. "Thanks for this and for opening up the bar after you'd already left. I really appreciate it."

"Not a problem. We'll walk you out." Lane motioned toward the door.

I repaid Lane's kindness by giving them a ride home. Both got out at her apartment building where Iris had left her car earlier in the day. Back on the road, it was another four blocks into the drive before I remembered that Iris had left the bar with someone earlier in the evening. Riley's buddy Devon made a comment about Iris's seductive prowess when she left. I wouldn't have made note of it, otherwise.

So, if she'd left with a conquest earlier, what the hell was she doing back after closing to leave with Lane?

18

Almost done with my workout, Iris came into the gym to join me. Seeing her sent a calming ripple through me. Last night's mad dash around town kept the adrenaline pumping well into the night, and I'd barely gotten any sleep.

"Hey, Vega," Iris greeted, taking up the treadmill next to me. Within seconds she stepped into a dizzying pace, putting my elliptical glide to shame.

"Morning. What have you got planned for today?"

"Fourth day on a ride along." She must have seen my confused look. I'd made a trip over to Spokane for part of last week, so I hadn't heard about her latest job. "A beverage company thinks one of their drivers is taking kickbacks from their clients. I'm their new trainee, riding along with every driver."

Having taken a few odd assignments over my lifetime, I knew what it was to enmesh myself in my subject's life. Willfully working as a beverage delivery trainee until I caught someone taking a payoff would have pushed my patience to the limit. "That'll take a while, won't it?"

"You'd think, but these guys don't think what they're doing can be seen, or they think I'm an idiot female who doesn't understand numbers or something."

"You've already seen evidence of it?"

She shot me a confident look. "Two of the three drivers I've ridden with, yeah."

"That's amazing. I can't believe it takes hiring a PI to get this info."

"Not to discourage anyone from paying my fees, but it doesn't. They could have had their interns ride along. That's how blatant the two drivers were."

"They thought it was only one driver?"

"They did," she confirmed and annoyingly ramped up her pace on the treadmill. Her well-defined arms swung with each stride, prompting me to apply more pressure to the elliptical handles for extra resistance. I wanted her arms and the chef lady's calves. My arms and calves looked and worked just fine, but it was good to strive for something. Iris's arms and Helen's calves.

"So why the extra days?"

"They want me to ride with all the drivers now."

My head tilted in admiration. "Nice job."

"Thanks. It's been hard work unloading all the beverage trays and stacking them in fridges. I definitely wouldn't want it as a real job." She acknowledged my confirming nod. "What about you? Writing or interviewing today?"

"I did some writing this morning. Helen invited me to go kayaking with her and her husband this afternoon. I was going to see if you wanted to join, but you've got beverages to haul and idiots to entrap."

"Not entrapping them." She laughed at my wording. "Helen? The chef?"

"I met her the next day when she came back to the bar. We chatted some, and I got her to agree to an interview with her husband that night. I like them, and they've got irregular hours."

"Flexible-hours friends are hard to come by. It's why you like me so much."

"Who said I liked you?"

Her arm came out and shoved me almost hard enough to topple me off the elliptical. She, on the other hand, kept up the annoying Olympic pace on the treadmill.

"Speaking of liking you," I started, a tease in my voice. "Did I see you leave with some cute brunette last night? Can't remember what Devon said her name was."

Iris glanced over, a curious expression on her face. "Did you?"

Even more curious. We hadn't discussed her bar exploits before, but since she'd teased me about Greer, I thought I could touch on the same territory with her. "I'm pretty sure I did. I don't think I've met her, but I've seen her before."

"And you think she's cute?"

Wait, what? What was going on here? "I thought she was attractive. Not for me, I was just complimenting you."

"Ah." Iris pushed buttons on the console and went into a warm down. I still had five minutes left on my hour of elliptical training. Iris tended to move from machine to machine for the hour.

"So?"

"What?"

"Really?"

"Yeah, really."

"You're going to make me ask?"

"Ask what?"

I growled and slammed the buttons harder than necessary to end my session and step off. "You leave with this cute brunette, but a few hours later, you're back at the bar and walking out with Lane."

All traces of the smile left her face. She jumped onto the sideboards of the treadmill and stopped the machine. "What are you implying?"

Her sharp tone surprised me. My hands came up. "Hey, nothing. I just—"

"You think I have something going with Lane?"

"No." Although I had the first time I met them. Not sure why the idea would be so offensive to her, though.

"That I'm taking advantage of women at the bar?"

I took a step closer to her and felt my stomach sink when she stepped off the treadmill and away from me. "No, Iris. No. I don't think you're taking advantage of anyone."

"So why'd you bring it up?" She pulled at the neck of her t-shirt, annoyed. "I know what people in there say about me."

Crap. She knew that her so-called friends thought she was a player. "It's not," I cut myself off. "I don't think anything of you. I'm not judging you. Judgment-free zone." My hand waved between us. "I didn't know it was a hot button issue for you. I'm sorry. I won't bring it up again."

Feeling about an inch tall, I turned and made my way to the door. I'd never seen her react this way before. That easy, no-limits friendship we were developing just ran into the invisible fence of a big fat limitation.

"Vega, wait." Her hand gripped my arm to stop my retreat. "I'm sorry. I overreacted."

I turned and saw the pleading look in her eyes. "No big deal. Really." Only it kinda was. I hated angering my friends. "I picked the wrong way to tease you. Didn't realize the sensitivity. Forget it."

"No, I was an asshole. I shouldn't have bitten your head off." Her eyes pleaded with me. "I just get that from a lot of people at the bar, and I thought it would be..."

"Different with me?" Now I felt even smaller. It seemed to be her one and only issue, and I'd stomped all over it. "I shouldn't have tried to tease you about striking out. It was stupid of me."

Her hand tightened on my arm. "Striking out?"

"Yeah, I know. Asshole me. I'm sorry." I placed my hand over hers. "I do want to be different, Iris. I'm genuine about that wish."

She turned her hand up to squeeze mine. "You are. I thought you were going to say something else, and I jumped down your throat before you could. Can we forget this conversation ever took place?"

I wouldn't because I definitely wouldn't be teasing her about leaving the bar with anyone. Ever again. Never ever. But I could try to forget how my stomach knotted up to the point of wanting to puke from causing her mistrust of me. "Only if you can. You're becoming very important to me, Iris. I don't want to do or say anything to make you uncomfortable. I might bungle things a bit, but understand that I have the best intentions."

"I know, and I forgot that for a minute. I feel the same way."

"Good. Then, I better go get ready for my kayaking adventure. I'll be thinking of you riding around stacking energy drinks and taking bribes while I'm relaxing on the water."

She laughed, and right then, nothing sounded better.

19

HELEN & JOE

Water slapped against my kayak as I pulled my paddle through Lake Union. We'd dropped in across the street from Joe's kayak shop. At first, it was difficult to battle for space among an entire lake filled with sailboats on this gorgeous afternoon. After an hour, I was getting the hang of it and enjoying myself and the company immensely.

"You ready to head back?" Helen asked as she smoothly slid up next to me. She and Joe both maneuvered their kayaks as if they'd been born in them.

I wasn't ready. I wanted to stay out on the peaceful water, stroking through the sometimes rippling, sometimes calm lake. After three or four thousand more times, I might be as good at it as they were.

"You're arms and shoulders will be killing you tomorrow if we stay out any longer today." Joe glided up on my other side. "It's not a normal motion for most people. You have to build up to a longer stay on the water. Trust me on this."

Since he built, sold, and rented kayaks for a living, I had to assume he knew what he was talking about. My arms and shoulders felt fine right now, but other than playing tennis, using the occasional weight machine, and typing, I didn't use my arms for anything else too strenuous.

We made our way back to the launch clearing and hauled our kayaks out of the water. I'd managed to stay fairly dry but had worn my one pair of outdoorsy, nylon blend pants in case I got soaked. Based on all the other activities Helen and Joe offered to introduce me to, I knew I'd be ordering more of these quick drying clothes.

"Hope you're hungry," Helen said as we loaded my kayak onto the rental rack and walked their custom jobs to the back of Joe's shop.

"I am and looking forward to dinner with a chef." I turned to Joe as he locked his shop. "Or does she make you cook at home since that's her job?"

He grinned, showing a ridge of teeth with prominent canines. "We share if we're not eating at the restaurant."

Sounds nice. Really nice. A true partnership. Rare from everything I'd experienced and, after all these interviews, heard about. I wondered if it had to do with the fact that they'd both waited until their late thirties to get married, and therefore, knew what they wanted and needed to make for a good life together. It could also be that they matched up well with the same muscle tone, each sporting different wash-and-go hairstyles, and healthy tans that indicated how much they liked to spend their free time outdoors.

We went to the doorway between his shop and her restaurant. They both kept odd hours for their businesses, staying open only Thursdays through Sundays. As I'd told Iris, it would come in handy when hanging out together.

"Nice place," I commented when they let me into their condo on the third floor. Open spaces and exposed brick walls gave it a loft feel, but the bedrooms were closed off and drywall wrapped the ceiling and ductwork. Condo-loft was probably the correct term for the place. A view of Lake Union filled the large windows lining both sides of the living room.

Joe gave me a tour of the space as Helen got started on dinner. Two dogs joined us from the massive laundry room. Golden retrievers that were well mannered but anxious for a run outside. Helen took them while Joe got their chef's stove fired up and I set the table.

Feeling as comfortable here as I'd been at Iris's and at my own place, I could envision spending more nights in their company. Perhaps I had found my home for the next year or more. I'd need to find something other than my pricey executive rental without the ability to write it off as a temporary housing expense. It shouldn't be too hard to find a nice but cheaper place close by. I'd have to give this a long think.

"We invited another couple to join us. The one I told you about?" Helen said when she came back with the dogs.

My brow rose. I remembered her mentioning another adventurous couple they knew with a good story. After hearing theirs, meeting while rock climbing—not on the trail near the cliff, they'd been on the rock face when they met—I was eager to interview this other couple. I could feel myself smiling, glad I wouldn't have to arrange the interview on my own, even if it meant working when I hadn't planned to work.

"I meant to ask," I said to Joe as he turned the pork chops to brown the other side. "What was your opening line with Helen as you two dangled off a cliff?" I tried for a cheesy impression of his voice, "Hey, beautiful, do you hang on this rock often?"

They laughed at my impression. Mellow seemed to be their overriding common character trait. As business owners, they should face stress every day, but they either hid it very well or got it all out with these outdoor activities. I should pull a page from their manual for life. Didn't think I'd enjoy the whole cliff dangling part of it, but I could embrace a little mellow to tame the critical a smidge.

"You make it sound like we'd fallen over the side of a mountain," Helen said through the laughter. "We were clipped in, scaling the rock face. On purpose."

"But not together?" I asked because I'd liked their story and wouldn't mind hearing more details.

"I'd never been there." She started chopping vegetables without looking. "Just read about it and had some time off, so I jumped in my truck and made the trek."

"I'd been there a few times with my climbing club," Joe said. "It wasn't hard to strike up a conversation when you're the only two people on a cliff wall."

"If ever there was a situation that didn't need a come-on line, that's probably it," I agreed.

Of all the couples I'd interviewed, they were the most suited to each other. The acrobats were a close second, but these two found partners that enjoyed the same things and were adventurous enough to explore other things they might like. My mind flitted to Iris. That dynamic was hard to find in a friend, let alone a partner. I'd lucked into that kind of friendship with her. Even if I'd put my foot in my mouth earlier.

"Our friends met on a whitewater rafting trip," Helen told me.

"One of them almost drowned," Joe inserted. "But we'll let them tell the story."

It wasn't the first time I'd gotten an interview when I hadn't planned on it. If their friends were the same easygoing types, the interview would be more of a conversation than work. Enjoyable work, which was my favorite kind.

"What about the sister who might help Lane. Is she married?" Iris had mentioned that the investor was gay. It would be interesting to put them in the same article. One gay sister, one straight, and see if people could pick which was which.

Helen chuckled. "Yeah, but she won't talk."

I laughed at the phrasing. "She doesn't talk at all, or she won't talk to me?"

"She doesn't talk about her relationship and certainly not to be published."

"Who, Willa?" Joe asked as he came back from settling the dogs into their crates. "I'd love to see Vega try. Can you imagine? She'd probably make a hole in the wall escaping the loft as fast as possible without stopping to open a door." He laughed and slung an arm around his wife.

"That or find something hard to hit us all with, hoping to knock us unconscious and wipe our memories," Helen added.

Now I really wanted to talk to her. I had a way with getting people to open up. No matter how hardheaded they might be. Someone this private would be interesting to try to crack. "Wow, she sounds interesting."

"She is that, but intensely private." Helen's face gave away her fondness. "It was a year before she finally admitted to her relationship with Quinn, and that was only when I caught them kissing after I'd walked into her house without knocking."

"Kinda hard to deny being in a relationship with someone you're kissing, you know?" Joe confirmed.

"Kinda hard," I agreed.

The doorbell heralded the interesting couple of the night. Over the course of the next hour, I gave serious thought to finding a more permanent place here. I liked these people. Add in Iris and Lane and a few others from the bar, it was all the incentive I needed to decide a change was in order.

20

In another airport, I settled in and thought back on the meeting I'd been summoned to. My editor, who'd loved the competition angle to the articles, now joined the worry of the other editors and her boss as to their mass appeal. They wanted to run a test article before announcing a contest and its extravagant prize. What I thought was a done deal now needed proof of popularity to rate what they offered. The test article's online poll response would decide if a wedding prize was offered. If it didn't garner enough interest, they'd offer a staff photographer to take photos of the winner's wedding instead.

More people than necessary had packed into the four meetings. More people with differing opinions on how to go about this series. I thought going freelance would be easier than working as a staff reporter. If these meetings were anything to go by, my assumption was wrong. The only benefit so far were the added interviews I'd picked up in the evenings near the paper's headquarters in northern Virginia. I also routed my return flight through Atlanta, Dallas, and Salt Lake to take advantage of the free airline ticket to pick up more interviews in different cities. Seattle was proving to be diverse among the locals and tourists, but it would help add legitimacy to the series if I talked to people in more cities.

My phone rang as I was charging it among a phalanx of six other phones and three laptops. Seeing who it was, I unplugged and walked toward the quietest corner I could find.

"Hey, Iris." A tremor rippled in my stomach. I'd had to leave for Washington DC the day after our misunderstanding in the gym before we could put our friendship back in solid order.

"Hi, Vega. Where you been?" Her voice held the same hesitation as mine.

"Had to fly out for a meeting with the paper."

"Oh." Relief this time.

"Last minute. I basically got on a plane as soon as they called."

"Okay, good. Yeah," she filled the void. "I thought, it's stupid, but I—"

"Thought I'd left because I said something careless to make you angry?" I guessed, not normally so direct with people because they could become overwhelmed or easily turned off. Iris believed in direct. It was one of the reasons we got along so well.

Her nervous laugh was loud and calmed the tremors in my stomach. "Yeah, something like that. When I didn't hear from you after two days, I thought I really screwed up."

"You didn't. We're bound to run into sensitive topics from time to time. We should just agree to talk it all the way out before we walk away."

"Good plan." She cleared her throat. "So, when are you coming home?"

Home. I liked the sound of that. Hadn't really had one for a while. Not the two years in Chicago nor the few in DC before that. Not since I left home after high school, but Seattle felt different. "I'm headed to Salt Lake in thirty minutes. I'll stay one night, then I'm back."

"Did you want to try for tennis?"

Our standing Thursday tennis game. I looked forward to them as much as any other time we spent together. "Absolutely. And maybe lunch to catch up?"

"Or dinner." Her voice held hope this time. "Whatever works."

"We'll figure it out," I confirmed, freeing some of that dread I'd been carrying around since ticking off my one true Seattle friend. "See you Thursday morning, Iris."

"Looking forward to it, Vega."

I hung up and surveyed the busy gate. Being in the third airport in three days no longer bothered me. I went back to the jungle of wires and reconnected my phone to sip up the last of the charge before I trudged onto a plane again. One more connecting airport, and then I'd be back.

* * *

One hundred and eighty-five square feet. As a living space. The condo manager thought this was an apartment. To rent. For thirteen hundred dollars. Gulp. We barely had enough room to turn around in this studio. I'd thought Iris's place was small, but this was miniscule. A studio in my current building, the only thing I could sensibly afford if I were going to give this book and freelance thing a try. The entire apartment would fit into my bedroom upstairs. It was hard to believe what seven hundred extra dollars would do to the size of an apartment. Seven hundred I didn't want to spend if I couldn't write it off or didn't own it.

Iris was trying to look positive. Her fake smile wasn't even fooling the building manager. "It's, um, cozy."

"Iris." I didn't need to say anymore.

"Your current place is available, Vega." the building manager said, yet again.

"Yes, you've said. Unfortunately, it's out of my price range now that I'm making this my home." I could afford a couple hundred more, but that was as far as my budget with sporadic income could stretch. Unfortunately, that meant I'd have to go small or live in a dump if I wanted to stay in this neighborhood. Super small, it seemed.

"We have another building on Olive. There's a studio there almost twice the size. Older building, but a larger studio."

Not even four hundred square feet. A dorm room, essentially. Ugh. "Thanks, I'll think about it. We've got a couple other appointments today."

Iris nodded her head enthusiastically. As much as she wanted me to stay in the neighborhood, she could tell that I was past the college space living phase of my life. She grabbed my arm to propel us into motion out of this closet of an apartment. "I was afraid to keep breathing in that place or use up all the oxygen."

I laughed but sobered quickly. "I'd forgotten how expensive cities can be on your own dime."

"You didn't live in the city in Chicago?" She started walking us down Madison toward the next building on our list.

"Nope, a bit up on the Blue Line. Took the train every day. Same with DC and New York."

"The bus system here isn't too bad." Again, she tried to sound positive, but I knew she was hoping that I could find something close enough to keep hanging out with her regularly.

"I'd rather stay as close to downtown as possible." I slid a grin her way. "I don't want to move out of that radius where it's too much of an effort for you to hang out."

She shoved my shoulder, making me stumble before righting myself. "Fifteen miles, max."

"There's another in Capitol Hill and one across the freeway to look at if you're truly up for the hunt today." I consulted my list, trying not to put pressure on her to accompany me.

"Absolutely."

"No PI work today?"

"Nothing that can't wait. I'm more vested in this."

I glanced at her. No teasing smile, no smirk. She was seriously invested in helping me find a place. My heart thumped at how happy that made me. "Thanks."

"Let's find you a place."

21

Nykos & Mariah

An hour spent laughing was just the medicine I needed after not finding an apartment yesterday. This guy should have been a comedian instead of a software executive. His wife added amusing tidbits to the conversation, but this guy was hysterical. He'd come into the bar with Helen last week. As her sister's business partner, he was there to perform due diligence on the investment's feasibility. When Helen introduced us, she basically ordered me to take down his story. I was glad I followed the order.

"The shark just swam away?" I interrupted his latest comedic riff to ask a clarifying question because how could I not? Sharks were involved; clarification was vital.

"Oh, normally I attract all kinds of animals and mammals. There's no end to my attraction level. You'll fall for me before we leave. Guaranteed." Nykos tapped his nose and gave a wolfish grin that was pretty hard to resist. His puffy face looked as if something venomous had stung him, but it went well with his barrel shaped body. Even if I went for guys, nothing about his looks would attract me and his personality would be exhausting twenty-four-seven. I was about to snark back when his hand came up in a stopping gesture. "Sexuality aside, lady, I attract."

"Except for sharks."

His eyes lit up at the banter. "Yeah, so maybe one species can resist."

"We were on the boat, screaming at him to swim faster." Mariah gripped his hand without realizing it. "This shark comes right up on him, gigantic fin, *Jaws* music blaring. I thought he'd lose a foot or something."

"And nothing happens, seriously, nothing." Disbelief showed on his face. "The thing skated right past me and went back out to sea."

"No way he confused you for a seal, babe."

"Something that ate a seal, maybe," he joked, which made me like him even more.

"And you're a little hairy." Her wide face crinkled into a grimace.

"Hirsute, buttercup. And you married it."

We all laughed at that one. "That's when you fell for him?" I asked Mariah.

"I was definitely more scared than I should have been for someone we'd just met on vacation."

I looked down at the sparse notes I'd taken, too involved in listening to their tale to actually scratch any notes. "You'd been hanging out together for how long?"

"It was a ten-day all-expenses paid couple's resort," she told me.

"On a private island?"

"Yep, just the resort and a little village owned by the resort. Stupidest idea I've ever had." He rolled his eyes. "I thought I could relax on the beach and read for hours to decompress from designing and coding."

"Relaxing was all I wanted to do," Mariah agreed.

"But?" I wanted to hear this one more time.

"Our significant others didn't." His shoulders heaved. "When you're at a couples-only vacation place, it's hard to do anything alone. You book a spa treatment, and it's supposed to be a couple's spa treatment. You book a jet ski, and it's a two seater. You want to go to yoga? Guess what, every stupid pose needs a partner. Everything is couple oriented. Idiotic."

"When in your life have you ever been to yoga?" His spouse gave him a playful punch.

"Hey, I can yoga with the best of them."

"Right, like you can make anyone fall for you?" she shot back.

"You did."

"Temporary insanity."

"That's lasted six years now?"

"Just plain old insanity, then." They both cracked up at that.

I was happy to have my digital recorder for this interview because I didn't want to miss a second of it. They'd been like this for an hour, and we'd barely scraped the surface of their story. "I have to ask, you were a foursome when you went to the island—"

"And two never came back," Nykos joked dramatically.

Mariah smacked him again. It was a large part of their relationship, joking and smacking. "We met on the plane ride down there. Got along great, ate together, went on those stupid excursions together."

"One of which involved a shark snubbing your man here?" I goaded and got a huge laugh from Nykos.

"It only took a day before Kos and I figured out we'd rather just relax and sit on the sidelines of the excursions while our partners took on the sometimes bone jarring adventures together."

Which is why I had to finish my question. "Did they also get together?"

"Oh, we didn't actually...no, not on the vacation. That would have been just wrong," Mariah assured me, looking sickened by the idea of cheating on her boyfriend while on vacation with him.

I sighed in relief, not realizing I'd been that hung up on whether or not they'd done something skeevy to get together. "How long after before you got together?"

"I broke up with Gavin a week later. It was mutual."

"Becca and I didn't even make it past the plane ride home," Nykos said.

"Because you'd fallen for each other on vacation?"

"No," Mariah said and my esteem for her shot up. She hadn't romanticized a fabricated romantic situation. She had the wherewithal to understand her feelings and act appropriately. "We just got along really well, which made it clear how much

Gavin and I no longer did. Kos makes me laugh, and he's considerate. We enjoy a lot of the same things."

"Like reading on beach chairs to relax instead of taking part in crazy stunts that involve death defying heights supported only by nylon or a zip line," Nykos inserted.

"Or snorkeling in shark infested waters," Mariah added.

"I gave her a call after a month or two back home. Like I said, nothing can resist this hunk o' man." His thumbs jabbed at his chest.

We all laughed again. I was too curious not to ask. "Do you know if your exes got together since they enjoyed doing the same things?"

"That isn't Gavin's style," Mariah assured me. "He's more into convenience than connection. Becca was a convenient partner for the escapades on the island, but she lived up here and he's in Tacoma. That would have been too much of a hassle for him to pursue."

"But not you?"

She shrugged. "Nykos was fun and I liked him. In my line of work that's rare to find."

"What line is that?"

"Construction. Most of the guys I work with are all trying to prove that I shouldn't be on the team with them, so it's refreshing when you run into a guy that treats you like an equal."

"Sounds nice," I murmured because it really did. Equality was part of many lesbian relationships, but being the sporty type and usually going for the more feminine type, it wasn't always the overriding dynamic in my relationships. I was tired of having to be the accommodating one, the one to pay or give gifts or take care of them.

"That's all I have to do to get on your good side?" Nykos asked her.

"Not anymore, buddy."

"I know, I know. You're the boss, I'm just here to be your boy toy."

She laughed, a delightful sound for such a sturdy woman. I liked her, too, but he was the highlight of this duo.

"You like this place?" Nykos asked, his finger waving a circle in the air.

I glanced around the bar. "I do. I think Lane does a great job of running it." Wouldn't hurt to put in a good word for Lane with the guy who might help push the investment through.

"What if it changed a little?"

My head tilted away from them. "How little?"

"Not exclusive anymore."

I shook my head. "I don't know that she'd want to run just another bar. There are seven within a four block radius as is."

His stopping hand came up again. "No, it would still be geared toward a gay crowd, but maybe less…flag bearing. Not so much with the Beware All Straight People Who Enter, but more subtle, classy."

Interesting. This guy designed and coded software and ran a group of engineers. What did he know about subtle or classy bars?

"It's Lane's bar." I couldn't guess how she'd react to toning down some of the aggressiveness in here. I wouldn't mind it. The first time I walked in with my long blond hair, light makeup, and professional dress code that was more feminine than androgynous, the foursome at the pool table had glared at me. They thought I was some yuppie straight chick who wandered into their territory. It wasn't until I'd conversed with Lane and Charlie that they'd lost their adversarial expressions. In fact, all throughout this interview, people had been shooting us glances that could be interpreted as hostile. They seemed equally bothered by a straight couple taking up one of the tables on a busy night and by me clearly interviewing this straight couple. Since the test article wasn't due out until next week, no one knew about the competition angle to my story yet. The people in here thought I was only interviewing gay couples.

Nykos glanced over to the most unfriendly couple in the bar. They'd been shooting make-me glances at him all night. The one time I tried talking to them, I became uncomfortable enough not to care if they had the best story in the whole city. After my attempt, Iris told me they were firefighters with massive chips on their shoulders from being the only women in their department and not being welcome there for years. I could understand the need for the chip, but that was more than twenty years ago. Why take it out on people now?

His gaze returned to mine. "Helen's talking to Lane about it now. What I want to know is if you think some of these regulars you've been interviewing will continue to frequent the bar if it changes some?"

"From what I've seen, they need something to help boost the crowds on certain nights. A change might be cheered as long as it doesn't turn into another bar where we're stared at for any public displays of affection."

"That's good info. Thanks," Nykos said, being serious for the first time all night.

"Would it be a company investment?" I still wasn't sure how these software people would be interested in the bar business, but if it meant Lane gets her bar, I was all for it.

"Willa will do it on her own. She's the hyperactive one. I want to relax in my free time. She likes to play venture capitalist."

"Yet you're the one scoping out the bar."

"She's tied up in our Virginia office, and she trusts my judgment."

That's a lot of trust. Lane hadn't mentioned her coming into the bar at all. Perhaps she'd been here at one time in the past, but now that she was evaluating it as an investment, she sends her sister and her business partner. It made me want to talk to her even more. "What is your judgment, or is it too soon to tell?"

"Helen's in. I just had to make sure the building was in good shape and give a second opinion. With some renovations by my talented wife and her crew, this place could be great."

My eyes widened. "Does Lane know?"

"Helen's telling her right now. Provided she's open to a few changes, I'd say it's a done deal."

"That's amazing." I searched the thin crowd and spotted Iris. I wanted to run up and hug her and tell her the good news, but that was for Lane to share. She'd be ecstatic. I couldn't spoil that, no matter how much I might want to.

22

Rubber gloves and various cleaning tools in hand, I knocked on the front door of Lane's bar. The official transfer of ownership happened last evening. She'd already submitted reno permits and was waiting on approval. Until then, Iris said they'd be doing some cleaning and painting. I knew how to do both, so I finished my writing quota early this morning and headed over to help out.

Iris appeared behind the glass front door and smiled when she saw me. Her eyes shifted down to take in my overloaded shopping bag and came back up with a questioning glance as she unlocked the door.

"You said you were doing some cleaning, right?" I lifted the bag.

"That wasn't a hint for your help." She looked embarrassed about possibly having guilted me into helping them clean.

"Does that mean you don't want help?" I turned away as if to leave.

She grabbed my arm and pulled me inside, making me laugh. Her guilty look disappeared at my tease. "Lane, look who's here to help."

Given Iris's response to my offer, I shouldn't have been surprised that no one else was here. I expected a few of their other friends to be helping, or at least pretending to help for any free beer they might get. Instead, the bar, which looked decidedly grimier than the last time I was in here a week ago, was empty.

"Vega," Lane greeted with a massive amount of relief in her tone. She should be ecstatic to finally be the owner of this bar, instead she looked worried. "Thanks for coming. Did Iris force you?"

"There might have been a gun involved," I joked and watched her face pale. Not that she believed her friend would hold me up, but she probably thought Iris had to plead with me to come. "She said you'd be taking over today and doing some cleaning. Thought I'd lend a hand."

"I doubt you'll still want to when you see the state of this place. I knew I shouldn't have taken that vacation."

Helen insisted she take last week off for the only break she'd get in the next year of bar ownership. I wasn't sure why it was distressing her so much. "I've got all the elbow grease you'll need."

"There's all other kinds of grease in the kitchen. That bitch didn't bother to clean once when Lane quit." Iris pushed a hand through her hair in frustration. The strands stuck out in mismanaged chunks. Made her look a bit harried, matching her tone.

"Iris," Lane said quietly. She wanted to sound admonishing, but a quick flick of her eyes around the decidedly dingier bar kept her from sounding too harsh.

"What?" Iris retorted, her chest visibly expanding. Another hair swipe settled some of the more outrageous wisps. "You gave her seven years, running her business for her lazy ass, and she gets pissy because she doesn't get the price she wants and doesn't have you to run it for the last week? That's juvenile."

It was. Not that I expected anything less from Charlie. Other than on the first day I'd walked in here, she hadn't shown much interest in her business at all. Of course, if I had Lane as my second in command, I'd probably feel fine with leaving the bar in her hands as well.

A knock sounded from the back door, causing us to jump at the disturbance. Lane and Iris went to see who it was while I looked more closely at the bar's interior. Not only had it gotten grimier, but several of the tabletops now had gouges in them. The chairs were scratched up as well. Moving closer to the bar, I spotted a chunk of the bar top missing. My glance went to the pool table area and found the felt ripped on all three tables. Charlie obviously took her frustration at the deal out on the bar.

"Damn," a loud swear sounded from the kitchen.

I headed back and found that Helen and Joe had joined my friends in the kitchen. A filthy kitchen with burners and handles missing on the equipment, dents in the stainless steel prep counter, and shelves destroyed. The negotiations really mustn't have gone Charlie's way. Without the leverage of a long-term lease, Helen's sister was able to buy the building obligation-free. All that was left was the value of the inventory and equipment.

"We thought you'd have to replace some of this, but..." Helen trailed off as her hands expertly checked hidden compartments in the equipment. She frowned more and more with each new discovery.

"The floor's trashed, too," Joe pointed out.

I glanced down. Large broken pieces of tile littered almost every walkable area. Whatever they'd budgeted had just doubled, possibly tripled.

"I'm going to be bankrupt before I even start the business."

"Hey," Helen reassured, grabbing her shoulders. "This happens sometimes. Nothing we can't handle. Willa has the renovation covered. It'll be a little more extensive than planned, but it'll raise the value of the building for her. You budgeted to replace some of the equipment. We'll get floor models or find the ones that have dents in the sides and backs. Those are always massively discounted because chefs with huge egos never buy them. That'll leave money for the ones you didn't budget for."

Lane looked partially relieved, but the weight of this burden settled uncomfortably on her. "You'll help pick them out?"

Helen's mellow smile glimmered. "I'm here for whatever you need. I couldn't have started my restaurant without help. We'll stick together."

"Starting with a little cleaning right now," Iris suggested. "Not that you have to stay for that part, Helen, but we're in, right, Vega?"

"All set." I grinned my most untroubled grin. "Show me where you want me to start."

Iris gave my shoulders a squeeze. She looked like she could hug me for the support I was showing, but she didn't want to disturb Lane with how much work this was going to be.

* * *

So far it had been a grand Grand Opening. Lane looked exhausted but she couldn't stop beaming. The mostly lesbian wannabe cocktail lounge turned modern lesbian-and-gay-fashionable-but-not-exclusive elegant public house was a hit with the old patrons and the new. On three occasions, I'd had to stand at the entrance and prohibit more people from entering. Lane couldn't stop squeezing my shoulder or hand in thanks whenever I walked past her. My social media pages helped to drum up a quarter of the crowds throughout the night. Almost every local interviewee stopped by as well as a lot of the Seattle residents who followed me on the various pages. Some left pretty quickly when they discovered it was a mostly gay pub, not just gay-friendly as I might have labeled it online. It didn't make them homophobic in my eyes. Most straight people needed a gay friend with them to feel comfortable being in a gay bar. As long as they ordered one drink before they left, Lane didn't care. It left more room for others who weren't as uptight.

"Can you believe this place?" Riley came to a stop beside me and surveyed the busy bar. She wore her standard cargo shorts and tank top. I hadn't seen her wear anything else. It was possible she didn't have anything else in her wardrobe.

"I can," I said because I'd seen it form over the past two weeks.

"Thought she'd gotten rid of the pool tables. I was gonna be pissed about that."

"You found the game room upstairs," I guessed. The three-floor building used to have two apartments over the bar. Helen recommended that they renovate one of the apartment spaces into the office and a game space. Moving the pool tables, dart boards, and adding a shuffleboard table to the second floor kept regulars like Riley happy but away from the new direction of the pub. A new dance floor took up the original space occupied by the pool tables and dart boards. Before, couples would just start dancing in between the tables. It hadn't been conducive to dancing, which was the reason several lesbians I'd interviewed stopped coming to the bar in the first place. Hopefully this new layout would entice them back as regulars.

"It's awesome. Love the new bathrooms, too."

I laughed. The new bathrooms took up the space of the old office with enough room for three stalls instead of just a lockable single bathroom. In the past, impatient, frisky women would lock the door for a sexy tryst, leaving any of us who needed to use the restroom out of luck or ducking into the men's. Now those sexed-up hornys would need real guts to have sex in a bathroom stall if there was a line waiting for the other two.

"Didn't see you pitching in when Lane could have used you," my thoughts tumbled out unsolicited.

Her head tilted back, surprised by my comment. We'd become acquaintances. I was pretty sure she thought of me as a friend, and here I was chastising her when another friend could have used her help. "Charlie was a friend. I didn't like how this all went down."

She didn't like how it went down, but she'd show up for the grand opening? "How what went down?"

"Lane got some rich chick to back her and screw Charlie out of a fair price."

I scoffed loudly, sick of how the rumor mill at this place never bothered with the truth. "That rich chick offered Charlie a fair price for her bar, but Charlie thought it was worth three times as much. If she were smart, she would have signed the lease for another five years. That would have given her leverage and close to the price she wanted, but she wasn't. So the rich chick bought the building and gave Charlie more than she should have for the contents of this place, all of which Charlie damaged before she left."

Riley's eyes grew wide. Yeah, didn't think she'd gotten the whole story. "What do you mean by damaged? The place was in okay shape the last time I was here."

"Not one piece of equipment in the kitchen or behind the bar could be used when Lane took over. She had to replace practically everything, even though she and the investor paid Charlie for the equipment. Iris, Lane, and I spent four days cleaning then sanding down all these tables and chairs to get rid of the scratches and dents Charlie added."

"Damn." Regret showed in her brown eyes.

"Yeah, so like I said, your friend Lane could have used another set of hands."

"You did that?" She chose to ignore my gripe.

"Of course I did. Lane's my friend. I've been in here every day. I don't have the skills to do a lot, but I can clean, sand, and paint after I was done working for the day. It was the least I could do."

"Yeah, well, Lane's been kinda closed off for a while now." Riley clearly didn't appreciate being called out on something. "She hasn't exactly welcomed help or anything from her friends. Ever since—"

"Cut a rug with me?" Iris interrupted, gripping my arm and tilting her head toward the dance floor.

I laughed at the old fashioned term. "This thing right here," I pointed to my body, "doesn't dance, but thanks."

"Just follow along. C'mon, it'll be fun." She sighed playfully when I shook my head again. Her eyes went to Riley, a bit of challenge in them. "Maybe I'll see if Adrian's up for a turn around the dance floor."

Riley's jaw clenched. "Maybe she is, but I'll be the one dancing with her. See ya, Vega."

I turned back to Iris when Riley stormed off. "Was that planned?"

A shoulder lifted in an innocent shrug. "Heard what you said about her not helping Lane. She was going to become really defensive in a second."

"And you came to my rescue?" I patted my heart dramatically.

"I didn't think she'd tie you to the train tracks or anything, but she can be a little abrasive when she gets defensive."

I laughed at the idea of being a damsel in distress for the first time in my life. "I thought you all were friends, yet no sign of her when Lane was getting this place together."

Iris glanced away, blinking a few times. It almost looked like she was keeping tears at bay, but that didn't make sense. "You know what they say, good friends help you move, great friends help you move bodies."

"Yep, heard that one before. So Riley's what kind?"

"Good-time friend for the most part. She'll show up for a party, celebratory drinks, meet for a game, all that casual good stuff you can enjoy with friends. I'm sure she'd help her foursome any way they needed. Everyone else falls into the good time category."

My sweep of the bar took in another dozen or so regulars that should have shown up to offer help for a couple of hours, but no one had. "They're missing out."

She turned back with a pleased look. "I knew you were a move-bodies type of friend even before you showed up that day with your cleaning gloves on."

I swallowed hard at the intense and almost worshipful look Iris was giving me. "Can't move bodies without wearing gloves."

Her look softened into a more familiar grin. "Probably shouldn't admit that to a former police detective."

I raised my hands. "Speaking of helping, does Lane need another set of hands back there?"

Iris had been drifting behind the bar to help pour drafts all night. Helen and her former sous chef, who was now the head chef here, were running the kitchen for this busy night. It freed up Lane and two others to make the more complicated drinks while the servers worked the table orders. I'd been bussing tables occasionally and keeping the crowd flow below capacity.

"You just don't want to dance with me," Iris joked, making her way back behind the bar.

I swallowed again. Dancing wasn't my thing. Never had been. But for a second, I'd been tempted.

23

Marty & Tate

If these two used the word "adorable" one more time, I might have to shove their faces into the fryer in the back. It wouldn't be on; I wasn't a monster. But I couldn't help thinking that adorable belonged to puppies and babies. Adorable did not fit a thirty-something woman who looked like she'd been around the block so many times she couldn't remember which house was hers anymore.

"I just melted, you know?" Marty sighed, shooting a gooey look at her wife.

Oh, yes, and the melting. Let's not forget the melting. They'd used that word almost as often. Along with drowning in her eyes, forgot to breathe, and needing to break off kisses for oxygen. They tossed out every overused line in a romance novel. Aside from the constant eye rolling moments, they had a pretty nice story.

They were waiting for me to react to what they'd said. The melting at the proposal. Tate used the jumbo screen at a baseball game—not an actual live shot of her presenting the ring—just a notice that read: *Marty, will you marry me?* I shuddered at how much that must have cost for the ten second notice and how impersonal it was and what if Marty'd been in the bathroom at the time and why anyone would decide that between the fifth and sixth innings at a ballgame was the opportune time to propose marriage. Not that I'd spent a lot of time thinking about proposing to anyone, but I'd rather it be more personal and in a place where someone wouldn't slosh beer on me as they slapped my back and pointed at a two hundred foot wide screen.

"You were melting?" I prompted, barely managing not to gag when I said the word. If adorable slipped from my lips, I'd probably staple my tongue to the roof of my mouth as punishment.

"I couldn't believe what I was reading. It was so romantic."

Yes, romantic to have 45,000 people read a marriage proposal with you.

"Our entire section went crazy." Marty flipped her dark brown hair over her shoulder in a practiced move.

"She was so adorable." Tate gave her wife the gooey eyes thing.

My teeth clenched, but I kept my hands in my lap rather than reaching across the table to haul her into the kitchen where a surprised Lane and her chef would likely try to keep me from committing homicide. "Did everyone in your group know?" I'd spoken to four couples from the season ticket holders group so far. All mentioned the ballpark big screen proposal.

"For sure. They had to help me keep her in her seat and looking at the screen so we didn't miss the message."

The message that lasted maybe ten seconds among probably two other marriage proposals and a dozen birthday messages.

"This place is nice. I was in here years ago and got the wrong vibe from it." Marty's eyes scanned the remodeled interior.

"New owner. She put a lot of work into it."

Tate looked over to Lane behind the bar. "That's Iris's friend, right? Yeah, I heard about her. Glad she has this now."

What a curious thing to say. It was too similar to Riley's comment at the grand opening about Lane being closed off. People seemed to know Iris but not Lane, and yet Iris and Lane were best friends. People should know both.

"How's everything going here?" The very Lane we'd been talking about placed a palm on my shoulder and leaned slightly toward Marty and Tate. "Can I get you anything else?"

Somehow she always knew when I was wrapping things up. Perhaps she gauged when I stopped making copious notes to know I was ready to end interviews. When she'd been the bartender, she rarely came out from behind the bar. As the owner, she was taking on that role a lot more.

"I had my eye on those sliders I saw go by a couple of times." Tate patted her slight belly.

"We only planned to meet Vega here for a drink, but Tate's right. The food looks scrumptious. We'll have to try it out."

"You're in for a treat. Our chef has brought pub food to a new level." Lane tapped their order onto her mini tablet and raised her brow at me.

"I'm good, thanks, Lane. Just wrapping up, but I'm sure Deb will turn these two into regulars with one bite."

The look of relief and pride was a permanent fixture on her face these days. With the help of Deb, who'd left Helen's kitchen with her blessing, Lane could concentrate on bartending, managing her staff, and keeping her customers happy. Deb relished having more responsibility and full-time hours here. She handled everything in the kitchen and came up with a tasty menu consisting of lighter fare, varied appetizers, and modernized bar food. I'd tasted everything and had a bunch of favorites. If it weren't for the lighter fare, eating here almost every day would have wreaked havoc on my waistline.

"Thanks for the story, ladies. It's been a pleasure chatting with you."

"So, we're in?" Tate asked, hope apparent in her eyes. "We read your first article and loved it. Had to get two logins so we could each vote. We disagreed on which couple was which. Can't believe we didn't know."

That made me feel good. As did the number of people who voted in the online poll. My editor was the hero of the day. The paper had no problem offering the wedding package now. They even upped the number of articles they'd be publishing. More pressure for me, but I had plenty of articles banked thanks to my non-procrastinating ways.

"Glad you liked it." I tried to keep pride from making me look like an arrogant fool.

"Does that mean we're going to make the series?" Marty asked, holding her breath because she'd probably forgotten to breathe again. I'll be lucky to leave without her calling me adorable.

"Read and see." I winked and headed up to the bar.

"They're adorable, aren't they?" Iris spoke into my ear.

I nearly jumped at her sneak attack and stifled a fit of giggles. Never before had I needed to stifle a giggle fit. One giggle, maybe, but a fit? Never. Sporty andros didn't giggle. "So adorable they melt on a regular basis."

Iris snickered and turned away to keep from laughing outright. With Tate and Marty still occasionally looking our way, it wouldn't do to show how rude I could be at times. "You aren't the type to believe in the public messaging system at ballgames?"

"Not my choice for communication, no."

She brushed an invisible piece of lint off her dark jeans. "You don't think anyone would wish you a happy birthday or congratulations on the big screen?"

The idea amused me. "I'd be more likely to have a friend put up a message like, 'Vega, someone might miss you if you died.' That's about the extent of the affection I'd get from people I know."

She laughed and gave me a look that said she didn't believe it. "I could come up with a better message."

"But then I'd just want to die."

Her hands came up in surrender. "A journalist who doesn't want to make news. Interesting bird."

"That's me."

24

Lorraine & Simon

Long fingers stroked the outside of the martini glass in a sensual rhythm. My eyes kept returning to the motion. Slender fingers attached to a remarkable beauty mesmerized far more than her love story. The husband was anything but remarkable. One glimpse at the wedding photo she had on her phone told me he'd been a looker once. When he didn't have a beer gut, back hair, and two separate bald spots slowly reaching toward each other. Two years younger than I was, he really had no excuse for letting himself go or not trying to groom some of that visible hair beneath the sleeveless t-shirt he was wearing. *Get some clippers, dude. Fifteen bucks at Target. Splurge a little. Your wife is a hottie; make an effort.*

"Can't say I was too thrilled to be here after reading your last two articles," Simon spoke up. He'd been civil throughout, but something had been hanging over the table since he sat down.

"Why's that?" I asked, wondering why he'd kept the appointment if he wasn't "thrilled" about it.

"I was under the impression you were writing a series of personal interest stories on nice couples. Imagine my surprise when I read those articles and see you're plotting two couples against each other and letting people mistake some for gay."

Wow. That's what he'd gotten out of the articles? "I think you're missing the point of the series, Simon."

"What? Too politically incorrect of me to say I don't want to have people reading our story and putting us in the gay column?"

Wow again. Seattle was pretty progressive. None of the other straight couples had made outright homophobic statements and many had no problem sticking around for Lane's opening night even when they figured out it was mostly gay couples crowding the place. Oh, well. Every city needed its quota of phobic idiots.

"Babe," Lorraine practically growled at him. She'd been cringing at several of his comments throughout the hour. Clearly their fifteen-year marriage was at one of those push-through-it points that all marriages endure. Her wandering eye didn't want to cooperate, though. She'd given me a hungry sweep on no less than four occasions. Perhaps their fifteen-year marriage was at the point where one of them decides to find something new and exciting to help spice up her own rut.

"What?" he growled back. "I said it wasn't politically correct, but I'm sick of people tiptoeing around the gays. Everyone's always so sensitive about their kind."

I clenched my teeth and released a pent up breath. "The point of the articles is to show people who think there's a difference between your kind and my kind that a love story is a love story, no matter the kind."

"Your kind?" He shoved his chair back.

"Hi, I'm Vega and I'm gay." I shot him a disarming smile. I'd never hidden my sexuality. Comments on my social media pages made it very clear that I was a lesbian. I never added it to my articles because I didn't insert myself into them. If he'd done his homework, he'd have known.

"No wonder," he mumbled when his wife gripped his arm in a deathlike vice to keep him from leaving. His eyes roamed the bar again, looking for boogeymen in the form of rampaging homosexuals who'd force him to watch them drink a cocktail or eat a meal. As if on cue, Riley and Adrian walked in the front door, smooching and laughing as they made their way up to the bar. I had to turn away to keep from laughing at how uncomfortable Simon now looked.

"Are we in a gay bar?"

"You're in a pub that doesn't discriminate," I clarified.

"Babe," Lorraine growled again, clearly used to being embarrassed by some of the things he said. She wanted the notoriety of being included in a publication that had millions of daily readers. Her eyes danced slowly over me again. Even knowing she was married didn't stop my heart from skipping a little. She was too hot not to be excited by the prospect that she might find me attractive, even as a straight married lady.

"Whatever," he sighed. "Are we done?"

Not really, but I'd had enough. They met in an internship program after college and had two kids. He was a boring exec somewhere, and she was head of the PTA and worked part-time somewhere else. Cute, quaint, and downright precious. As stories went, blah, but I needed more straight couples to balance out the number of gay stories I had from before I came up with the competition angle.

"Thanks for your time." I stood abruptly, surprising Simon enough to slide back in his chair again. Perhaps he thought I'd rub off on him if I got too close, which was pretty much the universal fear of all homophobes.

Up at the bar, I slid my empty cocktail glass toward Lane. She shot me an exasperated look, letting me know I didn't need to bus my own empties. I couldn't help it. I took pride in this place now. I'd run back and get Simon and Lorraine's glasses as soon as they collected all their crap and left. With the amount of stuff they had, jackets, sunglasses, phones, keys, purses—plural, he had a murse, which I'm sure he called a satchel or something less feminine, but he was walking around with a man-purse—and hats, they'd be there for a while.

"Waste of a woman right there," Iris said as she took the stool beside me. Her eyes grazed over Lorraine gathering her belongings.

"He was quite the looker back in college when they met."

"I find that hard to believe," she said. "Heard some of what he was saying as I passed by a couple times. Doesn't matter if he was movie star gorgeous, he had some stupid-ass things to say."

"Very true."

"She was loving some of that Vega view she kept taking."

My hand reached out and smacked her shoulder. "Stop."

"What? She was eye-guzzling you all interview." Both she and Lane laughed at that comment.

"She's straight and married."

"And you're hot and single."

Hot? Hmm. Something was going on here. She must be setting me up for something. She complimented Lane often and certainly said nice things about my writing skills, but this was the first mention of my appearance.

"I'm just saying the chick looked like she was not only ready to jump ship but switch oceans."

"Good metaphor. Might have to steal that one." Speaking of eye-guzzling. Iris wore a suit that lengthened and sharpened her appearance. I liked her better in jeans and cowboy boots, but this new look added dimensions. "What's up with the suit, sexy lady?"

Her eyes flicked away as her chin tucked against her chest, embarrassed. "Just back from court."

My eyebrows rose. Lane's did as well. She finished the two drinks she was making and turned to Derrick, the other bartender. Without a word, he took over delivering her drinks, allowing Lane to give Iris her full attention.

"You know the guy we followed from Pacific Place to the restaurant?" She waited for my nod. "He was held over without bail today."

"Thanks to your testimony?" I asked.

"To the overwhelming amount of evidence we had and a few words from me and the investigating detective."

"Congratulations, Iris. Well done." I patted her back.

Lane leaned over and hugged her. "I know how much this means to you. It's been eating away at you."

"One more down, a few more to go." They both looked too serious for a celebration. Whenever they did this, my reporter instincts kicked in. I wanted to know why they could look so solemn at times and communicate volumes without speaking.

"Dinner on me. C'mon, I hear this place has great food." I watched their solemn looks morph into smiles.

"Sure does. I'll get your orders in and bring them out to you."

"No, no." I waved her off. "It's a celebration, which means we're all having dinner. You're taking a break and eating with us. Derrick can handle the bar."

Lane wanted to protest, but one glance at Iris's hopeful face and she relented. She keyed in our order and joined us at the table Simon and Lorraine had finally vacated after packing up every possession they owned.

"Iris, congratulations on the win in court today. It must be a big relief." I tipped my glass at her and turned to Lane. "Lane, congratulations on achieving your dream. It's a great bar."

"And Vega, congrats on the success of the articles so far. More than three million votes online already. The paper must be going crazy." Iris clinked her glass against mine and did the same with Lane. "I'm so winning that contest. I know I got the first four couples right."

I laughed and gripped her shoulder. "Sorry to break it to you, Iris, but as my friend, you're not eligible to enter the contest." Her face fell, which shouldn't have made me snicker, but it did. "What would you do with a hundred thousand dollar wedding, anyway?"

"I could get married." She tried to look affronted.

"For a hundred grand?"

She shrugged and laughed. "Well, no, but I could pay Lane eighty-five to fake cater it and use the other fifteen to order wedding crap that I'd return so I could take a wicked good honeymoon."

"Yes, please." Lane perked up at the idea.

Now I was laughing. "Again, hate to dash your hopes, but I'll be there to cover the wedding for the paper. They're milking this thing dry. It's going to have to be a swanky affair and, most importantly, real."

Her eyes caught mine again. "So you're saying that you'll be at my wedding?"

I snickered at her playfulness. "You're not eligible to win. Especially since you already know half the damn stories I'll be publishing. You'd be considered a ringer."

"You'll still be at the wedding," she said with a cockiness only she could pull off without seeming cocky.

It felt good to sit among close friends. I'd had some in the past, but knowing how transient my life had been, following stories or stints with papers, none had really gotten under my skin. Keeping in touch wasn't as easy as we'd thought it would be. Deciding to make this my home base for a while, perhaps for a seriously long time, I knew these two would be friends I wouldn't let drift away, no matter the circumstance.

25

Pat & Marlowe

A hand came down and clamped onto a hairless forearm. Completely hairless and not attached to a baby. I'd never seen one before and certainly didn't think I'd find the first on a grown man. Perhaps he was a champion swimmer or bicyclist. Or a different species from a planet filled with hairless people who swam or biked competitively.

A voice interrupted my deliberation of the arm hair versus no arm hair argument. "We should back up," Marlowe, the owner of the clamping hand, said for what seemed like the hundredth time in the past three hours.

Oh, goody. Another excruciatingly long backstory of a backstory of a backstory. I'd gotten all I needed in the first half hour, but these two loved adding unnecessary details and offshoots and anecdotes and any manner of conversational tangents that had nothing to do with the point of the story.

"Actually," I began but got cut off by Pat, who'd already taken Marlowe's suggestion and began at the absolute beginning of time on the surely thousandth tangent of the night.

My eyes surreptitiously made a break for it, wandering the interior of the bar. It was odd not seeing Riley and her group over in what was now the new dance area instead of crowded by pool tables only they'd used. Moving the tables upstairs and making it a full game room had increased the usage and kept the celebratory noise to a minimum.

My eyes jerked to a stop when I saw Iris leaning against the bar. She'd left two hours ago with some dark-haired woman. Not someone tipsy that Iris would help into a cab. This was a completely sober, fine looking woman that she'd gone home with.

I'd watched it happen as another diversion from the backstory quagmire I'd been stuck in at the time. What was she doing back at the bar? Again. This was a bit of a pattern for her. Fourth time I'd seen this very thing. Did she take them home, have quick sex with them, and come back? Take them home, decide not to have sex with them, and come back? Take them home, leave them at the door, and then come back?

"...if he hadn't opened that door? Can you believe it?"

Huh? Oh, right, we'd backed up to go through some activity that in some way was responsible for the thing that brought them to the other thing that again led them to an event that brought them both to the same town where they ultimately met in the waiting area of a tire shop of all places. Couldn't for the life of me understand why walking through a door twenty years ago—sixteen years before he met Marlowe—had anything at all to do with how they got together. Not that I would ask. They'd have me here another three hours.

"Amazing," I said in that tone that any socially versed person knew was meant to wind down a topic. Pat's mouth opened to say more, probably a story of when he was in the womb and somehow knew that he'd find Marlowe thirty-three years later, but my sudden stand from the table prompted his jaw to snap shut. "It's been wonderful chatting with you. Thank you for your time and the great story."

"Oh, well, yes, yes." Pat stood and shook my hand.

I scooped up the notepad and left before they could ensnare me in story quicksand again. I probably should have headed outside to make sure they didn't find me for their second wind, but I couldn't resist saying goodbye to Lane and Iris first.

"How long did that last?" Lane asked as she lifted a beer glass in question.

I waved off the offer and nodded hello to Iris. "Honestly. At one point I wanted to say, 'Listen, I'm forty-six. I'm pretty sure my life expectancy won't extend past this story.' But I wasn't able to string that many words together before one of them started talking again."

They laughed as Iris gave me a questioning look. "Are they making the cut?"

"Met in a tire shop. Not exactly exciting, but unique. I'd say it's a damn good chance."

"They can be boring all they like as long as they keep downing beers like glasses of water after running a marathon," Lane commented before walking two more beers over to them.

"She's grateful, you know," Iris said, her eyes tracking Lane. She was dressed nicely again. Not the fancy suit tonight, but slacks and a button up shirt over a clingy tank. Different boots, black, a little dressy. I wondered if Lane owning the bar accounted for the constant upscale dress code Iris was sporting.

"About?" I asked.

"You, your social media efforts, having you conduct your interviews here. A few people have come in and asked if you're around over the past two weeks. You're a draw for tourists and locals alike now that your articles are coming out on a regular basis."

It felt good to know that Lane was benefiting from something I'd posted on social media. It felt really good that Iris noticed it as well. "I always wanted interviews to come to me. Think I could get them to just show up at my apartment?"

"You're joking, but I think you're underestimating your popularity."

"I'm glad my laziness is getting Lane some more business. How about that?"

Her smile flashed bright. "Are you sure you'll have time to help with the move tomorrow?"

"Happy to help." As part of the investment deal, Lane was moving into the newly renovated third floor apartment upstairs. She'd pay rent on both the apartment and the bar, while Helen's sister owned the building as an income producing capital asset. That was the extent of the deal. No demand for equity or co-ownership in the bar. It was a good deal for both, but Lane got more out of it. Helen assured me her sister made these kinds of beneficial deals when she or Helen had a personal stake in the investment.

"Thanks. She hasn't had much free time to pack since taking over the bar." She considered me for a moment. "What about your move? You really don't need any help?"

I was also benefiting from my friendship with Helen in more ways than just having a good friend. She offered to let me lease the vacant apartment she and her sister owned next door to her place. They'd been using it as a vacation home for friends. She would rather have someone she liked renting the place than dealing with time-consuming guests. I'd be moving in at the end of next week when my executive rental lease ran out. "Right now, it's just me and my suitcases. I'll be shipping stuff from my storage unit in Chicago, but it's nothing big. Thanks, though."

She assessed me, trying to make sure I wasn't playing down my need for help. "You staying to eat?"

"I've got to type up my notes tonight before I slip into a coma remembering this story."

She hopped off her stool. "I'll walk you out."

"That's okay. You look comfy here."

"I didn't see your car in the lot."

"When you came in the first time or the second?" I asked, testing whether or not we could broach this subject without her biting my head off again.

Her lips twitched. "Both times." She paused to run her eyes over me, contemplating.

I wondered if she'd finally admit to having had a nice evening in the company of the woman she now knew I'd seen her take home. She'd deflected all previous allusions to her dates. It didn't matter who was asking. Even Lane, but with my question, she knew I knew she'd left with someone tonight. She might let a tidbit slip.

"You're parked on the street and not near the bar. Let me walk you, please."

Then again, she could completely ignore the topic of her date tonight and go for that caring thing she does so well. "I'm fine, thanks," I assured her.

"Are you thinking your rep will be ruined if people see you leave with me?"

My grin flared. At least her sensitivity on the subject had waned. "I won't be leaving with you. You'll be leaving with me."

I turned and made her follow me if she insisted on the escort to my car. A glance back caught her matching grin.

26

My tennis game was failing me. All summer I'd handily beaten Iris with my serve and accurate ball placement. Her powerful forehand and athleticism kept her in most games, but until today, she hadn't stood a chance of winning a match.

"Today is the day I deliver that promised spanking." Iris's teeth gleamed at me from across the net.

"You're having the game of your life, sister. Live it up. It may be the only time you beat me."

"Ha!" she declared with the fierce ball strike down the line for a winner.

Applause sounded from the court next to us. The four women playing doubles had stopped their match to watch ours. The charmer across the net soaked in their applause and cheers over the next fifteen minutes to close out the third set 7-6. She broke out into a highly inappropriate victory dance and took a lap gathering high-fives from the spectators as they all giggled and swooned at her antics.

After ample time signing autographs and posing for photos with her fans, we started walking back home. "Feeling okay? Need a piggyback ride?"

I laughed at her taunts. "Yeah, yeah. One win. That's all I'm giving you."

"How'd the date go last night?"

My step faltered. Just the other night I'd tried to get her to tell me about her date. Not as directly as this, but she hadn't gone for it. I wasn't in the habit of telling friends about dates until they amounted to something. Last night's did not fit into that category. Maybe this was her way of opening up the subject. "Fine. How'd you hear about it?"

"Riley told me."

How did Riley know about it? I hadn't asked Cheryl out at the bar. We'd run into each other at a bookstore and went to grab a bite afterward. Maybe she went to the bar after dinner and told Riley then. Why would she, though? It hadn't been a stellar date. Although if there was one universal truth in the lesbian community, it was that dating gossip spread like a cold in a kindergarten class. Riley telling Iris seemed deliberate, not gossip. I'd need to shut down that protective thing she felt with me. It wasn't appreciated or welcome.

"Wasn't a good date?" Iris pulled me back from the rehearsed speech I was preparing for Riley.

"It was fine." It was. Just that, fine. The few times we'd spoken in the bar, Cheryl was intelligent and amusing. At the bookstore, she was interesting. Then we went to dinner, and she suddenly began working off a dating checklist when she wasn't focused on the things only she liked. "She's nice. Not for me, but that's what dating is for."

"Anything in particular?" Iris switched her tennis racket to her other shoulder. A movement that looked casual, but something in her tone rejected nonchalance.

"We talked about shoes for a long, long time."

She laughed and nudged my shoulder. The casualness was coming back. "How long?"

"More than a full minute."

Iris brought a hand to her stomach and doubled over, acting winded. "A whole minute? Just on shoes? How did you survive?"

"Listen," I started in a fake bothered tone to get her to stop the fake winded act. "One minute on shoes is enough to tell me she'd be overly concerned with the fact that I only own four pairs. She'd probably worn four pairs that day alone."

We turned onto Pike and had to dodge pedestrians for a block until we traversed over to a less populated street. I thought we'd moved on until Iris asked, "Just saw her and had to go for it, huh?"

The needling seemed a little intense this morning. She and Lane still gave me a hard time about Greer, but this felt like something else. "Cheryl's nice. How well do you know her?"

"She's FBI. Worked with us on a couple of internet fraud cases. Good agent, nice enough. She doesn't really do the bar scene, but her friends drag her out every once in a while."

"You never dated?" It just slipped out. I hadn't known I was curious about that, but apparently I wanted to know if Iris found Shoe Lady interesting.

She flashed a cheeky smile. "Never date anyone in law enforcement."

I grinned back. "Do you warn all of your potential dates off you, too?"

Her hands spread out innocently. "I'm not in law enforcement anymore."

"Which leaves you free to date indiscriminately?"

"Oh, I discriminate, all right."

I wasn't sure I believed that, having watched her leave the bar with all manner of women over the last two months. I knew several were just to get them into a cab or a ride home because they were too drunk for anything else, but a handful of others had to have been dates. "Sure you do."

"So? It was just the shoe thing, huh?"

"Of course not." Although it was a big flashing signal that we wouldn't be compatible in other areas. "There was just nothing there between us."

"Friends, then?"

"Doubt it." I didn't have enough opinions on shoes to interest Cheryl.

"Hmm," she murmured as we turned onto the block that housed my apartment building.

"What?"

"You don't stay friends with exes, do you?"

I turned my head fully to study her and nearly banged my tennis racket into a light pole on the street. "How would you know?"

"Just figured you'd be like me on that. All or nothing, right?"

"Yes." Where was she going with this? And why didn't she sweat as much as I did? My dry-wicking exercise top wasn't dry-wicking fast enough. Hers looked like she'd just pulled it out of the dryer. In fact, her only usual sign of overexertion was a red face and failed wispy hair. Perspiration occasionally. I had to bring a towel with me to these matches. She'd just pat her brow with the bottom of her shirt for three seconds and be done. Ruffle the wisps a bit and all was back to normal. Truly annoying.

"Any other prospects?"

My head shook, ponytail sweeping back and forth across my still damp back. I couldn't wait to jump in the shower. Defeat made me more aware of my perspiration habits. I didn't dwell this much in victory. Or perhaps it was her needling that ramped the awareness back up. "I'm good for about one first date a month."

"What's your conversion rate?"

I laughed. Only someone who scored as much as she did would use that kind of language. "I hope you're asking how often I get to a second date, not how often I get lucky with a first." Her hands came up to accompany the sly grin. "My last second date was more than six months ago. I don't usually date if I'm not going to be around for a while."

"But now you're sticking around, so time to start dating again?" She turned and faced me outside the entrance to my building.

"What's up?" I waved two fingers between us. "Why so interested? You want to share your notes on the women at the bar with me?"

A flicker passed over her expression before it rearranged into her usual blandness when people tried to tease her about her bar exploits. "What women?"

I did the imitation of someone gasping for air this time. "For serious? You leave with someone more often than not."

Her eyes clouded. "Not everything is how it looks."

"Remember, judgment-free zone." I moved my hand in a circle around us when it looked like I might have touched on that one nerve she had. Her face was getting red again. Not as much as when we were playing tennis, but red enough to let me know she was expending energy on this conversation. She'd started the conversation. She shouldn't be getting upset about it. "You're the one riding me about dating."

"That's because—" she broke off, pushed out a loud breath, and turned away. When she turned back, she repeated, "That's because—" And she broke off again.

Then her hands reached out and grabbed my face, dragging me to her as she stepped closer. In the next instant her lips were on mine. Or over mine, and for that first moment, other parts near my lips as if she wasn't quite sure where lips were situated on a face.

To say the kiss was unexpected would be like saying it was hot in Death Valley. It just was. Unexpected and shocking and stunning and staggering, which was why I pretty much just stood there, dumbfounded with her lips moving over mine and the other near-lips parts of my face. It was all the things a kiss was supposed to be: soft, giving, pliant, and provocative. And one thing a kiss wasn't supposed to be: not good.

Really, really not good.

She pulled away and searched my eyes. I'd always liked that part of a first kiss, the pull away and searching of eyes to make sure the kiss affected her as much as it did me. This time, the searching only lasted a second before she made some mumbled sounds, picked up her dropped racket, and practically sprinted away. In five seconds, she was turning the corner at the end of the block. Another five seconds, and my senses finally returned.

Huh.

27

Daydreaming was infinitely harder to accomplish with distractions. Arguing editors made for a mighty fine distraction. Nearly every editor and marketing executive on staff at the paper were assembled around the conference table, discussing what to do with my article series. Normally being called back to HQ for a meeting would have been intimidating, but the articles had increased readership by double digit percentage points in only three weeks. Anything that brought in new readers these days was considered a windfall. Hence, my required presence at this meeting, nearly three thousand miles away from where I wanted to be and where my mind still lingered.

She kissed me. Full-on kissed me, and it was not good. Bad, really. A bad first kiss. Not that there would be other kisses, but this was my first really bad kiss with someone I wouldn't think it possible to perform badly at kissing. In college I'd suffered through a few sloppy drunk kisses, but never as an adult. I might have liked kissing some women better for their technique or if feelings were involved, but feelings were involved here. Not romantic feelings, at least I hadn't thought so, but she meant a lot to me. The kissing should have had some emotional component to elevate it to a higher status. Should have been enough to mask any discomfort at kissing a friend rather than a date. But the clash of lips, scrape of teeth, mismanaged flick of tongue, and incessant pressure was just...bad.

Okay, I'll take fifty percent of the blame. More than fifty percent because I hadn't known I was going to be kissed. No prep usually paved the way for awkwardness in kissing, so sixty percent of the blame. Well, seventy percent because, after the initial awkwardness, I just stood there in shock. Had I even moved my mouth at all? Oh hell, was I the whole reason it was a bad kiss?

"Vega?" a voice interrupted my reluctant insight.

"Huh?" I replied eloquently and recognized the editor-in-chief addressing me. I shot up straighter in my seat and tried again, "Excuse me?"

"How many interviews have you conducted?"

I blinked, trying to bring my whole mind back into this meeting. "Dozens." I wasn't sure how many exactly. I'd culled through a lot of them.

"Two dozen, four dozen, what are we talking?" he persisted.

"Several dozen."

"Perfect." He smacked his hands together, glee stretching his mouth wide. He was impossibly handsome. Annoyingly so. Successful, rich, and handsome. Bet he didn't suck at kissing.

I wasn't sure what I'd missed while I was cataloguing my clinic on horrible kissing that was probably—likely—most assuredly—my fault for not responding at all and just letting her mouth kiss all over mine. But I needed to participate here. "Not all are useable."

The glee faded. "Why not?"

"Some weren't telling the truth. Others would be too obvious."

"Can't you fudge that a little?" His expression told me he had no idea that ethics even existed as a word much less a concept and should be applied to every article he published in his newspaper.

"Fudge meeting at an HRC rally?" I waited while the editor to his left whispered an explanation for the acronym. "I could say they met at a political rally, but the rest of their story is tied to LGBT activities." I was purposely using acronyms to irk him now. My lips were good at irking people. Kissing, no, they clearly sucked at that, but irking people, they had that down to a science. "Several met at church, and while it's possible for gay couples to meet at church, none of the ones I interviewed did. So, your readers would probably guess correctly on those. I have a bunch of repeats of people meeting online, at the gym, at a bar, and the rest of their stories aren't any more interesting."

"So how many usable?" he asked again.

"The agreed upon amount from our last meeting." Which had doubled the original number after the success of the test article.

"Surely, you have more than twenty-four from the several dozen?"

He must be bad at math like I was evidently bad at kissing. Which was worse? The kissing, definitely. A person could go through life with a calculator to solve being bad at math. "More. I need two articles week for three months."

"That's twenty-four, like I said."

Maybe being bad at math was worse since several of his editors had to look away to hide their mirth when they realized how bad at math their boss was. A person could go through life without kissing, if she was good at other things like math and irking people. "Each article has two interviews."

He blinked as realization hit him. He'd just done really bad math in front of all his subordinates, and a freelance writer called him on it. "Yes, right, well, that's why we're here. We'd like to run an extra article a week for subscribers only and extend it a month, possibly two or three."

I jerked forward. It felt like I'd just done the bad math. "That's a lot more work."

"With pay, of course."

Since he thought I'd agreed to this overload of work on a subject matter that I was already becoming bored with, I insisted, "We'll need to discuss that before I agree to anything. The cost benefit analysis might not work out for you."

"We'll pay you for each additional article. What's there to discuss?" Typical EIC behavior. He felt he was doing me a favor with this assignment that hadn't been his to begin with.

"The rate we agreed to the last time you changed the parameters of this article series won't suffice." I had his attention now. He knew budgets and advertising rates and how that applied to each new reader he obtained. He didn't know how to deal with freelance writers who weren't desperate to write for him. Editors dealt with those types, not the guy in charge. "That rate was acceptable when I could readily meet those weekly deadlines and be done with the series in two months. Now you're doubling down on the deadlines and increasing my time on this subject by months."

The editors of the various departments shifted uncomfortably in their seats. Normally they could greenlight articles based on their annual budgets, but this had taken on a life of its own. The EIC was making the decisions now.

"We can bring in a staff writer to help."

I cut him off. "If you'll remember, our contract states that I'll be able to republish each article in a book that chronicles the success of this series. Good publicity for you and royalties for me. No one else can touch this."

Several of the editors sat back in their chairs. They shouldn't be surprised. Freelance journalists were getting savvier with their negotiations now that so many papers had cut their writing staff. No longer would we just accept a standard pay-for-piece rate if we knew the piece could be reused.

"Give us the room," he barked, and all but my editor scurried from the room. "Why don't you tell us what you want, and we'll see what we can do. Mind you, we can always go back to our original plan of one article a week for two months and cut it off at any time. Your hope for a book contract would disappear with it."

I tried not to smile too widely, knowing he probably didn't study the content of his online pages as meticulously as I had. "Your online poll shows how many people have voted on each interview pairing. I did my research on your circulation numbers before I started. The online poll totals are significantly larger than that. Of course, not all of them are subscribers, but your new plan hopes to convert many of those larger numbers, right?"

"What's it going to cost us?" He sounded defeated this time. He shouldn't because he knew I was right. If the contest participants could increase their chances of winning by thirty-three percent with a subscription, they'd scramble to subscribe.

I asked for what I thought would be acceptable but higher than just twice the amount. My workload would increase exponentially, even if I'd fibbed about the amount of usable material I had. Several of the more common stories could be published. I'd just wanted to use only the best when the required number allowed me to be picky.

"Agreed," the EIC said brusquely and held up his hand. "Provided you write the press release about the subscriber option and record an announcement to run next to the weekly poll."

As much as I didn't like my face being part of my work, it would only help when it came time to getting a book contract. It made sense for me to do it, but it would extend my time here another day, perhaps two.

Too much time in a hotel, contemplating the ugly truth of how bad a kisser I'd become in my old age.

28

She was walking some pretty thing out of the bar and to her car. She'd kissed me, badly—not entirely her fault, or maybe not her fault at all—and gave me the impression that the kiss was supposed to mean something, and here she was walking yet another trollop out of the bar. Okay, not fair. The woman, Blaine, I think, wasn't a trollop, but she did get tipsy on the regular and left with a few women since I'd moved to town. But never Iris.

Not that this should bother me. It was a bad kiss. I shouldn't want to repeat bad kisses. I shouldn't want to kiss my friend, putting an end to the friendship with all the kissing, badly.

Yet, here, playing out in high-def, was Iris back to her usual practices of picking up women at the bar. Bad kissing didn't deter her. She'd put a hiatus on picking up women during the Grand Opening weeks, staying until closing to support Lane. But the hiatus must be up. Probably because I suck at kissing. I felt like calling my last three ex-girlfriends and asking if they thought I was a bad kisser. It never felt bad at the time, but I could have been deluding myself, and it took a friend to shove it in my face. What else are friends for?

Bad kissing and picking up other women, obviously.

I'd been in the act of parking down the street from the bar when I spotted Iris and her date *du jour* leaving together. Iris's hand was on Blaine's lower back, the other gripping her arm to help keep her steady on the five inch heels the chick was wearing to a mostly lesbian bar in a city where it rains three hundred days a year. My exit from the car was delayed by the complete disbelief that paralyzed me. I'd been dreading the discussion of the kiss— the off-the-charts bad kiss—with my friend who wasn't supposed to want to kiss, however badly, her friend. Dreading it so much that I'd stayed in my wonderful new apartment for two days before finally sucking up my bad kissing lips and dragging the rest of me over to the bar for the c.o.n.f.r.o.n.t.a.t.i.o.n. Lowercase because uppercase would imply it would be filled with anger and maybe fists if we were animals who couldn't control our emotions. But a confrontation, nonetheless. We needed a serious discussion about what the hell had brought on the kiss. An actual kiss, not just a grazing of lips to wish me a good trip. It was a hold my head and smash our mouths together in no way mistaking it for a friendly see-you-soon buss. I had to know what she was thinking. We could discuss the horrible technique at a later time. I just had to know what brought it on.

Then I watched her walk out the door with Blaine of the Spiky Heels clan. Get into Iris's car, and drive away, in the direction of Iris's house. Maybe Blaine and her heels lived near Iris, and she was just giving her a lift.

Sure. And I'm a good kisser.

I cranked the ignition on my daily rental and pulled into the street. I'd lucked out on the flights and sat next to a few couples that produced unintended interviews. I didn't have to get one tonight. A drive to clear my head might be the better option. One that would not go anywhere near Iris's place to see if she'd taken Spiky Heels home.

An hour later, after a drive up and down practically every street on Capitol Hill, my head wasn't any clearer, and I found myself back at the bar. Sunday nights, Lane closed early for a deep weekly clean rather than a wipe down after service every other night. I'd have fifteen minutes before she locked the doors.

"Hey, you're back," Lane greeted when I came inside. "How was the trip?"

"Good, thanks." My eyes wandered the nearly empty interior. She must have let the other bartender and server who usually worked Sunday nights go home early, but a couple of patrons were holding out till closing before choosing their conquest for the night.

"Kitchen's closed, but I can make an exception for you?" she offered.

Clanking sounds came from the kitchen, telling me that Deb and her assistant chef were busy cleaning already. "No, thanks, just thought I'd pop in and say hi."

Lane stared at me for a long moment. "She left already."

"Who?" I tried for casual.

"Someone drank a little too much to drive. Iris took her home."

My head nodded even as my mind fought to decide if I could take that statement at face value. Before the kissing—the awful, awful kissing—I would have smirked and been happy for my friend whether she was really just taking her home or "taking her home." Now the kissing screwed with my head. When I kiss someone, I don't want them to turn around and take someone else home days later, even if I didn't like the kissing. Made me feel a little worthless to be forgotten that quickly.

"Stick around," Lane said as she went to settle the checks for the final customers. At least two of them had paired up, but the others looked like they'd decided it was better to solo it home.

I studied Lane and wondered if she knew about the kiss. They were best friends. If Iris were a normal chick who liked to share with her besties, she'd have told her that bit of news. But Iris wasn't a normal chick. Neither was Lane. I certainly wasn't going to tell her, and not just because I'd probably have to admit to being a bad kisser because of how appalling the kiss was and all.

After checking the bathrooms were free of horny patrons, Lane threw the bolts on the front door and turned off the Open sign. She went to the first table with a disinfectant towel to wipe it down before flipping one of the chairs upside down and onto the table top. I reached over the bar top to the pile of cleaning towels and grabbed one to join her. She had a crew that came in for the bathrooms and floors every morning, but she and her staff cleaned behind the bar and the kitchen equipment themselves. Most nights it only took a half hour, but on Sundays, they did the deep clean.

"I wasn't hinting for help when I asked you to stay."

"I know," I said, even though I didn't know why she'd asked me to stay.

"Thanks." She worked on the chairs, leaving the tables for me, and stayed silent for longer than most would be able to handle.

"How'd your week go?" I asked a general question. It could refer to her bar take or her personal week or what she and Iris did.

"Good." She reached up and pulled the band from her messy bun. For a moment, the shoulder length, sable hair fell free until she swept it back up into another bun. I usually liked the hair-down look for women, but with Lane's longer jawline and chin, keeping her hair knotted at the back worked well with her features. "Saw the post you put up today. Thanks for mentioning the bar again."

I brushed off the gratitude. "It's as beneficial to me. Especially now."

"Did something change?"

"One more article a week and for longer. I won't have time to travel to many other places to collect the stories. If I post that I'm parked in your bar and want tourists with good stories to mosey by, the interviews will come to me. I'm tired of chasing them."

"Hope it works, and not just for my sake."

"Me, too."

We finished with the tables and chairs and moved back to the bar where I worked on cleaning the barstools and she emptied the shelves for cleaning. Silence stretched, except for the occasional clanging and chatter from the chef and her assistant in the kitchen as they cleaned. My curiosity finally got the better of me.

"Something on your mind, Lane?" I crossed my fingers that she hadn't been asked to give me the brush off. I'd just gotten settled here. I liked Lane and liked the bar and didn't want a stupid kiss to end what I had with Iris.

"She won't be coming back tonight. She doesn't need to anymore."

Blinking, I tried to assess what she'd just said. I knew who the she was, but was Lane saying that Iris usually came back, and why wouldn't she need to anymore if she did usually come back? Or did Lane think I was pitifully waiting around, helping her clean, just for the off chance the woman who was known for one-night stands would come back and pick me for one night?

"I wasn't expecting—need to?" I decided to go with the assumption that Lane didn't think me a pining loser.

"She's finally free to do whatever she wants every night."

That told me nothing. "She wasn't before?"

Lane sighed and went to the kitchen door to say a few parting words to Deb and the assistant. She waited for the back door to slam and the lock to throw. Handing me a stack of serving tins filled with cut lemons, oranges, cherries, and mint leaves, she brought out the cling wrap and turned to wipe down the back bar.

It was another full minute before she spoke again. I nearly cut my finger on the cling wrap box trying to free a section when she said, "I was attacked eight months ago."

Without needing to clarify, I knew what she meant by attacked. For someone like Lane and me and many other women who weren't overtly feminine, attacked was an easier word to say. My body pushed against the stool's backrest. A cold chill swirled through to land in my stomach. *Jesus, Lane.*

Her eyes glanced at me from over her shoulder as she continued to work. "I was thirty feet from my home. Thirty feet. I'd taken that same route home from work every night for years."

I kept my eyes trained on her but went back to fighting with the cling wrap box to keep my hands busy. I'd once written an article on the prevalence of college campus rapes and spoken to many women about their experiences. Making platitudes or sorrowful sounds didn't help matters. With someone like Lane, she might just stop talking.

"It wasn't something I wanted everyone to know, but I couldn't keep it to myself. I had...a broken nose, fingers, ribs, and visible cuts." Her eyes shot me a quick glance again. "I couldn't cover them all when I went to work, and my partner talked, so everyone eventually found out."

My eyebrows rose. She didn't have a partner when we'd moved her from her stark apartment to the newly renovated one upstairs last week. She didn't have a lot of anything, really.

"She left me." Lane read my mind. "Couldn't handle the thought of…Anyway, Iris would show up at closing every night to walk me home. She was usually here to hang out most nights anyway. But this…she supported me in the best way she knew how. She didn't keep asking me how I was doing. She didn't tell me how to feel. She didn't try to placate me by saying my feelings were justified. She was just Iris, and she treated me like I was me, not someone different because of what happened. The only change she made was to make sure women in the bar wouldn't walk home alone. If they weren't driving or getting a ride, she'd escort them and come back after. If she left with a date, she'd still be back for me at closing. Every night. She never once missed. I hated that I felt so much better for it. Hated that I needed it, even if it cut into her dating and social life." She let out a shuddering breath. "She's got her off duty cop friends walking the area on weekends, keeping it safer. They rotate weeks, but Iris is always on."

Because Lane wasn't the only one. And he hasn't been caught yet. She didn't have to say it.

"This job, working toward saving for this bar to take it over in a few years when Charlie left, was the only thing I focused on. It kept me going. When I thought I'd lose the chance to own the bar, I floundered. Iris didn't leave my side for two days until I got it together."

The one sunny day tennis game cancellation. I'd thought she had another undercover job and couldn't take an hour away. I was so wrong. It also explained why Lane had been so over-the-top miserable when Charlie announced her plans to sell the bar early. If the goal of buying the bar had been her steading baseline, having that drop out must have devastated her.

"My friends, they just...and the looks sometimes, it gets to be too much."

She pulled the stepstool over and climbed it to wipe down the light fixtures above the bar. I finished wrapping the tins and put them in the bar fridge. When she was done with the fixtures behind the bar, she carried the stepstool over to the first of the fixtures in the bar area. I pulled down a chair from a nearby table and began wiping the next closest fixture.

We worked for five minutes without talking. I wasn't sure if she'd finished everything she wanted to say or just needed a break. Either way, the busy work felt comforting.

"You haven't said anything," Lane finally stated, turning to face me fully.

I surveyed her defensive stance. She was expecting me to disappoint her like I assumed her friends had, which explained why the "friends" hadn't shown up to help her when she was opening this place. There was no one best way to respond to a situation like this. Counselors knew a lot of techniques, but no one universal comment to make it sound like you're on her side no matter what. I was certain she'd heard, "I'm sorry," or, "How terrible," too many times before those same people got consumed with their own lives and lost the appropriate amount of compassion.

"You've been through something no one should ever have to go through." I paused to gauge her reaction. The folded arms dropped to her sides as her head tilted a few degrees. "And you've come through the other side."

She scoffed and resumed the defensive stance.

"You have. You're too close to see it, but I'm still new here. I see what I see."

"What's that?" Brown eyes slit to half closed, afraid of what I might say.

"You're sharp, you're strong, you're funny, you're caring and genuine. You're a worthy person. You own a thriving bar and have a dedicated staff. More importantly, you have a best friend who would die for you. You're on the other side. Some days it might not feel like it, but that's what you show people." I gave her my most definitive stare. "I'm a journalist. My career is dependent on how accurately I can observe people and situations."

A tiny smile stretched her lips. "And you've got a successful career."

"That I do, and a great place to further that career, thanks to an amazing friend, who is kind enough to let me camp out in her bar."

Her smile widened, and some of that hesitancy I'd always seen with her dropped away.

29

Eleven a.m. on Thursday morning, I came to a stop on a borrowed bike at the tennis courts. We hadn't texted or called or anything since I'd been back. This was the scene of the bad kissing crime. Well, not really the scene, but the catalyst to the kissing incident. Would she show up?

The foursome from last week was loudly banging balls around, warming up on one court. Two teenagers were on another, a middle-aged pair of guys beside them. A few singles were sitting on benches by courts waiting for their partners. My eyes swept the area before going back to one of the singles. Long, toned legs showed past a mid-thigh pair of soccer shorts that hugged the tight backend of a woman leaning over her tennis bag. Not that I'd spent a lot of time staring at Iris's ass, but it was pretty unmistakable.

"Hey," I said to her backside until she swung upright and around.

"Hey," she replied, shooting a glance at my mouth, before focusing back on my eyes. "Good trip?"

"More work and for longer."

Her eyebrows shot up as she continued our shorthand way of speaking, "Good thing or no?"

I studied her. She'd shown up for our standing tennis date when it was possible she would have ditched because of the unexpected move she made and how badly it had gone. She'd shown up and smiled like she usually did and didn't act like she was at all uncomfortable. "It's a very good thing."

"Saw your last post. Thanks for mentioning the bar again."

I shrugged as we separated and went to opposite ends of the court. "I told Lane it benefited me just as much. Several people have already responded to tell me they'd be in the area and want to share their story."

"Out of towners?"

"So they've said. It'll keep me from having to hit more cities just to get the interview quota."

"Definitely a good thing."

We played as if nothing had happened between us the last time. As much as I appreciated the forget-it-ever-happened attitude when it came to something really uncomfortable, I couldn't forget. How could I forget the worst kiss of my life?

"New bike?" Iris asked after I'd thrashed her on the court, making all right with the world again. We stood beside the bike as I tried to remember Helen's four digit code on the lock.

"It's Helen's. I have to go car shopping after an interview today." My new place didn't have the same walkability score as the executive rental, not if I wanted to keep going to the bar and hanging out with Iris and Lane. Daily rental cars weren't practical, so it was car shopping for me. Or car shopping for Joe, who was salivating at the chance to pick out something for me. This would be my first car in six years. I was happy for the help. Even considered taking Riley up on her offer, but she couldn't get away till the weekend.

A smile slid across Iris's face.

"What?" I tried not to focus on how the smile made her lips look so inviting. My brain didn't remember that those lips and mine didn't match up well enough for another invitation.

"You're really sticking around." She nodded. "Yeah, you are, and it makes me happy."

That was a good sign. Meant the bad kissing didn't color her attitude toward me. "Me, too."

"I thought you might be tempted to stay in DC after your meeting." A faint flush crawled up her neck. Not the same flush that came during tennis matches. It was the kind of flush that could cause flutters if it weren't for our combined ghastly lip skills.

"I worked for a different paper there before and had enough of it." The city was fine to live in, but having to report on political maneuvers every day got old quickly. "I'm trying something new."

"This is good for new." Some of the flush retreated. "Are you settled into the new digs?"

"Yep. I've arranged for my storage locker to ship out the rest of my stuff from Chicago. Not that there's much, but some stuff to make it feel like a home."

"What about furniture?" Her mouth drew into a line.

"It was furnished for visitors." Lots of visitors, apparently. Helen kept expressing how pleased she was that I had taken over the apartment. "I bought a new desk chair and mattress, but the other stuff will hold until I'm ready to go shopping for replacements."

"I never got the whole story on how this place was miraculously available."

It did seem miraculous after all the apartments we'd looked at. The next stop for us would have been someplace called Shoreline since Northgate hadn't panned out. I was overjoyed not to have to spend more mornings looking at yet another tiny space that depressed me.

"A friend of theirs used to own it, but she moved. Since then, it's been a vacation place for her sister's friends. Helen got sick of them knocking on her door to play tour guide."

"You're getting to be good friends?"

"We are, and Joe. He's the one taking me car shopping." I gave a carefree flick of my hand, still not believing my luck. "I guess she figures if I start to bug her, she doesn't have to renew my lease."

"I'm just glad it worked out. Having you in Shoreline would have sucked."

"Out of the radius, huh?"

She stared at me, all mirth leaving. "I would have made an exception."

I felt some of her flush transfer to me. "Good to know."

The ladies foursome passed us and loudly clambered into their cars, two of them checking Iris out before finally starting their cars and pulling away. They'd briefly flicked their eyes over me, but Iris's muscle tone and flirtatious ways drew most of their attention.

"I kissed you," Iris blurted.

My eyes snapped back to hers. Yes. She did, and it was bad, but I couldn't say that, could I? What if she didn't think it was bad?

"It was..." she trailed off, watching their cars disappear from the parking lot.

Wrong? Shouldn't have happened? Horrible mistake? A grimace pinched her features as she struggled for the right words. I threw out my own guess before I could stop my faulty kissing lips. "Bad?"

She laughed, surprise hiking her brow up. "It was, wasn't it? Colossally bad. I think I chipped a tooth."

I joined the laughter. "Teeth really shouldn't be involved in kissing unless it's intentional, in case you needed a refresher on the subject."

"Oh, you're giving me lessons, now? You were half of that bad kissing display."

She was being kind about the percentage of blame, but I still had to make a crack. "The surprised half."

Her eyes flashed with mischief. "Since the invention of the kiss—"

"Really? *The Princess Bride?*"

She shrugged without apology. "Great movie."

"Even better book," I interjected.

"As I was saying before you interrupted me with movie footnotes—"

"Footnotes are critical."

She pushed at my shoulder to stop the teasing gibes. "Since kissing was invented, the rating for that kiss—"

"Ours, you mean? The one that was a complete surprise to me?"

"That very one would have rated just above the horrid display in *Dumb and Dumber*."

My whole body cringed as the kissing clip from that movie flashed through my head. Yeah, that was a bad kiss. Far worse than the one Iris had given me. "You just felt like you had to kiss someone and any surprised mouth would do? Hadn't had your quota of kissing for the day?"

Her eyes skimmed over me. "Lane talked to you."

I stepped back, surprised by the change of topic. The very serious topic. A nod was all I could manage.

"I'm glad. She hasn't talked to many people. Just her mom and me, that's it. It's good she could tell you."

"Her friends suck." I spoke the thought that had been running through my mind since the other night.

"A lot of them were my friends, too, and I couldn't agree more. It didn't take long for them to become gossipy, judgmental assholes."

On top of everything Lane had gone through, to find out her friends weren't who she thought they were must have been devastating. "Some people can't deal with anything heavy. She may not know it, but she's better for dropping those friends."

"She knows that now." Iris slid a hand down my arm and squeezed my hand. "Thanks for being different."

"I like Lane."

"Simple as that?"

"Yes." I shrugged because it was a simple code that not many people understood. I'd always thought of friendship as quiet joy. In a life filled with complications and difficulties, quiet joy wasn't easy to find.

"That's why I had to kiss you."

I swallowed, accepting that she got my simple code. "Because I'm different?" She nodded, but I couldn't help one final tease. "Yeah, bad kissers are pretty different. Even teenagers often get it right."

That got a laugh. "Half my fault."

She didn't seem as distressed by her kissing performance as I'd been by mine. Maybe she knew something I didn't. Maybe she was willing to overlook my terrifically horrible, dreadfully awful performance because I was different and good to her and her friend. Come to think of it, being good to someone and her friend, when they needed good friends, compensated for any and all lousy mouth sucking techniques.

HAYDEN & BILLIE

Stubby fingers kept sweeping the bob haircut behind the ears of the woman directly across from me. At first I thought she was just anxious that her hair might appear scraggly after she'd walked in from the windy evening outside. After almost an hour of constant hair sweeping, she clearly had a nervous habit. Her partner didn't appear to notice, when it was stole my whole focus. I wanted to reach across the table and trap her arms by her sides to stop the incessant fidgeting.

"At first, you think you'll be an hour late. That blows, but it can't be avoided. No reason to yell at the gate attendant. Then, as all the flights start switching over to delayed, you think, damn, it might be a few hours." Billie swept only one side of her hair behind her ears. The other was still tucked in safely, as it had been during the last ten sweeps.

"After a few hours, we started getting antsy." Hayden gave her spouse a fond look. She left her own lighter brown hair completely alone.

"I was a nervous wreck," Billie admitted. Sweep, sweep. "My job depended on me getting to San Diego to land that account. My boss basically told me that if I didn't come back with a signed contract, I shouldn't come back." Double sweep again.

"Yikes." Deadline pressure paled in comparison to career ultimatums. "Did you have the same stressor, Hayden?"

"God, no. I was glad to have less family time. Everyone was going there for my brother's wedding. Being stuck in an airport was a great excuse."

"After five hours waiting, you did start to freak a little," Billie said with a momentary pause in the hair sweeping to snake an arm around Hayden.

"I did, when it looked like we might not get out of there in time for the ceremony. It's one thing to skip out on all the family drama before the wedding, but to actually miss it? Mama would have roasted me and served me for dinner."

"By the time we figured out we weren't going anywhere that night, all the hotels were booked up. I was going to rent a car and drive the rest of the way." Billie pushed her fingers through her hair three times to indicate how seriously she meant to get the hell out of that airport.

"There was fourteen feet of snow out there." Hayden's voice pitched up to a near screech.

Fourteen feet of snow didn't dump in less than three hours. Not in Denver, and what the hell were they doing choosing a flight path from New Orleans to San Diego that put them through Denver in the middle of December? First, it's not on the way. Second, it's Denver in December. There's bound to be weather.

"You convinced her to sit tight, I take it?" I asked Hayden.

"I did. I'd noticed her, of course, who wouldn't?" She batted her eyes at the less than noticeable Billie. In baggie jeans and a tank top under a plaid shirt, she looked identical to a third of the women in Lane's bar tonight. Other than the constant motion of her arms to tuck her hair back, nothing really stood out about her. At a crowded gate, someone wouldn't pick her out as the most noticeable. Now, Hayden was a different story. Curvy and pretty, she wore a patterned summer dress that flattered her well-proportioned, plump frame. Many of the women in here had given her the look.

"You saw her making a break for it and did what?" I prompted.

"She practically vibrated in her seat with tension. I gave up my prime location next to an electrical outlet and went over to sit next to her."

"She tried to be funny."

"I was funny!" Hayden slapped Billie's hand as it came down from a hair sweep.

"She thinks she's funny," Billie corrected.

"That right there is what hooked me," Hayden told me. "Her sense of humor. That's always been number one on my list of things I needed in a girlfriend."

I bit back a long suffering sigh. Even before this series of interviews, I'd grown tired of friends saying their number one requirement in a mate was a sense of humor. Everyone has a sense of humor. Everyone. They may not be funny, but that doesn't mean they can't sense what makes them laugh. Most people think they want someone who's funny, but seriously funny people often use humor to mask whatever pain they've gone through. I'll stick with someone who amuses me because we have similar senses of humor over someone who is constantly trying to make me and everyone around us laugh.

"Your attempt at humor captivated Billie enough to ditch the plan to drive to San Diego?" I got back on track.

"Through fourteen feet of snow," Hayden piped up.

"No cars were left either." Billie's hair sweep hitched at the admission of checking on cars first before resigning herself to enjoy Hayden's humor.

"Truly stranded in the airport?" I made a note: *Stranded*. At least it wasn't on a deserted island, then I'd know they were LARPing a lesbian romance novel.

"It was pretty awful," Billie said, one-sided sweep again. She looked at Hayden and added, "But pretty wonderful, too. Who knew you could fall in love between a Cinnabon and an Orange Julius?"

"Oh, God, Cinnabon," Hayden moaned. "We need to hit a mall soon and grab one, sweetie."

Billie laughed and slung her arm around Hayden again, severely limiting her ability to double sweep the hair. "Anything you want, ladybug."

"How long were you stranded?" I tried not to make air quotes around the word. Stranded implies going for days without any luxuries. Cinnabon may not be luxurious dining, but it's still available food.

"Until noon the next day."

"Did you make it to the wedding?" I asked Hayden.

"I came in right at the end."

"Did you get your contract?" I asked Billie.

She shot an affectionate look at her spouse and proceeded to swipe first one side of her hair, then the next with the hand not around Hayden. "I went with her to the wedding."

Good for her. Screw work ultimatums when love was on the line. Especially a love that came about between food vendors in an airport that was nowhere near their original destination.

After gathering a few more details, I bid them goodbye. I'd been lucky to sneak them in before they left town tomorrow. They probably had another haphazard flight path back to New Orleans through Cleveland or some other out of the way airport. At least they shouldn't run into another weather system that forced them to sleep in airport chairs and eat heavy fast food.

As I approached the bar, I heard a familiar voice speaking from the group to my left. "Hey, she's hot, she's new, she's famous, and no one but Iris has had her yet. Of course, I took a shot."

My ego showed up and guessed they were talking about me. I didn't think I was hot or famous, but I was still new and somehow people think Iris has bedded me. I recognized Greer, of the Wallet Stealers, along with a few other regulars, and Cyrah, the one who'd been talking. Over the weekend, we'd run into each other at a barbeque Nykos and Mariah hosted. She'd asked if I wanted to chat over a drink, but Nykos was in the middle of introducing me to hundreds of people. As hot as she was, I wasn't upset to have missed out on the chance to get to know her better at the party. I had a much better time hanging out with the hosts, Helen and Joe, and Iris and Lane.

"You don't have a chance," another voice said.

"You're just jealous because your phone swipe didn't net you anything."

"I didn't swipe her phone," Greer sulked.

"You swipe everyone's phone. How else can you cyberstalk them?" another voice said.

It amazed me how often people didn't bother to look around before they start talking about someone. Lane caught my eye and smiled. Her eyes flicked to the group, and the smile stretched wider. Great, she'd overheard as well. She made an obvious throat clearing sound, and all heads turned in my direction. Only two of the faces looked guilty. The one belonging to the woman who perpetually wore the 1950s' garb grinned broadly. Three others slinked off to avoid being caught up in whatever they thought might happen when confronted with the object of their gossip.

"Hey, Vega," Greer greeted as if we were buddies. I'd called her out on stealing my wallet the last time I saw her. She looked appropriately shamefaced at the time, but apparently, she now thought we were back on equal ground.

"You ready for that drink you promised me?" Cyrah asked, stepping to the front of the crowd.

I glanced back and caught the delight on Lane's face. At least she was finding this amusing. Everyone in the group waited on edge for my response. I couldn't put my finger on precisely why I felt like being a bitch. Maybe it was the sweet love-blossoms-between-airport-fast-food-vendors story I'd just heard, or maybe I wasn't a fan of feeling like a prize to be won instead of a person. "You sure you want to have a drink with me or just the famous fresh meat that no one but Iris has had?"

Wannabe James Dean guffawed. A true guffaw, bending at the waist to hold her stomach. Greer looked triumphant. Cyrah looked apologetic, which made me feel bad that I'd had fun at her expense.

"What have I had?" Iris asked from behind us. Now, I was guilty of not looking around before talking about someone else. Not that it was a bad thing I'd said, since it wasn't true and I'd only been trying to make a point.

"Me."

The grin she wore slipped momentarily, and I could feel my cheeks warm. Damn, I'd somehow forgotten about the kiss for ten seconds. The colossally bad kiss, as she'd put it. I should sign up for kissing lessons. Classes must be available for all those people who suffered kissing setbacks like me. Instructions on how to push through the yips to get back to amazing kissing. Yes. I'd be on the lookout for those. I wanted my next kiss to be amazing. It certainly couldn't be any worse. Either way, I probably shouldn't be joking about her having had me.

Her eyes flicked to the group, noticing their eagerness. Her grin came back, and she played along. "Right."

"Not all that new, then, am I?" I said, turning back to Cyrah.

She held up her hands. "Listen, I didn't mean…we were just gabbing. You know how it is."

I gave her a long look. She was nice enough, and it wouldn't do to piss off every lesbian in this place if I ever wanted to date in this town. "I do. I was pulling your leg."

"Oh," she sounded relieved. "The drink, then?"

Another mental sigh before I agreed. A drink wouldn't hurt anything. She'd probably just been showing off for her buddies. She might turn out to be really decent.

Lane smirked as I placed our drink orders while Cyrah went to secure a table. Iris's head shook but a tiny smile pulled at her lips. "When did this 'having you' take place?"

"Ask them." My chin tipped at the now dispersing group. "Or Riley's group because they seem to think the same thing."

She scrutinized me, amusement twinkling in her eyes. "I should really go find out if it was memorable."

I glared and shot back, "It was memorable."

"Our imaginary night that never took place?" Iris teased, and Lane started laughing.

"Memorable," I barked and stomped, well, walked away toward my semi-date for the evening.

31

Bike shopping was serving as my mid-morning break today. Since I'd been spending most of my mid-morning breaks bike riding, I couldn't keep borrowing Helen's bike. Remembering the couple with the bike shop, I looked up their address and headed out for a little shopping.

Several recommendations later, I was about to take a test ride in the store's parking lot when a text came in. Normally, I would have ignored the text since the cute saleswoman was giving me all her attention. Flirty good attention. Ignoring texts was the polite thing to do, but I had this feeling. The kind of feeling that said this was not something to be ignored.

"Excuse me a sec," I said to the bike cutie and fished out my phone from the light jacket I'd had to tie around my waist halfway to the shop when this odd city couldn't figure out if it would stay warm all day.

YOU BUSY? NEED A FAVOR.

That feeling flared again as I read Iris's text. This wasn't a favor to put off.

NOPE. WHAT'S UP?

LANE NEEDS TO COME DOWNTOWN.

A RIDE?

AN ESCORT. FOR A LINEUP. SAYS SHE'LL TAKE A BUS BUT WANTED TO CHECK W/YOU.

They'd found him. My heart pounded. They, more likely, Iris, found him. Lane must be freaking out. I didn't doubt that she could make it to the police station by herself, but this was big.

I'LL GO GET HER.

SHE MIGHT

I waited for more, but Iris apparently couldn't find the right words to describe how her best friend would be reacting to this.

On my way. I'll be persuasive.

I turned back to the cute saleswoman. "Sorry, bit of an emergency. You on tomorrow?"

She flashed a smile that was both hopeful for the commission and disappointed that she hadn't closed me. "Sure am. Ten to four, ask for me."

"Will do." I was already at my car when my phone beeped again. I glanced down and read the two simple words of thanks. Like she even had to say anything.

Minutes later, Lane answered my buzz up to her apartment. Hope painted her tone. She was probably thinking that Iris had broken away to come get her. At hearing my voice, she adopted a fake casual tone. "I'm headed out, actually."

"I know. Iris texted."

There was a long pause. "She shouldn't have."

"Lane, please. Just come down."

She didn't take long to come down from her apartment. She looked hesitant and shaky but determined. "I can handle this."

"I know you can."

She waited for me to turn and go back to my car, but I didn't budge. "You don't have to go with me. I told Iris I was fine."

"Lane." I reached out to grasp her hand. It was a nice hand, soft, with long fingers. I curled mine around it with a slight squeeze. "Let me be here for you. That's what friends do. If I could have dragged you into my last editors' meeting for support, I would have done it."

She studied me, a ghost of a smile forming. "Editors. That's asking too much."

"That's why you weren't strapped into the airplane seat next to me. This," I waved toward my car, "is a ride downtown. Iris is meeting us there, and in no time, we'll be right back here."

"Sounds too easy."

I turned serious. "We're going to be with you every step of the way."

Her brown eyes glistened as she nodded and walked to my car. "Is this new?"

I recognized her need for distraction and played along. "New enough. Couldn't keep writing off a rental for those days I needed one. Joe went with me. Started drooling the second I told him I needed a car and had no idea what to get." He'd taken me to three too many dealerships, but we'd found the perfect used coupe that looked brand new.

She turned to face me when I slipped inside. "I'm glad you decided to stay here."

My hand grasped hers again. "Me, too."

Once we got to the station, Lane's tension ratcheted up. We'd kept the conversation light on the ride rather than getting into what Iris had told her on the phone. I was there for moral support only. My curiosity could wait.

Iris came through the security door with a shorter woman dressed in a badly wrinkled linen suit. They both looked exhausted. No doubt they'd caught him last night and spent many hours questioning him and organizing a defense-proof lineup. She nodded at me and waved Lane over for an introduction. Seconds later, they disappeared behind the security door.

I plopped onto a bench in the lobby. The building was newer, damn nice for a police department. People-watching helped me refrain from biting my nails. Lane had been nervous enough in the car. I couldn't imagine her fear at having to see this guy in a lineup.

Before my nails were bitten to the nub, Iris resurfaced from behind the security door. Her expression this time was unreadable. She waved for me to follow her outside.

"How's Lane?" I asked when we'd cleared all the people clusters around the building.

"She's coping."

I wanted to wait for more, but I'd been waiting long enough. "Did she pick the right guy? Can you tell me without jeopardizing the case?"

She glanced back and forth, making sure we were alone. "She picked the guy we brought in last night, yes. It was a good identification. His lawyer doesn't have a prayer of throwing it out based on the usual crap."

"What's the usual crap?"

"When only one suspect in the lineup is wearing a hoody like the guy who committed the crime. Or when only one suspect has a goatee and everyone else has a full beard. Anything that differentiates our suspect from everyone else in the lineup."

Too bad I hadn't met Iris when I'd written that article on police procedures years ago. She would have been a great help. Instead, all the officers I called thought I was going to report on the police brutality charge they'd faced the year before and weren't very forthcoming.

"So today's lineup was good, defense wise, and Lane picked the right guy."

"She and last night's victim, yes."

I made a noise with my mouth that indicated surprise and repulsion that he'd attacked someone else last night. "Oh."

"Yeah. She was worried she wouldn't recognize him. It's been months. That's always an issue when the defense attorney watches the lineup. If she showed any hesitation at all or said she wasn't sure, they jump all over that in court."

"But she didn't."

Iris released a short breath through her nose. "No. She didn't. Neither did the woman from last night. We're getting two other victims in later. The others couldn't give a specific description of him at the time, so we'd rather stick with the ones who were sure they could identify him if they saw him again."

"Is there DNA?" As much as DNA evidence would clinch the case, having it there made me sick to think about.

"No sperm, but skin scrapings and blood. Those tests take a few days."

I took that in, trying not to let my mind wander to how blood and skin scrapings would have gotten there. "Did you or linen suit catch him?"

"We, Daphne and I, came across him and the victim. He ran for it, but we called two others and converged on the guy a block away. Daphne was on him and cuffing him in a second. We interrupted him before he could do more than bruise the woman from last night."

"Thank God," I said.

"I know. If not for Lane's identification, we'd only have him on attempted rape. If we can get the other two to identify him, he's looking at a serial rape conviction along with assault. Based on the injuries he inflicted, we might even try for attempted murder to get him to plead." She released another calming breath. "All the criminals we've tracked, none meant as much to me as catching this guy did."

"It's all thanks to you." My hand rested on her shoulder for a comforting squeeze.

"I was beginning to give up hope. He's been targeting lesbians from the gay bars on Capitol Hill. We were within blocks of the other three attacks since Lane. That's been killing me for months."

"Iris, you've done everything you can." My other hand came up to grip both shoulders. "These detectives and officers volunteering their time to patrol that area, that's down to your influence. This guy is done because of you."

"Everyone, really. I owe them all drinks for a month."

"I'll chip in for that."

She gave me a soft smile. "Thanks for being here. Can you wait for her to finish her statement? I'm stuck going through mine and wrapping things up."

"Absolutely. I'll be ready whenever she is."

"And can you—"

"Yes, I'll be pushy and invite myself in if I have to. She shouldn't be alone."

Iris leaned in to put her arms around me. The whole of her body caressed mine and felt really good. Relief and celebration and a little gratitude all wrapped up in one delicious hug.

Well, we weren't bad at hugging. At least there's that.

32

Kelly & Vic

Bright blue eyes twinkled at me. Mischief danced in the woman's expression spurred on by the look of complete disbelief on my face. "Hard to believe, isn't it?"

My eyes bounced between Kelly and Vic. I wondered if they were pulling my leg. In all my years as a journalist, all the interviews, all the stories I'd listened to, never once had I come across someone with long-term amnesia. I'll say that again: AMNESIA. It wasn't just the can't-remember-what-happened-right-before-my-traumatic-event kind. No, this was the real no-memories-from-this-point-backward kind.

"Nothing. You remember nothing?" I repeated my earlier question.

"Not one thing. Skied right into that tree, or so they tell me, and nada." Her blue eyes twinkled again, unaffected by the fact that she had no memories from before she'd turned thirty-one.

Her partner, Vic, was a muscular brunette with lips so full it looked like she'd used a suction cup to plump them up before arriving. Other than the full lips, not much else was feminine about her. Sheer short hair, sleeveless t-shirt that showed good muscle tone and cargo shorts that displayed unshaven legs. Not just an oops-forgot-to-shave-this-week-before-I-decided-on-shorts-tonight look, this was a statement that said she didn't succumb to the patriarchal view on the subject of shaving. I was all for equality and flying in the face of how men think women should look and act. All for it. I just really enjoy running my hands over smooth, non-hairy skin. That was one of the many benefits of dating women. Whether the skin belonged to me or someone I was seeing, I liked it smooth. During the winter, go ahead, take breaks from daily or weekly shaving routines. I certainly did, especially if I wasn't in a relationship. But when spring rolls around and shorts or swimsuits are the daily attire, meet a razor every once in a while. Just my preference. Others, like Kelly, obviously had a different perspective on the subject. Since she was in a committed relationship and I wasn't, this peculiarity of mine showcased how picky I could be when trying to find the right woman.

"Where do you come into the story?" I asked Vic.

"I was an EMT on the mountain. We got her strapped in on a sled and brought her down with a snowmobile. She was in a coma for four days. I'd go back to the hospital every night just to check on her. When she woke without knowing who she was, it freaked everyone out."

"She was the first person I saw." Kelly snuggled into Vic's embrace. "She was so nice and soft spoken. I didn't realize until the doctor finally joined us that I couldn't remember my name."

Vic smiled a really nice smile with those full lips. "I started spending all my evenings in the hospital."

"I don't know what I would have done without Vic. It got so frustrating when the doctors kept trying to get me to remember." A touch of the frustration she must have felt crinkled her brow.

"Was your family there?"

"I'd gone up for the day on my own and my phone got ruined in the crash." Her shoulders shrugged, taking on that unbothered posture again. "The hospital had my ID and insurance card. That's all we could work from."

"Must have been scary," I prompted because the ever chipper blue-eyed brunette wasn't fazed by anything.

"Frustrating mostly. I was happy to be alive. The doctors said my memory could come back, but they kept trying to force it back right away."

Vic rubbed her hand along Kelly's back. Her calm nature probably helped with Kelly's initial frustration. "She'd figure it out sooner or later. I just tried to be supportive."

"You were, baby." She kissed Vic's cheek.

"How was the mystery of your background solved?" The grip on my pen tightened. If I was doing an amnesia story, I wanted to get every detail.

"My insurance was through an employer. From there we tracked down my sister, who was my emergency contact. My parents and sister showed up the next day with a lot more pressure to remember and pressure to recuperate with them and pressure to get back to work."

That didn't sound like a respite from the ordeal she was going through. "What kind of work?"

"I was an accountant. My family thought I could go right back to that, but have you ever tried to be an accountant when you can't remember much of the Internal Revenue Code?"

My head shook automatically. I wouldn't try to be an accountant if I *could* remember *all* the Internal Revenue Code.

"All the better, right, honeybun?" Vic encouraged.

"Right." Kelly pecked Vic's full lips this time. "Apparently, I was a rigid type-A personality with few friends and pretty fixated on money."

"You were an accountant," I commented.

"Yeah." She laughed as if it just made sense to her that, as an accountant, money would play an important role in her life. "My family took it personally when I couldn't remember them. According to some of my friends, we hadn't been on the closest of terms anyway. When the pressure got too much, I just walked away, from my job, from my family, and moved to the ski resort for the one and only true friend I had."

Likely it was transference to begin with. Vic had been there for her from the beginning of her new life, and she didn't care for the people trying to force her into her old life. Obviously, she'd feel great affection for her. As a former type-A personality who no longer felt type-A, she was probably relieved to ditch that persona.

"She was right handed before the accident, now she's left," Vic told me. I wondered if Kelly experienced any other one-eighties. Like perhaps she had a hunky male fiancé before the accident.

"Lots of things changed if I'm to believe what my sister and mom say about how I used to be." Kelly gave another unbothered shrug.

"Do you keep in touch with any of your old friends?"

"Most were work related. After I quit, we didn't know what to talk about anymore."

I'd had friendships like that. Floating from paper to paper, I made plenty of friends in the office and on assignment. Every time I left, it was difficult to keep in touch without that commonality. It was one of the reasons I liked Iris and Lane so much. They weren't part of this assignment. We'd built a friendship outside of my work. Same with Helen and Joe and Mariah and Nykos, more reasons I knew this stay in Seattle would be different from my other posts. "Were they more understanding than your family appeared to be?"

"At first, yeah, then they'd bring up things we did in the past and get upset or embarrassed because I couldn't remember them. I thought a clean slate with my clean brain was probably the best move I could make."

I sat back and finished the notes I was making. Her logic made sense. Although I'd been living a no-ties lifestyle for many years, I still couldn't imagine what it would be like to wake up with absolutely no idea of who I was. Would I find writing again? Would I want to play tennis every Thursday? Would I forget how important Iris and Lane were to me?

"You seem distressed." Kelly scrutinized me.

"I was just thinking how hard it must have been for you."

"I'd have been lost and hopeless without Vic by my side. With her friendship and later love, I felt like I could do anything. Learning more about how I used to be, I was thrilled not to be that way anymore."

That was the perfect attitude to make a full life after suffering amnesia. "What do you do now?"

She let a delightful sounding giggle slip. "I'm a chainsaw carver. Bear statues and the like. I wasn't artistic at all before. I have the love of my life by my side and we're happy. I don't want to go back to being an uptight anal-retentive who does nothing but count numbers so people can make more money. That crash was the second best thing to happen to me."

My eyes flicked to the loving gaze Vic was giving her. I didn't need to ask what the first best thing to happen to her had been. "I've got to say this is definitely one of the more unusual stories I've heard."

"Oh, goodie. We're going to make the list, then?" Kelly asked.

"Normally I don't promise anything, but yeah, your story will definitely make it in."

She squealed with glee and grabbed Vic's face for a loud kiss. I chuckled as I closed my notepad and clicked off the recorder. I thanked them for making the trip up to the bar from their hotel where they'd suspended their tourist activities to tell me their story.

Iris was talking to Lane when I approached the bar. She tipped her chin at the couple I just left. "Where are they from?"

"New Hampshire."

"Nice," Lane said. She'd been steadily gaining back her confidence from the police station visit the other day. It couldn't rival Iris's yet, but they had a lot more in common than I'd originally thought when that previously unexplained hesitation seeped its way into her demeanor. I liked both versions of Lane, but it made me happy to see her get her feet solidly under her. "Can't believe people want their stories in a paper so much that they'd take part of their vacation time to go through an interview."

"Good story?" Iris asked.

"Amnesia," I said and watched their mouths drop. "I know. Major cliché in lesbian romances."

"Any romance." Lane blushed when she realized her tough persona just collapsed with the admission that she reads romances.

To save her from the sure ribbing Iris would start in on, I asked, "You know what's more cliché?" They turned their attention to me. "A lesbian PI."

Lane and I cracked up at Iris's expression. Now that I knew Lane also read romances, we could spend some time going over some of our favorite themes. Or more likely, mock them while secretly showing just how much we liked them.

"Even better, a lesbian PI with amnesia. Now that would make for a great romance," I suggested and looked at Iris. "Should I knock your head against something?"

"Then write about it?" Lane offered.

Iris shook her head and joined our laughter. "You both should be locked in a room and forced to read classic literature for a week."

After the week I'd had with the step up in interviews as well as worrying about Lane's case, I wouldn't mind being locked in a room to read. My eyes flicked to Iris. Maybe not. I'd miss our tennis match and daily teasing sessions and just being around them.

33

EMORY & ROBIN

As stories went, this one couldn't be true. In no way could it be true because I swear I just read it in a lesbian romance novel a couple of weeks ago. It was an older book as far as the genre went, ten years at least. Maybe that's why they thought they could recite it back to me.

"I thought I'd lost her forever." Emory leaned over the table to express just how imperative it was that I empathize with her loss of love. Tall and slim, she stretched well into my personal space.

"But you didn't?" My mind kept cycling through the various authors, trying to remember where I'd read a story similar to theirs.

"It's a miracle." Her lean brought her attractive tanned face into mine and prevented her from being able to drag her miracle Robin to her side in a show of affection borne by said miracle. She stayed suspended over the table for another second before slamming back into her chair and reaching with both hands to practically haul Robin onto her lap.

Robin, a short, hair-sprayed vixen in the latest designer clothes, gave a little giggle and happily scrambled the rest of the way onto Emory's lap. "A miracle," she agreed in a perfect breathy imitation of Marilyn Monroe.

I glanced down at my notes to stop the endless ruffling of mental library catalogue cards in search of their story's author. Reading through each point, I felt I had to confirm their story. Give them a chance to back down on some of the more outrageous aspects.

"You," I started with Emory, "returned home for your father's funeral."

"Didn't want to," Emory inserted for the—let me count it up in my notes—sixth time in the story.

Because he'd kicked her out of the house when he couldn't force her to change her lesbian ways. That sucked, I'd give her that. Still, if she really didn't want to go back for the funeral, she wouldn't have.

"To a horse ranch in Oklahoma where your family needed your help securing capital to cover the mortgage they didn't know your father had taken out on the farm?"

"I'm in high finance. Of course, I could help them," she proclaimed proudly.

Did anyone use the term high finance anymore? I was pretty sure most people just referred to them as financial pricks or the asshats who caused the world economy to meltdown for no other reason than their obsessive greed.

"And you went?"

Her brow furrowed. "I couldn't let my mom lose the ranch. It's been in our family for generations."

I glanced down at my notes. Her father's family, but financed by her mother's money because her father was land rich and married his wife for an influx of money. I'd heard that one before, too. Where had—No. No. I was not listening to *Downton Abbey: On the Ranch*. No, I refused to make that connection.

"You returned and ran into Robin—"

"The lovely and demure Robin," she interrupted and planted a loud kiss on said Robin.

Nothing about that Robin was demure. "Your first love." From high school when love was more of an infatuation than an actual feeling.

"We were going to run off together." Robin's breathy voice was hard to hear over the increasing noise level at the bar, but it didn't prompt her to drop the fake breathiness and speak like a normal person. "Emory was going to Princeton. I was going to go with her to style hair."

Without meaning to, my eyes ran up to the sheer volume of hair on her head. They now lived in New York. Big hair might play in some places in Jersey and on a horse ranch in Oklahoma, but must be out of place as the spouse of a high financier. "Sounds like a nice plan."

"But my dick of a dad put a stop to it," Emory spat in a menacing tone.

Her dick of a dad who was now dead. I wasn't a big believer in turning the dead into saints, but I also didn't think calling the dead "dicks" was appropriate either.

"By?" I prompted to get her to tell me this scrumptious plot point again.

"He threatened my squishy cupcake. Scared her to death."

The squishy cupcake turned her head and buried it in Emory's neck. A soft whimper sounded from the small crevice she allowed between their conjoined bodies. My notes hadn't included the scared to death comment, and the threat had come in the form of a payoff. "He paid you how much?"

Pink suffused Robin's cheeks, battling with the addiction to her orange spray tan. "Ten thousand." The breathiness was a barely audible whisper this time.

He'd paid her ten grand to leave his daughter alone, and she'd taken it. The squishy cupcake currently glued to the front of the daughter whose father bribed her. Bribed her, and she'd taken it. It would be one thing if she'd accepted the bribe, then screwed him over by leaving with the daughter as planned, but she hadn't. She'd let him pay her off to leave the supposed love of her life alone. That bears repeating: she took the money and left the daughter alone. Until his funeral, that is.

"I was in despair," Emory took up the narrative again. "I didn't know what was going on. She didn't meet me in the hayloft like she usually did. I thought something might've happened to her. So I snuck out that night and went to her window."

Her window? Now we're quoting songs not just books?

"She told me she couldn't see me anymore. She didn't want to go to Princeton with me. Despair!" Emory was leaning again, only she couldn't finish the lean because her squishy cupcake was taking up the space between her and the tabletop.

"Yes, I can see how that would cause despair." If we lived in the 1800s and suffered from the vapors whenever something difficult in our lives came up.

"When Daddy figured out I wasn't going to get in line and become the perfect girl who would marry the rancher's son next door, he told me to get out and never come back."

But she did, when he died. And Daddy? Come on. A New York investment banker that still called a father who'd disowned her "Daddy" was too unbelievable. They had to be putting me on. I couldn't wait to verify this story. Maybe one of the brothers, who probably didn't like that she'd come back to save the ranch when their beloved father couldn't, would have a different version of this thing.

"Yet, you returned for the funeral?"

"After she'd made it in the Big Apple," Robin said, pride and something else jumbled her expression from cowering in fear over the supposed threat that was actually a bribe to genuine delight.

"That's right, squishy. I showed my dad, didn't I?"

"You did. He had no idea what he was throwing out."

Wonder how she made it through Princeton or even got to Princeton if her father truly disowned her. Oklahoma's a long way away. Hitching was unlikely, and even if she had a full-ride scholarship, she'd need money. Mommy probably helped out, which was why she must have felt compelled to return for the funeral of her homophobic father. It surely wasn't a sudden need to forgive in order to move on with her life that compelled her to return for the funeral.

"Take me through the getting together part again?" I tried not to cross my fingers in the hopes that they were actually telling the truth. That they'd be able to get all the points out in the same order and with similar language. I should ask them to tell it to me backwards. That always trumped liars.

Clichéd Love | 197

Emory's eyes narrowed. She, being of the high finance set, could recognize when a deal was going bad. She wasn't sure if I was questioning her genuineness or if I was simply stupid and needed things repeated. "I invited Robin to the funeral. Kind of an 'F-you' to Daddy, you know?"

Daddy, who paid off her girlfriend, who in turn took the money and shattered her deeply fragile first love heart. Yeah, he was the only one who deserved the F-you.

"I was nervous." Robin trembled to make it obvious.

Nervous that she wouldn't bag the high financier while she was back for a brief visit, more like. How else could she be kept in designer clothes and orange spray tan for the rest of her life?

"Some of the family sure didn't like it." Sly delight danced across Emory's face. "Too much time under Daddy's thumb, you get me?"

Oh, I got her. A family funeral was *the* perfect place to try to make a point. Every guide to proper conduct said so.

"She must have kissed me a hundred times." Robin went back to giggling. With the breathiness, it sounded more like wheezing.

"Whenever one of them looked our way." Emory smooched Robin as if to prove she knew how to perform the act of kissing. Perhaps I should take notes on this. Robin looked pretty satisfied with the kisses, even if I wanted to cringe with every overtly public display. That could be what I was doing wrong. All of my kisses should take place in public from now on. It might solicit suggestions from onlookers to improve my failing technique.

"We wanted them to know that he couldn't stop our love," Robin whisper-talked and smooched at the same time.

Except for all the years after he bought her off.

"We all went back to the ranch," Emory said, her eyes glazing a bit. "God, it was run down. I couldn't believe my dad and brothers let it get like that."

"It's beautiful now," Robin told me as if that was something I should admire.

"It is," Emory confirmed, giving Robin the admiration she'd been looking for. "Only after I secured the financing, calling in every favor I had, mind you. We hired the right people to fix it up. Then I got Mom to fire my oldest brother and hire a real ranch manager."

"Oh, boy, did Ernie get mad at that," Robin bragged, the giggle back in breathy effect.

"Back to the part about you getting together," I encouraged.

"Right, yeah, so there we are at the ranch house, surrounded by family and Daddy's friends. People were shooting us glares and whispering. I just couldn't take it. I hauled Robin upstairs with me to my old room."

And this was where the story got really good.

"We made love." Robin's breathy giggle showed absolutely no remorse.

They'd had sex. At a funeral. In Emory's childhood home. On her childhood bed. With all of her family and father's friends milling about only one floor below. She had way too much faith in the sound dampening quality of a door and floorboards. She also had zero respect for her mother. Forget her father, the guy whose funeral they were attending. She didn't have to have respect for him. He was a homophobe who rejected her. But still, it was a FUNERAL. Who sneaks upstairs to have sex during the wake? It takes someone with pretty much no soul to think that would be an appropriate thing to do. Wait to get back to the hotel, at least. Don't make everyone attending a funeral listen to sex sounds from one floor away.

"I couldn't keep my hands off her. I'd just found her again. Found out she still loved me. How could I not?" Emory's expression was one of expectation. Expectation that I'd do the exact same thing in her place.

I could bring up the fact that the love of her life didn't love her enough to tell her father to go to hell when he thought he could buy her off. Which he did. I could bring up the fact that if she truly hated her father, no amount of begging on her mother's part would have made her attend the funeral of someone she hated. She wasn't the type to go to a funeral for a sense of closure. She'd gone to show her family up. I also could have brought up the fact that had she not come back clearly wealthy—as evidenced by the thirty thousand dollar watch, the four thousand dollar suit, the five hundred dollar haircut, and the twelve thousand dollar earrings—the love of her life might not have acknowledged her when she returned. But I didn't. I simply jotted another note: *VERIFY*. In all caps, because if anything deserved all caps, it was this. Then I rose from the table to shake their hands.

Breathy squishy cupcake didn't understand that we were done. She must have wanted to continue talking about all the possessions they'd amassed since their inappropriate joining at a funeral of a man whose money she'd taken to leave the daughter alone.

Lane appeared as I took a seat at the bar and placed a gin and tonic in front of me without me needing to ask for my usual recovery drink. "That one took a while, and you look dazed. This'll help." Her left hand flicked to get someone's attention. My current hazy state kept me from being too curious about her gesture. I relied on muscle memory to deliver the drink to my lips. The cool, sharp taste helped clear some of the daze enough to recognize that Iris had joined us.

"So?" Iris tilted her head in the direction of the now departing couple.

So many words flitted through my head I couldn't sort through them all. "They…I just…If you had to…It's really unbelievable."

"Sounds like," Lane commented and settled down across from me on her elbows. That was one of my favorite things to get her to do. She didn't take enough breaks. Iris and I did what we could to encourage them.

"Start with where they're from," Iris encouraged.

"New York," I managed to answer that one.

"With that hair? No." It was a statement, not an argument.

"By way of Oklahoma."

"Ah," they both said.

"Is it a good story?" Iris asked.

"If it's true," I admitted, even as much distaste as I had for it.

"What's the crux?" she prodded.

"They went at it at her father's funeral."

"Eww," Iris said while Lane asked, "They fought at a funeral?"

"No, another f-word. *The* F-word," Iris said as if she'd been sitting next to me at the table. They both turned for my verifying nod.

"With the casket there and everything?" Lane was so enthralled she ignored the four customers who were trying to get her attention because she made better drinks than the other bartender.

"At the gathering afterward at her mom and dad's place."

Iris pulled in on her lips. "Marginally better."

"But still," Lane added her thought on the matter.

"I'm so happy you both see this my way."

"How could we not?"

"Apparently he was a homophobic dick, who threw her out after high school and disowned her. Hadn't talked to him in years."

Iris's eyes dulled. She'd probably heard that kind of story many times in her career. "Then why'd she go back?"

"I know, right?" I declared.

"And she thought having sex at her father's wake was the way to get back at him?" Lane guessed.

"I can't believe she was actually thinking, but that's the result anyway."

"Wow," Lane breathed out. "You hear some real whoppers, don't ya?"

"This was a good one. In a completely wrong way, that is."

"Sometimes completely wrong makes for something quirky. Good quirky, though. Not disrespectful quirky." Iris's shoulders hitched up once as if she were apologizing for feeling that way.

I wanted to hug her for feeling that way. Quirky was my customized setting, and not many people in my life had learned to value that. "Good quirky," I agreed.

"Can you use it?"

A frown formed on my forehead. "I'm going to have to find an equally distasteful straight story to publish with it. The last thing I want is to give any readers the ammunition they need to think love between gay couples is inappropriate."

"Glad I don't have your job," Lane said and went back to doing hers.

"Yeah, quirky's good," Iris confirmed, staring after her friend before turning that appraising gaze on me.

That it caused a slight riffling in my stomach was something I could ruminate on after writing up the story on inappropriate funeral sex.

34

Another baby picture appeared on the screen thrust in my face. "Isn't he just the most adorable thing you've ever seen?"

He was pretty cute, for a baby. Babies all looked alike to me. His pink, pudgy face wasn't any different than the pink, pudgy face of my nephew as a baby. He was adorable, as she insisted. It was a baby. I could allow adorable as a descriptor.

"He's so smart, too. Started talking at seven months."

Sure, he did. A baby genius.

"Walked at nine months."

Uh-huh, because he's a future Olympian.

"Scored off the charts on development."

Yeah, a verbal, speedy Einstein. She had a winner with this one.

"How old is he now?" I asked the cute bike saleswoman currently boring me into being snide on our first date.

"Seventeen."

"Oh, wow." I couldn't help the surprise. So far she'd only shown me baby pictures of her son. A lot of baby pictures. "Has he decided on a college?"

"Well, he's thinking he might take a year or two off first. I'm trying to get him to go to community college. Get some credits done with. That's how all the kids are doing it these days."

Ah-ha, baby genius turned out to be the typical lazy teenager. His prospects were: living rent-free in his mom's basement while she rides his ass to get a part-time job, or going to an open admission community college to keep her happy enough to let him stay rent-free in her basement.

I thought about my progression from high school, spending year-round at college to take advantage of the summer sessions, which were cheap, fast, and cut a year off the time. After graduating, I developed my writing style at two papers over the next decade before my favorite editor coaxed me up to New York for a stint. As prestigious as that paper had been, I couldn't stay in that city for more than two years. It wasn't until I headed to Washington to work for the *Post* that I felt I'd made it in journalism. There, I spent several years mired in political-centric reporting, then looked for something broader in Chicago with the *Trib*. All of that experience finally led me here. I'd never once stayed in my mom's basement, partly because she didn't have a basement, but also because I wasn't about to leech off my hardworking parents. Cameron, the cute bicycle saleswoman, didn't have that attitude.

"Sounds promising," I commented. Like with Cheryl and Cyrah, this first date with Cameron wasn't going well. Although, I *was* the common denominator in those first dates. I should probably adjust my expectations. Yet, discussing the relevance of hot shoe designers with Cheryl or the latest gossip about every person in Lane's bar with Cyrah or how adorable and brilliant a baby who was no longer a baby was with Cameron did nothing for me. The one thing I realized over this lunch was that I only seemed to want to date women whose names started with the letter "C."

"Tell me about these articles that you're writing. I think I saw one the other day." The sparkle in her eyes wasn't just interest in my chosen profession. I'd been getting a lot of this kind of interest in the bar lately. This was the give-me-the-answer-key-so-I-can-win-the-contest interest.

"If you saw one of the articles, then you've got the gist of them."

"The one I read was tricky. I had to guess."

"That's been my hope all along."

"What about the soldiers' story? Were they the straight couple or the gay one? I thought at first they had to be the straight couple because it was the military years ago, but then I thought that might be too obvious..." And she continued with her thought process on how she voted on that article—one of the first in the series. She wasn't fooling me with the "think I saw one" indifference.

We were on this date because I enjoyed her flirty nature in the store. She'd offered to show me some of the bike trails in the area. Yesterday, I called to see if she had some free time for one of those trails, and she suggested lunch instead of the proffered bike trail guidance. Once again the date I'd hoped would be different from others turned into a sit down meal to go through topics that didn't interest me. Now that she was clearly trying to get me to give her tips on how to choose among the couples in my contest, I lost all hope of salvaging this thing. None of the other dates had ended in a kiss. This one wouldn't either. After the eight, nine—jeez, could it be ten-month hiatus?—from kissing anyone on a regular basis, I had no hope of practicing my technique to see if the kiss I'd shared with Iris was just a one-time fluke. Was I doomed to wonder if my kissing skills had completely left me?

"Those people are trying to get our attention." Cameron's eyes were trained over my shoulder.

I turned to see Iris and Lane waving at us from up the block. Both were in shorts, and Iris held a volleyball. I'd never seen Lane wear anything other than her standard bartender attire that usually showed off her slender arms and tight ass. I knew where they were headed. A lunch hour volleyball game broke out between two nearby companies in a park a block away. Iris had done work for one of the firms and had an open invitation to play whenever she liked. I refrained from sighing with my desire to join in.

"You know them?"

I looked back at the turquoise eyes that had enticed me in the bike shop. "They're friends."

"Don't think I've seen them before."

"Get up this way much?" Other than for this lunch date that was supposed to be a promised bike riding date.

"Not since college, no. It's definitely improved. Before it used to be only Broadway that had anything going. Now it looks like there are a lot more developed areas."

"They both live up here and stay pretty close. It's probably why you haven't seen them."

Her eyes flicked back in their direction. I was afraid to turn around again because I didn't want to see them coming toward us as much as I didn't want to see them leaving me here to toil away at this non-bike riding date that wouldn't end in a much needed practice kiss. "Are they a couple?"

"Nope, just friends."

She let out a disbelieving sound. "Does that really happen with lesbians?"

I sat forward, now a little more interested. "What?"

"All my friends have slept with each other. Most of them didn't become friends until they'd tried dating first." Her shoulders lifted like it was a given. "Unless they're both butch. For some reason you guys can be just friends. Must be that whole top thing. Not that you're butch-butch, but you know what I mean."

I didn't identify as butch, certainly not like most of the butch women I'd met in my interviews. It wasn't just my looks either, long hair and occasional light makeup; or the way I dressed, absolutely no cargo anything or tank tops; it was more my attitude. While I tended to want to date more feminine women, I didn't adopt the take-care-of or take-charge-of attitude that some butch women possessed. I wanted an equal. Someone to take care of me as much as I wanted to take care of her.

"They're just friends," I repeated and signaled the waitress for our bill.

"I was thinking we could go to that coffee shop across the street and talk more about your articles. You're a really talented writer."

"Thank you." My eyes flicked across the street to the coffee shop that was just as busy as this restaurant. We'd been lucky to get a table on the patio, and I certainly didn't need to move across the street to sit down again for more beverages when I didn't need any more beverages or sitting down. "I should get back to work, actually."

Her eyes lit up, not the expected response of someone who really wanted to extend this date. "Who are you writing about today? I know some couples that would be perfect. My ex and I wouldn't mind being interviewed."

One of the main points of this article series was how couples got together and stayed together. She and her ex were no longer together. "If you're in the series, you're not eligible to win the prize." Not true. They just couldn't vote on their own story, but I wasn't going to tell her that.

Her face fell. "Oh, well. It's just so compelling."

The prize sure was.

"This has been fun." I stood after paying the bill because, of course, I was the apparent butch in this twosome.

"Yeah, let's figure out when we can do this again."

I had several options. In Chicago, I would have blown her off and never called her. Here, now that my current income depended on staying on the good side of lesbians, I probably shouldn't do that. "I'd love to get together for a bike ride sometime."

"An activity date, okay, sure." She didn't sound that enthused by the prospect.

"I was thinking more as friends." I tried to be gentle about it, but her shocked expression told me I might not have accomplished that. "I'm sorry, did you feel like we made a connection?"

"Well," she paused, trying to figure out how to play this. If she were really hurt, she'd probably get weepy. "I guess not. You seem like a really nice person, but you're right. There's not much here."

Or anything at all here, but I'd take her observation if it got me out of this. "Thanks for keeping me company." I went to shake her hand, but she slipped into my arms for a hug.

"Keep me updated on the articles. I know I'm getting most of them right."

Goody. Based on some of the comments I got in the bar, everyone thought they were getting them all correct. According to my editor, only about twenty percent of the readers were still in the running for the grand prize. Everyone else had been mathematically eliminated.

I turned in the direction where I'd last seen Lane and Iris. They wouldn't still be there, but I could wander by the park on my way back to the car. If I stopped to say hello and watch them play volleyball for a bit before I went back to writing today, it might give me a little inspiration.

35

Jamie & Glen

In the midst of another interview, I scribbled furiously on my notepad to prevent myself from plundering through all the problems this couple would face throughout the life of their child. A child born to two mommies using the sperm of one of the mommy's brothers. A baby daddy uncle. It happened, possibly a lot in the lesbian community, but all I could see were the pitfalls.

The one that birthed the baby, whom they hadn't stopped talking about despite my many attempts to get them back on the track of their love story, had the habit of sighing heavily every few minutes as if something was bothering her. I'd asked several times if something was and gotten another anecdote about her baby. Her genius baby, of course, because heaven forbid, some lesbian had a baby that tested below average.

My eyes shot to her partner after another loud sigh. Glen looked like she hadn't slept in four years, wore a rumpled business suit that pulled tight across her chest and shoulders, and wasn't as thrilled as the birth mother to have their story published. Her short blond hair could use a good brushing, and by the way she was shoveling the second order of sliders into her face, I guessed the stretched suit wasn't a result of impatient shopping habits.

"Oh, you can definitely tell from the picture that he's going to be president one day." I'd learned that questioning their highly unlikely prophesies for the six-month-old baby boy just got me another earful of arguments as to why he would skip all of elementary school, land directly into high school for a year before going to college at three, and then becoming an attorney at nine, a governor at eighteen, and president at twenty-five. I almost went searching for a copy of the Constitution on my phone to shove in their faces and prove at least one of their predictions could not possibly come true because it was against the Constitution. They had pictures of their baby on their phones; I had a picture of the Constitution on mine.

"He is. I just know it." Jamie heaved another sigh and took the phone back to search for even more pictures of the future president, who was, at their insistence, adorable. Of course.

"Getting back to how you proposed." I directed my query to Glen without knowing for sure she was the one to ask, just using the typical stereotyping to deduce it.

"I rented out the whole pavilion," she said in between bites. She was a managing director of some pharmaceutical company and probably had the funds to rent out an entire pavilion just for a proposal. At least it was private, but she didn't need to spend a fortune for privacy.

They'd met when Glen was a pharmaceutical saleswoman and Jamie was a nurse for a doctor's office. Jamie no longer worked as a nurse, as she'd painstakingly explained to me. Glen wanted her to do whatever she desired. As long as she took care of the cooking and cleaning and any babies. Only she didn't say Glen wanted that, it was simply expected. I could put it up against several of the straight couple stories where the husband held the job and the wife took care of the house and kids. Straight people would be extra confused by the dynamic because they didn't think two women or two men would take on those traditional roles.

"It was such a romantic night," Jamie sighed again. Just as heavily, so perhaps these sighs were not a harbinger of dissatisfaction. "We almost chose that night to get pregnant, but Gene wasn't available for a donation."

Gene, Glen's brother, the father of the baby and also the uncle of the baby. Since they weren't moving off the subject of their baby with a father who was also his uncle, I started pecking at the dome surrounding their parental bliss. "Why did you decide not to use a sperm bank?" A facility that would afford many of the legal barriers they'd need if anything ever went wrong in their perfect family unit in the future.

"The baby had to be mine, too," Glen said as if I were an idiot.

I smiled my idiot smile and said, "I thought you said that Jamie was the birth mother and your brother was the birth father?"

"Well, yeah, but he's my blood."

"And that's important?" my idiot self asked. There was no mention of Jamie wanting to experience pregnancy. That would be a completely understandable argument. This was all about a blood tie to Glen.

"Of course!" She leaned into that one. "Blood is everything."

"So if you're not blood, you're not family?"

"It's the definition of family." Glen was liking this superior stance she got to take.

"What about kids who are adopted? Are they not also family?" This was a particular hang-up of mine. I probably shouldn't be letting my personal feelings on the subject affect this interview, but Glen's superior attitude pressed the wrong button.

She sat back, a mixture of guilt and embarrassment overtook her expression. "Obviously, if someone adopts a child, he'd be family. I just wanted a kid that looked and acted like me."

"Because you think it's all genetics that dictates actions and looks?"

"Yes," the former nurse spoke up when it became clear that her partner was getting flustered.

I let that settle over the table before deciding to push it one step farther. "My extended family is filled with biological and adopted kids. We all have similarities and differences in the way we act, and some of us look as if we're siblings, not just cousins."

"That's what I'm saying," Jamie spoke up for Glen again. Only she hadn't said it, Glen had.

I considered how much I wanted to share, then pulled out my phone and found a photo to show them. "This is everyone together at my cousin's wedding. Can you tell which of us are adopted?" They each took the phone and zoomed in on all the cousins before making wrong guesses. I pointed to the bride. "She and I could be twins, and she's adopted. These two," I pointed to my brother and my ranching cousin, "look most alike among the boys, but nothing like me. The three of us act most alike because we spent so much time around each other growing up. My brother's adopted and our cousin's biological. Our bloodlines may have accounted for some similarities, but they certainly didn't prevent similarities, either."

"Well, well..." Glen tried to come up with an argument that wouldn't belittle my family nucleus but would prove her point that it was absolutely necessary that her offspring were biologically tied to her.

"I'm not saying one way is better than another." I backed off after she got stuck on what else to say. It was hard to back down when I thought about all the kids who needed adoptive parents. How different my life would have been without my brother. How it took a situation like this to remind me that he was adopted because it never occurred to me otherwise. He was as much my brother as any other baby my mom could have had. "I'm just saying that choosing your brother as the sperm donor was an interesting choice."

Curious, really. I could never get past how I'd explain my child's parentage to anyone who didn't know us. "My baby's father? Oh, uh, he's my brother." It would need more explanation to deflect the immediate conclusion that most people would come to after that statement.

"He's been very understanding," Jamie inserted.

"We wanted our son to have a male role model in his life," Glen added.

And the close uncle wouldn't have been an appropriate enough male role model? He also had to be the father? "Will he be involved in decisions about the kid?" Who will one day become president if he can somehow make it through the intense scrutiny that comes with any campaign. Intense scrutiny that will include, among every mistake he's ever made, finding out he has a father who is also a biological uncle.

"He's not raising our son. He's there for talks when our boy wants another man to talk to."

Mm-hmm. And when the boy decides he hates both his mommies, because all kids get to that stage with their parents at some point, will he scream that he wants to live with his dad? If the boy decides he wants to become a ballet dancer instead of play football like his uncle daddy, will daddy stay quiet about that?

"Was this a casual arrangement, or do you have legal documents?"

Glen clamped a hand on Jamie's arm to stop her from answering. "Why do you want to know? I thought this was supposed to be about how we met and fell in love."

"It's about your love story and much of it involves your child now."

"What does it matter if there are legal documents?" Glen slanted a skeptical look at me. She was picking up on my opposing stance and didn't appreciate it. Most likely she thought me selfish because I didn't have kids of my own. Thought I lived a life without responsibility. That belief always made me laugh. I'd responsibly chosen not to inflict my bad parenting skills on some kid, and the planet had enough people without me adding to the population count.

I responded in my most informative, nonjudgmental tone, "Some states don't recognize sperm donors unless the sperm is acquired from a facility and implanted by a medical professional."

"We know he's the sperm donor." Glen shot me another pitying look. She really thought I was an idiot. A selfish, irresponsible idiot. "It doesn't matter if the state recognizes him as one."

As suspected, they hadn't thought through all of the ramifications. My reporter's training forced me to look at all sides of any situation. At most, people without the same kind of training thought all the way through their chosen path. Glen and Jamie wanted a biological child; they figured out how to accomplish that with someone they loved and trusted. Thought process ended. It may turn out that they didn't need to look at any other angle of this multisided issue. I certainly hoped that would be the case for them, but it didn't stop me from analyzing everything they might have missed. And the smug, pitying look on Glen's face didn't stop my mouth from voicing some of those concerns.

"If you're in one of those states and something happens to one or both of you, your brother will be given all the same rights and responsibilities as any other father. He won't be let out of those responsibilities just because you say he donated sperm only."

Jamie fidgeted and gave a whimpering sigh this time. She was the one in the precarious position. Many things could go wrong in the future. They could get divorced, and with Gene being a known donor, he could insert his own parental rights at the custody hearing. All of a sudden, Glen, with Gene's help, gets the kid two-thirds of the time. Or worse, if Glen's eating and sleeping habits wreaked havoc on her health to the point that she dies prematurely, Jamie might find herself fighting a legal battle over the child's custody if she ever tried to move on with her life and marry someone else. Those were just two problematic scenarios based on using a friend or family member as the sperm or egg donor. Find the right homophobic judge, and the biological mother might end up sharing equal custody with the sperm donor. Or the judge doesn't have to be homophobic. He might have just gone through his own custody battle and understands the plight of a father who now wants to be part of his child's life.

"I've read a few cases, that's all. Not the norm, certainly," I rushed to say because Jamie was looking more and more perplexed. With Glen's career experience, she should have known to protect themselves with a contract. In some states that would be sufficient, but not all states.

"We won't have to worry about anything, kiwi." Glen turned Jamie's face to focus on her. "Gene won't ever be a problem."

As long as you two stay together, possibly not, I wanted to tell Jamie. The law on this issue was way too fluid to predict all that could happen. Especially with known donors, which is why using a sperm bank can offer more protection.

"Of course, sorry," I apologized because Jamie was getting upset. We'd gotten off track, even if they insisted on talking only about the baby and their family unit. "I'm just a worrier. You obviously have a close relationship with Gene."

Jamie looked like she might vomit. Perhaps the closeness Glen talked about was all for show. Hopefully this little chat would be good for her. She could institute some ground rules on how much influence Gene would have. Set the right boundaries from the start, and he might never be a problem, so long as they stayed together.

"Yeah, she's a reporter." Glen kissed Jamie's cheek and patted her arm in sympathy. "Her whole job is following bad news."

Yeah, bad news reporter, that's me. "I think I have enough here. Thanks for sharing, and those baby pictures sure are cute." Even if he looked exactly like the pictures of Cameron's baby from yesterday. They could honestly be the same baby.

"You did a good job of scaring them off," Lane said as she came up behind me and leaned down to scoop up the ticket book.

My eyes tracked their progress as they walked past the front window outside. I gave my own heavy sigh, which prompted Lane to drop into the seat next to me. "I'm a cynical doomsday bitch."

Lane blinked twice and chuckled. "Doomsday?"

"That's the word you have a problem with?"

"You are cynical, but I like that about you."

"And bitchy, which you also like."

She squeezed my shoulder. "It's always good to have a friend that's bitchier than you are."

"For comparison purposes you mean?" I teased, and she gave me the same deadpan look she gives Iris whenever her friend says something cocky or lame.

"What's with the doomsday?"

"They used one of their brothers as the sperm donor for their child—who's a genius future president, by the way—and all I could think of is that if the brother wants to become a real dick, he could make their lives hell."

Lane crinkled her brow. "I'm with you on the many complications they could face."

"Let's just hope it all works out. The kid could become the most well-adjusted, lovely human ever to live because he's got two moms *and* a dad in his life."

"Well, he is going to be president, so yeah, everything will be perfect." Lane smirked and left to tend bar again.

"Vega," Riley called out as she slapped my back in greeting. "I so guessed right last Wednesday." She'd been bragging about her guesses on my articles for weeks now.

I thought for a second before a grin tightened my lips. "That's because you introduced me to one of those couples." Montana and Mac to be exact. I wasn't sure if Riley might be eliminated from the contest because we were acquaintances, but I wouldn't burst her bubble right now. The probability that she would be one of the finalists was slim. Many of her other guesses had been wrong. She wouldn't have enough of a cumulative correct total to win.

"Like I said, got it right. Give me a bunch more of those, and I'm taking that trip." Another back slap and she disappeared up the staircase to the game room where she practically lived. We'd played a few games together when her friends weren't around. I liked her better without her friends, which probably made me even more of a bitch.

"You're going to need a chiropractor if you keep hanging out with Riley," Iris said as she took Lane's vacated seat. She hadn't been around when I started the interview. I wasn't sure she was coming in tonight.

"If you wanted to have a baby, where would you get the sperm?"

She gave me a blank stare. "I can't even give that a hypothetical answer. It'll never happen."

Once again, I marveled at how identical her view on a specific subject was to mine. "Just say, where are you getting the sperm?"

She continued to squint in confusion at me. "Are you trying to get me to say I'd pull a gun on some dude or something?"

I laughed and shoved at her shoulder. "No, I'm trying to see what you think of as the first option for getting sperm?"

"A sperm bank?" she responded like it was a trick question. "Isn't that where the available sperm for purchase lives?"

I laughed again. "It does live there. All that sperm, and yet so many women go to their brothers."

"Oh, ick. Now I get what you were looking for." She glanced around and back at me. "Was that your story tonight?"

"Part of it. They wouldn't stop talking about the baby as if he was their whole love story. He's a genius, by the way."

"What baby isn't?" Iris joked. "Especially if it belongs to a lesbian."

"I know, right?" I smiled at her. "What're you up to tonight?"

"Stopped in to see if you were around. Want to hit a movie, or do you have to write tonight?" Her blue eyes sparkled and I knew something else was coming. "Or are you going on another date?"

"Another date?"

"Weren't you on a date yesterday when we saw you?"

My mouth nudged ajar. "She doesn't come into this bar, I didn't tell anyone in the bar about it, how would you know?"

"You were sitting with a cute woman at a restaurant without your notebook. Odds were good you were on a date." She studied me closely, more anticipation than I would expect to see.

"Another…blah. Dating bites."

"Yeah it does."

Not that she needed to worry about it. Her idea of dating was escorting someone home from the bar. "She was nice in the bike store."

"Good pickup spot. What was her story?"

"She, like the couple tonight, kept showing me baby pictures. Only her kid is seventeen now, and she's still clinging to the baby pictures and talking about how high he scored with development."

"Is he headed to MIT or something?"

"More like serving burgers at the fast food joint down the street so he can 'take a few years' as his mother put it."

She pulled in on her lips to keep from laughing. "Dating sucks. C'mon, let's hit a movie." She grabbed my arm, and I didn't resist being yanked up and over to say goodnight to Lane. A movie would be just the thing to temper my critical eye tonight. A movie with a friend would be better than any date I'd had in months. Years actually.

36

The rain splattered against my window. On a Thursday morning. Everyone talked about the rain here, but it mostly rained late at night. Any rain during the day was more mist or sprinkles than rain. The downpours I'd been through in the Midwest could soak me in thirty seconds, causing many a train ride home in wet clothes. Nothing like that had happened here yet. Of course, it was still summer and, according to the locals, a dry summer. But it was raining today. On a Thursday when I was supposed to be playing tennis.

The phone buzzed with a text from Iris. My mood lightened when she suggested we get together anyway. Since I'd been living for our scheduled Thursday tennis as a reliable and fun break from writing and interviewing, I jumped at the chance to see her.

Fifteen minutes later, I was buzzing her into my place. "I'm so glad you still wanted to get together."

A smile touched her lips. "Thursdays are my favorite, Vega."

My ears heated, which almost never happened to me. I'd get embarrassed occasionally and feel my face flush. Generally, I could will it to stop. Only when something happened that I didn't quite understand or couldn't get a handle on did my ears heat. The lower lobes, inner canals, and space between my jaw and ears flashed almost to boiling.

I took stock. I didn't feel confused about anything. Didn't feel like something was too much to handle. It certainly couldn't be that I was—no, absolutely not. Okay, yes, Iris was attractive. We've already established this. Hot and alluring and yes, sexy. But not for me. That couldn't be what this was.

"Something wrong?" Her eyes wandered my face. I'd never checked to see if my ears got red when this happened. Surely, she would catch that.

"Nope. Everything's fine." Except my ears were on fire for some unexplained reason in the presence of someone sexy but not for me. "Coffee? I've got some banana bread that Helen made."

"Yes, to both, thanks." She took off her overcoat and joined me in the kitchen.

"Is this what winter's going to be like around here?" I looked at the rain sprinkling against my windows.

"It's a lot of overcast, gets pretty chilly, and yeah, rain." She glanced at me, tentative. "Are you regretting the move?"

I tilted my head at her worried tone. "Chicago winters are brutal. This'll be soggy but fine."

"You learn not to let the rain keep you from doing things. If it rained in San Antonio, we'd have a bunch of indoor activities to tide us over. When it rains here, it really depends on how hard it rains. There are some days that staying inside is the only option. But days like today, throw on a jacket and do whatever you need to."

"Except tennis," I guessed.

"Well, yeah, the court would be too slick, but the walk we're going to take won't be an issue."

"We're taking a walk?" I smiled at what I thought was a joke.

"As soon as we have the coffee and banana bread."

"In the rain?"

"It's barely sprinkling. You don't even need an umbrella. Throw on a hat or put up your jacket hood, and we'll tour the campus."

I gave her a disbelieving look. The difference between walking through rain when dashing from the car to the grocery store and walking in the rain for no reason at all was obvious to me. To a Seattleite, walking in the rain was a way of life. "For serious?"

"Has a U-Dub graduate taken you through campus yet?"

My eyes darted to the window where I could make out the tops of a few campus buildings in the distance. I'd walked the bike trail that traversed the lower parts of campus and over to the athletic fields, but I hadn't really walked through the campus. "In the rain?"

"Get out of that mindset, darlin'. You're going to learn to love it."

"Let's walk in the rain, yay." I gave a little fist pump.

Once I got used to the constant feel of mist on my face, I had to admit I liked being wrong. Iris told me a story about almost every building on campus. I soaked it in, knowing the college was the reason she'd converted to being a Washingtonian. With cowboy boots, because she couldn't give up everything about Texas.

"That library was under construction the entire time I was on campus. My tuition paid for that damn library, and I never got to use it." She shook a fist at the elaborate brick building next to an equally ornate gothic structure.

"I can see how that would still get to someone twenty-five years later," I joked and her fist made contact with my shoulder.

"I loved it here." She slowly made a circle in Red Square, taking in the variety of architecture surrounding the red brick expanse. "Did you love your college?"

"UMass was okay, but I was ready to leave when I graduated. Ended up with a paper in Boston for a few years, but I didn't feel an overwhelming need to stay in the state. Unlike you."

"Yeah," she sighed. "I didn't know I'd like it that much. The weather was a huge deterrent at first, but I'm glad I picked it over my second choice, Florida."

"Not Texas?" She hadn't reminisced about Texas much. Like me, she didn't return to her home town often.

"God, no, I wanted out of there fast." Fast enough to get rid of any accent, if she'd ever had one.

We walked past the fountain and between some buildings to get back onto the bike trail. I checked my watch and saw that we'd been walking for two hours. Aside from a slight chill on my exposed skin and my now wet sneakers, I hadn't noticed. The fact that it didn't bother me at all, made me feel like I'd passed a huge milestone in becoming a local.

"You had fun," Iris told me as we keyed into my apartment. That cocky attitude should have made me want to throttle her, but she pulled it off better than anyone I'd ever met.

"It sucked."

She shoved me inside. "I don't even know why I try with you."

"I get you."

She gave me the cop stare again before breaking into a smile. "That you do."

"I never asked, but are you a video game or board game kind of person?"

"Card games."

My eyebrows rose. I liked a good card game, but someone who had to enjoy adrenaline as much as a former police detective and current PI must, I was surprised she hadn't said video games.

"Poker?" she asked.

"Without at least two others? Not much fun."

"It would be if we played strip poker."

"Ha!" I laughed but could have sworn something devious flitted through her eyes for a moment. And for an even longer moment, I had the urge to see her naked. An overwhelming can't-control-myself urge.

"Why are you looking at me like that? I didn't take you for a prude."

My earlobes fired up again. I knew exactly the cause of the burning this time, yet couldn't understand it. Desire, hot, explicit desire didn't just suddenly turn on with someone who previously played the role of your best hang. A best hang with an indiscriminate eye and a high libido. Mount Rainier level libido. Mine was more of a trench, a deep trench at the moment. Ten, no, eleven months without sex, and I hadn't even missed it.

She kept looking at me as if she were expecting a response. To what, I didn't know. I was too busy nuking every brain cell I had fighting off the bewildering desire that was making its way through my body. She stepped closer and reached her hand out. If I was going to be successful in putting a halt to this uncharacteristic yearning, I had to prevent that hand from touching me. It reached and reached and reached, and I stood and stood and stood, not doing a damn thing to prevent the touch. The one I wanted to avoid but wanted to experience even more.

It landed on my upper arm, squeezing lightly. "I was kidding about the prude thing. You okay?"

Yeah, I've just gone a little nutso at the moment. Don't mind me.

"Vega?" She stepped even closer.

"Yes, yes. I'm here. Spaced out a sec."

"Writing an article in your head?" That distracting hand squeezed again. "Am I keeping you from doing more writing?"

I should tell her that she was keeping me from working so she and her distracting hand and unbelievably hot body that somehow suddenly sparked an onslaught of craving would leave my apartment. "I always get my writing done first thing on Thursdays." Except my mouth and nuclear wasteland of a brain apparently didn't want that.

"Thursdays," she repeated in a reverent tone. "Then, what's with the look?"

"Hmm?" I managed.

"You're looking at me like…"

"Like?"

"Like it doesn't matter how awful our last kiss was, you're willing to overlook it."

My mouth nudged ajar. She couldn't have just guessed that. I wasn't broadcasting that much. "It was an awful kiss."

Her eyes drifted to my mouth. "It was."

"No one's ever told me I was bad at kissing before."

"Me, neither." Her eyes came back up to meet mine. "I wasn't telling you, either."

"Neither was I." My eyes dropped to her mouth. "It was just one really bad kiss."

"Chipped tooth," she said.

I would have smiled if the hand gripping my arm didn't move up to seize the back of my neck.

37

Our eyes locked. I wasn't sure if it was her hand that gentled me closer or my own lean, but our breath now mingled. Her lips were a sliver away. Lips that I wanted on me so much I didn't care that I could fail epicly at this again.

Her mouth touched mine. Tentative, just a light touch. The grip on my neck tightened as my hands slid onto her waist. We each took a step closer. The whole of her lips situated against mine, a try-out for the real kiss. The kissing minor leagues. Seeing as how we'd botched it the last time, letting these lips run through the farm league first wasn't a bad idea. Problem was, I wanted so much more.

I dared to move my mouth first. Hers parted slightly and repositioned. Another move, added suction, and we were full-on kissing now. Kissing with moving lips and, oh yes, nudging tongues. It wasn't awful. The technique nor the feelings the kiss evoked. Not awful at all.

She opened her mouth and pressed against me at the same time. My hands moved around her, clinging to her back. She snaked her other arm around me, pulling to eliminate the space between us. My lips opened, meeting her demand, but it was my tongue that surged forward first. Hers met mine in an expert tangle that skimmed sparks up and down my nervous system.

No, this wasn't awful or bad or horrible or anything like the last time. This was the best second kiss of my life.

The length of her body pushed up against me. Every curve, every plane, every breath, every heartbeat, I felt as if they were my own. My hands skimmed over her back, exploring the same way our mouths were. Her hands began to massage. The sexy kind of massage, one that could guarantee a happy ending if I wanted. Did I want? Oh, damn, her mouth, and her hands, and her body, I wanted. I wanted so much.

Her lips slid off mine, kissing over to my ear, still burning to amplify my desire. "We're not bad at this," she murmured, and my ear flashed even hotter.

I turned my head and pressed my lips to her jaw. "Not bad at all."

Then her mouth was back on mine, proving again how not bad at kissing we'd become. Her hands slid to my waist and, in the next moment, tucked up under my shirt. Tingles sparked on the bare skin she found there. I wanted to slide down the wall to urge her fingers higher. It was all I could do not to start grinding against her. No control. Zero, and that never happened to me.

I gripped her hips and pushed, turning us so that her back was against the wall. There, better control. I needed it. My mouth moved against hers, wanting to be on her throat, her breasts, her abdomen, everywhere, but not able to leave her luscious, not at all bad kissing, mouth.

Her fingers fiddled with the buttons on my shirt to let her hands map out more of my bare skin. They pushed against me to give her some room to move. As much as I didn't want to lose the press of my body to hers, those hands needed space to make me crazy.

I skimmed mine up her sides, thumbs brushing over her breasts. A groan was swallowed by my open mouth. Nothing sounded better. Nothing. I wanted so much more of that. My fingers popped the buttons on her shirt, slowly at first, then hastily when her own reveal grew desperate. I could have ripped her shirt off by the time I got to the last button.

My hands slid onto her stomach, her hard, wonderfully chiseled stomach. Another groan sounded, possibly mine, couldn't really care because her hands danced over my chilled skin, bringing fire to every surface. Mine skimmed across her abdomen, dipping fingers into the ridges of her muscle definition. I wanted to look, but I couldn't stop kissing her.

Her thigh slid between mine, multiple groans this time. She turned us again, my back crashing against the wall. Her mouth popped off mine and traced the column of my throat down to lick at my collarbone. Hands moved up to brush the undersides of my breasts. Her thumbs tested the weight before she reached around to unclasp my bra. My simple, white cotton, so not sexy bra. No time to dwell on that as her hands pushed the loose bra up and her mouth locked onto a nipple.

"Damn, Iris," I exhaled, pushing forward into her mouth. My hands went from tracing her stomach to gripping her head. Directing her head, really, trying to keep it from moving off my nipple. My unbelievably sensitive nipple. I never did this. Never needed something so much I directed where it went. I was always in control of my actions, keen to please my partner, my own responses and needs were secondary. Today, slammed up against the wall after a walk in the rain with a friend, I was gripping her head because I couldn't get enough of her mouth on me.

Her teeth grazed my nipple, a little sting. My pelvis pulsed against hers. She made a sound that was part moan part chuckle as she grasped my wrists to allow her head to move to the other nipple. So unfair. I didn't want to just stand here. I wanted to feel everything of hers, kiss everything of hers, rub everything of hers. But her mouth and my gripping hands wouldn't stop what they were currently doing.

When another chuckle sounded, I pulled myself together and yanked her mouth from my breast, bringing her up for another kiss and turning her against the wall. My thigh pushed its way between hers, my hip thrusting into her core. Her chuckle collapsed into a long groan that poured into my mouth. There, better. Although, not quite. For the first time I wanted her on me as much as I wanted to be on her.

"Vega," she whispered, pulling back to look into my eyes. "I want you so much."

"Yes," I managed before my brain blitzed at the sight of her open shirt and bra pushed askew to reveal two small breasts.

Dusky pink nipples puckered tight and so taunting. I ducked forward and latched my mouth to an enticing nipple.

"Oh, yeah," Iris breathed, her hands now gripping my head.

My tongue lapped at the hard bud, lips pulling on the areola. I used a finger to pop the front clasp of her bra. The hand followed to close around her other breast. It felt so good, small and firm. The nipple spiked under my finger swipe. My thumb and index finger wrapped around it and tweaked.

She keened softly and dropped her grip on my head. Reaching to cup my breasts again, she teased my nipples until they stung with unquenched need. Her thigh pressed up against me in a slow rhythm that drove me wild.

My hand drifted down to cup her ass and pull her into me harder. She dropped her hands from the magic she was making on my breasts to open my pants and dip down over my ass to help speed our thrusts.

Lifting my head to kiss her fully, I reached to unsnap her pants. I pulled back from the kiss to watch her as my hand snaked into her underwear, skimming over bristles to meet copious wetness. Her eyes pinched closed when my palm cupped her sex.

"So wet," I murmured and nibbled her lips.

Fingers circled her engorged lips, teasing but not targeting. Her thigh gave a harder thrust, and I bucked under the move. She slid her hands off my ass and shoved my pants lower on my hips. When a hand came back, it slid under the band of my underwear and teased the top of my mound. I bucked up again, helpless to do anything but try to get her to touch me more.

This need consumed. Unrecognizable need. Not just to have her. For her to have me. This had never happened to me. Always able to hold back, give my partner what she needed, wait for what I wanted.

"Look at me," she said, and I glanced up from the hand in her pants to see her blue eyes open and fixed on me. Layers of desire and burning and pleasure swirled through the gorgeous color.

She drove downward, determined fingers searching and wanting. I let out a gasp as they landed on my clit. I'd been teasing her, and she tossed that nonsense right out. Her legs opened to encourage my hand to stop the teasing. A finger grazed her swollen clit, swiping once, twice, and pressing down, over and over. She was giving me a similar treatment. Soon our hips were thrusting, breaths pouring out audibly as our hands worked each other toward climax.

We moved again, her back to the wall, or maybe mine, we'd turned so often I couldn't feel who was where. She felt as if she were part of me. Every pleasurable ripple she experienced transferred to me. So in tune with her needs and she with mine, it muddled every thought I had.

My fingers plucked at her clit, hand trapped by the band of her underwear. Her forearm was bumping against mine as she caressed me expertly, pulling want and need to the edge, backing off, and pulling again. Her breath came in truncated huffs when she wasn't using her mouth to torture me further. I'd stopped trying to cut off my groans and gasps and moans to stay in control. Screw control. Control had no place under her mouth and hands and body.

"Ah, Vega," she panted, letting two moans slip before a final, long audible groan.

Pulsations drummed against my fingertips as she climaxed in my arms, shuddering violently. Her fingers, so deft at making me want everything she could give, had seized with her orgasm, giving me a moment's break from the precipice I was teetering over. A moment was all I got before they convulsed with her pulsing rhythms, tearing an orgasm from me. My mouth made a sound I didn't recognize as my head and shoulders jerked forward, knocking against her time and again in a powerful climax.

Unbelievable, amazing, out of this world. No other thoughts could push their way inside, and for once in my over-analytical life, I didn't care.

38

My face was buried in the crook of her neck. Breath still heaved from me and matched the rhythm Iris was setting. She was clutching me to her, which was a good thing since I couldn't stand up on my own. Not after that shattering orgasm.

Perspiration slicked my skin and slid against the bared strip of Iris's stomach. God, we hadn't even bothered to get undressed. That kiss—that unbelievably, phenomenally, not bad in any way kiss—had led to upright sex against several areas of the wall and one of the windows. My wonderful voyeur proof windows. Not that anyone could have seen much because we were still mostly clothed.

And I was still practically collapsed on top of her as much as one can be while standing. Her lips brushed my neck in a leisurely crawl. Each smooch would have made me shiver if my body wasn't completely drained of all energy. I touched my tongue against her neck, tasting the perspiration and triggering small tremors. She must have a tad more energy left than I had.

My hands drifted up from my stabilizing grip on her hips to brush under her unbuttoned shirt and skim across her flat stomach. It quivered under my caress. My lips widened against her neck. She'd been nothing like I expected. I now felt stupid for expecting anything with her. Just because she wasn't ultra-feminine didn't mean I should have assumed she'd insist on a particular role. The same role I usually took and had once before been a problem when I'd attempted to date another non-femme. Iris seemed happy to share, which I really, really liked.

"That was..." Her voice sounded drugged.

My smile returned. I slid my hands up and cupped her small, tight breasts. She shuddered and moaned. The sound made my sex clench and again when her nipples hardened against my teasing palms. Her hands shot under my loosened bra to mimic my actions. Fingers tweaked my nipples when she didn't initially pull a moan from me. My teeth sank into my bottom lip to prevent any more moaning. I'd done enough moaning and groaning and even whimpering under the assault of her hands and mouth and press of her body. But one expert tweak, and she got what she wanted.

When she chuckled at the sound, I pulled back and seized her lips. I should have been afraid that the sudden kiss attack might prompt another horrible episode of surprised kissing, but I didn't have the energy to worry. Great sex, hell, out of this world sex, must have reset my brain and deleted the prior insecurity about my lack of kissing prowess. Or the brain reset came with an upgraded factory setting for kissing abilities. Either way, I didn't care. Kissing her was the second most enjoyable thing I'd done in my life.

She was savoring the kissing just as much. Her mouth slanted perfectly against mine, opening when mine did, tongues reaching for more. It was so intense I'd forgotten that I was teasing her breasts, those luscious mounds that barely filled my palms. Smaller than anything I was used to, but damn if I didn't ever want to stop touching them. They were absolutely perfect in shape, size, and texture.

A soft beeping sounded and would have annoyed me if not for her amazing lips making love to mine. It sounded again, and a groan poured into my mouth.

"Tell me you're going to ignore that," Iris spoke in between kisses.

My head cleared just enough to register what she said. "Not mine."

Her head jerked back for a second when the beep sounded again. "Then I'm definitely ignoring it." She placed an unhurried kiss on my lips. "You have the most gorgeous eyes. I can't stop staring at you."

Heat blazed on my face and settled on my telltale ears. "I could say the same about you." Violet blue eyes, the exact color of an iris flower, and she thought my drab olive green could compare? Sex must have blitzed her brain as well.

She ran her fingers through my hair. A tantalizing scrape over my ears and down through the strands to where they ended at the swell of my breasts. Those beautiful eyes tracked the progress and slammed shut when my fingers tweaked her nipples again. Her hands switched to my wrists and brought them away from her breasts. She laughed when she saw the disappointment on my face.

Her head tilted toward the back hallway. "We need to take this to a flat surface."

Mine tipped up toward the loft. "Will a bed do?"

She grinned and circled my wrists to place her hands in mine. "Upstairs?" Her gaze went back to the hallway just beyond the kitchen.

"Master's upstairs."

A ringtone sounded from her phone this time. She stiffened a moment before brushing it off. "Don't know if I can make it all the way up the stairs."

I chuckled. "We better. The guestroom still has the bed that's been used by Helen's friends. No telling how many people have had vacation sex on that thing."

Her tongue darted out in a show of distaste. I was tempted to try to capture it in another kiss, but I conserved my energy to start pulling her up the stairs.

When her phone rang again, she stopped. "Sorry, that's Lane's ringtone. Twice now. She usually just texts."

Probably those beeps before. I tried to gauge what she wanted. Even as much as I wanted to continue this upstairs, if Lane was texting and calling, it might be a problem. "It's Lane." Was all I needed to say to give us both permission to be distracted from our path momentarily.

"I'll just check and tell her I'm busy." Iris dashed to her hanging jacket, her opened shirt flapping with the effort. Too bad I hadn't been on the right side of that dash for the enticing view.

"Hey," she said into the phone and started to talk again but stopped to listen instead. "Hold tight. I'll be there soon."

My stomach knotted in disappointment. "What's wrong?"

She shook her head, her eyes expressing the same kind of disappointment I was feeling. "Her ex just walked into the bar and wants to talk."

"The one who dumped her after…" After Lane was attacked and vulnerable and reeling.

"Yeah, that one. After six years together, she gives her all of two months to 'get back to normal' as she put it before walking out on her. It's the first time Lane's seen her in months, and the bitch walks into her place of work. She's got drama tendencies, and Lane's freaking."

"All right." Lane would be freaking; anyone would. Lane was my friend, too, but Lane's ex was preventing more sexy sex with the sexiest woman I'd ever known.

Iris came up and kissed me fiercely. Another excellent kiss. Seems like we've gotten through our kissing yips. "I wouldn't go if it weren't something important."

"Sure, yeah, I know," I said, but still felt disappointed.

Her fingers deftly hooked her bra and started buttoning her shirt. I watched for two seconds before I realized that my shirt was hanging open still, and my pants. When her hands reached to hike her jeans up from their mid-hip slouch and button them, she said, "This has been the best Thursday ever."

Yeah, it was, and I'd really liked our Thursdays before. She leaned in for one last kiss, gentle but thorough, and turned to walk out of the apartment. I could have gone with her, but she hadn't invited me. Our amazing Thursday was over.

39

Dylan & Reese

Sitting through the second interview of the day, I was growing increasingly more frustrated. I'd left Iris and Lane alone last night in case Lane was in a bad way. Then I had to dash out this morning to get to an interview with a couple. I hadn't had time to call Iris before needing to leave.

The interview turned out to be a good distraction. He was a car salesperson, and she'd come in for a test drive. They hit it off well enough that she test drove every model at the dealership over the next two weeks. His manager threatened to fire him if he couldn't close her since she'd wasted so much of his time. He decided he'd rather have a date with her than a sales commission, so he asked her out the next time she came in. She admitted to holding out on buying anything just to spend more time with him. Very sweet and easy to write up, which had taken me well into the afternoon.

A lesbian couple scheduled for next week called to change their interview to tonight. I didn't like conducting two interviews in one day. Crankiness always set in during the second interview, which wasn't fair to the couple. Adding to that mood, I'd gotten so caught up in the morning interview and afternoon write-up that I'd forgotten to call or text Iris today. I wasn't a clinger. Never had been, but I felt a morning-after check-in was the decent thing to do. My phone hadn't buzzed either. A little frustration, but also a little anxiety.

Enter Dylan and Reese. Compared to Manny and Vanessa this morning, these two could put a hummingbird to sleep. Dylan was a doctor who liked nothing more than to describe her surgeries in detail. Reese had been a receptionist until she married the doctor and spit out the requisite number of kids.

"...then I thread the stent through the..."

Yep, she was still talking about her latest heart procedure. She was a cardiac surgeon, which she felt made her one of the gods. A lesser one, in my opinion. My eyes wandered the bar area again. It was a busy Friday night, good for Lane, but getting tougher to hear the responses to questions I posed. If I could pose any after hearing about a mitral valve replacement or a pulmonary aneurism repair without feeling queasy. I wanted to talk to Lane about the callous ex-partner visit, but she'd been too busy when I got here. At this rate, I wasn't sure I'd still be awake at the end of the interview to chat with her.

The surgery descriptions allowed for time to contemplate my relationship shift with Iris. I'd been sure it was a shift when she left, but after sleeping on it, I wasn't as sure. Not having heard from her or being able to contact her started screwing with my mind. What if the text and call from Lane had been a standard SOS that Iris always set up before she seduced someone? But I didn't think she came to my apartment yesterday with the intent of ending up in bed. Or against a wall, having hot, hot sex. Ear burning sex. No, the phone call had to be genuine.

The door opened to reveal three women and a guy. Not regulars and possibly not gay. The bar's reviews were making it clear that anyone was welcome as long as they understood gays and straights would be mingling. I was so caught up in tuning my gaydar on the foursome that I almost didn't see Iris come in behind them.

My lips spread wide. Her eyes found mine almost instantly. A corresponding smile appeared and the belt cinched around my heart loosened. Nothing in that smile said she'd used Lane's call as a blow off.

"Vega?" Dylan said when she realized my eyes weren't glued to her godlike existence.

I scolded myself. This was work after all. I should be focused on this interview. Even if watching ants trek in single file was more interesting. "Yes, sorry. I was making sure we weren't about to be pressured into leaving this table."

She swiveled in her chair and finally noticed the others in the bar for the first time tonight. "Oh, I guess we've been here a while, haven't we, snooks?"

Snooks squeezed her arm as she checked her phone. "We still have two hours with the sitter service, bones."

Bones? Ah, sawbones, got it. We wouldn't want to forget Dylan being a doctor, would we?

"Excellent." Bones relaxed back against her chair. "Things in a Los Angeles trauma department can get crazy. I almost missed her case because we were expecting a busload of patients involved in a multiple vehicle collision. One suffered a massive heart attack. If I'd gotten to the ward ten minutes later, I would have been in a nine-hour surgery instead of repairing this one's valve."

"Wait," I sat up. Had she already told me this part, and I'd glossed it over because I'd been too busy reliving a surprise sexual encounter? "Reese was your patient?"

"Yeah, didn't we say that?" she responded.

"Isn't that against hospital policy?" Not to mention the medical board's ethical standards.

"Technically, sure, but what are policies when you fall in love at first sight?"

With a woman needing a heart valve replacement. Reese must have looked unwell, short of breath, probably in a lot of pain. Not exactly the appropriate time for Cupid to strike.

"How long were you her patient?" I asked Reese, who also didn't see anything hinky about having an affair with her doctor while being her patient.

"A few months until Dylan transferred me to another doctor so we could go public with our love."

Or they got caught by another doctor on staff and were told to put an end to their doctor/patient relationship before Dylan was brought before the hospital board. I had to look away to stop from shaking my head. There was a reason it was ethically wrong for doctors to become involved with patients. Transference, confused gratitude, position of authority—hold the phone. What was Iris doing?

I rubbed my eyes to make sure I was seeing what I was seeing. She had her arm around a woman, another spiky heeled woman, and was escorting her from the bar. She might just be seeing her to the door. Or into a cab since she was now holding the door open for her. Spiky didn't look drunk or tipsy, but Iris was a considerate woman. She could hail a cab with the best of them, even if the woman didn't really need help hailing a cab.

My eyes landed back on Doctor Unethical to get my thoughts back online. Dylan had diverged from the excruciating particulars of her many surgeries to the excruciating particulars of their wedding. A destination wedding—that must have thrilled their guests. Not only did they have to buy the couple a wedding present, but they had to spend a lot of money to watch them get married. Stupendous idea. Whoever the hell came up with the concept deserves applause and fanfare. A punch to the throat, too. Yes, that's a little more fitting than applause and fanfare.

What I'd noticed most about Dylan, taking out the whole doctors are gods thing, was that she liked to talk. Craved it as much as someone craves food or water or sex. It would almost be funny if it hadn't been four, no, five whole minutes since Iris left the bar with a woman. Twenty-six hours after we'd had dazzling, heart valve replacement worthy, sex. Which, unlike talking, was something that merited craving.

I didn't expect a bouquet of flowers—that actually would have made me run for the door—but a word or two before she went and seduced another woman would have been nice. Seven minutes now. With the abundance of cabs that drove this route in front of the bars, she wouldn't need seven minutes to get her into a cab. She couldn't be walking her home. Those of the Spiky Heels clan didn't walk great distances. She had to be getting her a ride. Unless she wasn't. I'd watched her take women home before, but never two nights in a row. After sex with a friend, she couldn't float me a two-day buffer?

"That all sounds lovely," I said without knowing exactly what sounded lovely. I just knew I had to wrap this up and get out of here. I was tired and, if I allowed myself to admit it, hurt. How many women had warned me about Iris? I didn't believe them. She didn't act like a player. She didn't. And the way we were together yesterday, the regret that she had to leave, the promise in her eyes at the prospect of more. I read people for a living. She wasn't a player, but maybe she realized friendship was a better option for us, and this was the best way to get that message through to me. Sometimes words weren't enough. Actions drove things home.

"It has been. I take it you're not married?" Reese asked, her eyes on my ring finger.

"I'm not."

"You'll know it when it's right," the doctor told me with all the certainty of a mother knowing her child will be a genius.

That was the smartest thing she'd said all interview, including all the descriptions about every surgery she'd ever done. I stood and thanked them both again before heading to the bar. I really just wanted to talk to Lane and get out of here, but no less than three people stopped me to talk about my articles, ask if I needed more couples, and gossip about a few regulars. Iris, included. Had I seen who she bagged tonight? Had she ever said anything to me about liking them? Etcetera, etcetera. If the subject didn't rankle so much, I'd give them a hard time about passing notes in homeroom. All I could manage was a polite nod before breaking free.

Lane was still slammed, but she finished her current slate of drinks and came over. "Hey, Vega. Good couple tonight?"

"They were fine." I searched her face. "Heard you had a bit of an event yesterday. Everything work out okay?"

She let out a long breath but kept her bartender expression on. "Sort of a shock." She looked away then back. "That's a lie, actually. I didn't expect to see her again. Ever. Threw me, big time."

"I'll bet." My eyes scanned the crowd at the bar. "I know you're busy. I just wanted to let you know I'm around to talk any time you're free and want to."

She smiled, a full smile. One that came out more frequently since becoming a bar owner. Made me happy to see. "You leaving?"

"I should type up these notes while they're fresh, but I can stay if you need me to."

Her eyes went to the front window. Maybe she was hoping Iris would've been back from her escapade with Spiky Heels, too. She glanced back at me. "I'm good for tonight. Thanks."

"I'm headed to Boise tomorrow, but let's go to lunch when I get back." I was dying to hear about how the visit from the ex went, but it could wait until she had some free time. Wait until I wasn't still hung up on a sexual encounter that I should have guessed wouldn't mean as much to my chosen partner as it did to me.

"More interviews?" Lane asked about my scheduled trip.

"Six." With requests for others, but I hadn't wanted to stay away longer. Now, perhaps it wasn't a bad idea to stay on longer. Come back with a fresh attitude. One that wasn't still wishing Iris would come back through that door after finally finding a cab for Spiky Heels.

"Does Iris know?" Concern marked her tone.

I was certain Iris hadn't told her about yesterday, yet she seemed overly troubled that Iris know I was going to be out of town. "She gave me a hotel recommendation."

"All right." She glanced at the front window again. "See you when you get back. Have a safe trip."

"Thanks." I squeezed her arm and headed out. Alone because I couldn't even think about having sex with one of these lovely ladies in here, let alone actually go through with it. Not after yesterday. I could only hope that in a few months, I'd be ready again to give dating that might lead to sex a try.

40

My ass was falling asleep. Driving more than three hours always did this to me. Into the fifth hour, the scenery had changed from beautiful mountains to flat, wide open plains. Regret seeped in at not having stopped for lunch and to gas up before crossing into Oregon. What was the point of not being able to pump my own gas? Did we live in the fifties?

Even with that educational stop—nearly getting tackled when I went to pick up the pump and being lectured on Oregon's gas station policies—my rump was starting to feel those stinging prickles every time I shifted. I'd hoped to make the eight-hour drive to Boise and conduct the first of the scheduled interviews tonight after checking in at the hotel. Given the way my back was getting stiff and my behind smarting, I may have to adjust the schedule.

Turning off the audiobook I was listening to, which was the only thing making this trip bearable, I swiped through the numbers on my phone. I could handle two interviews tomorrow to avoid a lot more discomfort tonight. Unfortunately, when the call connected, my interviewees couldn't accommodate my requested change.

I turned up the audiobook, checked the distance to the next rest stop, and drove on. I'd chance looking like an idiot by sprinting a few short dashes at the next rest stop. Anything to get rid of this dead feeling in my lower half.

A ring sounded through my audio system, signaling an incoming call. My foot tapped the brakes when I saw Iris's name on the display. She'd finally texted last night, asking if I was busy working. I was, so I didn't have to lie. I hadn't wanted to see her freshly sexed from some other woman a day after she'd done the same thing to me.

I pressed the display button to accept the call. "Hey." Cool, casual, in control.

"Forgot you were headed to Boise today. Where are you right now?"

"Pendleton, I think. It's hot as hell, and I almost got shot when I tried to pump my own gas."

She started laughing. The sound eased some of the tension. At least I could still make her laugh. "I forgot to warn you about that. Do you have an interview tonight?"

"I just tried to get them to move it because I'd forgotten what eight hours in a car can do to a body. They didn't go for it."

"Oh, well, you'll be done sooner, then. When are you back?"

I hesitated. She sounded eager, like she usually did. Like nothing had changed. In her mind, it probably hadn't. The wonderful thing about two days of contemplation was that I could put this into perspective. Just because I was past the one-night stand stage of my life didn't mean the women I had sex with had to be. We'd made no promises to each other. Even if it turned out we both wanted to continue a sexual relationship, we hadn't talked about exclusivity. It didn't help with the pinch of hurt I felt every time I thought about watching her walk out of the bar with that woman from last night, but I couldn't let her more casual attitude about our sex blip affect how I felt about her as a friend.

Avoiding her sexy self for a few days would help. A lot. I'd have enough time to stop remembering how she felt and all that she'd done to me. Start thinking of our afternoon tryst as I thought of my past sexual relationships, which was not at all. Then we could go back to being friends with no other expectations.

"Vega?"

I paused, trying to recall her question. "Tuesday, maybe Wednesday. Could be longer."

"Oh." Now she sounded disappointed. "The employer I just finished working for gave me tickets to the Mariners game on Monday."

"Lane has Mondays off." Like she didn't already know that, but I was struggling for something to say.

"I've got three tickets."

Oh, she'd planned for us all to go together. Prior to last night, I might have changed my plans to go with them. "Sorry. Work, you know?"

"Sure." Silence ensued for longer than I liked on phone calls. "I wanted a chance to talk last night."

Then you shouldn't have gone off to have sex with someone before I left the bar, I thought. Bitter because I hadn't had enough time to get to the cavalier point yet. "That couple moved up their interview to last night." *And you were busy anyway.*

"Can we talk when you get back?" She abandoned her trademark cockiness.

"Sure." Was there any other answer I could give her? Even if it was one of the worst questions someone can ask another person in any kind of relationship. Nothing good ever came from a "Can we talk?" talk.

"Okay. I just, we should have, but we got sidetracked and now it's awkward. I don't want it to be awkward."

Neither did I. As much as I wished it could be more because, dammit, I liked her, I'd rather it not be awkward than tension-filled with the potential to accidentally find ourselves smashed up against a wall with our hands shoved down each other's pants and lips locked. Awkward-free, amazing friendship like no other, or occasional, partially-clothed, upright sex that led to confused feelings?

No contest.

* * *

This article was shredding every writing attempt I made. None of the right words fell into place, making it too obvious which couple was which. I'd been trying all morning to generalize it and still make the love stories compelling. Been at it since six to meet a one o'clock deadline. I'd let writing slide for more than a week, thinking I could bang this one out easily. After that, I could start building another cache of completed articles in case I had to go out of town for more interviews later. I'd stayed in Boise one day too long, and now I was in deadline mode.

The front door buzzed. My eyes jerked up from the screen. She cannot be early. Not today. She wasn't due till lunch. It was going to be a reward for getting this article sent in. Work past the awkwardness to our friendly banter and maybe convince her to hang out for the rest of the day. But I had to get this done first.

When she appeared at the top of the stairs, my heart set out on an obstacle course. Tripping, clenching, tumbling, swinging, it went through every movement, matching each of the emotions at seeing her. Usually it just broke into a happy dance to be with my friend, but this morning, it also faced trepidation, embarrassment, dread, and fear. That last one because I was in danger of missing this deadline, and she was so early.

"Hi." I waved to have something to do with my hands. "You're early."

She'd been smiling and moving toward me, but she frowned as her eyes dropped to her watch. "No."

"Huh?" Then her response registered. Panic took over everything in my heart. "Are you saying it's noon?"

She took a step back at my panicked tone. Whatever greeting she'd planned to give got ditched when she saw how freaked I was. "Yeah. What's wrong?"

"Dammit! Sorry, I have an hour till deadline. I thought I'd be done by now."

Her hand reached out and rested on my shoulder. "But you're not?"

"I don't know what happened. The morning slipped away."

"Okay." Comforting but distracting hand squeeze. "I can come back later or go get us some lunch to kill time." The two options were too plentiful for me to contemplate when I only had an hour to work on this frustrating article. We stared at each other until she made the decision for us. "Go finish. I'll come back later."

My hand reached out on its own and clamped onto her arm. "You can stay. I just can't talk until I finish."

She weighed my invitation. "Get in there. I'll go get my laptop and do some background checks while you're working."

I watched her disappear down the stairs and felt both relief and anxiety. I should have just let her go get us lunch or something to kill an hour. I'd never written with anyone around before. Even at a newspaper office, I did most of my writing at home.

Before I could text her to say I'd changed my mind, she was bounding up the last flight of stairs. Jeez, she was fast. And hot. She couldn't have toned that down today? Damn those well fitted jeans, sexy cowboy boots, and green check shirt. This was the first outfit I'd seen her in. Dammit, I shouldn't remember that. Friends didn't remember first outfits.

"You're not working," she chided and pushed me back inside. "Just one thing before I shut up till you're done."

I watched with wide eyes as hers slipped down to my mouth. No, no, can't happen. I'll never get this article done, and we hadn't settled on what we were yet, and no, just no.

"Key in your Wi-Fi password for me, will you?"

The question didn't make sense given what I'd been thinking about. "What?"

She shoved her laptop into my hands. "Type, and I'll leave you alone."

My eyes flicked down to the screen where it showed the available Wi-Fi networks and the space for my password. I would have appreciated that she didn't just ask me for it if I weren't so hung up on meeting my deadline and willingly submitting myself to writing in front of another person. With several keyboard clicks, I'd entered my password and connected her.

"Thanks, now get to work."

Like a zombie, I went back to my desk and read through the last several lines before starting to type again. Four paragraphs later, I got up and walked into the kitchen for a drink of water and came back to sit again. Two more paragraphs, I took my laptop and set it on the standing portion of my desk and did another circuit into the kitchen and back. It's how I work. Don't judge.

My cell beeped. I glanced at the display as I was typing the third to last paragraph. "I'm going to make it. I've got forty-five minutes. Stop bothering me," I told my editor as soon as I picked up the phone.

"Just making sure." And she clicked off. That's how we work. Don't judge.

Another paragraph, and I was feeling less panicky. Making the circuit again, I sat back at my desk to pound out the last two paragraphs. One spell check and word count later, a few descriptive adjectives were added here and there to make up the count requirement. I sent the draft to the printer and read through the pages as I walked the circuit all over. Every once in a while, I'd stop, grab a pen from the nearest surface, scribble a correction, and continue walking. After my proof circuit, I sat to make the corrections and gave it a final read-through on screen. Two changes, and finally, I attached it to an email and sent it off. I reached for my phone to text my editor, who snark-texted a warning not to leave it to the last minute ever again. *No duh, lady.* This was too stressful.

My head fell back. I let out a relieved sigh and threw my hands up in the air. I would have started singing if I didn't feel singing was the worst talent I possessed. For a while there, singing and kissing were neck and neck. Oh, yeah, kissing. I turned and saw Iris leaning back on my couch, her twinkling eyes giving away her delight.

"That was quite possibly the most interesting work routine I've ever witnessed."

I blushed, my whole face, not just heated cheeks or ears, whole face and probably neck and onto my chest. One paragraph in, I'd completely forgotten she was there. She would have been in my periphery vision as I made my desk, kitchen, and back hallway circuit, but I didn't hear her. When I had to work in those awful cubicles at the paper, I could hear every little sound. See anyone who moved. Awareness was my thing. So she'd sat quietly and worked or watched me work and didn't draw attention to herself or bug me in any way. No one did that. Everyone bugs me. Everyone. I didn't get upset or angry about it. It was simply a fact. People make noise or movements or whatever when I need complete silence, so they bug. Nothing against them. They just do. She hadn't.

"I have to apologize again. Time got away from me. I should have texted to push back the time. And I'm such a jerk; I didn't even offer you coffee or water or anything."

"I helped myself. I didn't want to bother you." She lifted her water glass.

She'd moved and I hadn't noticed? "Good, yes, and in case this ever happens again, just know to make yourself at home." I walked the path from the couch to the kitchen with my eyes and still couldn't get over how I'd missed her making that trip. "You must be starving. We were supposed to go to lunch." And talk without me thinking about her hands and mouth and body on mine. Or about her leaving the bar with another woman the next night.

She stood from the couch and came toward me. I felt my heart thud with each step. Now that the article deadline panic was over, I was free to feel the other kind of panic. Other than a couple of texts, we hadn't spoken since our phone call. Our short phone call after we'd had sex in this very apartment not far from where we were standing now.

"Lunch can wait a minute." She stopped in front of me. And damn she smelled good. Looked good, too. Criminally good. "I missed you. I'm sorry we didn't get to see each other before you had to leave."

We did. We saw each other at the bar. Before she went off with another woman. When I was still feeling how her hands felt making love to me, she was using those hands on someone else. I could still feel them.

"Yeah."

She waited for more but I didn't know what to say. "See? This was the awkward I wanted to avoid."

I let out a laugh, forced, but a laugh. "You're right. My head's still recovering from the whole almost missed my deadline thing."

"Never happened before?" she teased and looked even sexier.

"Never. It was a bad move to put off writing last week to focus on getting interviews."

"I could tell by the way you took it out on your keyboard. It never did anything to you."

Yeah, I press hard on the keys. It's how I work. Judge that one if you want.

"Did you get any work done, or just stare at me the whole time," I teased back but warmed at the thought of her staring at me.

"Little bit. You were more entertaining." She stepped closer and raised her hand to cup my cheek. "I'm glad you're back."

I swallowed, trying to get some moisture back in my mouth. She tilted toward me. Uncertainty overwhelmed me, and I stepped back. She blinked and dropped her hand. Dread gnawed at my gut, but I had to get this out. "I probably should have told you that I'm past the point in my life where casual works for me."

Confusion dotted her expression. "What are you saying? Because the last time we kissed was anything but casual. It seemed like you enjoyed it."

"I did. It was..."

"Amazing," she supplied, and my heart squeezed at her awe-filled tone.

"I like you too much to lose you as a friend just so we can have casual sex occasionally." There, I said it. "Totally old fashioned and completely cliché, I know. I listen to these stories every day and think that nothing is ever original. I want to be original, but I have old fashioned ideas about seeing only one person at a time."

"I'm not sure I understand your objection." She searched my eyes. "You want to keep our friendship as is because you think this would be casual? Or you want exclusivity and originality?"

"Both, all, I don't know what I'm saying." I stepped toward the kitchen, but her hand clutched my arm to stop me.

"I like you, too. Let me just say that first. We got over the bad kissing hump together. I don't know about you, but I lost my confidence there for a minute. Then we shared an amazing afternoon together. I've never been with anyone like you. I think we're good together. That's all the originality I need."

That sounded so promising. If only she thought about relationships the way I did. "Like I said, I'm too old and there are too many diseases out there to be in an open relationship. Sorry, that's just not me."

"Okay." She raised her hand up to my cheek again.

"Okay?" I took another step away before her hand landed. "How could that be okay with you?"

"Why wouldn't it be?" She was the one who stepped back this time.

"Are we going to pretend that you didn't take a woman home from the bar the other night?" My hands came up. "This isn't about jealousy. We weren't...hadn't defined what we were. You were free to see anyone you wanted. I just don't work that way."

Hurt spiked on her features. My stomach knotted at the sight. I didn't want to hurt her feelings. I was trying to be open about what I could and couldn't handle in an intimate relationship. I wanted a one and only, and she wanted to be free to take women home from the bar.

"I see." Her head nodded repeatedly. "You think I'm a slut."

My mouth popped open. "No, I don't. I didn't say anything like that."

"Fine, a player, which is just a more polite name for a slut."

"No, I don't." I didn't think she was slutty. I didn't think people who had multiple sex partners were slutty. I wasn't a prude about sexuality. People could sleep around all they wanted. I just didn't want to be with someone who wanted that. "I'm just trying to tell you what I need from a relationship."

"And it's not me, obviously," she said, turning and walking back to the couch where she scooped up her laptop and slipped it into her bag.

"Iris, please don't be like this." I moved to stand in front of her. "You want one thing, and I want something else. Can't we just recognize that and not completely ruin our friendship?"

Her eyes closed slowly, and she let out a long breath. "Yeah, we can."

"Good," I said and breathed out my own relieved sigh. "I feel at home here because of you, Iris. You're the best friend I've made in years. I don't want to screw that up." By thinking what we'd shared was special and something she would cherish as much as I had. Stupidly outdated ideals, but still.

She slung her bag over her shoulder. "Me, neither." She walked to the door, ending what should have been an afternoon together. I couldn't blame her. This conversation was going to be awkward no matter the outcome. In the open doorway, she turned and gave me a long look. "Just so it's been said, I didn't sleep with Kaylee last Friday. She was about to walk home without the friends she came in with. I wanted to make sure she got home safely. Just because we got one guy doesn't mean there aren't other predators out there. I thought you were still going to be at the bar by the time I got back so we could talk."

I opened my mouth but nothing came out. It wouldn't have mattered anyway because she'd already walked out the door. A second later I heard her footfalls on the stairs. Each sound like a punch to my stomach.

41

ALICE & NEIL

As a professor of literature, the woman chatting with me knew far more about writing than I did. I was a little surprised she'd agree to be one of my subjects when my writing couldn't hold a candle to some of the classics she taught every semester. I was an okay writer. I knew how to tell a story. My strength was making complex subjects relatable and understandable. They weren't always lyrical or prophetic. Memorable, sure, but no one would ever accuse me of being Brontë or Woolf. I could only imagine the critique she'd apply when she recognized her story in one of my future articles.

Her husband, an equally smart guy as a philosophy professor, probably wouldn't be as harsh a critic. He'd complimented me on the articles he'd read so far and told me how much fun they were having registering their votes every week.

"The best lesson I learned in grad school?" Neil looked first to me, and then with a kind smile at his wife. "Don't treat your grad assistant like a gofer."

I flicked my eyes between them. This was my fourth couple with an age difference of twenty-plus years. Unlike the others, these two were now at the point where that age difference was very, very noticeable. Alice was about to retire this year, and he'd still have another couple of decades working at that university. What I liked most was that they'd been together more than twenty years already. Also, she didn't color her hair and didn't look like she'd gone through any cosmetic surgery to suspend aging. She looked like a sixty-seven year old woman. The new sixty-seven, still very active and as fresh faced as someone on the planet almost seven decades can be. Neil looked like a guy my age. They would be mistaken for mother and son at times, I was sure of it. Yet, because they'd made it twenty plus years, they knew what they had and who they were. It still wouldn't work for me, but of the age difference couples I'd interviewed, this one was the most solid.

"Wait, you were her grad assistant?" I asked because all they'd said so far was that they met at their employing university.

"Oh, heavens no," Alice interjected. "That wouldn't have been right. It was bad enough as it was."

"As it was?" I prompted.

Her cheeks colored. "He was the grad assistant for another professor on our office floor. I'd see him running back and forth carrying coffee, dry cleaning, walking the guy's dog, picking up the guy's kids. He was being treated like a lackey. My colleagues and I kept trying to encourage him to apply for a different position. He wasn't getting what he needed from that professor."

"The guy was a complete gasbag." Neil chuckled like it never bothered him to be the errand boy of some gasbag professor.

"You stayed as his grad assistant for how long?"

"A year. I was going to stay on, but Alice was pretty convincing. Grad students should help with research or grading. She was right. He wouldn't further my academic career."

"Did your relationship start then?"

Alice pinched her lips together and looked away. Yeah, even twenty years later she still knew it wasn't kosher to have gone for a grad student when she was a professor. The only thing that probably saved her career with the college was that he wasn't in her department or taking any classes from her.

"It did. She's the smartest person I know. I could listen to her for days," he said proudly.

"Years," I said. "Twenty-one to be exact."

They laughed and she slipped an arm onto the back of his chair. "We've been lucky."

Took a lot more than luck to overcome a huge age difference, working for the same employer, and having their colleagues all know that they'd had what most would consider an inappropriate affair at the start.

I asked some follow-up questions and wrapped it up. Rather than high tail it out of the mostly gay bar, they went over to the dance floor. They stood watching for a moment before joining in. From what I could see, they were the only straight couple on the floor and didn't seem self-conscious about it.

A hand landed on my back. Gently, so I knew it wasn't Riley. No goosebumps, so I knew it wasn't Iris. Lane took the seat next to me. "Interesting couple."

"They were. Don't really get the age chasm thing, but it works on them." I faced her and caught fatigue in her eyes. "Can you take a break?"

She glanced back at the bar and saw that Derrick had things in hand. "Good idea. How've you been? Did the trip go okay?"

"Got four more interviews than I expected. Didn't realize Boise had such an impressive gay population."

"I've heard that. Only been there once."

"How've you been, and don't tell me about the bar. How have you been?"

Skin crinkled at the corners of her brown eyes. "Better."

"Do you want to tell me about the ex visiting?"

"Iris hasn't told you?"

My stomach knotted at hearing her name. I'd stayed home, writing up the rest of my interviews over the past two days so I wouldn't get caught out like I had been on Tuesday. Thursday brought rain again, giving me yet another reprieve from having to face Iris and the hurt I'd seen on her face and the hurt I'd felt. I needed to get out tonight, though.

"We didn't get a chance to talk, no. I'd rather hear it from you."

Her lips pressed into a line. "She just walked in like we'd seen each other only last week."

"Instead of how many months?"

"Seven." She glanced at me, checking my reaction. When I didn't say anything, that barely-there smile widened. "She's decided she wants to talk. Maybe try again."

The brashness of some women. I'd had ex-girlfriends call months later to see how I was doing. Almost always, they were trying to find out if I'd be open to getting back together. I never was. Only one of the relationships had lasted more than two years. Lane had been with this woman six. They'd lived together, considered themselves partners, not just girlfriends.

"It was so unexpected." Her hands went to check that the ever-present bun was still secured at the back of her head.

"Freeze, scream, run, hit something, or tell her off?"

Confusion creased her brow. "What?"

"When something's unexpected, those are my usual go-to reactions."

She gave a single nod. "You don't strike me as a screamer."

I shoved at her shoulder. "Shut up."

"I wanted to hit something or tell her off, maybe even run, but I guess I froze. She didn't care that the bar was busy. Just expected me to drop everything and want to talk to her." Lane waited, thinking I'd ask her something. I was pretty sure this was her bartender training. Let the patrons do the talking. "I told her that it wasn't a good time. She ignored that, like she ignored a lot when we were together. I had to text Iris. I couldn't even confront her without my best friend backing me up. How pathetic is that?"

I laid my hand on her back and swept it up to grip her shoulder. "Nothing about that is pathetic. We all need support. An ex showing up out of the blue is always shocking. An extremely selfish ex who thinks the world revolves around her and doesn't take a hint or your wishes into account? Anyone would need reinforcements, and Iris is the best kind."

Even if Iris had to halt what would have been another round of amazing sex to be here for her friend.

"The best kind of what?" Iris's unexpected voice made us jump.

"Support," Lane said, reaching back to grip her hand and pull her into a chair at the table.

Iris shifted her gaze from me to Lane and back. She looked amazing as usual. Slacks and a shirt that caressed her torso. I tried not to remember how that torso felt under my hands and mouth. We were better as friends. Even if she hadn't slept with the spiky heels lady, at some point, she'd sleep with someone she took home from the bar. She wouldn't be a celibate nerd, pounding away at work for the next ten months, which was my usual after ending a sexual relationship. "Thanks. Are we talking about the bitch?"

Lane gave a tiny shake of her head but didn't protest much more. "I was telling Vega how I needed you to come to my rescue."

Iris's eyes shot to mine, probably remembering exactly the moment those texts and calls came in. Regret showed in her expression. Regret at having to leave or regret at having taken that step that now put us in this temporary holding pattern, not sure which. "She shouldn't have come in here. She couldn't just be a normal bitch ex and drunk dial. No, she had to demand face time in your place of work and completely ignore what you wanted."

"Did you toss her out?" I joked, but her expression told me it wasn't out of the realm of possible reactions.

"Wanted to," Iris muttered and Lane jabbed her. "She doesn't like me much, so it didn't take a lot of persuading to get her to leave once I got here."

"Thankfully." Lane let out a sigh.

"Won't she just come back when she thinks Iris is gone?"

"I told her I didn't want to talk to her." Lane made it sound like that would be enough.

"But now you own this bar and have a nice place to live." I figured that was at least part of the reason the woman showed up now rather than a couple months after she'd walked out.

"You are irresistible, darlin'," Iris teased and got another shove from her friend.

"Maybe now that you know this can happen, you'll be better prepared for her next drop by," I suggested. Or she could get prepared because there was no way a woman like that wouldn't attempt to regain a more successful Lane.

"Most of the time, I like people dropping by," Lane told us. "Not so much that time. If it happens again, I can handle it."

Iris gripped her other shoulder. "I'll be here if you need me."

They shared an affectionate glance. Their close relationship, how good of friends they were to each other, made Iris even more attractive. I really didn't need more things to make her attractive.

42

Helen and Joe looked like they'd only walked a block rather than the bike race they'd incited up from our building to Lane's bar. Three miles of all out racing. Mostly uphill. Way too intense for me. When they'd invited me on the ride, I thought it would be like our kayaking trips, leisurely and enjoyable. They apparently took bike riding seriously. Their vacation pictures should have been the biggest clue. Every one of them showed the couple decked out in biking gear and riding steep mountains in beautiful places.

Lane bit her lip when she saw us walk up to the bar. Helen and Joe were chatting and laughing like we'd just walked over from the parking lot where we'd left a car. I wasn't chatting or laughing and barely walking. She slid a glass of water across the counter to me and asked what Helen and Joe were having. They turned their gazes on me when I downed the water in five seconds.

"You okay, Vega?" Joe asked, surprise evident on his face.

"If you were trying to kill me, there are easier ways."

"You ride all the time," Helen reasoned while fighting a smile.

"I ride, at a normal pace. Nobody is chasing me, and my job doesn't depend on dropping off a package before the office closes. We could have taken an extra, I don't know, ten minutes to get here."

They laughed. At me. Not with me. They were laughing at the fact that I considered a bike ride to be leisurely fun, not a race to win. Laughing about how I looked like I'd been working all day on my cousin's ranch, hauling heavy ranch things, rather than having just ridden only three miles. Uphill at a breakneck pace.

"Who are we laughing at?" Iris's voice sounded from behind me. For the first time in a week, it didn't make me jump. I was slowly getting back to thinking only of friendship whenever we got together.

They all pointed at me as I turned and shook my head in exasperation. "They're trying to kill me."

Her eyes flicked over them and back to me. In an unconcerned tone she said, "Somebody should call a cop."

Now they were back to laughing at me. I shoved the water glass across the bar top and pointedly looked at it. Lane took the hint for a refill.

"Be that way. I'm taking my delightful company away from you," I grumbled. "I came up here to share my good news, and you all couldn't care less."

Lane collected herself first, followed by Joe. Iris and Helen were still chuckling but looked interested and gestured for me to continue.

I waited, feeling a little huffy that they all found something so damn funny about me. But the news was too good not to share with my friends. "I emailed my book proposal to four publishers last week, and all four want it."

"Vega!" Helen cried in excitement. Her arms came around me for a hug that turned into a bit of a jumping dance.

Joe patted my shoulder and offered congratulations in between our hopping and hugging. Lane grabbed hold of me after Helen let go. No hopping, just a quick congratulatory hug. I glanced at Iris and saw a mixture of relief and happiness. She stepped forward and wrapped her arms around me. Suddenly everything felt so much better. Forget Helen and Joe trying to kill me with exertion, forget everyone finding my lack of a killer instinct hysterical, forget that I'd hurt her feelings and she mine; she was happy for my success that would allow me to stay on indefinitely here. And she felt so damn good.

"I'm proud of you, Vega," Iris whispered in my ear.

My insides wriggled at the compliment. It meant so much. Tempered all the anxiety I felt about our relationship and erased the missteps.

"Do you know which one you're going with?" Joe asked.

I reluctantly let go of Iris to answer. They'd probably think it was weird if I kept my arms permanently around her. "I'm meeting with a lawyer who specializes in publishing tomorrow. We'll comb through the contracts and do some negotiations. They're all good offers, so I'm pretty jazzed."

"So are we." Iris settled an arm around my waist. Maybe she didn't want to let go of me either. "We should all celebrate. Lane? H & J? You're all off Monday night. Let's let someone else make you dinner and drinks."

"Sounds great," Joe agreed. "I might even slow down on our next leg of biking. Just for you, Vega."

I held up my hands and waved him off. "No thanks. I'm off the ride as of now. You go on, do your speed trials racing, and I'll make my slow-ass way home after I've recovered here."

They laughed again, but it felt good this time. I coaxed Iris, Helen, and Joe into a game of pool before the bike athletes left to continue their ride. Iris got a phone call as I was racking up another game, so Riley joined me from the other table where she was waiting for her usual crew to arrive. Three games later, I went back downstairs.

"Anything up?" I asked Iris, wondering why she hadn't come back upstairs.

"My mom's plane is a little early. I have to leave in ten minutes."

Oh, right, her mom was in for a visit this weekend. They invited Lane and me to brunch on Saturday, so I could meet her. Or she could meet me. Apparently, she was a big fan of my articles. I was looking forward to it.

I glanced out the window and saw that the weather had turned dark. Thunder rumbled, and a crack of lightening followed. I checked my watch and saw that it was more than an hour since Helen and Joe had left. Hopefully they made it through the rest of their ride and back home before this rain started. Didn't help me much, but I could wait it out.

"Don't try to ride in this," Iris said, then looked sheepish. "Please."

My heart thumped at her caring request. "I'll wait it out."

She checked the weather app on her phone and gave me a bleak look. "Looks like it won't be stopping for a while. I might be able to run you home before I need to be at the airport." Her eyes moved up to the left as she calculated the travel times in her head.

"Don't worry about it. Go pick up your mom. I'll wait this out."

"Wait what out?" a voice from my right asked.

I turned to find Cyrah watching us. Our semi-date had gone okay. We didn't really hit it off, but she was nice enough. Neither of us had rushed to ask for a second date. I was fine with that arrangement. In a few weeks, I might suggest she sit with me at the bar so we could get to know each other as friends. We'd never date again, not after the feelings Iris had pulled from me. I wouldn't be content in a relationship of shared interests any longer. Not now that I knew what real passion felt like. I'd wait for that, too.

"The rain. It was so beautiful when we started our bike ride this afternoon."

"You guys on bikes?"

"Just me," I responded. "I was with two others that are serious riders. Told them to ditch me, only now I've stayed an hour too long, and I'm stuck unless I want to ride home in the rain."

"I can run you home," she offered. "You're not too far out of my way. Your bike won't fit, but you can chain it up here."

I was conflicted. I usually didn't like to take favors from acquaintances, even if we would become friends eventually. Favors were a big deal for me. Then again, riding home in this thunderstorm didn't appeal either. "Are you sure you wouldn't mind?"

"Not at all. You can invite me in for coffee so I can finally see Austy's old pad. She never let anyone inside when she lived here. I was always curious."

I remembered Helen mentioning that name. She'd been the original owner of my unit until she moved and it became a go-to vacation spot. I wasn't crazy about the idea of inviting Cyrah into my place, but coffee was a polite response for the favor.

"You can leave your bike in the back hallway here," Lane offered, her eyes moving to me from being on Iris. If they'd shared another silent conversation, I chose to ignore it. I still believed Iris wouldn't have told Lane about us, but I wasn't one hundred percent sure.

"Thanks. That's nice of you."

"You ready?" Cyrah asked, eagerness livening her expression. She must really want to see the place.

"Sure, just let me walk the bike to the back." I gave her a nod.

"I'm parked in the lot. A white BMW." She tipped her head at Iris and Lane and left.

"Guess I don't have to wait it out," I said. "You'll text the address of the brunch place?" I asked Iris and got a nod. "Okay, see you both then. Thanks again for letting me leave the bike."

"Wouldn't want something else to try to kill you on your way home." Lane's deadpan was in full effect.

I chuckled and waved on my way out. At least I'd avoid a miserable trip home, even if I'd pay for it by having to play host for a half hour.

43

It took two trips past her house before I got up the nerve to park on the street and approach her front door. We were going to be playing tennis later. I could have just waited. I probably should have waited, but I needed to know.

The epiphany had taken me by surprise this morning while waiting for my coffee order to come up. Nothing in particular happened to spark this realization of mine. No one said anything to me or around me. No emails or texts or headlines gave me the idea. I was simply taking a coffeehouse break after finishing another article that morning. Standing off to the side of the counter, I watched patrons add multiple extras to their already complicated coffee mixtures and waited for the guy to pour my small black coffee, then call some version of my name. It was only four letters, shouldn't be too hard to master. Yet the number of times someone pronounced it with a long "e" tripled the times people got it right. Vegas, Vega, drop the "s," not that difficult. Anyway, it happened as I was reaching for the coffee. The thought, realization, epiphany, whatever profound woo-woo crap people called it. At that moment, I just knew. Well, I didn't know, which was why I was here to check. But I was certain I was right. And if I was, I was the biggest idiot alive.

Iris gave me a surprised look when she answered her door. "Don't cancel. We've got to take advantage of the good weather before fall really hits."

"Are you Ferdinand?" I asked, forgoing any trivial greeting because trivial greetings shouldn't stand in the way of woo-woo epiphanies. "The bull?"

She squinted at me, her head tilting, confusion wiping away the surprised look. "I'm Iris, but you know that. You even met my mother, who confirmed my identity."

I had and enjoyed meeting her mom quite a lot. Retired now, her mother was able to sneak off for these mother-daughter visits while her dad got the house to himself and refused to retire from the consulting business he owned and loved. Iris got to see him a couple times a year when they both visited, but she really enjoyed the solo time with her mom. "I liked your mom. Now answer my question."

She reached out and dragged me inside. It felt more and more like home every time I crossed the threshold. So comfortable and fitting. "Am I a bull?"

"Ferdinand, to be exact. Do you know the book?"

She took a seat on her couch and patted the space next to her. "The kids' story about a bull who'd rather sit under his cork tree and smell flowers than fight in a bull ring?"

It didn't surprise me that she could recall the story so easily. Everything else about her fit so well, and she understood so much. That she'd know my favorite kids' book was on par for everything else that was great about her. "That very one. With the 'appearances can be deceiving' moral to the story."

"And you're confusing me with a bull who'd rather smell flowers than fight?"

"I'm asking if that theme applies to you." If I could make more sense right now I would, but this realization and being in her presence muddled my mind. "Iris, please."

"I'm trying to follow you here, Vega. I really am." Her hand darted out but dropped back to her side. Yeah, we'd stopped touching each other, even casually.

"Let me put it this way. Have I had more dates here than you have in the past three months?"

Her mouth nudged ajar. She looked away and gave a sharp nod.

"Damn, I have, haven't I?" My head jolted to the side, trying to toss off my stupidity. "You let everyone believe..."

"Whatever they want," she finished for me. "Nothing I say would have changed that."

But she could have told me. Then I wouldn't have assumed. Or I could have just been a better friend. "I made assumptions. I'm an idiot, and I blew it."

"What did you blow?" She leaned forward, still not touching.

"Any chance. I blew it because you're Ferdinand, and I'm one of the short-sighted men in the funny hats." I blew out a long breath. "I'm sorry I hurt your feelings. I was an idiot to assume anything when you were always so…"

"Different," she finished. "So were you. It's why it hurt so much."

"I know. I'm sorry. I don't know if it would have changed anything, but I am sorry." I stood and shook out my hands. "I like you so much. You've made good on your promise of being a great friend."

She stood with me. "So are you."

"Tomorrow for tennis? I could use a day to think about how I made stupid assumptions and was a lousy friend. Tomorrow, we can go back to being Iris and Vega, friends extraordinaire." I headed for the door.

"Tomorrow?" she questioned, following me out to her porch.

"Tomorrow," I confirmed and hurried to my car. If I didn't, I might be tempted to turn around and beg her to forgive me. To forget everything I said and give us another chance.

Back at my place, I opened my laptop. Writing another article didn't hold any appeal. Neither did starting another chapter of the book. I glanced at the coffee that had sparked the epiphany. It remained unconsumed and frigid cold now. Another trip to the coffeehouse might help jumpstart a new mindset. One that could get some work done.

Walking my circuit, I cleared my head and went to the laptop. I started typing, anything, didn't matter, knowing it was the best way to get writing when nothing came to me. Four paragraphs later, the words started making sense and even matched the story of the couple I was supposed to be writing about.

My editor texted some words of encouragement. Totally in character, which meant mostly snarky. Just what I needed to turn all of the words I was typing into something publishable. The life of a writer and her supporting cast.

The front door buzzed a while later. I jumped at the sound, so engrossed in writing. It was probably that neighbor's moronic friend who just buzzed everyone's door until someone let him in. Helen had to play the domineering landlord last week with the tenant, but obviously the friend hadn't gotten the message yet.

It buzzed again, and I gave a long sigh. That moron was going to get an earful. I was in the right mood for it. Forget Helen having to play the heavy again. I'd do it for free. I pressed the buzzer, ripped open the door, and marched to the top of the landing. All frustration drained from my body when, instead of the moronic random door buzzer, Iris bounded up the stairs. The same Iris who agreed to start over tomorrow.

"Hi," she greeted.

"It's not tomorrow."

She chuckled. "We really need to work on your greetings."

I tipped my head back at the open door and turned to lead her into my apartment. "Did we need more time to go over how I'm a faithless friend before we reset for tomorrow?"

"Two questions," she said as she closed the door behind her and faced me. "No, three, possibly, four."

I blinked, taking in her statement and a moment to just stare at her. "Okay."

"Did someone tell you, or you just assumed?"

"About sleeping with Kaylee? A few people in the bar said something. I thought you were just getting her into a cab, but when you didn't come back, I wasn't sure."

She gave me a long stare with those beautiful blue eyes. Eyes the color of the blue flower. Her mom's inspiration for the name. Iris had managed to stop her mom from sharing the name she'd chosen before seeing her newborn's beautiful iris-colored eyes. I planned to make it my mission on her next visit to find out that name. The way Iris reacted told me she thought it was embarrassing. For now, I was happy to return any stare she graced me with.

"I don't think you're a player, Iris. I never did. I thought you were friendly and gorgeous and sometimes you enjoyed company for the night. That's all."

She assessed me for a moment longer. "When I told you I didn't have sex with her, did you believe me?"

"Yes."

"Even though some people in the bar said I did?"

"I believe you. What you tell me, how you are. I trust you and I believe you."

Another nod, then a frown creased her brow. "Did you sleep with Cyrah?"

I flinched and backed up. "No, absolutely not." Not that Cyrah was repulsive, quite the opposite, in fact. I just couldn't imagine sleeping with anyone else after being with Iris. Not for a while, yet. But that couldn't be a random question. "Who's saying I did?"

"Some women at the bar are saying you invited her in for 'coffee' as they're calling it. With air quotes and everything."

I scoffed and growled, a scrowl. "What the hell is wrong with some of those women? They can't keep their traps shut."

"I know that." She sighed and looked back at me, tenderness in her gaze. "Looks like we both made some missteps."

My heart tripped and started pumping hard. I reached back and stabilized my stance by gripping the desk. "We did."

"Last question." She stepped closer, and my heart kicked into a double-time beat. "Did you believe the rumors that I was with Lane? Taking advantage of her?"

"God, no. That came up once around me, and I shut it down. Told them off."

"Without knowing for sure?" She moved closer still. Her presence felt like a physical touch, one I wanted so much.

"That first night we met, I thought you might have been together at one point. You have a closeness that some couples don't ever get to. But I discarded the idea after hanging out with you both. Now that I know more about her, there's no way you'd cross that line with her."

A breath of air puffed from her lips. She took in another deep breath and released it. "Thanks."

"You just had to clear that up today?" I felt marginally better than when I'd left her place. It gave me hope that we'd ditch the tentativeness that we'd shown around each other for the past couple of weeks.

"You know that all-or-nothing thing we both live by?"

I swallowed hard. "The 'if we're done being girlfriends, we're not going to be friends' all-or-nothing?"

"Or the 'friends or girlfriends, but not both' all-or-nothing?"

"I think you said we have that in common." My voice shook, not sure where this conversation was going. Just very hopeful.

"Here's the glitch with people like us." She reached out and cupped my cheek. My lids fluttered closed. "We're already great friends, and we practically imploded when we made love. At least I did."

My eyes struggled to open against the onslaught of emotions her words caused. My heart thrashed against my ribcage. It was getting more difficult to stand without the support of the desk behind me. "Me, too."

"We were friends before we made love. After, I still felt like we were friends, but we'd added so much more." Her fingers played along the nape of my neck, encouraging the twister that kept touching down over and over in my stomach. "We can have both."

"Both?" I whispered, hardly adding any volume to the whisper. I might have just mouthed the word.

"Friendship and a relationship. That's our all." She swallowed hard, her eyes studying mine. Red flushed her neck and cheeks. "If that's something you think we can have."

Think? Know. Definitely, know. It wasn't just my wildly beating heart, my swirling insides, my desperate need to touch her, and my burning ears. I knew we could have both with every thought and wish and feeling I possessed.

Throat tight, I let my actions speak for me at first. Turning my face, I kissed the palm cupping my jaw. "I want the all in that equation. Definitely, the all."

She fell against me in an embrace. I slipped my arms around her and squeezed. "I'm crazy about you, Vega. It tore me up to leave after we'd made love. I'd never let Lane down, but I was tempted that day. It broke me when you said we wouldn't work together."

A knot rose in my throat. "I'm sorry. I thought I knew what you wanted." My lips kissed the side of her head and onto her cheek. Anything they could touch. "I won't make any more assumptions like that."

"I won't either. Just tell me you're in this with me."

"I am, Iris. You're so special to me." I cradled her head and shifted it back to look at her. "Very special."

Then my lips were on hers in a scorching kiss, picking up where we left off last time. Absolutely nothing bad in our technique today.

44

"God, Vega," she moaned into my mouth, her hands already pulling at my shirt, desperate to get to the flesh underneath.

I surged into the kiss, soaking up every sensation her lips sparked inside me. "Iris," I murmured, jerking against her body when her fingers finally dug through to my abdomen. "Iris," I repeated and pulled back. Her eyes, wild with desire, gazed at me in pleading. "Upstairs. Flat surface, remember?"

A smile replaced the pleading look. Her hand grabbed mine, and we yanked each other up the stairs, pausing every other step to kiss, until we basically kiss-walked the rest of the way to my bedroom.

Fingers flexed, twisted, and plucked to get clothes out of the way. Usually I liked undressing women, but I was fine with the shared attempt at undressing each other and ourselves, anything to get naked with her as quickly as possible. My heart squeezed at the sight of her finally bared before me. I'd barely glimpsed her breasts the last time and never got to see all of her. Here she stood, splendidly naked, those feminine muscles shaping her form, small breasts with hard rosy nipples, hip bones looking like lethal weapons and leading my eyes to the trimmed bristles of the tapered triangle covering her sex. She was perfection, utter perfection.

"Vega," she whispered, her eyes busy running over my body. I'd felt self-conscious the first time. My breasts were a size larger, and over the past year, I noticed that gravity was starting to play a small part in their shape. Still high enough, but aging would factor in more over the next few years. Her small mounds probably wouldn't ever be affected by age. "You're so gorgeous."

And that wiped away all self-consciousness. She was beyond gorgeous, and I would have told her if she didn't smash up against me in another passionate kiss. My lips and hands could tell her how gorgeous I thought she was.

She pushed and I pulled and we ended up on the bed, our mouths trying to stay attached. Our hands skimmed over any available surface. She pushed against me as I pushed against her. It should have been awkward trying to get her under me when she was trying to get me under her, but it wasn't. I loved it. Every second.

"Vega." Her voice was strained.

"Iris." Mine mimicked the tone.

Her hands slid up from my waist to grasp my breasts, making me moan. "I don't care who is where. I just need to feel you against me, on me, under me, whatever."

I laughed, relief and happiness glowing from the sound. She wouldn't insist on being the top or any of the other juvenile assertions I'd dealt with in that brief relationship with another non-femme. "You're amazing. I don't care either, as long we're in this together."

"We are." Her smile gripped my heart. Then her fingers tweaked my nipples, and I forgot all about the rising emotions that were already far deeper than I'd ever felt with anyone else. Those talented fingers could make me forget anything.

I rolled on top of her, groaning at the feel of her warm flesh and muscle tone beneath me. Her fingers were still doing their little twisty torture routine, but they froze when my thigh slipped between hers.

"Ah," she exhaled softly. Her eyes closed as I nudged against her wet center.

My elbow dug into the mattress on her right side to give my other hand the freedom to roam. I kissed her chin and slid down along her neck. My hand landed on her breast, which spurred hers back into action. Breath surged into my lungs at the motions of her fingers. I could lie here and enjoy this for hours, battling the urgency to touch her. Usually the urgency drove my actions, but with Iris, I could learn to enjoy the give and take.

I continued on my journey down her chest until my mouth nudged against her rigid nipple. She released one of my breasts to grip my head, making another sound. Or it might have been me making the sound. I was too far gone to notice. My mouth closed over the nipple, licking a semi-circle on the underside before sucking it into my mouth. Her body surged upward, trying to get more of herself inside. Her wetness painted a trail on my resting thigh, and my hips bucked in response.

My mouth kissed its way over to her other breast, pausing on occasion to gasp at what her hand was doing to mine. This nipple was just as stiff and sensitive, surprisingly so, if her body's reaction to my ministrations said anything. I kissed a path down her stomach, licking the ridges of her muscles. My tongue dipped into her belly button, chin nudging downward. I paused, looking up at her. Waiting for her to meet my eyes and give me the okay. She wasn't like other women, so I had to make sure she would be okay with what I wanted.

Her eyes met mine, and she guessed what I was asking. "Yes, Vega, anything. I need that with you."

I pressed a kiss to the barely-there bristles. "You have it."

My thumbs parted her plump, dusky lips. I gazed at her, reveling in this moment. Her muscles strained under my arms as she waited. My tongue reached to touch her, and she jerked her hips. I added force to my arms to keep her thighs in place as my mouth went back, tongue extended to lick the whole of her.

"Ah, damn," she panted.

My lips surrounded her swollen clit, tongue lapping lightly at first, adding more and more pressure. Her hands clung to my shoulder blades, thighs straining to rock against my mouth. Her taste burst into my senses, marking out a space in my mind and heart as hers alone. I wanted to luxuriate here for days, but I needed more. My fingers probed, sluicing through her folds. Her hips pulled up, hands dragged on my shoulders. My mouth came off her, searching for her eyes.

"Up here," she groaned. "I want you up here with me when we do this."

I swallowed at the emotions clouding her voice. This was affecting her as much as it was me. Slowly, I dropped kisses on her torso as I rose to meet her. Her mouth covered mine as soon as it was within reach. We both moaned as we shared her taste.

Her shoulders twisted, and I found myself looking up at her. That smile scattered my thoughts of having her under me when I took her. This was perfectly fine. Taking her like this would be just as good.

She settled on my hip, our thighs intertwined. Those gorgeous eyes pouring into mine how much we both needed this. She kissed me again, her hand skating over my breast and along my sides then onto my stomach and down. Her fingers played in the trimmed strip of hair, teasing, mischief dancing in her eyes.

"Iris," I whimpered, not able to handle any more teasing.

"Yes?" Now her tone was teasing.

"Damn you," I growled.

She laughed and said, "Same to you."

I did the only thing I could think of to get her to stop screwing around. I reached down, passing everything fun and distracting and gorgeous and perfect, and went right for the good stuff. She grunted audibly when my hand cupped her.

I fought the desire to spread my legs more, but gave up to the losing battle. Seemed I'd be wanton with her. Never before, but with Iris, I could be anything. The only thing saving me from a full blush was the shift of her legs, succumbing to her own needs, spreading to let me do what I wanted.

Her fingers finally drifted over the crest of my mound and dove down. God, her hand. Felt so good the last time, felt erratic and explosive and buoyant this time. Mine tried to match her movements, not wanting to rush her, but needing so much. More than I've ever needed when I was with someone.

"Are you okay with…?"

My head was nodding at the unfinished question as I was asking the same, "Are you?"

"With you? Yes. Anything." Her words came out in a rush, matching the breathlessness I felt at being finally free with someone. Letting her have what she wanted, trusting that was okay.

"Anything with you," I repeated so she knew that I felt the same, every little feeling, the same.

My middle finger circled her clit, drawing more wetness and moans from her. She rubbed two fingers over mine, my hips rocking with each swipe. I'd never needed anything more. My lips pressed against the base of her throat and onto her cheek as she looked down to watch our joining.

She probed, nudged, prodded before slowly pushing inside. I sucked in a gasp, having forgotten this feeling, not allowing it for years. I never needed penetration to climax, but she filled me, enhancing every sensation. "You feel so good," she whispered and kissed my chest.

My finger stopped circling and dipped down to her opening. In the next instant, I surged into her. She gave another sexy grunt as her tunnel squeezed my finger. Her head lifted, and she stared down at me. I couldn't look away, didn't want to. We began to pump our fingers in rhythm, drawing out and surging back in. Our hips rocked, meeting each thrust. Never once did we look away from each other.

Her thumb added to the mix with crafty but targeted swipes. I lifted up to capture her mouth and swallow the loud groan trying to work free. My hips pumped harder against her hand. Hers came down against mine, my palm slapping her engorged clit. With one strong swell upward, my hand twisted, palm digging and finger caressing just so. She cried out, climaxing against me, body shaking, hand jerking. The motion grazed my clit precisely, and I yelled her name as I joined her bliss. My orgasm shuddered through me, my body twitching and spasming out of control. Only the weight of her body crushing against mine kept me from lunging up in wild contractions.

"Oh, yes, yes," she murmured as her body rippled above me.

I kissed that beautiful mouth that said and did such beautiful things. "The best," I mumbled against her lips, breath still erupting in huffs as my body worked itself down to boneless.

"You are," she gasped into my mouth and finally collapsed all of her weight on top of me.

My arms snaked around her, running up and down her back. I summoned all of my remaining energy to turn us onto her back. She smiled against my lips, not at all bothered that I'd just taken this position back.

"Let me catch my breath," she said, her lips crawling over my jaw to my still burning ear. "Then I'm going to taste you. I didn't get the chance before I had to have you."

I chuckled, lazy and pleased. Best sex of my life, and I knew without having to ask that I'd be getting as much as I wanted, whenever.

45

Tristan & Presley

A bodyguard. I was talking to someone who claimed to be an actual bodyguard. Like when Iris told me she was a PI, I wanted to grill this woman to make her prove she was truly a bodyguard. That just didn't happen outside of books. Or a bad movie. Good enough music, but a bad movie.

Iris. Deep sigh, stupid smile, zip of heat, flashes of flesh. And back to—nope, one more stupid smile and burning flush—now, back to business.

A bodyguard. The woman sitting next to her had been her protectee. The bodyguard used that word. Honestly. Like we were in a romance novel, and in the next moment, someone was going to take a shot at her protectee, and she'd have to cover her with her body, then drag her off to some remote cabin that absolutely no one but the bodyguard knows about. Of course, the cabin will be completely stocked and have working electricity, despite her not having been there for months because a bodyguard can somehow afford two places, one to live in and a remote cabin for convenient hiding of her protectees.

"I thought it was all nonsense." The protectee, better known as Presley, brushed her hand through the air.

My eyebrows shot up, and I refrained from nodding in agreement. It was kind of ridiculous. No one had been stalking her or threatening her, and she wasn't exposed to criminals who might want revenge. She was a software executive. A big software company. Technically, the biggest software company, but still, just a software company.

"Easiest damn job I've ever had," the bodyguard, who went by Tristan, winked at me. She was a winker. Not flirty, just someone who used the wink as part of her facial repertoire.

"How'd you get it?" Based on the expensive watch she was wearing, the cushy job paid extremely well. Could be the executive wife bought her the watch, but not the way she proudly flashed it.

"I was an Army MP. When I got out, I applied to a police department. Went through several rounds of interviews and background checks. Then it came down to an eye test and I failed. Colorblind."

My brain rattled inside my head from the confused shaking. I had several questions, but took them one at a time. "You're colorblind? Do you know how rare that is?"

Presley slid forward in her seat. "Not that rare. A couple of my colleagues are."

"Male colleagues, right? Not so rare with men. It's carried on the X chromosome and is a recessive trait. Women are far less likely to get both chromosomes with the recessive trait." I watched Presley turn her head and stare at Tristan, amazement in her eyes. She shrugged like it wasn't a big deal to be in a category with less than one percent of other women. I asked my second question, "Why does it matter to a police department? It's not like you're flying jets and need to be able to determine if lights go from green to red on the instrument panel."

She shrugged. "No one could actually tell me. The lieutenants who wanted to give me the job had no idea it was a requirement. One of them is still petitioning to have the rule changed. He thinks I'll drop this gig to become a beat officer at a third of the pay."

My eyebrows lifted higher. The watch told me she got paid well. It didn't tell me she got paid three times what police officers made. That was a little despicable. Not her fault, and I couldn't blame her for sticking with the well-paying job, but the fact that security detail personnel were paid three times the salary of someone placed in dangerous situations every day to protect the public at large made me sick to my stomach.

I thought of Iris again. All summer, she'd sprinkled little tidbits of what her job had been like. Extremely difficult at first because she was one of only a few women in her division and the only female detective for a while. I'd been proud of her accomplishments and her chosen career when I was just her friend. Now that our relationship had changed, I was impressed and honored to know her.

"Did anything ever happen?" I asked the executive.

"Other than being served bad chicken that gave everyone food poisoning at one of the conferences we had to attend, no. Not one scare. It's just a policy that the company has. Once you reach a certain level, there's a security detail that follows you anytime you leave the campus. Keeps the key-person insurance costs down."

"And Tristan was one of the security detail?"

Presley gave her a fond look. "She was. One of the few women, which almost always put her on my team."

"Lucky for me." Tristan winked again. "I couldn't stand guarding that marketing lady, and the IT exec almost never left the basement."

Presley pushed against her shoulder. "She doesn't work in a basement, and there are more than three female execs. Don't give Vega the wrong idea about our company."

I waved off their concern. It didn't matter what I thought of their company as long as their software kept working on my laptop. I only cared about their story.

"We were at the TED conference. Tristan was on call twenty-four hours a day because all the execs were attending, and there weren't enough females on the detail to go around clearing public restrooms and department store changing rooms."

I slid back in my chair. "You were out shopping at a TED conference?"

Presley's shoulders hitched. "Some of my colleagues would go shopping after hours or between talks. They go a little crazy away from campus at conferences."

"Presley was the only one not darting off to find other things to do," Tristan reported. "I had seniority by then, so I got to assign others to the execs running around off the rails. One detail just stayed at a strip club as several of the execs rotated in and out of the place. Took them weeks to get rid of the glitter."

Good imagery. "You stayed with the exec who was there to work?"

"My favorite exec." Wink, wink. "Only she didn't know it, but spending twenty-four hours a day together for five days gave me enough time to win her over."

She had the same kind of arrogant but still charming quality about her that Iris did. I wondered if it might be a law enforcement trait. She wasn't quite as charming or good looking as Iris, and there was no way she kissed or touched or made love as well as Iris, but she had a chance at second place in the arrogant but charming race. A slower, less charming, more arrogant second, but still second.

"The stress of keeping up with all the business back at the office, making the right connections at the conference, prepping my part of the talk a colleague was giving, it got to me. Tris was the one calming influence throughout." Her left shoulder popped up and down. "I couldn't resist."

"Are you both still working there?"

Tristan nodded and winked, while Presley said, "Yes, but she's hardly ever on my team. HR likes to keep things in their places."

"I'd like to see them try," Tristan bragged and winked again. Her hands came up to roam Presley's body and had the executive giggling and slapping them away.

A few questions later, I was done with the interview. They were off to some tech event and cleared out pretty fast. I gave the bar a cursory glance, hoping to find Iris, but not having any luck. She was assessing the security needs of Nykos's office today. After spending almost every second together since Thursday, it wasn't easy to let her leave my bed this morning. We'd get to a routine at some point, after this can't-wait-got-to-have-her feeling tapered off. For now, I'd keep counting the minutes until she was back in my sightline.

I bounced my eyes among the regulars to keep from shifting in my seat while I decided on whether to wait here or go home to call Iris. Lane was conversing with an attractive woman while fixing her a drink. Greer looked like she was staking out her next victim as her friends prodded her into another questionable act to obtain information about her. Cheryl was talking to Devon and Sawyer. Cyrah was heading toward wannabe James Dean. My gaze narrowed. I needed to deal with that. She hadn't seemed the type to lie about conquests, but I'd see what she had to say about it before overreacting.

A slap landed on my back when Riley took the seat next to me. "Good people?" Her head tipped toward the door.

"They were, yeah. How're you tonight, Riley?"

She shrugged and looked away. Her grin hadn't been as forthcoming recently. My increased deadlines kept me from hanging out in the bar much after completing interviews, so I didn't know what might be going on with her. "Pretty good. Wanna play some pool?"

I turned to face her. As showy as she could be at times, I still liked her. More so than any of the others in her usual foursome. In fact, I thought all of them could be kinder to her. Devon was pretty nice, but they all took Riley for granted. "Tell me your story, Riley."

She pushed back and gave a loud guffaw. "Oh, now you want to hear it when you rejected us from day one."

I knew she was teasing, but she'd guessed right. I didn't think her story would have been that unique. I also didn't think they'd last as couples. I needed the couples I wrote about to stay together long enough to see the end of the series. "That's not entirely true."

"Just giving you a hard time." She was quick to let me off the hook. Another thing that would make for a good friend. I made a note to do something about that. Ask her to do something outside of the bar soon.

"What is it about Adrian that does it for you?"

She tipped back in her chair and folded her arms. "What do you mean?"

"Personal question, but do you like being the one to take care of your woman? Do you like always having to make sure she's happy? Is that what gets you going?"

Her eyes searched mine. They were a pretty light brown. I preferred Lane's reddish brown, but Riley's light brown stood out against her dark brown hair. I hadn't noticed that before. Her demeanor kept me from noticing anything beautiful about her. "Why?"

"I think you're pretty cool, Riley. You're funny and interesting when it's just us." I hesitated because I didn't know her all that well, and she'd probably take offense to anything else I said.

"Us? You mean without Adrian around."

I gave a slight nod, hoping she'd piece together what I was saying and not hate the messenger. "You sometimes disappear when she's here. You're there, I see you, but you're attending to whatever she needs or wants. Don't you want something for yourself?"

"That's what you've seen?" Her brow furrowed.

"I don't mean to offend. Like I said, I think you're cool. You just care more that Adrian and your other friends have a good time than if you're having one."

"Is that bad?" For the first time, a chip in her self-confidence formed.

"It makes you a good girlfriend, but you have to enjoy yourself as well or what's the point?"

"Yeah." She dropped her folded arms and heaved a sigh. "Yeah."

"Have you been realizing that lately?" I guessed.

Her gaze darted away. "A little. I thought I knew what we had, but you're right. I should be getting more out of it. As much as she is."

"When partners feel they're on equal standing, those are the partnerships for the ages."

She looked back at me, a grin forming. "Is that on a fortune cookie somewhere?"

"Probably," I said and laughed, but I'd always felt that way. It was why, until now, none of my girlfriends ever made it to the partner stage. I didn't have any doubts about where my relationship with Iris was heading. Even as brand new as it was.

"What about you? You've been here a while, but none of your dates are sticking." She threw up a hand when my eyes narrowed. "I know now that you and Iris weren't ever together, and I'm not sure what Cyrah's saying about the other week."

I wouldn't be telling Riley about Iris until we'd talked about it. "I don't know what Cyrah's saying either, but she gave me a ride home. That's all."

"Thought so. I'm pretty sure it's her friend Ruth that's spreading the rumor. Cyrah's not really like that." Her eyes flew to the group with Cyrah and Ruth, aka James Dean wannabe. "You're a hot commodity in here, you know. Beware that someone doesn't try to use you for that."

"Right there." My finger pointed at her. "That's what I'm saying about you. That concern for me makes you a damn good friend. Everything I said tonight is out of friendship and concern for you. That's what you deserve."

She clapped her hand on my shoulder. Much softer than her usual backslap, as if now that we'd had our first really serious chat, she didn't have to play the role of the tough butch around me anymore. "Thanks, Vega. I know you're right. It's time I did something about it."

"Good luck," I said as she stood and made a beeline for the game room upstairs. If Adrian had joined Devon and Sawyer up there, they'd be getting an earful. She looked determined.

"Is she okay?"

My lungs filled at the sound of Iris's voice. I let the breath out in a deep sigh and turned to look at her. "Hi."

"Hey," she said in an equally dazed tone and took the seat Riley had vacated.

"How was the job?" I shouldn't resent Nykos's need to increase security at his office. Iris and I needed the break. It was good for us. Made the vision of her before me now that much sweeter. I'd never been a twenty-four-seven kind of girlfriend. I liked breaks, needed them to do my work and keep from screaming about all the little things that bugged me in relationships. Breaks were good. Today had been hard. I found out I didn't need a break yet, which should have scared me a little. I'd never needed a girlfriend before. Wanted, sure, but needed, absolutely not.

"The building needs more security. It'll be good to get that squared away for them." She placed her hand on my thigh under the table, needing the connection as much as I did. "Nykos had my sides hurting from laughing so much. I knew he was funny, but he and Willa together are like a professional comedy duo."

So, we'd both had a good day. Not as good as the last two spent in her arms and in my bed and on a tennis court and on bikes and on walks and everything else we'd done together the last two days, but a good day otherwise.

"Helen's sister is finally in town? Will she be coming by to actually see the investment she made here?" I'd been wondering that for a month now.

"Didn't ask her. I'm sure she'll go over to Helen's before she leaves. You may actually meet her."

"If she really exists. So far she's been more like a fairy godmother, making things happen for the people she likes."

"Oh, she'll hate that description. Make sure you mention it if you meet her." She laughed and moved her hand to stroke down my arm. It sparked all sorts of tingles. "I was hoping I'd catch you here. I want to tell Lane about us. Is that okay?"

My eyes flicked over to Lane, who was talking to the same woman at the bar. My insides wriggled knowing that Iris wanted to share the news about us with her best friend. I was already in pretty deep with her. The slope got even slicker knowing that she wanted to tell one of the most important people in her life about something that was still very new. "Of course, why wouldn't it be?"

Her hand tugged gently on my forearm as she tipped her head toward the exit. "Let's take a walk. I don't want anyone to overhear."

I glanced around and caught one or two people looking at us. People were often curious as to whom I might be interviewing, but when it was just me and someone else from the bar, no one noticed. Until today. "All right." I followed her outside, and we started walking up the block.

"You look amazing, by the way," she said as soon as we'd cleared the door.

I flushed at the compliment. That was one of the best things about her, making the people she cared about feel good. "As do you." Slacks and a silk top never looked better on a woman.

Her eyes closed slowly, taking in the mutual admiration. "Was the interview interesting?"

"It was. Did you know some tech company around here pays massive amounts of money to have bodyguards for their executives?"

Her head bobbed. "I know a lot of retired cops who take those positions."

"That's how this couple met. Nice enough folks and a usable story."

"Good." Her hand slipped into mine. She gave it a squeeze, shooting more tingles up my arm. "About Lane. I want to tell her because I'm really happy about us."

The tingles spread all over. "So am I, and happy that you want to tell your best friend."

She brightened and slowed our pace. She must have been stressed about my reaction. "I'd just started seeing someone when Lane was attacked."

I stopped and faced her, my hand slipping out of hers. Two guys with their arms around each other walked by. I waited for them to pass us before saying, "Tell me she didn't make it harder for Lane."

Her hand came up to cup my face. She leaned forward to brush her lips against mine, and now the tingles multiplied exponentially. "That's why you're so amazing."

I wrapped my arms around her. "You're amazing yourself."

She leaned her forehead against mine. "She was understanding at first but started to lose patience. Got angry that I'd go over to Lane's every day and be at the bar every night. Or if I took Lane's calls all the time. She gave me three weeks before she issued an ultimatum."

"You showed her ass the door, I hope." My blood boiled at the idea that someone put pressure on anyone in that situation. Three weeks before she becomes a selfish bitch? Crazy.

Iris looked at me with awe in her expression. She glanced away and tugged me across the street to a small park. My back was soon pressed up against a tree, and Iris's mouth was on mine. The kiss was tender and exactly enough to forget that I'd had to wait a whole day for it. She pulled back and gazed blissfully at me. "I could love you forever for that."

I knew it was a just a saying. I shouldn't read anything into it. Just because my heart was beating like crazy and feeling that word with every pump didn't mean it wasn't just a saying in this situation. It still felt good to hear. "Because I would have kicked her ass out for being a bitch?"

"Well, that too, but that you understand about Lane." Her eyes took in every feature of my face, something I noticed she liked to do. As if memorizing every detail.

"She's your best friend. She needed you. Anyone who couldn't understand that doesn't deserve even a thought." My eyes took their own stroll over her face. Her beautiful, transfixing face. Eyes violet-blue, lips just plump enough, ears tucked tightly against her head, jaw tracing a path to her appealing chin. I'd spent the better part of the last two days staring at this face. I couldn't imagine ever growing tired of just looking at her.

"You're right," she agreed.

"Is that what this walk's about?" My eyes left her face to glance around the small park. A few people were walking dogs, but mostly we had the area to ourselves."

"I wanted to make sure you knew...were okay with..."

"Iris." I placed a hand over her heart. It was beating as hard as mine. "She's your friend, our friend, but your friend." I shook my head, confusing myself. Lane was my friend, too, but theirs was a special friendship that wouldn't ever break. I wouldn't muscle in on that. That loyalty and love she had for Lane was one of the things I loved about Iris. Made her who she was. "I don't expect anything with her to change."

"Even if her phone call interrupts us?" Her expression grew tentative.

So that was the issue. She was worried I'd resent Lane and use it against her. "As long as we get to pick up when we see each other next, I'll be good. We kinda screwed that up the last time. Missed the picking-it-back-up step." My hand pushed up from her heart, along her throat to palm her cheek. "Let's not do that again."

All tentativeness left her expression. "Do you have to work tonight?"

"I should write up this interview." I leaned forward and kissed her. For a while. Made out, really. When I pulled back, I said, "An hour, no more."

Her eyes lit up. "Want to come over after?"

I brightened. Hell, yeah, I did.

46

Lane's butt landed on another sofa. Helen dropped down beside her. I stood watching from the edge of this living room tableau. We'd already gone through several others. Helen looked like she could go through dozens more. Lane shared my expression, both of us ready to be done. Our trio had performed this shopping task once already when I'd needed replacements in my living room. Helen was an expert furniture shopper like her husband was an expert car shopper. She made it easy and fun. I'd asked Lane to come with us because I knew she spent too much time on bar business every day and needed something to draw her away. Furniture shopping wasn't a great draw, but she liked spending time with Helen and me, so she'd come along. This morning, she'd called me to return the favor. I was happy for the break from writing, even if we spent it testing out sofas.

"This one's nice." Helen's hand ran over the material of the backrest. "Good quality, and you can order it in other patterns. Or did you want leather like Vega's?"

Lane glanced at me and back at the sofa. "I've never had leather before, but I do like Vega's sofa."

"Over there." Helen's finger pointed to another setting of living room furniture, and like that, she was off.

"Damn, she loves this stuff," Lane said with an amused shake of her head.

"You asked the right person for help."

Her brown eyes looked up at me. "Still can't believe it sometimes. The bar and my new apartment. It's all so great."

My head bobbed as I grinned. "Want me to pinch you?"

She laughed and smacked my arm. The gesture so familiar it made my heart trip. All summer, we'd been getting closer, but I still felt like she considered me more Iris's friend than hers. Now that Iris and I were together, I was afraid she'd consider me permanently once removed. With that smack, I could tell she was letting me in.

"Let's choose the next decent sofa so we can get out of here and grab a late lunch," I suggested, knowing she wasn't particular about furniture style. Unlike Helen, who had already moved onto another setting, having rejected the first.

"You're just dying to get out of here to spend the afternoon with Iris." Another light smacking tease.

I could feel a blush touch my face. Iris and I were doing another stakeout later. She didn't need my help or anything. I just wanted to see her today, and she was happy to have company on a boring stakeout. And she wanted to see me today, too. So far, we hadn't been able to go a day without seeing each other. It would be ridiculous if it didn't make me feel so damn good.

"Jeez," Lane muttered, spotting my blush. "You two are pathetic."

Even Lane thought we were pathetic, but she didn't have this same feeling. This feeling that I'd stumbled upon a treasure absolutely no one else in the world knew about. After only a week together. How crazy was that? It probably helped that Iris was one of the best friends I'd ever had, but this desire to see her, hear her, talk to her, touch her, it was all so new. Not ever in my past relationships had I felt this kind of desperation. Made me shake all over when it overwhelmed me.

"Is it weird?" I had to ask because Lane was so important to Iris, important to me. She couldn't feel left out.

The practiced sexy quirk of her lips turned into a full, sly smile. "Please. You idiots were dating all summer and didn't know it."

My eyes popped wide. I hadn't expected that. "We were?"

"Well, not exactly dating, but I had a feeling it could head that way. You're good for her."

My insides warmed at the praise. "Thanks."

"No, really. I've known her a long time. Seen her in two other serious relationships. They couldn't handle the cop thing."

"The cop thing?" I questioned as Helen waved us over to test a simple brown leather couch.

"You know, the danger of the job, the case obsession, massive amounts of voluntary overtime. Don't know what they expected of her." She shrugged and started us toward Helen's find. "To take care of them, treat them as if they were precious gems to be worn out of the house all the time. I don't know, but it wasn't a partnership. You're not going to do that to her."

That could have been a statement or a warning. Either way, Iris's best friend recognized what we had was special. Different from Iris's other failed relationships. She didn't know it, but it was different from mine, too. Although, I still thought it was crazy to be thinking this way so early on. And yet, was it that early on? We'd been hanging out together for more than three months. I felt I knew her so well already. Felt it was only natural to feel this deeply so soon.

"This is it." Helen rubbed the seat of the couch she was sitting on. It didn't occur to her that Lane might not like it. I'd noticed this about Helen. She could be headstrong, very considerate and intuitive, but headstrong.

Lane's butt landed on this sofa. A smile hit her face. Helen was right, apparently.

After the promised late lunch, we were back at Lane's bar. I was going to drop them off to go find Iris, but she pulled into the parking lot behind us. My stomach fluttered, a minor earthquake of a flutter, and I had to look away or my face would flush red. I still had a reputation as a cool customer to uphold.

"Hey, Iris," Helen called as we piled out of my car.

"How ya been, Helen?" she called back, grabbing a shopping bag from the backseat of her car. "Brought over those camera upgrades, Lane." She held up the bag as her eyes shifted to me. The same kind of struggle to stay cool played across her face. "Hi."

"Hey," I responded.

Before I could decide to just screw the appearance of our fake coolness, Helen said to me, "Oh, just kiss her." Helen and Lane cracked up at our surprised faces. "You think I didn't see Iris sneaking out of your place the other morning?"

Now I knew how she felt with all those visitors staying across the hall from her. It was kind of hard not to be in each other's business. I glanced at Iris and smiled, completely okay with being caught. She looked a little stunned, probably thinking her cop skills kept her stealthy at all times. I walked up to her and cupped her face. "Hey," I repeated and slid my mouth over hers.

She kissed me back. We kept it G-rated, knowing we had an audience, but it still felt really good. We hadn't spent last night together because of her early client meeting. I could tell she missed me as much as I missed her.

"There now," Helen declared as I pulled back. "Everyone feel better? Let's get inside."

Headstrong. Like I said.

Iris wrapped her arm around me as we followed them into the bar. Still an hour till opening, it felt peaceful inside. Could be the woman at my side helping that feeling along, but I liked the atmosphere of the bar when things were calm. It never felt dead, as it had when Charlie owned it. Now the slow times or emptiness gave off warm and inviting vibes.

"Let's ask Iris's opinion," Helen said when she finished inspecting the kitchen. She couldn't help herself. If a kitchen was around, she needed to look through it.

"About?" Iris said, her hand started rubbing my hip. Sparks shimmered along my side, the touch reminding me of everything else she could do with that hand.

"Helen thinks closing an hour earlier on weeknights is a good idea," Lane reported, looking through the shopping bag that Iris set on the bar top. "It's a bar. It's supposed to stay open till two."

Iris shrugged. "I remember a lot of nights with just us here in the last hour."

Lane sighed. "I'll look over the numbers. If Tuesday through Thursday are slow, maybe I'll try it out. It'll mean one less person I have to schedule those nights."

"Or another night off that you can take?" Helen suggested. "You can't grind down to nothing in the first year, Lane. Find a balance."

"Like couch shopping?" Lane teased her.

"Exactly. Get out of this bar and away from the paperwork when you're not working." The carefree Helen replaced the headstrong one.

"I've been telling her that for a while now." Iris released me and walked over to Lane to wrap an arm around her shoulders. She didn't want Lane to think we were ganging up on her, but it was one of her main concerns. I'd taken to calling Lane once or twice a week for lunch out or an afternoon walk or bike ride or anything to get her away from the bar and thinking about the bar. It had been her protective shield when she needed it most, but with the attack behind her, the court case being plead out, she didn't need that shield anymore. Iris wanted her to live life to the fullest again.

"Plus, the couch rocks." I added a little levity to the well-meaning advice that her friends were giving her.

"It does. I'll start keeping track of the customer count and run a register tape for the last hour over the next couple of weeks."

Iris gave her another shoulder squeeze. "We'll put these up on Monday, okay?" Her hand swept over the security cameras.

Lane tipped her chin once. "Thanks for picking them up. I'm glad you looked over what Charlie had up before."

"These will definitely show more and at a better quality. The motion sensor flood lights are a must. It shouldn't take more than a couple hours to get them up on Monday."

"Sounds good." Lane's arm went around Iris's waist for a squeeze in gratitude. She tried for a detached attitude almost always. She didn't like showing weakness, more so than most. It warmed me to see her drop her guard around her best friend.

"You ready for that stakeout?" Iris asked me, a twinkle in her eyes.

"Ooh, a stakeout?" Helen spoke up, her eyes bouncing between us. "Is that code for hot sex?"

We all laughed at that. Iris reached out with both hands to grip Helen's shoulders. "It's code for stakeout."

"Oh," Helen sounded disappointed. She seemed delighted by the change in our relationship and eager to encourage us as much as possible. "Who are you staking out?"

"Suspected insurance fraud. Car accident, but the woman's injuries match exactly another case she was involved in years ago. We're going to see if she slips up and shows just how uninjured she really is."

"Yeah, that doesn't sound at all like hot sex." Helen made us laugh again. She had the same dry delivery that Lane had. No one would expect her to be funny. Made for a nice surprise every time she was.

I felt like assuring her that there would be hot sex later tonight, but I never bragged and this thing between Iris and me was still too private. Didn't stop my eyes from sending that exact message to Iris, though.

Hers studied mine, and her lips pulled wide in a sexy smile. Message received.

47

Riley gripped her thighs and sucked in deep breaths. After pulling our kayaks out of the water, she needed a minute to get her breath. This wasn't like when Joe and Helen had raced me three miles uphill. The kayaking had been at a beginner's pace. Joe helped her perfect her stroke as he toured us on an easy course, nowhere near boats. The extra weight she carried was the culprit here. Over the past three weeks, we'd spent a couple days doing something active and fun. She wanted a change from her usual routine since breaking up with Adrian and telling her buddy Devon to stop taking advantage of her good nature. Our friendship had stabilized now that she wasn't constantly trying to be the big bad butch all the time.

"Are you okay?"

Her hand came up to wave me off. "Got to get back in shape. This is good."

"Fun, too, yeah?" I asked, worried that the exertion might influence her opinion about this activity I'd grown addicted to.

She rolled upright. "Yeah, a lot. Thanks. We should try this again before the really cold weather comes in."

According to Iris that could start soon. We'd been playing more tennis before we had to hang up the rackets for the winter. Same with bike rides and volleyball and any other manner of outdoor activities we enjoyed together. Still in the midst of the can't-wait-have-to-have-her stage, we spent almost all of our free time together.

"Next week?" I asked.

"I'd like that. Thanks, Joe, that was a lot of fun," she said as he came back to get my kayak after already collecting Riley's. I would have taken it in myself, but I'd been worried about Riley's recovery.

"Next time it'll be a lot more fun. Ice some of those muscles tonight," he told her and waved before heading back to open up his shop for the flood of returns at the end of the day.

"True that," she said, rubbing her right shoulder. "You hanging with Iris tonight?" She gave me an eyebrow flutter. "Still can't believe you guys are together. Didn't think she had it in her, and with someone like you."

I stopped our progression toward her car. I'd been getting similar comments when Iris and I were together at the bar, so I should be used to it after a month. "What am I like?"

"You know, two chicks who aren't feminine."

I gave an amused huff. We weren't, and yet, we were all woman. "I live to buck tradition."

"Makes sense, considering all those articles you've written. You'd want something..." She searched for the right word.

"Singular," I supplied for her.

"I'm going to have to get used to having a friend who's a writer. Just don't correct my English, 'kay?"

"I wouldn't, so long as you stop being so confounded by Iris and me."

Her hands came up. "You got it. I'm happy for you. Iris has always been cool to me, and I like her even more now that I know those women were all talk."

Yeah, they were. Apparently some of the women in the bar would use Iris as their imaginary lover whenever they'd gone without dates for a while and their friends were giving them a hard time about it. She never bothered to get involved in those discussions, which made her an easy scapegoat for their lackluster sex lives. I didn't have the same attitude regarding the rumors circulating about me. One comment to an equally surprised Cyrah, and we both tracked down the source. Her friend Ruth mistook the meaning of being invited up for coffee. She didn't look all that sorry about misleading everyone, but at least the rumor got shut down that night. I didn't want anything else interfering with what Iris and I had.

"Well, thanks. Glad we could do this. Text me about next week, yeah?"

"Will do," she said and limp-walked her way to her car, holding her back the entire way. I didn't envy her sore body tomorrow. After many excursions with my crazy-ass neighbors, every previously unused muscle group had worked through all the soreness.

My phone rang as I was unlocking my apartment door. I smiled at the display and picked up. "Hi, sexy."

"Hey, hotness," Iris greeted.

"Are you headed over?" We were going to hang out, maybe watch some TV tonight. Liked that a lot about her, too. We didn't actually have to do something when we were together.

"Lane's here."

"Oh," I said, adjusting my mindset. "Did you two need some private time?" We could hold off till later.

"Join us?" Hesitation marked her voice. She still wasn't completely confident that I wouldn't dangle her close friendship with Lane in her face any time I didn't get my way. Even before Lane was attacked, Iris's other girlfriends hadn't appreciated or understood their close friendship. Didn't trust that they didn't have feelings for each other.

"If it's okay with Lane, sure."

"It is," she said immediately, the hesitation now gone.

I chuckled at her eagerness. I was eager, too, but I wouldn't become that kind of girlfriend. "Ask her first. You know I can't stand when the g/f just horns her way into whatever you're doing with your friends."

She laughed and spoke to Lane in the background. "She's your friend, too, and she's wants you to join."

"All right, I'll be there in a bit." I hung up and headed for the shower. After an hour on the lake, I needed a good scrubbing, and I wanted to look good for my fiery hot girlfriend.

Out of the shower, I took the time to blow dry my hair. Normally I'd just put it in a ponytail, but it would dry with a kink. Didn't want a kink in my hair if I was getting lucky later. Kink was fine in other places, but not my hair. Choosing jeans and a formfitting top, I stepped into some shoes and applied a touch of liner to my eyelids. I stuffed clean undies, another pair of pants, and a shirt into a backpack. Last week, we'd left toothbrushes at each other's places. We were taking it slow, not making any assumptions. I was fairly sure we both felt this was for the long haul, but not assuming that we'd spend the night or take over a drawer or not bother to ask each other what we wanted each day solidified the relationship foundation.

Finding a spot on Iris's street at the weekend was the only negative thing about getting together at her place. Her car took the one available spot in her driveway. She didn't have a garage, so I fought for a space on the street. Tonight, it was six houses down.

Iris opened the door as soon as I stepped onto the front path. "Hi."

I met her on the porch and gave her a kiss hello that lingered much longer than hello.

"We have a surprise for you." She pulled me with her through the front door.

"A surprise?" I asked and smiled at Lane once inside. "Hi, Lane. Fun day?"

"Ha!" Lane practically growled.

Iris ignored her and made an elaborate hand flourish toward the left. I followed the flourish and spotted an ergonomic desk that could be converted from a sitting desk to a standing one. It took up the nook space that used to house an unused coat tree. A small window looked out to her side yard beyond the desk.

My eyes shifted to a very smiley Iris and back to a still scowling Lane. "What's this?"

"Took us all damn day to put together. Do you know how many pieces are in that thing?" Lane grimaced and wrapped her hands around her hair to whip it into her characteristic messy bun.

Iris shot an elbow into her side and did the hand flourish again. "You like?"

"It's nice, but you have a nice desk in your loft up there." My finger pointed to the tight space above her kitchen. The roofline didn't allow for standing. Well, Lane might be able to, but Iris and I couldn't stand upright in the space. It was fine for sitting at the desk, and it helped her separate work time from home time.

"This one's for you to use," Iris said. "Whenever you work here, you're stuck trying to get comfy on the couch or at the island. Neither works as well as your setup at home."

"You got this for me?" I felt my throat tighten. My eyes flicked to Lane. "You put it together for me?" It was far more than just a desk. It said that she understood and encouraged my work habits. That she wanted me to work at her home. That she wanted me to feel as comfortable here as I did at my place.

"Do you like it?" Iris couldn't read the emotions showing on my face.

"Please like it," Lane added, looking worried by my misty reaction.

"Thank you," I whispered to Iris and turned to Lane and repeated, "Thank you. This is perfect." I reached for Iris.

Her arms folded over my back. Tension drained from her as she realized she hadn't overstepped by buying me a piece of furniture that would stay in her house. Not an overstep at all. We might get to those drawers sooner rather than later now.

"Thanks." I offered again and kissed her. Then, I turned to Lane and wrapped her in a quick hug, no kiss for her. "You wasted your off hours doing this? You've still got a full shift tonight, don't you?" Saturday nights were her busiest.

"Anything for a friend."

I liked that she meant both Iris and me. Things could get a little murky with relationships when two friends got together and one friend was on the outside.

"Nobody lost any fingers?" I reached out and ran my hands over the desk and used the lever to send it into a standing position. It worked without any hiccups, and the ergonomic kneel chair that fit under the desk would be ideal for the constant position changes I took when writing.

"Somebody almost lost a helper when she couldn't find the directions sheet in English," Lane teased her friend, slapping a hand against her shoulder.

"They were in French for some reason." Iris gave a sheepish shrug. "Had to look online for the English version."

"I'd love to stick around and review every little nut and bold we attached, but I'm already late for work." Lane started toward the door. "Derrick is probably rearranging the tables as we speak. He's been dying to try out a new pattern for the servers."

I checked my watch and saw that the bar's opening time passed more than a half hour ago. "Thanks again for spending your free time doing this. It's beautiful."

She laughed at the reverence in my tone. "It's a desk, Vega." She looked at Iris. "You still okay with me borrowing your car on Monday? I know you've got that new investigation starting. I can drop you off first, or should I just get a rental for the day?"

"If you can drop me before you get on the road, I should be fine. I'll see if I can't persuade my awesome girlfriend to pick me up if you aren't back in time." Her gorgeous eyes blinked seductively at me.

"Take mine," I offered. "I'm taking tomorrow off and no interviews on Monday. This way, Iris will have her car if she needs it on the investigation."

"You sure?" Lane showed surprise at my offer. She'd been without a car since her ex left her and took the car they shared. Living on Capitol Hill and working nonstop, she rarely needed one.

"It'll be sitting in a garage for a few days otherwise." Lane still looked like this was the biggest favor anyone could ever do. "You spent all day building me a desk, and you let me use your bar as my office. It's the least I can do." I pulled the key fob from my jacket. "Take it."

Her hand came up. "I only need it Monday."

"You need a ride to work, or we're walking you. Take it now." I whirled and looked at Iris. "Unless you can't give me a ride back home...later." I lost my confidence for a second when I realized

I'd just invited myself to stay over tonight. We usually spent the night whenever we got together but some morning appointments ended our nights early a few times.

"I'll give you a ride home whenever you want. Tomorrow, hopefully." She gave me a suggestive grin, and the confidence I'd had returned full force.

"Thanks, this is great." Lane took the key from my outstretched hand. "I'm thinking about getting a car, so I don't have to keep borrowing Iris's to visit my folks in Arlington."

"If I'm not using it, you're welcome to it." I meant that. I spent a lot of time writing at home. A friend might as well get some use out of the car.

We walked Lane out to where I'd parked. She slipped inside and adjusted the seat and mirrors for her shorter height, gave us a wave, and pulled out.

"I'm going to thank you properly when we get inside." Iris said and wrapped her arm around me to start us back.

"I think I'm the one who needs to thank you for the desk, Ms. Thoughtful." I waited until she closed the door and pushed up against her. My lips followed and she met my kiss with a groan. I loved that sound. I'd do just about anything to hear it. For as long as she'd share it with me.

"You're my captive now, you realize." She smiled against my lips.

"I'm okay with that...for tonight. You can be my captive another time."

She nipped at my lips. Like me, she'd been surprised at how easy we were together. Both of us had always been the aggressor in relationships, always the ones to take charge. It was expected of us as much as we chose it. With her, I didn't always have to be in charge. I could allow myself to be vulnerable and trust that she wouldn't think less of me. I could tell she felt the same.

I fell for her a little more every moment we spent together.

Epilogue

Iris & Vega

Eight Months Later

Before I had time to completely unwind at home after my return flight, my front door opened, and Iris came through. If not for her trained observation skills she wouldn't have noticed me over at my desk until she was already well inside. As it was, she got one step in before surprise brought her to a halt.

"Vega!" Her sexiest grin, the one comprised mostly of surprise and delight, stretched her mouth wide.

"Hey, Iris." I stood, having really just sat down, and held my arms out. In the next instant she was in them and kissing me. A wonderful welcome home, so different from our standard hello kisses.

"You're not due back for hours." She cupped my face. "I was stopping by to tidy up."

"Really?" We were both fairly neat, but neither of us liked to clean.

She shrugged and squeezed me tight again. "You like for us to stay at your place whenever you come back from a trip."

I was no longer surprised by the things she knew about me without me having to tell her. She knew I'd want to stay here tonight and that I liked fresh sheets when I came home from a trip. Ah, that was the tidying up she planned to do. "I love your place, but my bed's better. Do you mind?"

"As long as we're together. How is it that you're here already?" Her hands drew down the length of my arms and up my sides. She liked mapping out the planes of my body whenever she or I returned from a trip. I never asked her why. I assumed it was part of her police training in making sure someone was all right. Or she could just like touching me after missing me for four days.

"Got an earlier flight. Lane picked me up."

"She did?" Her eyes blinked, hands pausing in their examination. "Your car wasn't in the garage."

"She still has it. I'm not going anywhere for a couple of days, and she wanted to take the new g/f out to La Conner for lunch tomorrow."

"She likes driving your car more than you do." Her hands had made their way up to massage the base of my scalp. "They're cute together, right? She's a good one, I think."

"Yeah, she's pretty great and good for Lane. Much better than the other one." Although, that one had been good to get Lane back out there. Hot, but self-absorbed to the point she never asked any questions as to why Lane hadn't been with anyone in more than a year. I'd given them two months; they didn't make it six weeks. A couple of months later, the new girlfriend moves to town and falls head over heels for Lane almost from the moment they met.

"How could you not like a woman who gives up the prime shift at work to match Lane's work schedule?" Iris finished her touching perusal of my body by gripping my hands.

"How could we not? Plus, she's nice. I like nice. It's underrated."

"You're nice." Her lips scraped down my neck.

"I'm a cynical bitch, and you know it."

"But I love you anyway." She leaned back and loosened her grip on me. "How'd the trip go? Is the publisher happy?"

They were very happy with the planned book launch. I could still find little tweaks I'd like to make with the book, but they had a point about the urgency. Now a week after the coverage of the contest winner's grand wedding—a lesbian couple, much to my delight—it should hit stores before everyone completely forgot about the article series. If I hadn't been sending draft chapters to my editor all along, it wouldn't have been ready in time.

"They seem to be. Want to see it?" I fluttered my eyebrows.

Her eyes went wide. "You have one?"

"Just the review copy."

"Give it here, author lady."

I retrieved the bag from outside the laundry room and dug out the book. She was at my side, impatient, telling me the book was as important to her as it was to me. She held it reverently, studying the cover before opening it and flipping to the back flap.

"Damn, you look hot." Her eyes looked up from the photo of me on the book jacket. "I have the hottest, most talented girlfriend alive."

I laughed and swept my arms around her, looking down at the book as she leafed through it. "How'd the investigation go today? Any closer to catching the guy?"

"I'm getting there." She'd been investigating a series of incidents at an assisted living facility where residents were being conned out of money in all manner of schemes. Five days investigating, which included awareness talks for the residents, and she was finally getting somewhere. I envied her ability to focus and stay sure even when faced with an almost impossible task of tracking down someone like that. It was what made her a damn good detective. "I spotted a recurring charge on several residents' credit cards. I plan to stake out the place tomorrow. See if I can't catch him making more of the fake sales calls."

I rubbed the small of her back as she kept flipping through the pages of my book. "I'm proud of you." I leaned in and gave her a peck on the lips. "You're hot and talented, yourself."

She set the book on the kitchen counter and faced me, caging me in with her arms. "We have a few extra hours today thanks to your brilliance at catching an earlier flight." Her forehead touched mine. "What do you think we should do with all that time?"

I laughed and tipped my chin up to capture her mouth. It still amazed me how horribly our first kiss went when all I could think about now was kissing her all the time. "I was thinking about writing one last story."

She pulled back, surprised. "Thought you were done interviewing couples."

"I am. This'll be our story. Just for us."

Her chest expanded, and a slow grin inched across her face. "I like the sound of that." Her gaze flicked up to the bedroom and back at me. "I've been thinking."

"About?"

"Us living together."

I drew in a sharp breath. We'd been consistently spending our nights together with only the occasional night off, depending on our schedules the next morning. As much as this step had suffocated me in past relationships, I couldn't get enough time with Iris. It didn't bother me to work with her in the house. It didn't bother me when she came through my door using her own key without calling first. It didn't bother me when she'd call to check if we had plans for a specific day before she agreed to something for us or on her own. All the things that used to bother me about girlfriends making presumptuous moves or deciding they would insert themselves into my life, none of it came up with Iris.

"Or we can stay like this. That's fine." Iris stepped back after the moment of silence. "I don't want to rush you."

I reached out and snagged her arms, bringing them back to cage me in. "I love you, Iris."

"I love you, too, Vega." Relief sounded in her tone.

"You make me very happy."

"Same here." Her eyes studied mine. "Why do I feel like there's a 'but' coming?"

I shook my head and collected my thoughts. This had to be said the right way. "I don't want to just move in together. Not if it's a trial stage."

"A trial stage?" Her brow furrowed.

"A lot of the couples I interviewed said the same thing. When they started living together, they used it as a try-out for getting married. If it didn't work out, no biggie. Many kept their old places or rented storage units just in case."

She nodded slowly. "Okay."

"I don't want it to be a try-out. If we move in together, it'll be because we want to share the rest of our lives together." I searched her gorgeous blue eyes. "So take some time to think about that. If it's not the way you think of living together, then we keep things as is until you get to that point."

"Vega," she started, but I pressed my fingers to her mouth.

"I don't want a ceremony, and I don't need a legal document." My insides knotted into a nest of nerves. I hadn't meant to bring this up today. Soon, but with candlelight and soft music, something worthy of her and this. "But I would like to make promises and exchange rings. I want very much for you to be mine for good." A nervous laugh slipped out. "Not in a creepy way." Then I shrugged. "Maybe a bit of a creepy way because you know I'm a little off."

"I love that about you," she said in a shaky voice. Nothing in her expression said she didn't want everything I wanted.

"I love you, Iris. More than I love writing. I never thought I'd love anything or anyone more than that. I want us to be together, to keep this great friendship, to cherish our love, and to share in everything we go through."

Her eyes were filling as I spoke. My heart expanded at the emotions so clear on her face.

"When I listened to all those couples, I thought so many of their stories sounded cliché. That they were doomed to live lives of routine, stealing moments right out of books or movies that they thought were original." My head shook. "I was wrong. Look at us. You're a private investigator. I'm a journalist. Seems like every other lesbian romance published has one or the other in it. Hell, we met in a bar. Is there anything more cliché than that?"

She chuckled and moved her hands to grip my sides, anchoring both of us.

"But what we have and where we're going is completely original. Everything about us."

"Yeah?" She leaned in and kissed me softly. "I think we're very original. You have no copy, my dear."

"You're just the same. It's why we work." Off-beat, quirky, imaginative, special. Every word I could think of to describe us together as something different. The way we both liked it.

Her forehead touched mine again. "So, you're saying that you won't move in with me until I'm ready to consider it a permanent arrangement, not just a try-out for a permanent arrangement."

My pulse raced, not sure if I was reading her tone correctly. "Partners, that's what I want for us. No wedding or anything. Just us making a promise in private."

"To love each other and be together for the rest of our lives." She filled in with absolutely no hesitation or question, as if she'd been thinking the exact same thing for as long as I have.

"But not in a creepy way."

She laughed. "Not in a creepy way, except for how off you are, of course."

"Of course," I agreed.

"You're okay with my house, aren't you?" She looked so hopeful. I liked my place, but it was temporary. Always had been.

"Your house feels like home."

"Especially now that you don't have to park on the street anymore?" she guessed. Over the past month, she'd had Mariah's crew extend her driveway into the backyard and build a detached two-car garage. It was just as useful for her, but I suspected she'd gone through the building process mostly for my benefit.

"I dig that garage. Thank you again, by the way." I planted a kiss on her cheek as I'd been doing for weeks every time I came into her house from the easy parking spot that wasn't on the street three blocks over. "And I like your house." I grinned slyly. "I will be bringing my bed, though. Yours is too soft."

"Picky and cynical. I'll have my hands full with you." Her hands spread wide to encircle my waist. "I was nervous to ask. I should have guessed you'd want exactly what I've been hoping for." She brought a hand up to rub her knuckles against my jaw. "I think I told you that you'd be at my wedding."

I remembered that. Back when she wanted to spend the contest winnings on a fake wedding to benefit her friend's business. I'd laughed at the time, but my heart pounded now, half afraid she might be serious. "You don't actually want one, do you?"

"No, but we could invite our parents and a few friends in for a party at Lane's bar to celebrate." Her eyes searched mine for the response she wanted to hear.

That sounded just about right. My mom would probably have a conniption if I started referring to Iris as my partner, not just my girlfriend, without having done something to mark the occasion. Something she could be invited to. My dad and brother were more like me. A text would be fine with them, but they wouldn't object to a visit if there was a party planned.

"We could do that." I raked my fingers through her soft, wispy hair. It was turning lighter again with the spring sunshine. Over the winter I'd loved counting all the different hues that made up the sandy brown shade.

Her knuckles slid down my neck and back up again. She pulled a shiver from me. "I love you so much, Vega."

My head tilted into her caress. "I knew you were special from the day you told me you'd make a great friend." I pressed up against her and gave her a passionate kiss. "All my life, I thought I'd be happy writing other people's stories. Now, I get the chance to live my own. Thanks to you. You're my original love story, Iris, and I can't wait to live out every page with you."

About the Author

Lynn Galli resides in the Pacific Northwest where she enjoys long walks on rocky beaches in the rain and standing in everlasting lines for a complex cup of coffee that will sustain her on a fifty-five minute, ten mile drive to her job writing software programs that allow her to build airplanes, save wildlife, and promote recycling. Her chilly summer evenings are usually spent writing about places that are much warmer and drier but nowhere near as beautiful or bursting with coffee, airplane manufacturing, and software coding.

OTHER PUBLICATIONS BY LYNN GALLI

VIRGINIA CLAN

Wasted Heart (Book 1) – Attorney Austy Nunziata moves across the country to try to snap out of the cycle of pining for her married best friend. Despite knowing how pointless her feelings are, five months in the new city hasn't seemed to help. When she meets FBI agent, Elise Bridie, that task becomes a lot easier.

Imagining Reality (Book 2) – Changing a reputation can be the hardest thing anyone can do, even among her own friends. But Jessie Ximena has been making great strides over the past year to do just that. Will anyone, even her good friends, give her the benefit of the doubt when it comes to finding a forever love?

Blessed Twice (Book 3) – Briony Gatewood has considered herself a married woman for fifteen years even though she's spent the last three as a widow. Her friends have offered to help her get over the loss of her spouse with a series of blind dates, but only a quiet, enigmatic colleague can make Briony think about falling in love again.

Finally (Book 4) – Willa Lacey never thought acquiring five million in venture capital for her software startup would be easier than suppressing romantic feelings for a friend. Having never dealt with either situation, Willa finds herself torn between what she knows and what could be.

Forevermore (Book 5) - M Desiderius never thought she could have a normal life filled with love. She gets all that and more when she marries Briony, including an amazing foster daughter named Olivia. Every wish she'd never allowed herself to voice became real. When someone from Olivia's past threatens M's newfound family, can she carry on in the face of loss or will it push her back into a life of solitude?

ASPEN FRIENDS

Mending Defects (Book 1) – Small town life for Glory Eiben has always been her ideal. With her rare congenital heart defect, keeping family and friends close by preserves her easygoing attitude. When Lena Coleridge moves in next door, life becomes anything but easy. Lena is a reluctant transplant and even more reluctant friend. Their growing friendship adds many layers to Glory's ideal.

Something So Grand (Book 2) – A designer for the wealthy, Vivian Yeats doesn't have time for relationships, yet she longs for romance. She's had to settle in the past when it comes to women but won't bother to again. If romance is going to happen for her, it'll take someone special to turn her head. Natalie Harper, the new contractor on her jobsites, might just be the woman to do it.

Life Rewired (Book 3) – Two years ago, Molly Sokol decided she wanted to get serious about finding that special someone. She could picture her perfectly—petite, feminine, excitable, adoring, and ultra-affectionate. When the opposite of all that comes along in the form of Falyn Shaw, Molly never thought they'd be anything more than friends. Being wrong has never felt so good.

OTHER ROMANCES

Uncommon Emotions – When someone spends her days ripping apart corporations, compartmentalization is key. Love doesn't factor in for Joslyn Simonini. Meeting Raven Malvolio ruins the harmony that Joslyn has always felt, introducing her to passion for the first time in her life.

Full Court Pressure – The pressure of being the first female basketball coach of a men's NCAA Division 1 team may pale in comparison to the pressure Graysen Viola feels in her unexpected love life.

One-Off – Weddings have never been Skye MacKinnon's thing. When she's put in charge of planning her friend's big event, she's less than thrilled. Finding out she'll have to work with the bane of her college existence, Ainsley Baird, may push her right over the edge. Knowing there's nothing she can do to change her circumstances or the company she'll have to keep, her only plan is to make it through the happy occasion without setting fire to the whole show or one person in particular.

CPSIA information can be obtained at www.ICGtesting.com
Printed in the USA
BVOW05s2316150616

452222BV00001B/13/P